yu

Zoran Drvenkar was born in Croatia in 1967 and moved to Germany when he was three years old. He has been working as a writer since 1989 and doesn't like to be pinned down to one genre. He has written over twenty novels, ranging from children's and young adult books to the darker crime novels *Sorry* and *You*. In 2010, *Sorry* won Germany's Friedrich Glauser Prize for crime fiction. He lives in an old mill outside Berlin.

A Note About the Translator

Shaun Whiteside has translated more than fifty books from the German, French, Italian, and Dutch, including novels by Amélie Nothomb, Paolo Giordano, Marcel Möring, and Bernhard Schlink, as well as classics by Freud, Nietzsche, Musil, and Schnitzler. His translation of *Magdalene the Sinner* by Lilian Faschinger won the 1996 Schlegel-Tieck Translation Prize. He lives in London.

D1112916

Also by Zoran Drvenker

Sorry

you

Zoran Drvenkar

TRANSLATED FROM THE GERMAN BY
Shaun Whiteside

HARPER

Harper
An imprint of HarperCollins*Publishers*
1 London Bridge Street
London SE1 9GF

www.harpercollins.co.uk

This paperback edition 2015
1

First published in Great Britain by HarperCollins 2015

Originally published in German as *Du* by Ullstein
Buchverlage GmbH, Berlin in 2010.
Copyright © Zoran Drvenkar 2010, © Ullstein Buchverlage GmbH

Translated from *Du* (German translation) by Shaun Whiteside

This edition published by arrangement with Alfred A. Knopf, an imprint of
The Knopf Doubleday Group, a division of Random House, Inc.

Zoran Drvenkar asserts the moral right to
be identified as the author of this work

ISBN: 978-0-00-746526-2

Printed and bound in Great Britain by Clays Ltd, St Ives plc

For you.

I

did you ever know
there's a light inside your bones

Ghinzu
BLOW

THE TRAVELER

As much as we strive toward the light, we still want to be embraced by the shadow. The very same yearning that craves harmony, craves in a dark chamber of our heart chaos. We need that chaos in reasonable portions, because we don't want to turn into barbarians. But barbarians are what we become as soon as our world falls apart. Chaos is only ever a blink away.

Never have thoughts made waves so fast. Stories are no longer passed on orally, they are transmitted to us at breakneck speed in kilobytes, so that we can't turn our eyes away. And if it gets unbearable, we react as the barbarians did, and turn that chaos into myths.

One of those myths was created in the winter fourteen years ago, on the A4 between Bad Hersfeld and Eisenach. We won't write down the exact date; anyone can do the research for themselves. And in any case, myths don't stick to dates; they are timeless and become the Here and Now. We return to the past and make it Now.

It is November.
It is 1995.
It is night.

The traffic jam has been growing for an hour now, thinning into three lanes, then two, and finally one, before it comes to a standstill. The highway is blocked by snow for over twenty miles. You can only see a few yards ahead. The snowplows creep along the secondary roads toward the traffic jam, and get stuck themselves. The skies are raging. The headlights look like lights under water. It isn't a night to be out and about. No one was prepared for this change in the weather.

People are stuck in their cars. At first they keep the engine running and search optimistically for a radio station to tell them that the traffic jam will soon be over. They search in vain. It's one o'clock in the morning, there's no sign for an exit, and if there was one it would be impassable anyway. Standstill. The headlights go out one after the other. Engines fall silent, the only sounds are the wind and the falling snow. Coats are pulled on, seats reclined. There is an inconsistent rhythm—the cars start up, the heating stays on for several minutes, before the engines fall silent once more.

You are one of many. You are alone and waiting. Your navigation system tells you you are an hour and fifty-seven minutes from your house. You can't believe this is actually happening to you. That this can be happening to anyone in this country. A simple traffic jam and nothing goes.

You're one of the few people letting their engines run uninterrupted. Not because you're cold. You know that as soon as the silence envelops you, resignation will set in, and you're not the kind of person to give up willingly. You even leave the satnav turned on and study the display, as if the distance from your destination might be reduced by some miracle. And the more you look at the screen, the more you wonder how something like this can happen to you.

One thousand one hundred and seventy-eight people are asking themselves the same question tonight. They're sitting there uncomfortably and cursing their decision to set off so late. In the end they give up and come to terms with the situation. Not you. Your engine runs for two and a half hours before you turn the key and are engulfed in silence. Your gas is running low. The satnav turns off. No light, no radio. Every few minutes you turn on the windshield wiper to sweep away the snow. You want to see what's going on out there.

And that's why you see the first snowplow parting the snow on the opposite side of the road. It looks like a weary creature dragging the whole world slowly behind it. At the side of the road the snow makes waves that immediately freeze. *If they're clearing one side, then they're bound to be working on ours too,* you think, and study the snowplow in the side-view mirror until only the glimmer of the taillights can be seen. It's only then that you close your eyes and take a deep breath.

Years ago, your sister gave you a yoga course as a present, and some of the exercises stayed with you. You go inside yourself and meditate. You become part of the silence and within a few minutes you fall asleep. An hour later your windows are white with snow, and a pale light fills the car, as if you were sitting inside an egg. The cold hurts your head. The windshield wipers have stopped moving. You rub your eyes and decide to get out. You want to free the windshield from snow and see if there's any sign of a snowplow up ahead.

The disappointment is as keen as the cold. You stand next to your car, and in front of you there's only darkness and behind you there's only darkness. *I'm a part of it,* you think, and wait and hope for a gleam of light and suddenly you burst out laughing. *Alone, I'm completely alone.* Only the wind keeps you company. The wind, the snow, and the desperate peace of cars that are stuck. The laughter hurts your face; you should move, otherwise you'll freeze.

You take your coat off the backseat. Needles of ice hammer down on you, snowflakes press against your lips. You put on gloves, take a deep breath, and feel surprisingly whole. As if your existence had been striving for that moment — you, getting out of the car; you, turning around and feeling the falling snow and smiling. It's a good smile. It hurts less than laughing.

A truck creeps past in the opposite lane and flashes once as if to greet you. Its tailwind reaches you with full force seconds later. You don't duck; you feel the wetness on your face, stumbling slightly and wondering why you can't wipe this stupid grin off your face. The truck disappears, and you're still there looking at the apparently endless snake of vehicles in front of you disappearing into the darkness. You turn around and look at the darkness behind you. *Nineteen years,* you think, *it's nineteen years since I felt like this.* You wonder how so much time could pass, and decide not to wait another nineteen years before continuing your search.

I'm in the Here, and the Here is Now.

You can't go forward, so you decide to go back.

In the months that follow, there were countless theories about what happened that night. Was it an argument? Was it drugs, revenge, or madness? Some people thought it had something to do with the moon, others quoted from the Bible—but there was no sign of the moon that night, and if there is a God, he was looking the other way. There were all kinds of conjectures, everyone had a theory, and that's how the myth came about.

At first everyone agreed that several people must have been acting together. No human being could have done all that on his own. It was only over time that theories came to focus on an individual perpetrator, and the Traveler was born.

Some people thought it would never have come to an end if the snowfall hadn't suddenly stopped. Others suspected there was a system behind it.

Many claimed the Traveler got tired.

Conjectures through and through.

You go to the car behind you and get in on the passenger side. The windows are covered with snow. You don't have to look. You know what you're doing and leave the car three minutes later.

You leave the second car after four minutes.

You skip the fourth and fifth cars because there's more than one person in them. How can you tell when the passenger seat is empty? Perhaps it's instinct, perhaps it's luck. Two men are asleep in the fourth car, and in the fifth there's a family with a dog. The dog is the only one awake, and sees you passing the window like a shadow. It starts whimpering and pees on the seat.

In car number ten you encounter your first problem.

A woman sits wrapped up at the steering wheel. She can't sleep, she's absolutely freezing because she's too stingy to turn on the engine even for a moment. She's wearing three pullovers and her coat over the top. Her car windows are damp on the inside, the drops of condensation are frozen. The woman's face is sore with cold. Her hands are claws. She regrets not bringing any drugs along. A sleeping tablet or two and it would all be more bearable.

The woman gives a start when the passenger door opens. For a moment she thinks it's the emergency services bringing her blankets and a thermos. She's about to complain because it's taken so long.

"Don't panic," you say and close the door behind you.

You smell her body, the fading deodorant. You smell her weariness and frustration, it is clammy and sour and leaves her mouth with every breath. She asks who you are. She tries to shrink away from you. Her eyes are wide. Her throat feels brittle under your hand. The inside light goes off. You press the woman against the driver's door, you put your whole weight into the movement—your left arm stretched out as if to keep her at a distance. You don't take your eyes off her for a second, feeling her blows against your arm, against your shoulder, watching her hands change from claws to panicked, fluttering birds. She gasps, she chokes, then her right hand finds the ignition key and starts the engine. You weren't expecting that. In car number six the driver tried to climb onto the backseat. In car number eight the driver repeatedly banged his head against the window to draw attention. None of them tried to drive away.

The woman puts her foot on the accelerator; the car's set to Park. The engine roars and nothing else happens. She hits the horn; the honking sounds like the bleating of a lost sheep. You clench your right hand and strike the woman in the face. Again and again. Her jaw breaks, her face slips to the left and she slumps in on herself. You lower your fist, but you keep the other hand on her throat. You feel her bones shifting under your strength. You feel the life escaping from her. That is the moment you let go of her and turn off the engine. It took less than four minutes.

The Traveler moves on.

In car number seventeen an old man is waiting for you. He's belted in and sitting upright as if the journey is going to continue at any moment. There's classical music on the radio.

"I was waiting," the old man said.

You close the door behind you; the old man goes on talking.

"I saw you. A truck went past. The headlights shone through the windows of the car in front of me. I saw you through the snow. And now you're here. And I'm not scared."

"Thank you," you tell him.

The old man unbuckles his seat belt. He shuts his eyes and lets his head fall onto the steering wheel as if he wants to go to sleep. The back of his neck is exposed. You see a gold chain cutting through his tensed skin like a thin thread. You put your hands around the old man's head. A jerk, a rough crack, a sigh escapes from the old man. You leave your hands on his head for a while, as if you could catch his fleeing thoughts. It's a perfect moment of peace.

The next day on the news they talk about an organization. The police were trying to make a connection between the twenty-six victims. The families were grieving, everywhere in the country flags were flown at half mast. They were talking about terrorists and the Russian mafia. They were thinking about a cult; the subject of sects was given prominence once again. Only the gun lobby didn't get involved, because no guns had been used. Whatever was said, whatever people conjectured, no one dared to use the phrase "mass murder." It never takes long. Eventually a tabloid newspaper put it in great big letters on the front page.

MASS MURDER ON THE A4.

It was a dark winter for Germany.

The big question on everyone's mind was what made the Traveler get out of the twenty-sixth car and think, Enough's enough. Did he really think that? Did he hear a voice, did demons speak to him, or did he get bored? Whatever the answer, it had nothing to do with the snowfall, because the snow went on falling till dawn. No, the truth isn't complicated, it's relatively simple.

You leave the twenty-sixth car and don't think anything at all. You feel the wind and you feel the cold and you feel safe and you're moving to the next car when you notice a glimmer on the horizon. Perhaps the snowfall is reflecting a light in the far distance. Whatever it is, it makes you turn around and set off back to your car. You follow your own overblown track and it is opening up like an old wound. At your car you wipe the windshield free of snow and sit down behind the steering wheel. You take a deep breath, put thumb and index finger around the ignition key, and wait. You wait for the right moment. When you start the engine, the cars in front of you come to life, and the headlights of over a hundred vehicles light the blocked motorway with a pale light. After exactly four hours the traffic jam gets moving again, because the Traveler was waiting for the right moment.

You put the car in gear and you're very pleased with yourself. The pain and throbbing in your hands are insignificant. Later you will discover that you've broken two fingers on your right hand, and in spite of your gloves the knuckles on both hands are swollen and beaten bloody. Your shoulders ache from the uncomfortable posture you assumed in the cars, but none of that matters, because there's this indescribable contentment within you. There's also a sweet taste in your mouth that you can't explain. The taste prompts a memory. The memory is nineteen years old. Glorious, dazzling, sweet. You know what it all means. You thought the search was over, but it had only taken a breather. It's the start of a new era. Or in other words—the beginning of the end of civilization as you know it.

In retrospect you still like that thought best.

No beginning without an end. A man gets out of his car, a man gets back into his car, and the traffic jam in front of him slowly starts to move. The Traveler travels on.

RAGNAR

This isn't the end, and a beginning looks different. This is the moment in between, when everything still looks possible. Retreat or attack. We're in the present. It's eight o'clock in the morning. The spotlights are turned on you, because this Friday morning you're making a decision that will change all your lives, as you are standing at the edge of the pool unable to believe your eyes. The light gleams blue and cold up at you. What you are seeing is a soundless nightmare. Not one of you dares to break the silence.

You wish you were far, far away.

Leo has moved back a step; he is waiting for your reaction. His hands are deep in the pockets of his jacket and he's struggling to stay still. David is standing on the other side of the pool, rubbing the back of his head. He's only been working for you for three months, and you're still not sure what to make of him. He's young, he's ambitious, and he's one of Tanner's many grandchildren. Family means nothing to you. You wanted to give the boy a chance, because Tanner is putting his hand in the fire for him. It's the only kind of family bond that you respect.

You take a deep breath. The air is warm and clean, the air-conditioning system is working without a sound. Oskar had the arched basement dug out four years ago. Walls and ceiling are new and covered with terra-cotta tiles. They don't just reflect the light; every breath is clearly audible and echoes in the silence like the panting of dogs. Your hands tingle. You want to hit something, a bag of sand or just the wall. Something.

How could she?

You rub your eyes before you look again. You still don't believe it. Leo shifts uneasily from one leg to the other; he knows there's going to be trouble soon. A whole lot of trouble.

"I don't believe it," you say.

"Maybe—"

You raise your hand, Leo falls silent, you turn to David.

"What do you think how much is it?"

"Thirty, maybe forty kilos, it's hard to say."

Footsteps can be heard from the floor above, none of you is looking up, you are standing motionlessly around the pool. On the surface of the water you can see your elongated reflections quiver slightly. Maybe there's an underground line nearby, or else one of those massive great trucks is dragging itself along a side street and sending its vibrations far underground. Your faces look like the faces of ghosts that have seen everything and are tired of being ghosts. *Tired is exactly the right word,* you think, because you're seriously tired of all this bullshit. You felt something dark coming your way, you should have been prepared, but who expects something like this?

"I've never seen anything like this," says David.

"And you should never have seen anything like this," you reply and hear Tanner coming downstairs. He stops some distance behind you. Tanner is your right hand; without him you'd only be worth half of what you are. He turns sixty next year and wants to retire slowly. You have no idea what you'll do without him. He taught you everything you know, and it's only when he's no longer there that you'll find out whether you can cope on your own. One of your customers once said that Tanner scared him because he didn't emit anything at all. Tanner's a transmitter who only transmits when he feels like it. Now, for example. He says, "Nothing. It's gone. She's taken all of it."

You don't react; what should you say to that? "Thanks" would be inappropriate. The quivering on the surface of the water vanishes. You look up from the pool. Your fury and frustration need an outlet. So far you've ignored Oskar. You didn't want to talk to him, you couldn't even look at him because the mere sight of him would have made you explode. This is all his fault. Correction. His *and* yours, if you're honest. You should never have done business together.

Never.

Take a look at him, how peacefully he is sleeping there on that stupid leather armchair as if he hadn't a care in the world. It's eight o'clock in the morning, and you wouldn't be surprised if he was drunk.

"Wake him up."

Leo bends over Oskar and shakes him. No reaction. Leo slaps him in the face with the palm of his hand. Once, twice, then he steps back. It doesn't suit him. When Leo takes a step back, it means there's a problem. You react immediately. Your bodily functions are shutting down. The breathing, the heartbeat. Your blood is flowing slower, your thoughts move like molasses. *Reptile, I'm turning into a fucking reptile,* you think, when Leo confirms what you were thinking: "He's gone."

A few steps and you're beside Oskar, crouching down in front of him. His skin is pale and shiny in places. It reminds you of dried sushi.

"What's up with his skin?"

"That's ice."

Leo holds his hand out to you; his fingertips are damp.

"He must have frozen to death."

You want to laugh. It's over twenty degrees down here, and out there it's early summer. *No one just freezes in the summer,* you want to say, but not a word comes out. David comes and stands next to you. You'd rather he kept his distance. It's your own fault. David is anxious for your acknowledgment, and you aren't making it easy for him.

"May I?"

You nod, David crouches beside you and taps Oskar's forehead, there's a dull *tok.* David looks for a pulse and then shakes his head.

"Leo's right. Oskar's gone."

You feel Tanner's and Leo's eyes on your back, and David is looking at you too. There's nothing to say, your mind is blank. Oskar deep-frozen on a chair, the vanished merchandise, and then this fucked-up swimming pool. When you can speak again, you say, "I want her to suffer."

"I'll see to it," David replies.

The answer comes too quickly. David wasn't thinking, even though an order like that doesn't call for much thinking. He reacted automatically. You hate that. Your men should think and not react.

Both of you get up at the same time; you're close to one another, so that you can smell his breath.

"David, what did I just say?"

"That she—that she should suffer?"

You grab him between the legs. He tries to move away, thinks better of it and stands still. Only his torso bends slightly forward, that's all that happens. You press hard.

"What is that, David?"

Sweat appears on his forehead; his answer is a gasp.

"Suffering?"

"No. This isn't suffering, David. Suffering is when I pull your balls off and let you dive after them in the pool, that would be suffering. Now do you understand what I meant when I said she should suffer?"

"I understand."

You let go of him. His nostrils are flared, a tear runs down his cheek, his chin is trembling. David is twenty-four, you're nineteen years older. You understand each other.

"Bring me the boy."

"But where are we supposed to—"

"Ask Darian," you interrupt. "He'll know where you can find him. And David, this is serious. Leave no stone unturned and don't even think about coming back here without the boy."

You turn to Tanner.

"Go with him. Leo and I will wait here. You've got an hour."

Tanner nods and leaves with David. You tell Leo to get two chairs. Leo disappears too. At last you're alone with Oskar, and the tension leaves you and is replaced with a heavy weariness. *It should never have come to this*, you think, and although you are weary you still want to yell at Oskar and behave like an idiot. *He's gone.* Leo couldn't have put it more appropriately. Once you're gone, it's final. It has no beginning, it just has an end. You put your hand on Oskar's head for a moment. His hair feels greasy; through his scalp you can feel the cold emanating from his body.

What on earth happened to you?

You lift one eyelid as if his gaze might tell you what's happened here. *Come on, talk to me.* Nothing. The gaze of a dead man is the gaze of a dead man. It isn't the first time you've seen it. When you let go of the lid again, it closes very slowly.

Leo comes down with the chairs and says, "Christ, it stinks up there."

You sit down opposite Oskar. Leo's bulk obscures the chair next to you. Eight years ago, he was still in the ring and it was shaming. As a young man Leo had been national champion twice in a row, then the fire went out, and everyone apart from Leo noticed it. He kept going. When a man turns forty, he can stand wherever he wants, just not in the ring. Leo was one of those stubborn guys whose brain can come trickling out of their ears and they just pull back their shoulders and go on boxing. His second passion almost cost him his life. His gambling debts were in six figures, and if it hadn't been for Tanner, Leo would have had to go on tour—Thailand and Indonesia loved European flesh. Fights without rules, but the money was good. Tanner bought the aging boxer's freedom and saved him. Since then Leo's been working for you and he is at the same time Tanner's shadow. You don't know what kind of aftereffects boxing left him with. His face is scarred, most of his nerves don't work, the hands are deformed paws. He is married to a former model. She treats him like a god. You know you can always rely on Leo. He's loyal and he can take a beating like no one else. And he hardly misses a thing.

"There's no TV."

"So?"

Leo points at Oskar.

"If there's no TV, then how come Oskar's holding a TV remote?"

You're surprised; you hadn't noticed the remote control. It sticks out from his fingers like a black popsicle. Focus—how could you have overlooked something like that? You bend forward and take Oskar's hand in yours. For his last birthday you gave him three watches and a watch winder. Oskar was allowed to choose the watches, the watch winder was your department. Its frame is covered with black piano lacquer, and as soon as you touch it, four little lights come on inside. You remember Oskar calling you up after his birthday party and telling you he'd spent an hour sitting in front of the box looking at the watches being rocked to sleep.

There were days when Oskar was like a ten-year-old. What he hadn't been able to experience as a child, he'd more than made up for as a grown-up. And you were always by his side, like a proud uncle with an overflowing billfold.

The watch on Oskar's wrist cost you ten grand, but it's still not cold-resistant. The date tells you that Oskar was deep frozen on Saturday. The watch stopped at twenty to twelve.

Leo asks you if you have any idea what might have happened down here.

"Not a clue," you answer, and let go of Oskar's hand. "But if we wait till Oskar's thawed, I'm sure he'll tell us."

Leo doesn't laugh; even though he knows you were making a joke, laughing would be a mistake. You ignore him, just as you ignore the vaulted basement and the swimming pool and stare with a full focus at your brother's frozen body, as if it could suddenly give you answers to all your questions.

STINK

Stink you got from your brother. It's miles better than Isabell. As if you were like from Spain or something. Not normal. Like that girl in 9C, the one with the braids. Like a hippie, except a techno one. Wall. Why Wall? As if there was something wrong with her. No, you're Stink and you want to stay that way. The name stuck, even though your brother left school four years ago. You thought they'd give it a rest after that, but that was wrong, everyone went on calling you Stink, so you started getting used to it. Stink's okay. Nobody ever says anything about toilets or whatever. And why should they. You smell nice. Perfume is a protection against the outside world.

Protection against guys like Eric, who turns around two seats in front of you and looks at you as if you're naked from top to toe. You shut your eyes, you really don't want to see him. Hairless ass. Of course you don't mean his ass, just his dumb shaved head. As if he's a soldier on the way to the front, acting cool and shaving his head twice a week, though he's only got fluff on his chin anyway, he'll never have enough for a goatee. He'd need to drink more coffee. At least that's what your aunt says. Aunt Sissi. *Drink a lot of coffee and you'll grow a beard.* Hormones and crap. Thanks a lot, Auntie. That's exactly what you don't need. Hair all over the place. The only thing that works is Epolotion or whatever it's called. You're sure Schnappi can spell it, Schnappi's always up-to-date like a radio station without ads that collects all the important information and feeds it back to you.

"That hair thing doesn't take a second," she explained to you all, "a hot needle goes in"—she showed you and poked it around in her wrist. "It goes into your pores, you know? Or you do it with wax, but the hot needle lasts longer, right? So it goes in where the hair is and then burns your roots and it hisses and it hurts like fuck."

"Ouch!" yelled Ruth, blond, almost transparent and with no visible hairs on her legs.

"Stop wriggling," you told her and asked Schnappi how long it would keep working.

"A few months."

"A few months?"

"What did you think?"

About a year was what you thought, but it probably isn't.

"And quanta costa?"

Schnappi rolled her eyes.

"No idea what it costs. You think I own the shop or something? Ask for yourself."

Epolotion's out, you've checked. Incredibly expensive and incredibly painful. Two incrediblys too many. And anyway you like shaving. It takes a long time, but your legs like the feeling and your skin prickles afterward. You could get Indi to do it. It'll be like in a movie. *Pretty Woman II.* Indi sitting on the edge of the tub, your foot in one hand, the razor in the other, desperate to suck your toes. *No, Indi,* you'll say, *shaving first, then sucking.* And Indi will say, *Okay.* And then he will shave your legs, making you completely nervous with his touches as you doze in the tub and sip your champagne, all queasy and woozy and—

"Hey, are you awake or what?" Ruth wants to know.

"'Course I am."

"Then take your stupid head off my shoulder."

"Okay, okay."

"Slobbermouth."

You wipe your chin. No dribble, what a bitch! You narrow your eyes to get a better view of the screen. Stupid cinema. Stupid seat. Stupid movie. Come on, who wants to sit at the back? You can hardly see a thing. Stupid eyes and stupid half-price Tuesdays. Next time you'll pay two euros and watch a DVD. More fun anyway. If you have to pee you don't miss the whole story.

"Stupid movie," you mumble.

Schnappi jabs you with her elbow.

"Bitch!"

Nessi sits next to Ruth and bends over and hands you her Coke. At least there is one person thinking about you. You drink and clink the ice cubes. Again Eric turns around and gives you the Look. Zombie.

"You a Nazi or what?" you ask.

"Dyke," he hisses back and turns away.

"Could you shut the fuck up," Schnappi whispers, drumming her feet on the floor so people can feel it four rows down. Every time things get exciting Schnappi turns into Speedy Gonzales. *An Asian girl on speed,* you think, and it makes you laugh and you say, "Speedfreak."

"Are you having fun?"

"Shut up, Ruth."

"Come on, if all you want to do is get on our nerves, just go to the can and talk to the toilet," Ruth tells you without looking at you.

"Or the soap dispenser," says Schnappi, and they giggle together like two little girls on the way to the candy store.

You look at them. They don't look like sixteen.

"I'm leaving," you tell them, mature and grown-up as you are, and then you leave.

The door shuts behind you, and you inhale with relief. The air in there was horrible. As if everyone had farted at the same time and then fanned it around. You fumble your cigarettes out of your jacket, a new pack, fresh out of the machine, you've never liked bumming from the others. You take off the cellophane and pull out the silver paper, tap one out and stick it between your lips.

"Oh, come on."

You hammer your lighter on the palm of your hand. The flint crunches, there's no spark. Great. Now what? You can't just go back in there and ask for a light, they'll lynch you. Go to the counter, they're bound to have a light.

You're half the way there when this guy comes from the bottom of the stairs. He was probably in the john, hasn't missed anything anyway.

"Got a light?"

He takes out this enormous golden flamethrower.

"It's my dad's," he tells you, as if he'd inherited it, as if he had to explain it, as if you'd asked. He probably swiped the lighter when his dad was looking the other way, wanna bet? Guy as tall as a basketball player, much older than you. Mid-twenties. Gives you a light and smiles. Nice.

"Thanks."

"You don't like the movie?"

"Boring."

"That's the word."

That smile again; you smile back. It's better than standing around on your own anyway.

"How about an ice cream?"

You tell him you're waiting for your friends. You're not that easy. He looks around, probably checking that he's not dreaming and he really has met you. Hot mama that you are. Then he winks at you. He really winks. Maybe he's gay or something.

"We could wait outside and eat our ice cream. My treat. But only if you want to," he adds, with a big fat question mark at the end. He's actually really friendly, but let him twitch for a minute or two. Friendly's only half the battle. You're not naïve. *Don't trust strangers who offer you candy,* Aunt Sissi drummed into you, and if you've grown up without parents you listen to your aunt.

"Hm," you say and pull in your stomach and check the guy out—black T-shirt, jeans, Doc Martens, leather bracelet, ponytail. No, he's not gay, you've never seen a long-haired gay; and if your nose doesn't deceive you he's got just as much perfume behind his ears as you do. Smells good. When he glances at his watch, you see gold again. You could bet that when he laughs the sun comes out.

"Why are you laughing?" he asks, and you just grin and he says, "We've got an hour, what do you think?" Questions about questions. Come on, Stink, behave yourself, he's not going to go straight for your shorts, and if he does, you've put up with worse. So just be cool, go with it.

"Ice cream sounds great," you tell him and your heart starts to flutter loudly.

Before you leave the foyer, you buy ice cream from the guy behind the counter. Of course you choose the most expensive one, you want to do this in style. The guy says *Go for it* and you laugh, and he laughs too, then you're standing outside nibbling at your ice creams and glancing at each other. These are really flirty looks, they fall like a veil over your eyes and make your vision a little blurry. Leaving the cinema wasn't such a bad idea after all. From a certain angle the guy looks like Alberto. Alberto wasn't an Italian, you just wished he was. Alberto came from the East and his real name was Albert, but what sort of a name is that? Alberto sounded miles better. That guy, oh hell, he could really turn you on. He was wild about you. *Wanna eatsch you up,* he said. Stupid lisp, but at least it made you laugh. And you didn't want to talk to him anyway. He made out with you wherever you were and nibbled away at your lips as if they were pink chewing gum. And once at the bus stop he shoved his hands down the back of your jeans and grabbed you by the ass. *Alberto, what're you doing?* you asked him and he pressed himself closer to you so that you could feel his erection, massaging your ass as if it were an overripe peach and breathing heavily. *I'm an ath fetishist,* he muttered in your ear, almost blowing your head off. And you weren't cool at all by then and murmured back: *Whatever that is.* You had no idea what an ass fetishist was and you didn't have much time to think about it, because Alberto was pressing and kneading your cheeks till you thought: *Help, he's going to tear me in two!* It didn't come to that, though, because Alberto suddenly went quiet and rigid and stopped breathing at all while having an orgasm pressed against your belly, and that happened all at the bus stop on a lovely day in May.

". . . never seen it. I went to Berlin a lot as a child. My father lives in Friedrichshain, my half brother in Zehlendorf. But my mother lives in Hamburg, that's where I grew up . . ."

The guy talks and talks and smiles at you and you think: *How long's he been talking?* You smile back and lick a bit of ice cream from your wrist and wonder if he's an ass fetishist as well.

"So you're just visiting?" you say, picking up the end of his last sentence.

"Right."

"Cool."

"What about you? Still at school?"

You show him your wrist. There's a little tattoo at the spot where they take your pulse. The writing's tiny, one word, not more.

"*Gone?*"

"Right, gone."

"School?"

You nod.

"High school graduation?"

"Nah."

You roll your eyes and laugh. Be honest, you don't look like graduation. You look like a wildcat in a petting zoo. But don't tell him that. And watch out, here comes the next question.

"And what are your plans?"

"We'll see. Maybe I'll open a beauty salon. Something like that. You?"

"I don't know where I want to go."

Funny answer, you think, and pretend to study the movie posters. Let the guy look at you in peace. Maybe he hasn't got a girlfriend, you could be with him for a while. But guys like him always have girlfriends. One of those smoothies who never have to go to the bathroom and in the morning they smell like flowers. That's the kind of girl he would have. He's much too nice for this world—he speaks nice, he smells nice and seems to have money. Maybe he'll lend you ten euros, then you'd have to see each other again so that you could give him the money back.

You feel him looking at you. His eye wanders up from your platforms up to your worn bell-bottomed cord jeans, the belt pulled tight, narrow waist, blouse under your velvet jacket, long pause on your breasts—of course he lingers there, he paid for the ice cream, he can linger. Perhaps he's noticed that your red hair makes you look a bit like the actress Kristen Bell, but he's probably never even seen *Veronica Mars* or *Heroes*.

"How old are you?" he asks and his eyes are on your mouth.

"Seventeen," you lie, adding a year. "You?"

"Too old."

"Come on."

"How about twenty-seven?"

"Definitely too old," you say and laugh.

He laughs too, takes a breath and tells you his name.

"Nice to meet you, Neil. I'm Stink."

"Funny name."

You wave dismissively.

"It's because of the perfume."

"You named yourself after a book?"

"What book?"

"You know, the novel."

"No, it's because I always smell so nice. Here."

He bends forward and sniffs your wrist.

"Smells good."

You look at each other. He knows there is more to this name.

"And because I'm mostly in a bad mood," you admit. "Mostly always."

"A real stinker, then."

"Better believe it."

He thinks for a moment, he looks to his left, he looks to his right.

"I have an idea," he tells you. "Will you come with me?"

"Now?"

"Now."

Now it is your turn to look around. Your girls will be gone for more than an hour. You could die of boredom or you could go on an adventure.

"You lead, I will follow," you say to Neil.

So he leads you down the street and stops next to a Jaguar, smart and red and with Hamburg plates.

"Wow, where'd you get that?"

"Swiped it off my mother," says Neil and opens the door for you.

RUTH

Once upon a time there were five girls and I was one of them. The fairy tale could start like that. *One of them.* That's exactly how you feel, lying on your back, above you the moss-green ceiling that you painted one afternoon with your girls because the pink was getting on your nerves and you needed a change. You're living with your parents in an old stylish apartment block they bought when you were born. Your top bunk is six feet up. Every morning it's like waking up in a forest. Now the green reminds you of the sea that you saw while traveling around the Bahamas with your parents. Of course you had to dive, and it nearly happened there in the water. You lost yourself for a moment. You were part of the deep and you didn't know what was up and what was down. It was the best experience you've ever had, and since then you've been wondering what would have happened if you'd made the wrong choice and gone on deeper. How do you lose yourself? Do you disappear or do you become part of the water?

Now you're lying on your bed, and the moss-green ceiling is within reach of your hands. Even though you're sure no one can just go missing like that, you're not so sure what's happening between your legs. *Is it his tongue or is it his finger?* You look down, his head is moving, so it must be his tongue. God, he's taking his time. You're sorry it has come to this. Why did you just let yourself go like that?

He asked so nicely.

That's all?

That's all.

You tug gently on his hair. Eric looks up. His lips glisten. He gives you a quizzical look, and you wish he would make another face.

"What are you doing?"

"What does it feel like?" he asks back and disappears between your legs again.

You wish it was his finger and not his stupid tongue, then you'd definitely be more aware of it. There are boys who don't know how to kiss. They swap gallons of spit with you and want to hear you gasping with passion. You want to be kissed so that your lights flicker. Flicker and not go out. Boys should learn from girls. Nessi kissed you once. It was New Year's Eve, you were sitting drunk on Taja's bed, and suddenly someone suggested making out and your mouth landed on Nessi's mouth and it was the hottest french kiss you've ever had.

Eric definitely doesn't know how to kiss, and you're annoyed with yourself for not telling him on the very first day. Now you are in the second week and he goes at it like a heartsick frog. Taja warned you, and this is what you've ended up with—a guy who busies himself between your legs as if he is working with his tongue on a scratch card.

You count the books on the shelf, you tense your belly and admire your belly button with its little ring. You wonder which pizza you'll have afterward and whether the movie will really be as weird as everyone says. Then you say the alphabet backward and at F you've had enough and drag Eric up to you by the ears. After a certain point enough's enough. You kiss him, and he does his frog face again, but it's better than all that fumbling. You taste yourself on his tongue, and your own arousal arouses you even further, and it's like something coming full circle. Eric's leg slips between your thighs, the pressure is good, you push back, your lower body twitches and it happens so fast that you have to grip the back of his neck so that you don't lose yourself completely. His mouth lands on your neck, you want to warn him that if he gives you a love bite he's dead, but you can't warn him, because all your lights have blown out, no flickering, just lights out, as the orgasm glides through you like a red-hot knife through a block of butter, without getting stuck once, and that happens twice in a row.

Eric isn't aware of any of that, he's too aroused to notice anything. He kneads your breasts and breathes in your ear. You let go of his neck and sink back. The knife has disappeared, now you're nothing but melting butter. It would be perfect if you were alone now.

"Oh God," sighs Eric, as you take him in your hand. He twitches, he presses himself harder against you, full with desire and the constant panic that he might come too quickly.

You look over his shoulder at your watch. You've got five minutes.

Your hand opens his zipper, you're lethargic and lazy, it's as if you're moving under water. His knees tremble. You push him off you and onto his back. He's so helpless, you could do anything you wanted with him. His boxer shorts are damp in two places. You touch him and he shrinks back a little. Eric said your face was too much for him, and you imagined him pleasuring himself while gazing breathlessly at the class photograph. Now his eyes are wide open, as if in terror. *This isn't love,* you think, *it's something else.* You pull down his boxers without breaking eye contact. You smell his cock before you see it. The scent, the expectation.

"Shut your eyes."

Eric shuts his eyes, as quickly as if his life depended on it.

You lean down and kiss the head of his dick. His skin is hot to the touch and he tastes bitter. You insisted that he wash beforehand. You have principles. You take him gently into your mouth and feel him twitch and grow and let him fall out of your mouth. He comes in frantic spurts, it's flowing out of him, onto your hand, his belly, the sheet. He whimpers. *Sweet,* you think, and put a finger on his bobbing cock and can feel his heartbeat. The twitching subsides, the fever has passed. You look up. Eric stares at the ceiling, he can't look you in the eye, it's been less than a minute.

Eric waits downstairs while you adjust your lipstick in the mirror and wonder what you'll look like in fourteen years' time. You don't plan on turning thirty, but neither did you plan to be licked by a frog when you were sixteen. Now you're sixteen and standing in front of a mirror with a pony sticker in one corner and a black heart in the other and wondering why time has to go by so incredibly fast.

Taja painted the heart three years ago with a felt tip, when your girls were on a sleepover. "Forever," it says below the heart. You don't know who it was who came up with that. Nothing is forever, everything has a sell-by date.

And sooner or later I'll turn thirty.

You're not a beauty. You're what lies between beauty and boredom. Your eyes are like cloudy water, your hair is smooth and so pale that it's almost white. You remind a lot of people of somebody, but no one can say exactly who. If it wasn't for your friends, you'd probably be invisible.

Your girls are alike in many things, but what fundamentally makes you different is your hunger. None of your girls knows how you feel. There's a hunger in you that never ends even when you're full. The hunger makes you start awake at night. You want more. More music, more talks, more time and sex and most of all more life. Your room has fourteen square feet. You lust for more.

Your girlfriends don't know anything about your plans. They think you're going to spend the next hundred years moving around Berlin, sharing everything and never parting. You have no illusions. Take a look at yourself; you won't get very far with your face, your mind will have to take care of the rest. And your mind's not really bad.

The tattoo on your wrist is barely visible, even though it's less than a month old. Needle and ink and a bottle of vodka. The writing's tiny. *Gone.* If the girls knew you were working hard to erase your tattoo with soap every evening, they would never forgive you. And if they knew you wanted to go to senior class at grammar school after the end of the year, they'd definitely go nuts. Your girls have plans. Stink with her ridiculous beauty salon, as if polishing pensioners' wrinkles was the crème de la crème. Schnappi just wants to get as far away as possible from her mad mother, who's been planning for ages to take Schnappi back to Vietnam to find a suitable husband for her. Schnappi in Vietnam is like you behind the register in Aldi. Nessi's plan is the weirdest of all. She wants to live with the rest of you in the country. Doesn't matter where. She's your personal eco-freak and dreams of a commune where you'll cook together every day and talk and be so contented that the outside world will dissolve. The artist among you is Taja. She inherited the gift from her dad and after school wants to travel with her guitar around Europe, which you find even stupider than opening some dumb beauty salon. Who actually likes those people who strum away on street corners? Or even worse, who likes it when you're sitting in the U-Bahn and then some entertainer stumbles in?

You wish you could steal a tiny bit of each of your girls—Stink's rage, Schnappi's energy, Nessi's warmth, and you'd especially like to have something from Taja, because she vanished just under a week ago and it doesn't matter what bit you get, you'll take it all—the gleam in her eyes, as if a storm was approaching, or her adventurousness, as if life was always dangerous and not just a tedious collection of school lessons.

You last saw Taja six days ago; there's been radio silence since then. No returned calls, no answers to your texts, nothing. Stink even went up to see her in Frohnau, but nobody answered the door. Schnappi thinks Taja might be traveling somewhere with her dad, like she did at Christmas—packed her things and lay on the beach in Tahiti until New Year's Eve.

Not this time, especially not just before the end of term.

Never.

You really miss Taja, and you check your phone a hundred times a day to see if she has written. You wish you'd argued, then there would be a reason.

"I wish you were here," you say quietly to your reflection and touch the black heart and think it's really time to get out of here. You glance at yourself one last time, weary from hunger, before you go down to Eric, who's already waiting impatiently for you.

The popcorn tastes like cardboard. The guy behind the popcorn machine says there's nothing he can do about it. He promises you a fresh portion next time. You ask him which next time that's going to be. He turns red and Schnappi laughs and bumps you with her shoulder, making you spill half the popcorn over the counter.

Schnappi leads on and you find row 45 and squeeze in. Because you're late the ads are on already and everyone groans and comments, particularly Jenni, and you give her the finger, tell her to be quiet or she'll get Sprite on her ugly hairdo. And then at last you're sitting down and Schnappi says, "We're late, the ads are over." And you say, "I've noticed that already." Only Nessi keeps her mouth shut, sits there looking as if she'd rather be somewhere else. The trailers start and at that exact minute Stink comes running in and everybody starts groaning again while Stink squeezes down the row and stands on everyone's feet, and as soon as she's sitting down, as soon as everything's quiet, Schnappi's phone coughs, which always sounds funny, because Schnappi recorded her cousin coughing as a ringtone, but it's only funny if you're not at the cinema, so everyone groans again and Schnappi says, "Sorry, sorry," and turns her phone off. At last the movie begins and you see a ship in the harbor and everyone on the screen cheers so much that you start yawning.

"Are we in the wrong movie?" asks Stink.

"Shut up."

Stink slips down in her seat slightly and says she hates half-price Tuesday.

"So why do you come?"

"Why not?"

You drink from your Sprite; Schnappi bends down, takes some of your popcorn, and immediately spits it back out.

"Is this stuff cardboard, or what?"

Stink snorts with laughter and you can't help it, the Sprite shoots out your nose and drips on your chest.

Well, thanks a lot.

On the screen the people are looking forward to a boat trip, they're wearing uniforms and they look the way you imagine Americans look on a Sunday. Eric turns around and winks at you, Stink asks him if he wants to take a picture, Schnappi throws popcorn at his head and you say, "That stuff tastes like old feet," then Jenni kicks your backside from behind and goes *Shh* and you're about to turn around, when everything explodes and your heartbeat just stops, flames and more flames, the whole screen is burning up, one explosion after another. It makes your jaws drop so you girls can't speak anymore. At least you're a hundred percent sure that this is the right movie.

NESSI

They get up and go outside, they look at their phones, talk, forget their crushed popcorn boxes and empty cardboard cups and call out to each other. They yawn, they grab each other's butts and have long forgotten what movie they were just watching. They're as superficial as a puddle at the roadside, looking at their phones as if they were navigational devices without which they wouldn't know where to go after the movie. They have too much, and because they have too much, they want more and more, because it's all they know. Greedy, never satisfied and never really hungry, because they get fed constantly before they can even feel the slightest hunger.

You wish you weren't part of it. They're so far removed from you that you could call to them and they wouldn't hear you. Your voice, yes; the words, no. And when they have left, peace settles in as if the cinema is holding its breath. The only sound is the murmuring from the corridors, then the door falls shut and it's completely still. The cinema breathes out and it sounds like a sigh. The world has been switched off. You are the world and you wish you were someone else. A tear in the curtain is a tear in the screen is a tear in your life. You look at your wrist, the tattoo gleams dully. *Gone*. You can't take your eyes off those four letters and wonder what would happen if you saw all the things in your dreams that you didn't want to see in real life. Things you close your eyes to. Things you don't want to imagine because they're so terrible. And what if all those things stepped out of your dreams and suddenly appeared in real life—and it doesn't matter if you want to see them or not, they're there and you have to see them. What then? Would you stop living and go on with dreaming?

I don't know.

"Sorry, I'd like to leave you sitting here, but I can't, I'll get into trouble."

She's standing at the end of the row, she's the same age as you. Short hair and those round glasses. You'd never dare go out of the house like that. She looks like she listens to Beethoven and bakes Advent cookies with her family. You'd like to ask her if she just feels like screaming sometimes. You'd also like to smell her skin and let her know she's definitely as real as you are. Even though it sounds nuts, that's exactly what you'd like to say to her. You're sure she doesn't know what she'll be one day, but she knows she'll be something. And who can say that with any certainty? Not you, just for the record.

"Sorry," she repeats, and you look at each other and you can't get up, you're bolted to the seat, however much you might try, right now you can't budge from the spot. Perhaps she sees that, or perhaps she knows the feeling, because she leaves you alone. Respect. She goes out of the cinema hall, the door shuts and again there's this silence, for one wonderful moment the world is switched off. You're sitting in row 45, seat 16. The movie is over, and the things from your dreams crouch growling on your shoulders and want to be real. You lean your head back, because whatever you do, your only option is to cry.

Everything about you is crooked; however you stand it all slips away. Your T-shirt, your jeans, your hair, your earrings, even your mouth is askew. You look as if Picasso's had a bad day. There's a pimple beside your nostril, and you know if you try to do anything about it it'll turn into a war zone. You lick your fingertip and dab crumbs of mascara from your cheek.

It could be worse, you think, when there's the sound of flushing behind you and one of the stall doors opens.

"I bleed like a pig!"

Schnappi chucks a tampon wrapped in toilet paper in the bin, then joins you at the basin, holds her hands under the tap and meets your gaze in the mirror.

How can her eyes be so beautiful? you think.

Schnappi's mother is called San and she's from Vietnam, her father's called Edgar, and he's been a subway train driver in Berlin for thirty years. He met Schnappi's mother on vacation. Schnappi insists on that version. She doesn't want anyone to think her father ordered her mother from a catalogue.

Schnappi soaps her hands and asks if you understood the movie. You don't like just her eyes, you like everything about her, particularly the fact that she's so incredibly energetic. No one in the crowd is more loyal. It would be ideal if she talked less.

"What kind of killer was that guy? I mean, didn't he play Jesus one time? Can someone who played Jesus suddenly become a killer? Nah, don't think so. You remember? Jesus had to drag his cross around the place and then he got tortured for two hours? I mean, somebody was trying to make us feel really guilty, right? Fucking church. Stink fell asleep in the middle, she hardly missed anything, we covered our eyes the whole time because it was so disgusting and all the time I was . . ."

Schnappi can talk as if there were no tomorrow. If you keep your mouth shut for long enough, she automatically starts over again, as if every conversation has to come full circle.

". . . mustn't think I'm not joining in. But I'm not decorating any gym! As soon as school's over you won't see me close to this prison, or were you going to the party? Let's do our own party. Maybe Gero will come, I could eat him up with a spoon. Look at this. I think my hair's looking tired. Maybe I should dye it. I think I'm getting old. If I end up looking like my mother, chop my head off, promise?"

"I promise."

"Okay, what's up now, are you coming to the playground or not? You've got nothing on at home, and then we might take a detour to the bar on Savignyplatz, or do you not want to because of Taja? I can see that, but you know what Taja's like. She'll come back if she feels like it, and till then none of us will hold our breath. Wait, let me just get rid of this for you."

She opens her backpack that looks like a weary panda, and takes out a blemish stick. You're thinking about Taja and all the messages you left for her.

"Stand still."

Schnappi's half a head shorter than you, and has to stand on tiptoes. She dabs at your pimple, puts the blemish stick away again and says it's perfect now. You look in the mirror.

Perfect.

Schnappi takes your arm and steers you out of the ladies' room and up the stairs and out of the cinema as only she can. She would be a great bodyguard, she always gives you the feeling she knows what she's doing. There's no one standing outside the cinema, just a few people sitting outside Café Bleibtreu.

"So did you get that movie or not? Because I didn't get any of it, nothing at all, cross my heart and die."

Schnappi laughs and deliberately puts her hand on the wrong side, stops laughing in the middle and looks at you, really looks at you at last, and says, "God, Nessi, stop looking like this."

You want to tell her that there is no other way to look right now. You have no idea what she wants to hear. Everything is a blur. You remember the movie as if you'd been blind and deaf for the last two hours. Everything that comes toward you flows around you and disappears without a trace, behind your back, lost and gone forever. But then your thinking apparatus clicks back in and you work out that this isn't really about the movie; Schnappi's language is a secret language, she says one thing and means another. She's been asking you the same question all along and just wants to know what's up with you and why you're not saying anything, while she goes on talking and talking. And of course she's right, you have to give her some kind of answer, but you can't come up with a good one, so you turn the answer into a question and say weakly and quietly, "And what if I'm pregnant?"

SCHNAPPI

Rather a big mouth than no tits, was always your motto, but maybe now's not the time to announce it. Nessi needs to hear something else. Something like: "Bullshit, you're not pregnant!"

"Why not?"

"You don't just get pregnant like that."

"But—"

"Have you done a test?"

"No."

"Without a test you're not pregnant, okay?"

Nessi can't reply to your logic, so you drag her up Bleibtreustrasse to Kantstrasse and then into the nearest pharmacy to buy her a pregnancy test, as if you were offering her a kebab, except that those tests are really expensive.

"Why are they so expensive?"

The pharmacist shrugs as if she didn't think that it was expensive. You read the instructions and whisper to Nessi that the pharmacist is one of those people who never get pregnant, that's why a test like that costs a fortune, and then you turn back to the pharmacist and say with a sugary smile, "Eight euros? Are you sure this really costs eight euros?"

The pharmacist puts the packet through the scanner again.

The price is right.

"We've got a double pack," she says. "It's 10.95."

"Well, that's a bargain, isn't it?" you say, and look at Nessi. "Do we need two?"

"Two would be good."

"We'll take the bargain," you say to the pharmacist and smile at her as if you'd pulled a brilliant trick on her.

From the pharmacy you go to the nearest café. Before the waiter can move, you tell him you just need to pee. In the bathroom both of you squeeze into one stall. Nessi is pale, it's all going too quickly for her.

"Come on, girl, take a deep breath."

Nessi takes a breath.

The sticks are wrapped in foil, you hold them up in front of Nessi.

"Now you pee on it and we'll know, because as long as you don't know, you're not pregnant. It's like math."

Nessi looks at you as if you've been speaking Vietnamese. It's a weird moment and you ask yourself for the first time why Nessi's actually worried. In your eyes she'd be a great mother. You other girls are either too thin or too young or too stupid even to think of being mothers. Nessi seems like someone who's experienced everything; in your opinion she can master everything if she wants to.

An old soul, you think with envy.

A few days ago your mother took you aside again and told you about the little village she grew up in. You know the stories inside and out and you know there's no point interrupting her. This time you found out that she can see things that other people can't. Souls. Your mother is full of surprises. She told you: *Some people have young souls and others have old ones, and then there are people without.* You asked what "without" means in this context, because your mother can't feed you any bullshit. Being without a soul is impossible, you know that. That's like someone coming into the world without a heart. Your mother tapped your forehead with her index finger and you had to promise her that you would never, never get within ten feet of one of those soulless people. *You will recognize them anywhere, because they have cold in their eyes, and when they look at you they steal your breath away. Promise me that you won't let one of those soulless get ten feet near you.* Of course you promised, otherwise you'd still be sitting beside her right now. Your mother also told you that your soul is young and inexperienced, and that your life will be a long and joyless journey.

Thanks, Mom.

You would like to know what your mother would say about Nessi, who now stands in front of you, confused and hopefully not pregnant, and asks, "Why is it like math?"

"What?"

"You said it's like math. Why is it like math?"

"If you think about it for a long time it makes sense," you tell her, and quickly go on talking: "Don't think about that right now, just concentrate and pee on this. And don't hold it the wrong way around. My neighbor held it the wrong way around, but she's kind of retarded. And don't pee on your hand, because that's disgusting. Even though lots of people say urine therapy's fantastic, I can't imagine washing my face with my own pee, it would be—"

"Schnappi!"

You raise both hands in apology.

"Okay, I am quiet."

Nessi tears at the packaging and can't get it open. You take it from her and peel the test stick out of its foil. You liberate the second stick as well so that it'll go more quickly. Now you only hope that Nessi can pee, because if she can't pee . . .

"It's working," you say with all the positivity you have.

Nessi shakes the stick dry and looks at it.

"How long?"

"Two minutes."

You pass her the second stick.

Afterward you both lean against the wall of the stall, each holding one of the sticks, and wait. Last year you caught your mother in the bathroom. She was sitting on the edge of the tub gnawing at a fingernail. Her skin was almost transparent, like one of those jellyfish you saw when you were at the North Sea coast. Your mother was holding the pregnancy test just as Nessi's holding it now—vertical and pointing upwards, as if it were important to hold the stick vertical and pointing upwards. You knew your mother didn't want any more children. She's in her late thirties, she has her hands full looking after you. You've never talked about it, but it's clear to you that she had an abortion. Since then you've been wondering whether it would have been a brother or a sister. You wouldn't have minded a brother.

"Look," Nessi says quietly.

You look, then you look at the stick in your hand, then back at Nessi's.

"I'm not going to cry," says Nessi, and bursts into tears.

STINK

It feels as if you're being dragged down the street on your ass. Except that it doesn't hurt. It is a weird feeling to sit so low. Glance to the right and you could scratch people's kneecaps. The Jaguar purrs. You don't say much, that's a good feeling too, just driving around and not having to say much, understanding each other without words, drifting through the city with an empty head and a cigarette between your lips. Pure luxury.

"Hungry?" asks Neil.

No, you're not thristy either, you're just more content than you've been for ages. Your heart is still fluttering, as if someone had placed one of those hummingbirds into your chest. *Flutterflutter.* You give Neil a sideways glance and without thinking you place your hand on his thigh. Neil doesn't react, doesn't look at you, doesn't say anything, goes on driving, hands on the wheel, wind in his face. You just have to ask, "Where are we going?"

"What?"

You are shouting it.

"Dancing," he replies.

"Good," you say, and leave your hand on his thigh.

The bouncer doesn't want to let you in, Neil waves a few banknotes, the bouncer still doesn't want to let you in, Neil draws him aside. He's exactly the same height as the bouncer, but only half as wide. He talks in a lowered voice. Very controlled. Then the bouncer looks at you again, rubs his forehead as if someone's hit him, and waves you in. No problem now. He even smiles at you. The asshole couldn't get close to you if he was the last guy in the world.

"What did you say to him?" you ask.

Neil makes a gun out of his thumb and forefinger, holds it to your temple and laughs.

"I threatened him."

You push your way through the crowd, the flickering lights are dazzling, the people are jostling each other, it smells of cigarettes and artificial smoke and very faintly of limes. A gap appears at the bar, you lean against it, shout into each other's ears, laugh loudly. There's a mirror hanging above the bar, at least thirty feet long, and for one terribly long moment you can't see yourself. Your palms are clammy. You see Neil, you see the people around him, light and smoke and fog, but you yourself aren't there. Like a vampire. Invisible. Then you spot your piled-up hair, your sulky mouth, and you meet your own eye and wonder if you're really as small and insignificant as the mirror is trying to tell you. You've never seen yourself like that before. *You're a sektschbeascht,* Alberto used to say. But he said lots of things.

"Do you like it here?" Neil calls to you, and you say *yeah* even though the music isn't your thing. Nonetheless, you bob up and down as if you listened to nothing but soul all day long. You're inches away from singing along. Before it can come to that, Neil hands you a beer with a wedge of lime in the neck of the bottle and you clink drinks and then the beer's gone too and you dance and touch each other and everything's as it should be, and a bit better.

You smell Neil among all those smells—his aftershave, the sweat beneath it—and he smells good, he smells so good that you press yourself against him, and he smiles and puts his arms around you and says in your ear, "Restroom?"

You wish he would go on dancing, and yet you take his hand and follow him to the restrooms. You notice that you're thinking too much. You're missing the special little moments. You want to stop and say it's going too fast.

He hasn't even kissed me. He's barely touched me. He's—

Stop thinking, you tell yourself and keep your hand in front of your mouth and hope your breath doesn't smell bad, and hope your makeup isn't too smudged with sweat, and try to remember what sort of underwear you're wearing.

Please, not the red ones with the little blue flowers, please not those.

Neil steps inside the men's room and pushes past a few guys. He rattles at the doors, finds a free stall and drags you in behind him.

Trapped.

The music is just a murmur now. The ultraviolet light makes Neil's teeth gleam, his eyeballs are like the magnesium flare you saw in chemistry. Cold and alien. Your nervous trembling is ebbing away in little waves, the hummingbird sinks exhausted to the bottom of your chest. You've lost your drive, you're fearful and shy. You don't feel the way you did when you got into the car beside Neil. You're an outstretched hand. Naked and sensitive. It would be nice if you could turn off the voice in your head: *If he kisses me now I'll do anything he likes. It's the only way. I won't cause any trouble. I'll go along with it all, because I think Neil knows what he's doing. He's going to—*

"I've got a problem," he says, interrupting your thoughts.

"Okay," you say far too quickly and try to smile.

"No, really," says Neil and then tells you about that girl, maybe you saw her? On the other side of the dance floor? Just below the DJs' cabin? Did you notice her? No? Doesn't matter, anyway it was because of her that Neil has driven from Hamburg to Berlin. Of course he wanted to see his father, too, but he's really here because of this girl and doesn't know what to do now. He needs help. Help from you.

"From me?"

"Yes, from you."

"Why from me?"

He shuts his eyes as if he can't bear the restroom any longer. When he looks at you again, you have the feeling he's just woken up. His expression is almost embarrassing, as if he's about to burst into tears. *Stop it,* you think, and regret going with him. Guys should solve their girl problems themselves. Is that why he talked to you in the first place? Do you look like Dear Abby or something?

"Do I look like Dear Abby or something?"

"No, you look real," says Neil and leans against the stall door and shuts his eyes again. "That's all I know."

Her name is Kira. Neil met her at a party in Hamburg, and hung out with her. Then he lost sight of her and Kira disappeared, she'd just gone. And Neil started burning, that's exactly how he puts it.

"I started burning."

He discovered that Kira was living with the girlfriend of a friend in Berlin, and that is why he borrowed his mother's car. Kira doesn't know he's here. Neil doesn't know what to do. And you sit between them and feel as if you're still in the cinema, back row, the picture's out of focus, the people are too noisy, and the movie's a dreary mixture of relationship crisis and sex comedy.

Let's see who laughs first, you think when you're back at the bar. Neil has organized two new bottles of beer and asks what you think of Kira.

"Look at her," he pleads.

You look across. Kira's one of those smoothies, what did you expect? Smooth hair and smooth face, and when she laughs even her teeth are smooth. She reminds you a bit of Taja, one of those girls everybody wants to have as their friend. Except that Taja isn't really smooth, she has hidden corners and edges, and that makes her especially beautiful. But you don't want to think about Taja now. Neil is waiting for an answer. What does he want to hear? His Kira looks great, and you wish that she'd get her period or a rash all over her face. But girls like Kira never get rashes, and they only get their periods when no one's looking.

"And?"

You roll your eyes. What's wrong with this guy?

"Look for yourself."

Neil shakes his head: no, he can't. He stares into the mirror above the bar.

"What are you scared of? She's just another beautiful bitch, she will definitely remember you. You're not sixteen anymore, why are you farting around?"

Neil turns the bottle in his hands, then lifts his shoulders as if to say *I don't know* and stands there like an idiot with his shoulders lifted. You've just got to ask him, "Are you in love?"

The shoulders come back down, his gaze avoids you and carves scratches in the mirror above the bar.

Bull's-eye.

You laugh.

All this because he's in love?

"I'm cursed," he says.

"What?"

"No, really. I've been this way for as long as I've been able to think. And it never stops. I search and search and I can't find the right love. I've been behaving like an idiot and I can't even . . . Have you never been in love?"

"It's nonsense."

"What's nonsense?"

"You know, falling in love. It's just nonsense. It's for people who have nothing better to do with their time. That's why I'm not going to fall in love, right? If I want pain I can pinch myself."

"It's not the same."

"You don't know how hard I can pinch."

Neil flinches when you reach for his arm. You take a swig of his beer, even though your bottle is still half full. What a spoilsport.

"So you've never had a boyfriend?" he asks.

"You want a list?"

"And you were never in love, not once? I don't believe it."

Neil looks away from the mirror and looks you straight in the eye. Real headlights. You feel some beer trickling from the corner of your mouth, and quickly set the bottle back down again.

"I'd fall in love with you in a blink," he says. "If Kira wasn't there, I'd be head over heels already, that's the way I am."

You cough. It's like in a slasher movie. Now all you have to do is go over there and cut Kira's throat and you'll have a new boyfriend, and one who's in love with you.

"Okay, I'll take care of her," you say and walk over to Kira.

As you shove your way through the dancing crowd, there's a sentence of Neil's that you can't get out of your head. *You look real.* It could have been intended as an insult. What did he mean? And why did he single you out, of all people?

Because I was standing on my own, because there was no one else around, because . . .

All nonsense. *There's no such thing as chance,* Schnappi said once, *everything happens the way it's supposed to.* Why should you doubt that now? Why are you so goddamn insecure? Just wait till your girls hear what's happened to you. They'll be green with envy and they won't believe a word of it.

"Hi."

You stop in front of Kira, your hands are shoved into your back trouser pockets, your pelvis is sticking out. She smiles at you, she's in her early twenties, just right for Neil. Kira leans forward and you lean forward too as if you were about to hug each other, then you tell her your name, your real name. She holds out her hand. Fingers cool as marble, green flecks in her irises.

Dammit, she's pretty.

"Do you know that guy over there? The one standing at the bar?"

Kira looks past you. Neil still has his back turned to you. You're sure he's watching both of you in the mirror above the bar.

"The guy who's looking away. The one with the ponytail. He's my friend. You met him at a party in Hamburg. He followed you here and he brought me with him. He wanted me to see who you are. You get that? He's completely confused. He doesn't know who he wants. You or me. Do you want him?"

"Who?"

Kira is confused, you can tell by her frown that she has no idea who you're talking about.

"Neil."

"Neil?"

"Yes, Neil."

"Never heard of him."

"Oh."

"Is he sweet?"

"Very."

"Sorry."

"Sorry about what?"

"That he's confused, but I don't remember him."

You nod as if you understand.

"He'll be devastated," you say and walk back to Neil.

"So?"

He asks without turning around, eyes on the mirror; you're sure he's been watching you all along and at the same time he's peeled the whole label off his beer bottle, total coward. But that's okay, even cowards have to exist. You press your lips to his ear and say, "She wants to talk to you," before you turn away, leaving him at the bar.

And there you are, it's too early, the night has just begun and you can go and meet your girls at the playground. You can if you want. But what do you want?

It feels as if a whole day has gone by. The time with Neil has stretched, as if someone had taken hold of the minutes and pulled them apart.

He could at least have kissed me.

You imagine what that would have been like. His lips, your lips, and off you go. Nothing happens in your head, you have no imagination, as soon as things get serious the screen goes blank. There's the taste of beer and lime in your mouth, and it reminds you of the beach and the sea, you think you can hear the rush of waves and there is the salty taste of the water on your lips, but you can't imagine a simple kiss.

Damn.

You look up at the sky. The stars above Berlin are always a marvel. *The city is far too bright,* Ruth once explained to you. *Because of all the lights you can't see the sky. Reflections and stuff.* That bitch always knows everything. But you wish she was here now. Ruth, and Schnappi, and Nessi. And Taja, of course, Taja too. She would know right away where you went wrong with Neil.

The longing creeps up on you, and you bite your lower lip. *Taja, where are you?* It's like a hole in your belly that the wind blows through, and there's always a cold spot, whatever you do, you can't keep that spot warm. It's been six days, and you can hardly remember her face.

What if she's gone forever?

"What're you doing up there?"

You look to the right. Neil is standing beside his Jaguar.

"Looking for the stars," you say, and slip off the car roof.

Neil rubs both hands over his face.

"Have you been crying?"

He brings his hands down. He hasn't been crying. He's just completely wasted.

"She doesn't remember me. She says she was so drunk that she doesn't even know whose house the party was at."

You wait to hear if there's anything else; there isn't anything else. Of course you can't leave it there.

"So? Are you still in love?"

He lifts his shoulders again and lets them fall, which could mean anything, then he opens the passenger door and you get in. He walks around the car. You belt yourself in, he belts himself in and starts the engine and drives off. You sense that there's nothing more to say. So you check your face in the side mirror and you smile at yourself and contentedly fold your hands in your lap.

They're sitting in the playground like a flock of fat crows, surrounded by pizza boxes and beer cans. Your crowd. Neil doesn't want to meet them, he doesn't even get out, he sits in the car and scribbles his number on the cinema ticket, smiles wearily and says, "Just in case." He probably isn't even aware of your kiss, but you are aware of the thin film of sweat on his cheek and imagine him driving back to Hamburg now, down the highway, on the road for hours, on his own for hours, even the trucks will overtake him. You know one thing for certain: he'll forget Kira quickly enough, but he won't forget you.

SCHNAPPI

Nessi looks down the street and avoids your eye. She doesn't want to go to the playground, she doesn't want to see the others, or speak, or do anything. The question is what do you want to do now? Your best friend is pregnant and you can't just disappear and leave her alone, that's not an option.

"Don't tell anyone," says Nessi.

"I'll take you home," you say, avoiding her request, which isn't all that stupid, because you don't know if you can keep your mouth shut. You've always had problems with secrets. They only exist to be shared.

"Thanks."

Even though it's not on your way, you take Nessi to Nollendorfplatz on your bike. It's a funny image. A dwarf who can hardly reach the pedals with her feet, and behind her a giant, clinging onto the dwarf as if the faintest breeze might separate them.

You cut across the Kurfürstendamm, come off the road at the Gedächtniskirche and onto the sidewalk, getting yelled at by the tourists. On the way you talk about your mother in the bathroom, even though you don't really know what your mother was doing. Your mouth is a machine gun, it never runs out of ammunition. Twice the word "abortion" slips sharp and jagged from your mouth and you bite your tongue to brake the onrush of words. Nessi doesn't react. She clings to your hips and rests her head against your back. When you stop at Winterfeldtplatz she doesn't move and you wait a minute and then another before you say you've arrived. Nessi straightens up, rubs her eyes and looks up at her block as if you'd dragged her to a gulag.

"Where are you actually going?"

You give a start. You look over your shoulder. Sorry, girl, but we're starting to worry about you. Nessi is still sitting on the luggage rack and you're still sitting on your bike and you feel her left breast warm against your back. Nessi asked you a good question. Where are you actually going? You're not outside Nessi's block, you're not even anywhere near, you're riding all the way through Charlottenburg in the wrong direction. More precisely you're on Krumme Strasse; even more precisely than that, you're on the way to Stuttgarter Platz.

At some point I'm going to be killed, you think, and try to calm the shaking in your arms.

The first time you had a blank, two years ago, it was when you were at school and the bell rang for break. You went outside to get a hot chocolate from the kiosk, and you talked to a guy you've always wanted to talk to. Stink brought you back to reality by kicking your chair from behind, and at that moment you were back in class and Stink was asking if you'd give her some chewing gum. You couldn't work out what had happened. It felt so real you could taste the hot chocolate in your mouth.

The second time was a month later at a party. You spent almost the whole evening playing strip poker, and when that got boring you went downstairs to dance a bit. Two songs later you were sweating and happy and wanted to fetch a drink when Ruth tapped you on the forehead and said she'd like to see if you were bluffing or not, because anybody who sweats bucketloads like you were doing must be bluffing. You looked helplessly at the people around you. You were still playing poker, your cards were rubbish, and there was a memory of dancing and there were drops of sweat on your forehead.

———

Your girls don't know anything about it. You're worried they'll think you're crazy and have you put in an asylum right away. Probably you got it from your mother. She calls herself a shaman and says she can sense when dead people are walking past her. She also firmly believes that everyone has to cross an abyss before he becomes a *real* person. Whatever a real person is, your mother says a lot of things when she has time on her hands, like that she has to die in Vietnam and nowhere else, she won't be persuaded otherwise. You've looked the word up, and you're sure your mother isn't a shaman, because she's never used her abilities for the good of the community. Witch would be better.

Two years have passed since then, and during that time you've had blanks at least once a month. It's your description for those daydreams that aren't really just daydreams. It's not a jump cut and it's not exactly a blackout. Whatever it is, no one writes on the internet about it. It's your very own illness. So you weren't surprised for a second when you rode your bike half a mile through the Berlin traffic with Nessi on the luggage rack without getting under a car.

Practice makes perfect, you think, and you'd be grateful if your arms would finally stop shaking.

And there you are now and you wish you weren't there. You made a mistake, you were supposed to bring Nessi home. Look at her: she's not really in the now, she's like one of those zombies who stare stupidly around the place and then go for your throat the minute you're looking the other way.

Nessi leaves half of her pizza and drinks a whole beer, then takes a drag on a joint and holds her breath until the smoke has disappeared into her and only hot air comes out.

Not good, not good at all.

You wish the boys would clear off, then you could talk. The boys are Indi, Eric, and Jasper. They could equally well be called Karl, Tommi, and Frank. It makes no difference. A year ago it made a big difference. Something has changed. As if your girls had switched off the interest when school ended. Ruth is the only exception. She's flirting with the three lads, and you could bet that at least one of them has a boner. You slide across to Nessi and can't help thinking of Taja. Alone you're nothing, together you're strong. First Taja disappears, then Stink. *Blood sisters never leave each other in the lurch.* That's what you'd love to whisper to Nessi, but Nessi would immediately think she's the one leaving you in the lurch, so you just shut up.

There are two beeps; Nessi fishes her phone out of her jacket. *Let it not be Henrik,* you think. *Let it be anyone else, just not Henrik.* You know a lot of idiots, but Henrik's right up at the top of the list. No one should be made pregnant by somebody like him. You know what you're talking about. You hooked up a few times with him and he dumped you when you wouldn't sleep with him. Henrik is like an advertisement on TV that everybody thinks is funny and then they forget all about it because there are so many advertisements that are just as funny.

Ruth points over your shoulder.

"Look who's coming!"

You turn around. Stink is getting out of a hot set of wheels. She sticks her hands in her back pockets and comes strolling over to you. The relief floods over you with such force that you explode with stupid laughter.

Now everything's going to be okay again.

"Hey, where have you been?" Ruth asks.

"Where do you think I was?" Stink asks back and doesn't even turn around as the red Jaguar drives off. "I took a trip. First Tenerife, then Malibu."

The crowd whistles and laughs, Nessi looks up from her phone and smiles wearily. Stink says she needs some chow, right now or even sooner. She is like quicksilver, nothing can hold her. Off she goes to the pizza stand. Ruth has the same idea as you and goes running after her. Nessi is forgotten for a moment. You want to know what Stink got up to with the guy in the Jag.

"I can hardly walk," she says, "it was that hot."

Ruth and you screech, even though you don't want to, the screech just slips out of you. You immediately hold your hand in front of your mouth and your eyes glitter with envy. If you rubbed them now, it would probably rain stardust.

"No way!" says Ruth.

"Yes way."

"Tell us it's not true!" you demand.

"But it is true."

"So what would you like?"

The pizza guy grins at you. He's in his mid-forties, he's wearing a stupid T-shirt, and his hair's so greasy he looks as if his head has spent all week in the food fryer. Stink ignores him and studies the menu, even though she always orders the same pizza.

"Who is he?" asks Ruth.

"Who's who?"

"The guy with the Jag."

"Oh . . ."

Stink pulls a face as if she's got a toothache.

"What's up?" you want to know.

"Hey, hot mama, what's up?" asks Ruth.

Even the pizza guy leans in curiously as if he knows what you're talking about.

"I forgot to ask him his name," Stink says, making the sort of big innocent eyes that people can only make if they know that innocence is a load of lies that would drop its pants for a measly slice of pizza.

You all walk down to the Lietzensee. The guys want to go to the park because they think that if the moon's shining and you're all sitting by the water it'll be romantic and they might cop a feel. You let them believe that, because then they'll shut their traps and try to behave properly.

By the shore you make a dip in the grass, scrunch up some paper, and lay dry twigs over it. Indi rolls the second joint of the evening, and then you are sitting there, blowing smoke at the mosquitoes and talking quietly as if you didn't want to disturb the night. Jasper is playing some kind of racket through his phone, a dog barks from the opposite bank, and now it would be good if you could shut your eyes and go off on one of your blanks, because you don't really want what's going to happen next.

One of the guys spots it first.

"What's up with Nessi?"

You look around. Nessi isn't sitting with the rest of you anymore, she's squatting down by the shore. And as you are looking, she slides silently into the water. Fully dressed, of course. The guys burst out laughing. You try to get up. Eric holds you back and asks if you're about to go for a swim too, or what.

"Nessi!"

Stink runs to the shore, suddenly everybody's at the shore and you're alone sitting in the grass like a parcel that someone's forgotten to send, and when you catch up with your girls at last, you see Nessi drifting in the middle of the lake with her arms spread. She's just lying there playing dead, and the guys are calling out and calling her Loch Nessi, and you call her to come back, even from the hotel opposite someone calls out of a window, but Nessi doesn't react.

"She'll come back," says Stink and points into the grass where Nessi has left her wallet and phone. "Someone who doesn't want her phone to get wet is always going to come back."

"I'm not going to collect her," says Indi and spits into the water.

"I'd have been surprised," says Stink.

The guys are sitting around the fire again. They're only interested in whatever's actually happening, and nothing's happening on the Lietzensee right now. You girls keep standing by the shore and Ruth says Nessi must have had a row with Henrik, and you say Henrik's an idiot, and Stink says what else is new, and adds, "The way Nessi's behaving, she must be knocked up."

"*I* didn't say that."

Your girls look at you in surprise.

"I really didn't say that," you add quickly.

"Oh, shit," says Ruth.

"Oh, shit," says Stink.

No one needs to point out that you're one of the worst secret-keepers in the world.

"I really didn't say that," you repeat, and it sounds so lame that you can't think of anything else to say for a while. You just stare at the Lietzensee and hope that Nessi will stay in the water for a bit longer.

II

so you lost your trust,
and you never should have

Coldplay
SEE YOU SOON

THE TRAVELER

The country heard nothing more about you for two years. You hadn't disappeared, and you hadn't gone into hiding. You're not one of those people who have a second identity. Jekyll and Hyde are a nonsense as far as you're concerned. You've returned to your life. Silently. There were eight hours omitted, eight hours when no one missed you.

Your life took its course.

In the morning you woke up and had breakfast. You were reliable at work. You had lunch with your colleagues and chatted. No shadow haunted your thoughts. You were you. On the weekends you did your family duties and visited your six-year-old son for a few hours. Your wife made lunch for you both and then tacitly handed you the bills. You parted in peace, no one mentioned divorce because no one wanted to take the last step. So every weekend you put the bills in your pocket, kissed the boy goodbye on the top of his head, and then drove back to your three-room apartment.

Some evenings you met friends or sat alone in front of the television and watched the world spinning increasingly out of control. You went on vacation, you set money aside and had two operations on your knee. You never thought about the winter two years ago and the traffic jam on the A4. You saw the reports and listened to the features on the radio. When there was a report on TV, you switched channels uninterested. You know what you've done. There's no reason to go on worrying about it. You're you. And after two years the Traveler is coming back.

―――――

It is October.
  It is 1997.
  It is night.

We're in mid-autumn, and you can't shake off the feeling that summer is refusing to go. The weather is mild. Storms rage on the weekend and it's only at night that the temperature falls to below ten degrees. It feels like the last exhalation of summer.

You've been on the road for four hours and you want to stop at a rest area, but all the parking lots are full of semi-trailers so you drive on and turn on the indicator at the next gas station. Here again there's hardly a free space. The semis with their trailers remind you of abandoned houses rolling across the country, never coming to rest. It's still a hundred and twenty miles to your apartment. You aren't one of those people who go to the edge and then collapse with exhaustion. Not you.

After you've driven past the gas pumps, you park in the shade of a trailer, get out and stretch. For a few minutes you stand motionless in the darkness listening to the ticking of the engine. In the distance there are footsteps, the click of nozzles, engines are started, the rushing sound of the highway. Then there's a croak. You look around. On the other side of the parking lot a row of bare trees looms up into the night sky. A crow sits on one of the branches. It bobs up and down as if to draw attention to itself. At that moment you become aware that you've never seen a crow at night before. Seagulls, owls, sometimes even a hawk on a road sign, but never a crow. You tilt your head. The crow does the same and then looks to the side. You follow its gaze. Three hundred yards from the gas station there's a motel. A red neon sign hangs over the entrance. A woman steps out. She walks to her car, gets in, and drives off.

You remember exactly what you were thinking.

You were thinking: *Now there's a free space.*

―――――

Seven cameras at the gas station and about eight hundred cars that fit
the time frame. The police checked all the number plates. A special
commission was set up, and over the years that followed it was dealing only with this case. Overtime, frustration, suspicions, and a lot
of idiots claiming it was them. The papers went mad, all other news
paled. And they had nothing to offer the reader. Except the dead.

You walk over to the motel and step inside the foyer. You aren't surprised that there is no one at reception. It's late. Above the reception
there is a black sign with a white arrow pointing to a bell. On the
sign it says: *Please ring.*

You don't ring.

A television flickers from a back room. You go into the room. A
woman is sleeping on a fold-out sofa. She is covered to the neck by
a woolen blanket. On the table in front of her there's a plastic bowl
containing a ready meal. The remains of peas and mashed potato.
A bit of meat. And beside it a half-empty bottle of Fanta and an
empty glass. You sit down in the armchair opposite the woman and
relax. The murmur from the television, the sleep of the woman, the
silence of the night. As you leave the room, you don't turn the television off. The blanket has slipped; you lay it carefully around the
woman's body and tuck it in at the ends.

The motel has two upper floors, each with sixteen rooms; there are
ten rooms on the first floor. You look at the plan. Under the counter
at reception you find a box. There are three skeleton keys in the box.

You go up the stairs.

On the second floor you open the first door and go in. You stop
in the anteroom and go back out again. You leave the second room
after a few seconds as well. Children. The smell of children. After
you've gone into the third room, you take a deep breath, a single
breath replies. You pull the door closed. The darkness embraces you.

This is the right place.

If you drove past the gas station today, you'd see a closed-down motel. The sight of it would remind you of the night twelve years ago—no light in the windows, motionless curtains, stillness. The flickering neon sign above the entrance is broken. And even though the rest area is always full, nobody parks in front of the motel. *Cursed*, they say. Weeds have fought their way through the cracks, they press against the building as though to support the façade. No one lays flowers outside anymore. The grave candles have disappeared. There's only an ugly yellow graffito on the front door: *Forever Yang*.

Almost two years after the A4 you've set off on your travels again, and everyone recognized your signature. The papers called you *The Avenging Angel*. On the internet you were *The Traveler*, sometimes *The German Nightmare* or *The Big Bad Wolf*. Fanatics called you *The Scourge of God*. By now the police knew you were acting alone. The clues were everywhere, and the clues didn't lie. You were aware of that. Clues mean you've been there. Honesty is important to you. There's nothing you want to hide. Everyone should know you exist. Of course your fingerprints were no help to the police. No previous convictions. You exist only in your own world.

Your myth grew beyond the borders of Germany, you made waves all around Europe. In England a bank cashier ran amok, in the Czech Republic it was a customer in a supermarket and in Italy a woman who said she couldn't stand the pressure anymore. Events began to accumulate. In Sweden a man killed his family and wandered through his apartment block with bloody hands until a Doberman went for his throat. In the Netherlands a boy put explosives in a McDonald's, joined the queue, and set off the explosives when his turn came. A television evangelist spoke of the Day of Judgment, studies were produced, prognoses filled the commercial breaks. Humanity seemed to be walking toward self-destruction with its arms spread wide open. None of it had anything to do with you.

Not rage, not despair, not self-destruction or revenge.

Not hate, not love, not religion or politics.

You're in no hurry. You go into the rooms one after the other and sit down on the edge of the bed. You watch them sleeping, the way you would watch a patient who has a fever and needs a cooling hand. You wonder what's happening to you. The Here, the Now, and you on the edge of a stranger's bed. With your hands around their neck and your fists in their face. You. Not hesitating for a moment. And they. Defending themselves and then giving up. And there's always this feeling of sympathy. As if they knew why you're doing it. As if at that brief moment of dying they understood. At least that's how it feels to you. As if they understood: that you're on a quest, that you have to explore the darkness. Because the darkness is always there. And in the darkness there's nothing to find.

That night you go into forty-two rooms and leave thirty-six corpses. After that you put the skeleton key back in the box and step out into the night like someone who has rested and can now continue on his journey.

The crow has vanished from the tree, the neon sign above the entrance still flickers. Three hours have passed. The traffic moves tirelessly in both directions. The world outside the motel has hardly changed.

On the journey home you look at your hands on the wheel. This time you didn't wear gloves. Your hands are bruised, the knuckles bloody, the pain feels good. *I am, I exist.* You're aware that you've left lots of clues. It feels right and good.

RAGNAR

Oskar isn't the first corpse you've found yourself sitting opposite. If you're not careful, someone might think this is a family tradition. Even if you don't think that's funny at the moment, a few hours later you'll make a joke about it and once again you'll be the only one laughing.

Your first corpse was a lunatic who behaved normally during the day and came home in the evening and went totally nuts. You've read a lot about mental illnesses and schizophrenia. You've engaged intensively with the mental effects of wars, because you wanted to understand your father. But how are you supposed to understand the paranoia of a man who's never been to war?

You found out that one of your uncles suffered from similar delusions. Perhaps it was a genetic defect. Everything's possible, but not everything's excusable. Everyone is responsible for his own life, and excuses are for cowards. Your father was definitely one of those.

He worked as one of eight bricklayers with a construction company and met your mother in Oslo in the early 1960s. He proposed and brought her to Germany. The first years of marriage ran smoothly, and it was only when Oskar and you appeared on the scene that everything changed. Your father started training you boys when you were six and Oskar was three. Outside of your apartment he was the most normal person you could imagine. But once the door closed, silence fell. The television was turned off, conversations lingered only as an echo in the rooms, sometimes you even held your breath. As soon as your father entered the room, a different life began for you.

Two decades later you asked your mother how she could have allowed it all to happen, and whether she'd never had any doubts about her husband's mental state. She didn't understand you. She wanted to know why you felt the need to drag your father's memory through the dirt.

After he had stepped inside the apartment, he took his shoes off and disappeared into the bathroom. Meanwhile your mother put the chain on and bolted the front door with extra locks. With your help she took the metal plate out from behind the wardrobe and pushed it against the door. Two clamps were placed around it and the door was secure. For you it was the other way round. You were trapped.

Once you made the mistake of opening the bathroom door, even though your father had forbidden it. You were curious, and in those days your father's madness seemed to be only a slight drizzle that would eventually pass. You were seven years old and just needed to find out what he did in the bathroom after work every day. You waited till your mother took Oskar into the kitchen to get the food ready, then you pushed the handle down.

Your father was standing naked in front of the wash basin, washing himself with a sponge. There was nothing else to be seen. You were so relieved that you nearly burst out laughing. It was all you had wanted to know. Your relief lasted only seconds. Your father told you to come in and shut the door behind you. He didn't look at you as he spoke, he didn't need to look at you. You obeyed. He set the sponge aside and told you to turn the light off. You obeyed. Your father pulled the curtain over the narrow bathroom window. It grew dark, really dark. Your father asked you if you knew what fear was. You nodded. Your father wanted to hear an answer. So you said: *Yes, I know what fear is.* Silence. You sensed him standing right in front of you. The smell of his naked body. He must have leaned forward, because his breath wiped over your face like a flame. *You have no idea what fear is,* he explained. Then you heard water running, and a moment later a wet towel was wrapped around your head. The towel was a shock. Suffocating and cold. You couldn't see at all, and he used a towel anyway. Your father asked you again if you knew what fear was. He also said: *I'll teach you fear. I'll teach you everything about fear, so that you venerate and respect it. Because you can't live without fear. Fear is air, fear is water, fear is everything.* You reacted instinctively, the towel was just too much for you, you couldn't breathe, so you started to swing your fists around.

That was all you could remember.

Later your mother picked you up from the floor and carried you to bed. At six o'clock in the morning she woke you again. You had to wipe up the filth in the bathroom. You caught your breath when you saw what you'd done. There was vomit on the tiles, there was urine and two bloody handprints on the whitewashed wall, which you rubbed away at with a cloth and soapsuds until two gleaming white patches remained. Never again did you make the mistake of surprising your father in the bathroom. You learned to respect fear.

As soon as your father was out of the bathroom, the preparations began. He checked all the windows, examined the front door, and the balcony door had to be secure as well before your mother was allowed to lower the shutters. You remember how she secretly reassured you, over and over again, that things would soon be back to normal, your father was going through a difficult phase. She was wrong. The drizzle was about to become a storm.

Your father had plans.

He took out library books about the conduct of war and taught you how to survive in the wilderness. Once he came home and told you and your brother to take a bullet out of his arm. He removed his shirt. There were his sinewy arms, there were the knotty muscles and no wound. Oskar knew what lay ahead. He burst into tears at the sight of the sinewy arms. Your father pointed at the box.

The box was a battered metal trunk that had belonged to your grandfather. If anyone didn't obey or burst into tears, he ended up in the trunk. You remember the smell, shoe polish and linseed oil. Your mother shut Oskar inside. No word of protest ever passed her lips. Oskar's whimpering emerged from the suitcase like the sound of a trapped insect.

Here, your father tapped you on the shoulder, *here's the bloody bullet. Get it out, Ragnar, get it out of there.*

You did everything right. You heated the knife over a Bunsen burner. You handed your father a bottle of schnapps and told him to drink it. Your mother held the bandage ready. You didn't hesitate for a second and cut into your father's flesh as if it were a slice of smoked pork on a plate. The picture is still very clear in front of your eyes—the way the blade sinks in and splits the skin, the way the blood runs down his arm, first hesitantly, then violently, and your father smiles at you and says: *Well done, you've saved my life.*

Throughout the years your father didn't let you and your brother go to bed before midnight. There were always shadows under your eyes. There was so much to do, so much to learn. He showed you war documentaries and taught you how to look after a gun. At the age of nine you could take a Luger apart and put it back together. You could tell the ammunition of different calibers apart and say which was best suited to which situation. You studied the human body for its most vulnerable spots.

Even though your father never killed anyone himself, you learned from him and became his tool, while Oskar stumbled after you and couldn't work out what was going on. He was simply too young. He was frightened, and you protected him. It worked. Your father focused his attention more and more on you, and Oskar was spared.

You gave your brother that protection until today.

From Monday evening till Friday night your family led a different life. Even though your father went to work during the day and you were able to resume normal life in the meantime, it was only on the weekends that you really had time to breathe. On Saturday and Sunday your father disappeared without a trace and no one mentioned it. For two days he stopped existing for you. You boys assumed he was carrying out secret missions or perhaps working for the army. Eight years passed before you penetrated his secret. Even now you don't know if your mother was completely unaware of what was going on. How could she not have known? She wasn't a weak woman, or a stupid one. But she had fallen for your father, which can turn any strong woman into a pitiful creature.

Worst of all were the days of discipline. Your father was testing Oskar and you to see if you could keep your mouths shut. He wanted to know how far you would go to protect each other. He thought up games for it. *Tell your brother a secret,* he said to you. And so you bent down to Oskar and whispered in his ear. *What secret did your big brother tell you?* your father then asked Oskar, who immediately widened his eyes, held his breath, and shook his head. Sometimes your father ordered him to lie on the floor and then pressed Oskar's little face into the carpet with one hand. Or else he pulled him up by his hair, until the tips of Oskar's toes scrabbled above the floor. *What secret did your big brother tell you?* The same question, over and over again. Tears flowed down Oskar's cheeks, he didn't want to disappoint his father, he wanted to be big and strong and show what he had learned. Your father grabbed him by the throat. *I can feel the secret,* he said, *it's hidden in here, I can feel it, I can feel it really clearly.* That was too much for Oskar, he slumped unconscious to the ground. Your father turned to you. *Your brother was brave, he didn't say anything. Now there's just you. What's your secret? What am I not supposed to find out?* He threatened you with a lot of things, and you were the brave soldier and stood stiffly and looked past him, because eye contact was forbidden. He hit your mother to make you speak. Nothing. He asked you if you wanted him to rape her in front of your eyes. You shook your head and held your tongue. That was a mistake. *You're saying no to me?* He took you into the bathroom, and there in the dark and with a wet towel over your head you cracked. It was too much. It was memory and it was the madness of a man who was your father and always found a way into your head. The secret came stammering over your lips. It was over. Your father led you in silence from the bathroom. He waited till your brother was conscious again, then he spat in your face and said, You're a traitor and you would have gambled away your whole family's lives. Your brother had to spit on you too and your mother wasn't allowed to look at you for the rest of the evening.

It was all a matter of discipline.

Since that day more than thirty years ago you have known exactly what silence is worth. Today your father could do what he liked to you, he wouldn't have a chance. You've learned from him.

It takes Tanner and David forty minutes to find the boy. They bring him down to the swimming pool. David tries to tell you all the places they've been looking. You wave him away, you don't want to hear it. They leave you alone.

He looks like he's about twelve, but you're sure he's older, otherwise he wouldn't be in your son's crowd and they wouldn't be friends. You wait for him to meet your eye before you say, "Do you know who I am?"

He shakes his head. He doesn't know your face, but he knows your name.

"My name is Ragnar Desche."

He ducks down, he actually ducks down. Good. His eyes flicker from left to right, he gradually realizes how much trouble he's in.

"Your girlfriend stood us up, that's why you're here, do you get that?"

He nods, even though you're sure he doesn't know what you're talking about. You let it go, you want to get it over with as quickly as possible.

"As I'm sure you'll have noticed, I have a small problem here. You see the man in the armchair?"

The boy turns his head.

"His name is Oskar. He was my brother. Now do you understand why I brought you here?"

The boy looks at you for a moment, then turns his head away. You can see the dark fluff trembling on his top lip. You should ask more questions, make him feel he has something to say.

"Where do you come from?"

"From here."

"And your parents?"

"Slovenia."

"Do the Slovenians get on with the Serbs?"

The boy's eyes wander nervously around the room.

If he bursts into tears right now, you think, *I will go crazy.*

"I asked you a question."

"I . . . I don't know."

"You're Slovenian and you *don't know* if the Slovenians get on with the Serbs?"

"I'm from Berlin."

Two steps and you're standing beside him, he's a head shorter than you, your face looms above his. You smell fear and the chewing-gum he has in his mouth.

"Spit out the chewing-gum."

He spits it on the floor, ducks down again; your voice is a hiss.

"Listen carefully, you little shit, I can rip your asshole open until your parents can't tell whether you're a human being or a sewer. I can rip open your parents' assholes too, if you like. I need clear answers from you, that's all I want to hear, you understand?"

He understands, you wait another few seconds, then you turn away. It is time for some calm words. You take one of the chairs and put it by the pool.

"Sit down."

The boy hesitates, then he sits down and looks at the pool.

"Sad sight, right?"

The boy doesn't know if he should answer. You stand behind him and put your hands on his shoulders. Like father, like son. You're sorry your son isn't there. He might learn something.

"What do you know about the girl?"

The boy flinches as if you'd stabbed him in the back of the neck. Your hands stay where they are. His collarbones feel as if they're made of chicken bones.

"Tell me everything. What her name is, where I can find her. Everything."

The boy's body is rigid, you take your hands off his shoulders. One blow and his neck would be broken.

"You know what she's done."

The boy says he doesn't know anything. He has to say it twice, his voice is so weak. Suddenly you sound friendly.

"My son told me lots about you. He says you're good, you'll go a long way some day. He also told me there's more between you and the girl. He said you're an item."

Silence, his face turns red, he stares into the pool; that's an answer too. He's probably one of those late developers who jerk off six times a day and bore girls senseless with stupid pickup lines.

"Do you know Taja?"

The boy shakes his head.

"Do you know Taja's father?"

He shakes his head again. You tell him that's Taja's father right there. He follows your outstretched arm, looks again at your dead brother and slowly grasps the connection. His eyes widen. It's time for him to understand you completely.

"A daughter kills her father, a man loses his brother, five kilos of heroin disappear, and a boy sits on a chair and doesn't reply. That's how things are."

You look at your watch.

"I'm going to leave the house in exactly half an hour. If I don't get an answer from you by then, you're staying here. Now look at me."

The boy looks up, he has tears in his eyes. He stinks of hormones and sweat and a little bit of shit.

"What's your name?"

"M-M-Mirko."

"Hi, Mirko, you've got half an hour to save your life."

MIRKO

A wood louse hides under a stone. That's exactly how it is. You're the wood louse, the stone's a car that you've squashed yourself under as if the sky was about to cave in on you. If someone tells you right now that Darian's father will be standing beside you in three days' time, giving you half an hour to save your life, you'd probably never come out from under that car. You've not met Ragnar Desche until then. He's a legend, he's a ghost and the father of your best friend. Nobody talks about Ragnar Desche. Never. Even thinking about him is taboo. Or as Darian once said: *If my father wants, I'm dead within a second.*

There's a nasty taste in your mouth, sweet and metallic, as if you'd bitten off some chocolate without taking off the silver paper. You spit, see the red stain on the tarmac and swallow down your own blood.

You ran away. That's it. The end.

I know.

How could you run away? Only an idiot would run away. You're the idiot. And what are you going to do now? You can't just stay under the car hiding. You just can't do that. Somebody will find out. These things always come out.

The wood louse rolls aside and pulls itself up by the door handle, it crouches beside the car, back to the driver's door, head thrown back so the blood doesn't drip from its nose. You know if the car alarm goes off the wood louse will have a heart attack and piss its jeans.

It's staying quiet.

You breathe out and look at the other side of the street.

It's staying quiet.

The derelict house makes you think of a rabid dog that's just waiting for you to make a false move. Lurking and rigid. Five lamps from the building site are flashing orange lights and illuminating the façade with a flickering light. It's one of those ruins that you loved as a child. Graffiti on the walls, not a soul to be seen and hidden treasures everywhere. You're not a child anymore, you don't find ruins exciting anymore. It's eleven at night and the city is a greedy hand hovering over you, wanting to stuff you into the darkest hole of the building site.

You rub the blood from your nose and wonder why no one's followed you. Things don't get sadder than this. No one's interested in you. They wanted Darian. They've got Darian.

Shit.

"What am I . . ."

Your voice is a croak. You're not great at talking to yourself. In horror movies the victims eventually start talking to themselves so that the viewer knows things are turning serious. Nothing serious is happening here, you're miles away from serious.

How could I have run away?

Your tongue checks if you've got a loose tooth. You're relieved, all your teeth are in place. And your nose isn't even broken. You banged it when you crawled under that car. A wood louse through and through. You shake your head to get your brain back in gear. You have to do something, doesn't matter what, you have to do something, otherwise you won't be able to look at yourself in the mirror again for the rest of the year.

Think.

A few bicycles are parked beside the church, you start tugging away at one of them, kicking the pedals. The chain snaps with a crack, your hands are bruised but hey, you've got the fucking chain.

"Okay, okay, okay . . ."

You wrap one end firmly around your fist and let the chain dangle against your thigh, then you pull yourself together and cross the street.

Whatever happens, one thing is certain, no one's going to be expecting you.

Darian sits in the ruins on an upside-down plastic barrel, staring into the distance. Elbows on his knees, hands slack. He reminds you a bit of a drawing in a book. Hercules sitting on a rock after a great battle, taking a break. Darian doesn't look up when you approach, and for a moment you're sure he's crying.

"Everything all right?"

Darian raises his head. There's a bloody scratch above his left eye, and his lower lip looks as if he's had a collagen injection. There's a second scratch on his upper arm, the muscles stand out angry, his T-shirt is a tight fit. It's a mystery to you how anyone would dare to mess with Darian.

"What's with the bike chain?" he asks, and his words sound as if he's got a pillow in his mouth.

"Sorry," you say and drop the chain.

And then there you stand, and there lies the chain at your feet, and there sits Darian who looks at you and says, "You ran away, right?"

You lower your head, you turn red.

"These jerks," says Darian, and lets you off the hook. "Look at my face, you see that?"

You lean forward and look at his face. Yes, you see it.

"I'm gonna kill them for that," he says. "And now . . ."

Darian holds his hand out to you. He doesn't have to say anything, you open your belt and take off your jeans. It's the least you can do for him. You're lucky he doesn't hit you. It would have been okay, he could even have whipped you with the bike chain, no problem, wood lice can cope with that kind of stuff.

Your jeans are too short, they stick to Darian's legs like a second skin, he can't fasten the top button, abs of titanium, thighs of steel. Since he filled the basement with dumbbells and an exercise machine, you'd been down there with the guys two times, but you'd had enough very quickly. Your body is your body, and that's how it's going to stay. Even if you wouldn't have objected to an extra pound of muscle. *Training is everything* is Darian's motto. No wonder he fucks the girls left and right.

"First they kick the shit out of me, then they steal my pants. You think that scares me?"

No, you don't think anything scares Darian. Apart from his training, he goes to the gym on Adenauer Platz twice a week, takes protein supplements, and looks as if he's in his mid-twenties when in fact he's only seventeen.

"That doesn't worry me, because I know exactly who did it."

Darian thinks it was the Turks, you mumble something about how yeah, it definitely was the Turks. You both know the Turks had nothing to do with it. Not the Turks, not the Yugos, not the gang from Spandau, not even those idiots who have taken over the Westend and nobody knows if they come from Poland or Romania.

Darian goes on.

"You should have heard them. They laughed. I swear, they're never going to laugh like that again. Just wait. I'm going to turn them inside out. I'll get them, just you wait."

"Perhaps you should—"

"Don't say it," he cuts in.

"I'm just thinking."

"Mirko, shut your trap!"

You shut your trap. Darian's very sensitive about his old man. He's the only boy in the whole of Berlin who's regularly made a target because of his old man. Like last night. Not for the Turks, not for the Yugos, but for six guys from the neighborhood. Darian's a challenge. How far can you go before the gods get furious?

"What are you going to tell him if he asks?"

"My father won't even notice."

"But what'll you say if he does?"

"That I had trouble with a few idiots, that's all."

You nod; one word to Darian's dad and those guys would vanish from the city never to be seen again. That's what they say.

Darian spits.

"I have my pride, you understand? I have my own pride. I don't need my father to wipe my ass. So they can work me over, they can drop by every day. It's called learning the hard way, get me? They want a mean dog, I will be a mean dog. I memorized their faces. One day I'll be ready for them and then they'll pay. Mirko, I tell you, they'll pay."

Today was your first official appearance. Darian went with you to the Columbiadamm to meet Bebe and his people. Bebe has twenty-four gambling places scattered around Berlin, which he inherited from his family. Darian's incredibly envious of Bebe. You spent two hours listening to them trying to outdo each other's successes. In the end Bebe said he was going to send a few girls onto the street while there was still a bit of summer left. Darian couldn't match that one, and mumbled that he'd better be going. It was just after ten, and during that time you hadn't learned anything new. Except if you have a dick you have to swing it around. You like learning new stuff.

When Darian and you left the subway, they were waiting. They came up to you, two in the middle, two on the left and two on the right. Darian didn't hesitate for a second, he shouldered the two guys in the middle aside and made a run. You were right behind him. Through the streets, through the backyards to the ruin, because Darian knows his way around the ruin. How was he supposed to know that the ruin wasn't exactly undiscovered territory for these six guys?

You wait at the traffic lights for a moment and jump a red. You're glad it's late. It wouldn't be funny if anyone saw you in your stupid underpants. Trainers, white socks and blue underpants with white clocks on them. A Christmas present from your mother.

Darian asks for the fourth time why you always have to wear jeans. Tracksuit bottoms would be a lot more comfortable. You don't know what to say. In a tracksuit you look like a guy who wants to play football.

"Jeans give you cancer," says Darian.

It's a typical Tuesday evening, there's nothing going on on your street, the usual two drunks are standing outside the falafel shop and whistle after you. The falafel shop is open until two, and until two they won't budge from the spot. Whatever the weather, those two drunks are always there.

Outside your front door Darian whacks you on the back of the head.

"Hey, pal, still there?"

"Yeah yeah."

"You'll get your pants back tomorrow. And keep your mouth shut."

"Okay."

"I mean it."

"I know."

He doesn't want to go, he still wants something from you. You feel the tension in your shoulders, as if you are going to have to dodge another blow.

"Is everything okay between us?"

"Of course."

"We stand up for each other, Mirko."

"I know."

He makes a fist, you make a fist, when your fists meet you look at each other and Darian says, "Glad we've sorted that out."

"We did."

"And think about tracksuit bottoms."

"If I wear tracksuit bottoms I look like I'm on my way to play football."

"You have a point there."

"Thanks."

"Say hi to your mom."

"I will."

"See you tomorrow, then."

"See you tomorrow."

After you've crept into the apartment, you creep on into the bathroom and wash your face. You turn on the shower and sit motionlessly on the edge of the tub, as if someone had removed your batteries. Every now and again you pass your hand through the running water. Your head is absolutely empty, the pain in your nose a dull thumping. The hiss of the shower calms you down. It's like a movie that you can watch as often as you want. And if you stretch your hand out, it gets wet and you're part of the movie.

You get into the shower. You scrub the panic off yourself and enjoy the water on your back. The hammering on the bathroom wall tears you from your thoughts. You turn the water off, rub yourself dry, and wrap the towel around your hips.

"Why do you have to shower so late?"

Your mother is lying on the sofa in the living room, romantic novel in her lap, cigarette in her left hand, right hand where her heart should be. Her question is one of those questions that don't need an answer. You say hi from Darian and go into your room. You shut the door behind you, let the towel fall to the floor, and get dressed as if the day had only just begun. You are still disappointed in yourself. It was wrong to run away. Darian will never forget that. Lucky nobody else was there. Imagine one of the guys witnessing your cowardice. Whichever way you look at it, you know you have to make it good again.

Somehow.

The smell of falafel and cigarette smoke drifts in through the window, the voices of the two drunks are clearly distinguishable from each other and sound hoarse. Some nights your mother goes down and complains. You live on the second floor, you're the only ones who complain. The drunks laugh at you.

You button your shirt; your hands are still dirty from the oil on the chain, it'll take a few days to come off. It looks as if the cops have taken your fingerprints. You check your watch. Uncle Runa will kill you. If you don't show up at the pizza stand before midnight, you might as well stay home. Your uncle was expecting you an hour and sixteen minutes ago. You wish you were Darian. The kind of person who doesn't get bossed around. *Apart from tonight, tonight he sure got bossed around,* you think, and are immediately ashamed of the thought.

There are no customers about. Not even an exhausted taxi driver taking a break and giving his hemorrhoids a rest. The night buzzes with insects. On the other side of the street people are sitting outside the cafés. Laughter every now and again, the scrape of chairs when someone stands up. You wish you were on that side. The telephone booth next to the café is like a yellow eye that flickers irregularly, blinking nonsensical messages at you.

Uncle Runa leans against the battered freezer and stares across at the cafés as if they were his very private enemies. He doesn't understand how four cafés can open up on one corner. There are lots of things your uncle doesn't understand. He wears a white apron and a red T-shirt with a silver Cadillac on the front. The T-shirt is tucked into his trousers, his belly hangs over the belt. You have no idea why he can't wear normal clothes. He isn't twenty years old anymore, he's in his mid-forties and acts like he knows what's cool. He should ask you. You know what's cool, because you're the opposite of cool.

"What are you doing here?" your uncle asks and spits between his front teeth. When you were six he wanted to teach you how to do it. The brilliant art of spitting. You never got the hang of it, so he called you a loser. Uncle Runa likes to say that he feels guilty about your father, and that's why you're allowed to work for him. He's doing you a favor. Which doesn't stop him paying you only six euros an hour. From ten in the evening until four in the morning you take charge of the pizza stand, and then you fall into bed or you're so wired that you stay up all night and fall asleep in class. It's been going on for three months. You'd rather be roaming the clubs with Darian, selling grass and pills. But no one respects you yet. You're still no one.

"Tell me, shitface, what are you doing here?"

Uncle Runa goes through the same routine every time you turn up late. There are no variations, always the same pissed-off face as if he'd stood in a pile of dog shit with your name on it. A train goes over the bridge. When it's quiet again, you mumble, "Sorry I'm late."

"What happened to your hands?"

You hide your filthy fingers behind your back.

"Your mother's a good woman, you know that?"

"I know."

Suddenly Uncle Runa explodes, as if you'd claimed the opposite.

"You never say a word against your mother, you hear me? Your mother's an angel! Don't you dare say anything against your mother! Your father is a son of a bitch! You can say whatever you like about him."

"He's also your brother—"

"That's how come I know he is a son of a bitch!"

Uncle Runa falls silent again.

"How else do you think I know, eh?"

He looks over his shoulder at the clock. You know he has a thing going with your mother. The way he touches her and how they kiss when they meet, the way he's sometimes sitting in your kitchen in the morning as if he's been there all night. You're sure your mother doesn't hit the bathroom wall when Uncle Runa spends too much time in the shower. His dressing gown hangs on the inside of the door.

He's probably glad my father disappeared.

Your uncle takes a deep breath as if to make an important decision. The Cadillac on his chest stretches. Someone starts a motorbike, a woman laughs.

"What am I to do with you, boy?"

You say nothing. Uncle Runa scratches his head and sighs. You know it's all fine now.

"Get to work. Just get to work and we won't mention it again."

It's fifteen minutes later and Uncle Runa raps on the back of your head as if someone lives there, and leaves you alone. You imagine him walking down the streets, nodding at the drunks, as if they were his very special guard dogs, climbing the stairs to the second floor and your mother opening the door to him, and then they're both laughing like the woman earlier on—high and superior— because they know you're busy for the next few hours, while they have all the time in the world to fuck each other's brains out. Eventually they'll pay for it. More than six euros an hour. You're sure of that. The justice of the world will recognize you one day. You have no idea what kind of justice that will be, you don't really think seriously about it either, because right now you're glad to be alone behind the counter at last.

Alone.

It's half-price Tuesday in the cinemas, the evening screenings will be over in half an hour, and this place'll fill up. You get ready and pull the drinks to the front of the fridge until they're lined up neatly, you cut vegetables and mix salad. Music whispers out of the radio, you turn it up, and no one tells you to turn it down. No one wants anything from you. Apart from the customers, but that's okay, they're supposed to want something from you.

While your uncle generally rolls the pizza bases out in advance, you prefer to make them fresh. The customer should see that you're doing something for him. Tomato sauce, a bit of cheese, then the topping, then a bit more cheese. You love the sound when the baking tray slides into the oven. A glance at the customer, asking if he wants anything else. Always a smile, always content. You.

Yes, me.

"Me?"

"Yes, you, what are you staring at?"

It's two o'clock in the morning, the wave of cinemagoers ebbed away at midnight, and after that you could count the customers on one hand. You've stopped counting the drunks a long time ago, because they're not real customers, they're alkies, gabbling away at you and loading up on one last drink before they roll onto some park bench and tick off another day in their lives.

"I . . . I'm not staring."

You are wondering how long you've been staring at her. Her green eyes gleam like distant fires, her hair is such a dark red that it's almost black. You can't concentrate on her mouth at the moment, because it moves and says, "Where's the guy who makes the pizza?"

"I'm the guy who makes the pizza."

"You're at best twelve years old."

You don't react, you turn sixteen in the spring but you keep it to yourself because you're worried that she might be older. She *must* be older, arrogant and loud as she is. You can't know that she's playing with you. She knows who you are and that you hang out with Darian, she sees you at school every day and knows you've noticed her too. If you'd known all that at that very moment, everything would have been a lot easier for you. As it is you're just startled and look nervously past her. She's alone, it's the first time you've seen her alone. Normally she hangs with a group of girls who buzz around her as if she were a source of light. You particularly like the little scar on her chin, it makes her look like she is truly fragile.

She snaps her fingers around in front of your face.

"Well?"

You don't know what she means.

"How old are you now?"

"Fifteen."

"Never."

You shrug and wish the moment would stay like this. Hours, make it days. You wouldn't even have to speak. You'd make her one pizza after another, give her free drinks and look at her the whole time. Nothing more than that.

It would be nice if she would laugh and say she was sorry that she thought you were twelve, you don't look twelve at all. That would be really nice. Only now do you notice that her eyes are glassy. She's either stoned or drunk.

"Your name's Mirko and you live on Seelingstrasse, right?"

"Above the falafel shop," you say and feel as if she's paid you a compliment. *But how does she know all this?* you wonder, as she says, "I've seen you coming out of your house a few times."

"Ah."

"Yes, ah."

You look at each other, and as nothing better comes to your mind you show her your hand.

"I was in a fight today. I defended myself with a bicycle chain."

She looks at your sore palm, looks at you, she doesn't seem impressed. But she goes on talking to you. She says she urgently needs a phone. Her forefinger goes up in the air.

"Just one call, I swear."

You don't point to the phone booth behind her, you don't ask what's wrong with her phone. Girls always have a cell phone. Just don't ask. Go to the back, reach into your backpack, and come back with your phone.

"Sure."

You go to the back, reach into your rucksack, and come back with the phone. She doesn't thank you, she takes two steps backward and taps away. You turn down the radio to hear her better.

". . . no, I'm stuck here . . . Don't . . . But I . . . I'll give you ten euros, I promise. What? Please, Paul, come and fetch me . . . What? The what? You know what time it is? There are no buses around here. And I hate them anyway, you know that. What? Aunt Sissi can go and fuck herself."

Suddenly she looks up, phone still to her ear, looks at you, caught you red-handed, you duck a bit but hold her gaze.

"Fuck this shit!" she says, and you are not sure if she's talking to you.

She snaps the phone shut. You ask if there's a problem.

"What do you know about problems?"

"I . . . I could take you home."

"How are you going to take me home?"

"I can if I want."

"But I'm not giving you ten euros."

"That's okay."

You laugh, you really don't know what you're doing. Uncle Runa will strangle you if you shut the place for as much as a minute. But you're making things even worse, because after Uncle Runa has strangled you he'll cut you into pieces as soon as he finds out you've borrowed his old Vespa.

"On that thing?"

She has walked around the pizza stand. You pulled the tarpaulin off the bike like somebody performing a magic trick. She stands there as if she wants to buy the Vespa, then she kicks the back tire so that the bike nearly tips over. You flinch but don't say anything. Uncle Runa drives around the block once a week to charge the battery. He got the Vespa from scrap and rebuilt it himself. He calls it Dragica.

"But I'm not wearing a helmet, just so we're clear on that."

She points to her piled-up hair. You nod: if she doesn't want a helmet then she doesn't want one. You untie the string of your apron and for a moment you smell her breath. *Definitely drunk.* The key to the Vespa hangs on a nail above the radio. You take it as if you do this every day. Perhaps you'll drive along Seelingstrasse afterward and beep two times. Perhaps Uncle Runa will recognize the rattle of his Dragica and come running after you.

Once you've shut up shop you put on your uncle's helmet. It's too big, but it doesn't matter. She stands there and holds out her hand.

"What is it?"

"Did you think I'd let you drive me?"

"But—"

"Come on, make a choice."

You hand her the key and imagine what it'll feel like sitting behind her. Her warmth, her presence. You'll lean into the bends together and be like a single person. Not just you, not her—both of you. And just as you feel your excitement growing into an erection you quickly think of your mother gutting a chicken and at the same time the Vespa springs to life with a cough and bumps over the curbstone and zigzags along the street. A taxi beeps, then the lights of the Vespa come on and it disappears around the next corner.

Without you.

TAJA

You don't exist anymore. When you move, the air around you is still. Not a breeze. You speak, and silence replies. You're there, without being there. And even though you don't believe it right now, it's a pleasure to meet you at last. You're always present in the thoughts of your girls, but we've learned as little about you so far as if you didn't really exist.

Don't worry, you don't need to talk, you don't need to think or, for a while, exist, we'll find out everything about you anyway. Why you became a shadow, why you don't want to exist anymore. Invisible. We'll open a window into your life and let the light in, and we'll shake you awake until you scream with fury. But there's time for that, that comes later.

The table in front of you is vertical, but nothing's falling off it. Not the glasses, not the magazines or the ripped bag of powder. Even the hand-knitted tea cozy doesn't move. Every time you look at it you wonder where the teapot's gone and how small you have to be to live in a tea cozy. Between sleeping and waking you see your phone vibrating, it quivers from left to right before freezing again. The walls stay horizontal, the light comes, the light goes.

———

Your nose runs all the time, sometimes it's blood, but mostly it's just snot. You smell urine and the acrid smell of vomit. But that's nothing compared to the stench coming from the kitchen. You shut the door because you thought it would help. Closed doors don't keep out flies. They come through the cracks, they come from all around and make straight for the kitchen. They're everywhere. You don't want to think about it. You take a sip of water, and a few seconds later it's as if you hadn't drunk anything. You wish it would rain. Your mouth is so dry that you're wishing it would rain in the middle of the room. You don't have the strength to sit up, you can't even stretch out your arm to reach for the edge of the table. You try, and you think you can hear the sinews in your arm creaking. Your fingertips touch the edge of the table. You give up exhausted, you pull back your arm and fall asleep again.

You believe in time. You pray to time and hope it hears you. *Just a bit, go back just a bit,* you think and know how absurd the idea is.

Still . . .

Sometimes you stare at the clock above the fireplace, at your dad's awards. Platinum—gold—gold—platinum—gold. And in between the clock, like a special prize for . . .

Nothing?

You concentrate. Sometimes you manage to make the hand of the clock pause. It lingers. That's all you can do, whatever you try, the hand never moves backward. It's like arm-wrestling with the world champion arm wrestler. Eventually there's no juice behind your will, and the hand unfreezes and ticks on a bit.

And another bit.

And another.

And time is time again and laughs at you in seconds and minutes and hours. You hate it for that. At the same time you yearn for it. You can't be without it, and you want it to disappear forever.

Time is your new religion.

Sleep is traveling inside your head. No packing, no waiting, just being there. And that's what your There looks like: a house on a

cliff, water below you, sky above you. You're sitting by a fjord.
Even though you have no memory of the place, you know: *I was
born here.* It's a gray day. Snow falls and turns the valley walls into
Japanese ink drawings. An icy wind scratches over the water. That's
where you are, that's where you want to be. On a terrace, wrapped
up in several blankets, on your right a table with a cup of tea, in the
background the silence of the house. You pick up the cup, you feel
the heat of the tea through the china, your palms warm up.

There's nothing more, nothing more is needed.

You wake with your face buried in the sofa cushion and sneeze
twice. Blood drifts down onto the pillow like a fine mist, you feel
dizzy and lay your head back so that the blood flows down your
throat like a gentle lava flow, feeding and warming you. Everything
in your body hurts and throbs. Your thoughts are sore. Your hand
claws onto the back of the sofa, you inch your way into a sitting
position. The table turns horizontal, the walls vertical and your legs
tremble, even though you're not standing. You set your feet down
on the floor and try to get the shaking under control. You stay like
that for a while. Your face in your hands, the trembling in your legs.
You look between your fingers at the powder and feel the stinging
in your nose like far-off longing. You know what will ease the pain
and let you sleep again. It's as simple as that. As if the thought has
reached your legs, they stop shaking. You lean forward, pick up the
teaspoon, and stick it into the plastic bag. You scatter the powder on
the tabletop and use one of the brightly colored straws. It doesn't
take long, it hurts and your senses greet the bitterness of the drug
with jubilation, then you feel like retching, you fight it and fight
it and sink back, draw your knees up to your chest and become a
warm, pulsating ball.

... *at last* ...
Sleep.

This time it's a different There. You're not at the fjord, you're with
your friends, time has been merciful and taken you along. In reverse.
It's right after school, you know the day and the year and it's reas-

suring, because you also know what's going to happen. *It's absolutely certain.* And right now you would give your soul for a little certainty.

You're in a freeze-frame. Your girlfriends are frozen in that moment that has already been and will never be again. You're sitting in Ruth's room. You know that Coldplay's first CD is going to play through the speakers at any moment. Ruth has all their albums, but is only allowed to put on this one, because you've decided that *Parachutes* is authentic and everything else is just homespun pop for teenyboppers. Whatever you are, you've never been teenyboppers. Or as Nessi once put it: *We're far too old to be young.*

You're lying stretched out on the floor with your head in Schnappi's lap. Above you is the moss-green ceiling that you painted together; sometimes flakes fall down on your heads because you had to go and apply the paint too thickly. Schnappi looks at you like a photograph that only comes to life when you let it.

Soon.

It's autumn, it's a good nine months ago. Your hair was long at the time, then before Christmas you went to the hairdresser and for the next few months your girls called you Frenchie. Yes, your hair has grown since then, but you keep it short because you've always thought it ridiculous that you've all got the same hairdo. Long, long, long.

Schnappi with her hair that's like black silk, Ruth and her blond fringe with which she tries in vain to hide the pimples on her forehead, Stink who's dyed her mane dark red as long as you've known her, and Nessi who looks like an angel and makes you sigh every time she piles up her golden hair and shows her neck. It was a good step on your part to change your hairstyle.

In a minute.

Ruth sits cross-legged on the bed with a magazine in her lap, she's flicking through it, her tongue peeps out between her lips. Stink sits opposite her on the windowsill with a cigarette in her hand, even though smoking's forbidden at Ruth's house, but Stink can't help it. You remember she actually squeezed out a tear when Ruth told her she couldn't smoke. Stink is no smoker, but on the other hand she doesn't like anyone telling her she can't do something.

You know what she's going to say next. She's going to ask you what's so funny about her not wanting to have anything more to do with that guy. You know your reaction, too. All thoughts and words are still frozen. Cigarette smoke floats like a charcoal line in the air.

You breathe out.

Now.

"... so funny about it?" Stink asks defiantly. "Axel's an idiot, do I look like someone who wants to be with an idiot?"

"For three months now," says Ruth.

"That was never three months!"

"Then a quarter of a year."

You laugh, Stink rolls her eyes and asks what's so funny about it. You think it is incredibly funny, and if Stink wasn't in such a stinky mood she'd laugh too, but of course that's not going to work, it would make the joke less funny.

A breeze drifts through the window and scatters the smoke around the room. You inhale the smell deeply and wish you were brave enough to have one too.

"Don't even think about it," Ruth says from the bed.

"I'll think what I like," you tell her.

Ruth holds up the magazine. You all look at it for a moment and shake your heads. You're evaluating actresses. You're cruel. Apart from a few exceptions you think they're all bitches who make too much money. Nessi's the only one who knows all their names.

"Cate Blanchett," she says.

"Show me," says Stink.

Ruth holds the magazine out toward her.

"That's not Cate Blanchett."

"That's Kate Winslet," says Schnappi.

Ruth looks at the magazine and reads, "Cate Blanchett."

"Shit," says Stink.

Nessi nods contentedly. She's sitting on one of those idiotic seats that are filled with beans and every time you move it sounds like a drunk jogger running down a pebble beach.

"If you fart into it," says Schnappi, "we'll have chili tonight."

You drink your Fanta. You're waiting for Ruth to hold up the next photograph when the door flies open. Even though you knew

Ruth's mother was about to breeze in you give a start, just like you gave a start then. The memory is so fresh in your head that you want to call out to your girlfriends: *I've been here before and want to stay here forever!*

"I thought I smelled smoke."

Ruth's mother looks around. She's thrown you out before, because the music was too loud. Stink makes eyes so big that she might as well hang up a sign. Her cigarette has disappeared, but of course Stink had to take one last drag and the smoke's still in her lungs.

"I don't understand you lot. You're girls, aren't you? What does this place look like?"

Typical Ruth's mother. Can see perfectly well what it looks like, and asks what it looks like. You take a look around as if you'd only just gotten here. It doesn't look great. All the scattered clothes and comics and pages from the school presentation that you really wanted to discuss but when that got boring Schnappi just dropped the pages on the floor. There's the tray of scraped ice cream bowls and a sticky stain on the carpet where one of the spoons was dropped. And then of course the nachos. Ruth's cat was desperate to get its head in the bag. Then it walked around for a while with the thing on its head, then it shook itself and the nachos flew all over the carpet.

"That was Freddie," says Schnappi.

"Maybe we should put Freddie to sleep," says Ruth's mother.

"God, Mom," sighs Ruth without looking up from the magazine.

"Don't 'God Mom' me, Ruth, or I'm throwing you all out."

Ruth pretends not to have heard anything and holds up the magazine. You shake your heads. No points. You're TV series junkies and you've seen all the episodes of *Lost* at least twice; as far as you're concerned the women have to look like Kate or nothing at all.

"Milla Jovovich," says Nessi.

"Julie Delpy," says Ruth's mother.

"Minnie Driver," says Schnappi.

You burst out laughing.

"Why are you laughing?" asks Schnappi.

"You wouldn't recognize Minnie Driver if she sat on your lap."

"Would too."

Ruth looks at the magazine. Of course Nessi's right. Ruth's

mother curses, she could have sworn that was Julie Delpy. Stink coughs out the smoke.

"What's the matter with you?" asks Ruth's mother.

"Cancer," says Stink and thumps her chest.

"You don't make jokes about that."

"Tell that to my doctor."

You all giggle, Ruth's mother narrows her eyes slightly. Dangerous.

"Isabell, I don't want you to smoke in our living room. How many times—"

"God, Mom," Ruth butts in and lowers the magazine. "Really, that's enough. Please shut the door behind you. Take a look . . ."

She points around her, as if her mother hadn't noticed where she was.

"—this is a girls' meeting."

For a moment you think Ruth has gone too far. You're the only one grinning, because you know how Ruth's mother will react. *My daughter*, she will say and smile.

"My daughter," she says and smiles.

"My mom," Ruth replies and smiles back and disappears into her magazine again as if her mother had left the room ages ago.

Schnappi strokes your head, you stretch and purr like you were Freddie. Nessi shifts her backside on the beanbag and says: *This is going to be a delicious chili.* You all snort with laughter, and when you've calmed down you notice that Ruth's mother is still standing in the doorway.

"You're such a bunch of bitches," she says.

Stink doesn't contradict her.

"We might be bitches," she says, "but we're sweet bitches."

Schnappi raises her thumb, Ruth raises her thumb, and you raise your left leg. Nessi just shrugs and says, "When Stink's right, she's right."

Ruth's mother leans forward, her mouth moves, no words come out, but you're used to reading her lips. Whether it's *Get out* or *Shut up.* You know the nuances. You're familiar with this one too. *I hate you.* It's meant nicely. No one hates you, you are loved. The door closes, and at that very moment *Parachutes* comes to an end, the last song fades away, and you know what that means—there'll be a little pause, followed by the song that Ruth found on the internet. A rarity that doesn't appear on any Coldplay album. At any moment a guitar will come in and you'll sing along the way you always do.

You taste the first lines in your mouth and realize why time has dragged you here—this song belongs to what has been, and it belongs to the Taja who will lie nine months later completely wasted on the sofa in her father's living room and lose her connection with reality.

But your hair's still long, your girlfriends are still with you, and you're not yet the loneliest person in the world. The song brings everything together. You wait, the pause ends, the guitar sounds and you take a breath and Stink says, "Don't imagine it'll be as easy as that."

You look at her with surprise. These are the wrong words. You're singing now, it's got to happen, but the music has fallen silent, no one's singing.

Wrong, you think, *that's wrong.*

"We'll sing along later," says Ruth and lowers the remote control.

"Did you really think you could avoid us?" Schnappi asks.

You sit up and slide away from her on your butt, a few nachos crumble under your hand, the girls look at you.

"We're waiting," says Stink.

"For . . . for what?"

You go quiet, you're just bluffing, because you know very well what they're waiting for. Nessi rummages in her jeans and throws you her phone.

"I've tried to contact you thirty-six times. Check, if you don't believe me."

"And I've tried just as many times," says Schnappi.

"I hate your voicemail more than I hate the fucking Simpsons," says Ruth.

Stink slips from the windowsill and crouches in front of you.

"Now will you tell us what's up with you?"

You smell her breath. Cigarettes and lemon ice cream. Stink takes your hand in hers. And the way she's looking at you, the way all your girls are looking at you, you tell them the truth.

"I'm not really here. I'm from the future."

Ruth crouches down next to Stink.

"Christ, Taja, we know that already."

"Do you think we haven't known that?" Schnappi asks behind you.

"But that doesn't explain anything," says Nessi. "Or do you think it does?"

You know it doesn't explain anything, you curse time and its little games and close your eyes tight as if you were in a dream, and when you open them again you're lying alone on the sofa in your father's living room and your mouth is dry as dust and your cheeks are wet with tears. *Where are you all?* you think longingly and grip the edge of the table and pull it across the carpet until it's right in front of you. Your hand seeks, your hand finds. You press your phone tightly to your chest and breathe out with relief.

Now everything's going to be fine.

You push your face back into the sofa cushion until you can't breathe anymore and that's a good way to vanish into merciful darkness.

NESSI

Above you hangs the night, below you lies the darkness, and you're floating between the two and hear your girls calling to you. You imagine it'll be like this forever. Just floating and not worrying about anything and forgetting that there's a child growing in you. *I could let go and sink,* you think and realize it's nonsense. You've never had a high opinion of people who killed themselves because they couldn't take on life. In books, in movies, in life. But who knows what you'll think in ten years; who knows what you'll think when you're lying in a bed somewhere sick and full of pain or when your heart is broken and the world seems as dark as the lake below you and the night above you. Who knows.

You turn in the water and only now do you feel the full weight of your wet clothes dragging you down. In no particular hurry, you move your arms and swim back to shore.

The boys think it's sexy, they say you should do it more often. You grin, you have humor, your teeth are chattering. The world is full of idiots, and you're one of them. Your clothes lie drying on the grass, Ruth has given you her jacket. You're sitting by the fire, your knees against your chest, your eyes closed. Schnappi said her heart nearly stopped when she saw you in the water, but as her heart stops every time a good-looking guy walks by, that doesn't mean much. What's much more noticeable is that Schnappi's avoiding your eye.

You don't need to ask. Your girls know you're pregnant. Schnappi's never been good at keeping secrets.

"Are you cold?" asks Stink.

You shake your head and feel as if you're six years old again and sitting by the fire with your parents after a long hike, so terribly tired and so terribly excited at being allowed to stay up so late with the grown-ups. Stink puts an arm around you. The boys talk on and on. You are all patient, as girls are only patient when they want to get rid of boys. You are looking into the flames, you are barely talking. One after the other the boys say goodbye. Eric mumbles: *Maybe we'll meet up later in the bar.* And then you're alone at last.

"What did you do that for?" asks Ruth, as if you'd just got out of the water.

"I don't know, it just felt right."

"And if we'd been standing in the station, would you have jumped onto the rails?"

"Come on. I wasn't planning on killing myself."

They all nod, they hoped you were going to say this.

"Let's all keep our mouths shut," says Stink, before Ruth can tear into you again. "If Nessi doesn't want to talk about it, then how about we don't talk about it?"

Everyone looks at you, it's your turn, the ball's in your court, you say, "Girls, I'm pregnant, and I don't want to talk about it now."

They nod again, it's accepted, and you're so relieved that you want to talk about it right now, but at the same time you're exhausted by the day and just want to sleep. Schnappi reads your thoughts and says that's enough for today. She offers to drive you home.

Ruth hugs you and tells you to keep the jacket. Stink strokes your back and kisses you firmly on the mouth. It's never been so hard to say goodbye to your friends. You get into your wet jeans. Schnappi takes you by the hand and you walk to her bike. When you've cycled two blocks she brakes, turns around to you, and swears she hasn't told a soul.

"They guessed, Nessi, they really guessed."

"You swear?"

"I swear."

"Thanks."

Schnappi cycles on, you rest your head against her back and shut your eyes.

It's just after midnight when you creep into the apartment. Your parents are asleep, any sound would give you away, so you take off your running shoes and walk down the corridor to the bathroom in your wet socks. You close the door gently behind you and lean against it. It takes some minutes before you dare to turn on the light. Your face is pale, your clothes still wet and heavy. You could never have pulled this one off in the winter.

I went into the Lietzensee, you think and flip yourself the bird in the mirror.

In the shower the water's so hot that you flinch for a moment, but you don't change the temperature, you put up with the heat and wait until it's passed through all the layers of cold to your innermost core and makes you glow.

You haven't been as freezing as that for years.

By the time you leave the shower, the bathroom is a landscape swathed in fog.

You wipe the mirror clear and look at yourself.

Go closer.

You try to see a change. *Nothing.* You look down at yourself. Everything is as it should be. Breasts, belly, legs. *As always.* You make a fist and press it against your belly button. You're furious. You're so furious with yourself that you want to shove your fist through your stomach.

And then?

You don't know what then.

But you have a clear vision of where it goes from here. You see your father shaking his head and calling you *my little one.* Your mother will burst into tears and get a bottle of white wine from the fridge. She won't understand you. She'll want to know how you imagine it will all be. On no account must you speak of abortion, bear that in mind. Abortion is taboo, because your mother had an abortion when she was nineteen and has never forgiven herself. The decision hurt both your parents. So no word about abortion, because then you might as well take a corkscrew and jab their eyes out. Your

mother with her tears and quivering shoulders, your father leaning forward, hands open, as if to catch you. After the first glass of
wine your father will say things will sort themselves out and there's
enough room in the apartment, which is already far too small, but you
won't point that out either. Your mother will hug you and promise
to take care of everything, because she is your mother, after all, you
should never forget that. She'll also say she's glad that you waited
until after school, as if you planned to get pregnant. Then she'll
look at your father and say emotionally: *I'm going to be a grandma!*

Your parents won't ask who the father is, because they're scared
of the answer.

That's how it is, that's how it always will be.

Fear.

And throughout all this your left hand would be clenched into
a fist.

Over the next few weeks you'll start getting fat. Not that you're
skinny now, but your mother looked like a whale when she was
pregnant, so you'll be exactly the same, she's shown you the future.
The months will pass, and the apprenticeship that Aunt Helga
promised you will go to another girl. You'll hardly see your girlfriends, because their lives are their lives and your life is your life
and you can't go in two directions at once. Every now and again
Stink will call and you will start crying and Stink will cry too and
after two hours your ears will be so hot from gossiping that you'll
hang up reluctantly. You'll read everything about babies, weigh up
the pros and cons of a home birth, and opt for the hospital. You'll
slowly come to terms with the situation. Your seventeenth birthday
will be sad. Stink will drop in with Schnappi and stay for fourteen
minutes. Ruth will phone in her greetings. And Taja? You'll never
hear a word from Taja, because still no one has any idea where she
is. There will be no presents for you, just presents for the baby. Little socks. Little jackets. Toys. People will look at you askance in
the supermarket and keep their distance. Everyone will know what
kind of girl you are. Mother. Mom. Whale. And sometimes they
will ask who the father is. And sometimes you will look at them and
smile, as if that was an answer. You know you're too young to be a

mother. You're too young to be anything at all. But life in reverse only works in the movies.

During the birth you will consist only of pain, and the pain will hollow you out and fill you with fire. *Nothing bad can happen to me after this*, you will think. And then the child. Red. Noisy. Yours. And everything will be fine.

And everything will be lovely.

It's the last thing you want. You want to live without responsibilities or obligations, and without parents. You want to be someone who leads a life that is a mystery. Not the life of a girl named after a pop star. Not the life of the many girls who run around like emotional building sites and get pregnant and accept it because they're just too idiotic to go a different way.

Not one of many, no.

But who knows whether you might not be better off like this after all. Take a look at Stink. Her mother ran off when Stink was still a baby, and after her father had decided that two children was too much work, he dumped Stink and her brother on Aunt Sissi and ran off to Argentina. Stink was nine at the time and until her twelfth birthday she thought her dad was coming back for Christmas. Stink's brother saw through it all right away, of course. Whenever you ask Stink about it, she shakes her head and says she couldn't care less. But you know that's not true. It is like an invisible itch that no amount of scratching helps. A mixture of hatred and resignation. You on the other hand love your parents, but you don't want them around, there's no getting past that.

You give a start when the phone in your jacket pocket rings. You seriously went to sleep on the toilet, your hair is dry, and the toilet seat has left two impressions on the underside of your thighs. Your phone beeps twice, then it's quiet. The text is so short that for a moment you think your phone has got bumped.

cm

Then you see who sent the text, and the thinking stops, your problems are your problems, this is more important. You run out of the bathroom into your room and get dressed. You put on a pair of worn-out running shoes, turn around and see your mother standing in the doorway.

"Vanessa, what's going on?"

You push past her and run out of the apartment like someone who's left herself outside and hopes to find herself again as quickly as possible, before it's too late.

SCHNAPPI

She yells at you. She yells at you through the closed door as if you were a stranger, as if your life were worthless and she had the right to spit on it. In the background you hear your father mumbling. She ignores him and goes on yelling at you. One of the neighbors calls up the stairwell, telling her to shut up. You call down telling him to shut up himself.

A door slams.

It continues.

She calls you a whore. She calls you a bastard. You wait till she is out of breath, then press the doorbell, you press so hard that your thumb turns white, when the ringing suddenly stops. You laugh out loud. She's seriously switched off the bell. You laugh until the tears come and the tears have nothing more to do with laughter. Your finger slips off the doorbell, you sit down on the doormat, your back against the door.

And I'm only three hours late, what's three hours?

Some nights you slip into the apartment unnoticed, a few times your father sits waiting in the kitchen, he shakes his head and says he was worried. But he isn't really bothered, he trusts you and calls you his little sunshine.

If it wasn't for her . . .

Your mother must have left the key in the lock. You wouldn't have credited her with so much imagination. She told you the houses in her village didn't have any doors, because people trusted each other, and if someone stole something, the whole family was chased from the place. So that's how things are back home. It's a mystery to you how someone who grew up without doors could come up with the idea of leaving the key in the lock.

You're so tired.

Now you'll wait till she's asleep, then your father will let you in. Wait for half an hour, an hour at most. The day rushes through your head like the subway train that you've been waiting for. You see Nessi in the water, you see yourselves in the cinema and you can taste the stale popcorn. You like looking back on the day. It's a bit like coming home late in the evening, turning on the television, and there's a program on that shows only you, going through life, all your mistakes, all your heroic deeds. You want to tell your father about the movie. He likes Denzel Washington. But how surprised will your father be when he opens the door in twenty minutes and sees that you've disappeared? And how surprised will you be in retrospect that your life has taken a new turn in a few seconds, and dragged you thousands of miles away from Berlin?

Anything is possible. And it all begins with two short beeps.

You're sitting in the dark corridor, because you don't feel like pressing the light switch over and over again. You sit there in the darkness, and there are two beeps. You take your phone out of your jacket and read the text on the blue display and react the way you all react to this message tonight.

You run.

RUTH

You get the message at the same time. You're lying next to Eric again and your ears are tingling. You were spared the sex this time. You're both too drunk. Your parents think you're sleeping over at Stink's. It's one lie more or less. You have very different problems, because you couldn't leave it alone. Four cocktails in the little bar on Savignyplatz, where you only get served because one of the waitresses is Eric's sister. Schnappi and Stink stopped after the second cocktail, only you couldn't stop yourself. Now you're lying beside Eric. In your defense, it would have to be said that there was no real chance of going home in this state. Your mother would have bitten your head off and your father would have pogoed on your corpse.

The mattress is on the floor and smells slightly of mold, and there's also the acrid smell of a sweaty boy who sprays himself with too much perfume—things you won't miss. You won't miss the hand on your shoulder either.

"Go away!"

Eric persists. He shakes you as if you were a fruit machine that had swallowed his last euro. You groan, you could puke, you could just lean out of bed and puke. But you don't. You've still got a bit of self-respect. So you open your eyes, and as if by magic your ears open too.

" . . . light is driving me mad. Really mad. How do you turn this little fucker off? Tell me how to turn this fucker off."

"What?"

Eric holds up a green star in front of your eyes, going light and then dark again. You feel spittle dribbling from the corner of your mouth and wipe it away.

"Please," says Eric.

You recognize your phone. You love that glow, it pulses like a light under water, you set it that way on purpose.

"Take it away," you say.

"Turn it off, Ruth."

"Put it under the pillow and let me sleep!"

Eric pulls the covers away.

"The fucker is vibrating *and* lighting up. Turn it off!"

You would like to strangle him. *Too dumb to turn off a phone,* you think, and grab it from him. You look at the message that's just come in and see double and then triple and then double again. You rub your eyes and look again. Your thumb taps in your PIN and the phone stops lighting up. Eric sighs with relief, but his happiness lasts only a few seconds.

"Shit, what are you doing now?"

You pick up your clothes from the floor and are about to clear out when you realize that you're far too drunk to negotiate a zebra crossing. You look back at the bed. Eric has his arm over his eyes. No, you can't rely on him.

Maybe it was just an illusion, you think, *maybe I'll turn my phone back on and there'll be nothing there.*

You go into the bathroom, drape yourself over the toilet bowl, and stick your finger down your throat. After that you feel better. You slap water in your face and rummage in your purse. Five euros. That's never going to be enough. You go back into your room. Eric is asleep, his arm still over his eyes. You take his wallet out of his trousers. Nothing, just a few coins. You drop the wallet, take a deep breath, and look at your phone again.

cm

You knew it wasn't an illusion. Phones don't lie. You pull on your boots, and then you run.

STINK

Of course there's an idiot in every story. Someone who does everything wrong, backs the wrong horse and gets caught in the rain. Someone like you, disappearing on a stolen Vespa and grinning to themselves as if they'd won the jackpot. You're the idiot, you're the marked card. At the same time you're the only one lying contentedly in her bed tonight. Your head is heavy from those two cocktails, the barkeeper probably slipped something into your glass. You hate it when guys flirt and then get nasty when you slap them down. If you said yes to every barman, you'd have died of alcohol poisoning years ago.

Eventually sleep overwhelms you and you dream of Neil going down on one knee in front of you in the disco and saying he isn't bothered by your flowery underwear. You also dream of Nessi, bobbing away like a water lily and disappearing into the distance, even though you call her name. It's a good thing you have a brother, otherwise you'd probably have slept through the rest of this story.

"Get up!"

The light goes on and off, on and off.

"Are you deaf or something? Get up!"

You wish you were deaf or something. You roll over. Your brother won't let go.

"One of your stupid girlfriends has been ringing up a storm, how can't you hear it?"

That's enough. You kick the covers away, bickering like a washerwoman. You swing your legs out of bed and a whole universe of stars explodes in front of your eyes. You feel dizzy and you bend down and look at your toes until the explosions subside. You didn't hear any ringing. Good thing your aunt's on night shift tonight.

"God, Paul, I didn't hear it ring," you murmur.

"Yeah, right."

Your brother slams the door behind him, you sink back.

Maybe it's all just a dream? Maybe I can just go back to sleep —

Your bedroom door flies open again.

You raise your head.

Ruth is standing there, and she says, "I hate it when you don't charge your battery."

And as she says it you know something has happened.

Something bad.

The clock by the door says ten past three.

Whatever it is, it's definitely bad.

The realization reaches your brain like a shock wave, your ears pop, you have to rub your nose because it's suddenly itchy.

"My goodness," you say, like a grandma whose shopping bag tears on the way home, then you totter to your feet and get dressed while Ruth tells you about the message she got.

Five minutes later you're sitting on the stolen Vespa, your hair blowing in the wind, Berlin is in a coma, the streets are deserted and the traffic lights have a weary pulse that looks a bit like slow-motion Christmas lights. How you hate Christmas, how you love the city at night.

III

drives up to the next seat and
onto the roots
drinking up the village

Portugal. The Man
THE DEVIL

THE TRAVELER

And then you disappeared.

Without a trace.

And chaos was left in your wake.

The special crimes unit has been searching tirelessly for you. They said you wanted to be caught after they found your blood on the corpses. They said you were losing your concentration. They were now as familiar with your DNA as they were with your fingerprints.

Did that worry you? Were you even aware of it?

You were aware of it, the way you're aware of things because people are talking about them. They said the Traveler was getting careless, and would soon fall into the special unit's clutches. It didn't occur to anyone that the Traveler didn't care what he left behind. You were moving forward. The past remained behind like the vague memory of a dream or a smell that gets blown away by the next breeze. Not that you woke up drenched in sweat and wondered what had happened. Things like that are stupid. That's what psychopaths do. The past was behind you, it wasn't pursuing you.

You're like a shark that always has to keep moving or it'll sink. In a flowing forward motion. There is no going back. And just as a shark has no swim bladder, you have no morals. If you hesitated, you would sink to the bottom of our society in an instant and disappear.

Stasis is corruption, so you stay in calm motion.

For six years no one heard a thing from you. On the internet they wondered if the Traveler had reached his destination. You're responsible for over sixty corpses. All inquiries have led nowhere, no one saw anything, the investigations washed out and the special unit was called into question. There was no pattern and no connection between the victims, there was no apparent motive. Even though the special unit would never have admitted it, they were waiting for your next step. They wanted mistakes. They looked at psychograms of serial killers, studied the behavior of frenzied attackers, and tried to force you into a category. They really had no idea who they were dealing with.

In 1998 you were offered a better job and moved to a bigger city. Your son turned seven and wrote his first letter, asking you if you couldn't have him for the summer. You wrote back to say it was a good idea, he should ask Mom. Mom said no. Life took its course.

Your girlfriend split up with you because the long-distance relationship was too uncomfortable. You started spending your evenings in theaters and at concerts. You started reading more books, and built up a collection of documentaries on DVD. You discovered culture and met a woman who shared your passion for architecture. Otherwise hardly anything in your life changed. You weren't calmer, you didn't drink to excess or call your existence into question. Your friends didn't notice any changes either. You were balanced. You traveled a lot throughout those years. Sometimes as a couple or in a group or on your own. And you never left any corpses behind.

When the new millennium was ushered in, your name was a legend. Someone wrote a book about you, someone put up a website that not only offered a forum for discussion but listed all your victims and was regularly checked by the special unit with the agreement of the provider. And of course someone tried to copy you and was promptly overpowered by his first victim. The day the two passenger planes flew into the World Trade Center, people started forgetting about you. The world was heading toward a new chaos. You

grieved with the Americans, spent that afternoon in front of the
television, and then got on with your life like the rest of us.

Year after year after year.

It was once again winter when you traveled across the country with
a lot of snow and a storm at your heels. The papers said: *The Avenging Angel strikes again.*

Avenging what, is the question.

You keep quiet.

It is November.

It is 2003.

It is night.

Fennried is a tiny village on the river Havel between Ketzin and
Brandenburg, so insignificant that there's no phone booth and no
public mailbox there. A main street and a side street, thirty-eight
houses, eight run-down farms, two cigarette machines. The bus stop
is by the entrance to the village, a van parks outside the bakery twice
a week, and once a week a van selling frozen food drives through
the streets and honks its horn. It seems like the village is all the time
asleep, the tallest building is a dilapidated church with a little cemetery, in which the gravestones have either fallen over or lean wearily against one another. In the run-up to elections the parties don't
bother to put up posters along the two streets. It's an in-between
place. It doesn't get bigger, it doesn't get smaller, it stagnates in its
insignificance.

One of your fans wrote that the challenge was so great that you
couldn't resist it. He wrote that after lengthy planning you had
finally decided to pay Fennried a visit. He made a sketch of your
journey through the town, as if he'd prearranged it with you, and
published the sketch on his blog. He spent four days in custody

for that. He knew too much. The special unit let him go when they found out that he'd got the details from a policeman who'd been part of the investigation in Fennried.

It's Thursday. After work you get into the car and drive toward Berlin. You had a premonition this time. Like a scratch in your throat. After you woke up you drank coffee and sensed the change. As if the wind had turned. You spent the day in the usual rhythm, you'd even gone jogging for an hour after work, and it was only then that you set off.

Just before Berlin you leave the highway and stop at a gas station. You eat a baguette with smoked salmon standing at a table and talk to the cashier. You learn that her husband doesn't want to see the children anymore, and that fourteen years after the wall came down hardly anything has gotten better and lots of things have gotten worse. But the cashier smiles when she says that. You like her optimism. She gives you an openness that she hopes will be reciprocated. You smile back and then you laugh together and you drive on.

Only when you've passed Fennried do you realize how small the village is. You turn around and drive back. One minute twenty-six seconds from one end to the other. Half the streetlights don't work. It's nine in the evening and almost all the windows are in darkness. The light of a television flickers here and there.

You drive through the village a third time. The wind tries to push your car off the road. You lower the driver's window and enjoy the cold. You stop by a derelict farm and wait. A strange car in a tiny village on a desolate winter's day. The snow starts enfolding you. The lights in the windows go out. It's a bit like that night when you were stuck in the traffic jam. Calm. Solitude. And it reminds you a little of the silence of the motel. Both times you surprised yourself. You knew your potential, but be honest, you didn't know what you were really capable of. Your new knowledge gives you a feeling of certainty now. As if a racing car knew its own strength.

Shortly after one o'clock you get out of the car and walk up to the first house.

_____

What are you looking for? What makes you kill? Is there a medical background to it? A tumor, perhaps, pressing against your cerebral lobe? A sickness that makes you bare your teeth? Did you learn it from somebody? Did somebody take you by the hand and show you that killing is liberating? Is it liberating? Is that why you're on the road? Are you looking for salvation, purification, absolution? Is it instinct? Is it desire?

Even though the shutters are down over all the windows and terraces, most of the doors are unlocked. You go from house to house. You ring the doorbell if necessary. Sometimes a dog barks at you, and sometimes there's a chain on the door. You're always polite and friendly. They let you in, you kill them quickly and efficiently. Most of the people who live here are pensioners. You happen upon two women under fifty. One is a nurse, the other a retired doctor. The doctor's bell is surrounded by dried flowers and her door is the only one that opens at the first ring.

A village, thirty-eight houses, fifty-nine inhabitants.

You don't leave a single soul alive.

RAGNAR

The house smells horribly of rotten meat, and you wonder where the stench is coming from. The kitchen is surprisingly clean, even the floor has been mopped, while the living room is a rubbish dump. The sofa is shoved across the floor, there are toppled chairs, broken crockery, and vomit on the floor. The table is scattered with colored straws, drink cans, and plates with dried-on leftover food. There's white dust in the cracks and you assume it's heroin. It looks very much as if there's been a party here.

"Looks like they had a party," says Leo.

"That's what I thought," you say.

Leo points outside.

"I thought we might sit in the fresh air."

The table on the terrace is laid. Leo has fetched pastries, coffee, and rolls from the bakery. There are napkins beside the plates. Leo knows what you like. Even if the situation doesn't call for it, you want to maintain a clear line. Your men must not think anything's different just because your brother is sitting dead in the basement and the merchandise is gone.

Tanner and David are already seated. David has opened his notebook. Leo pours the coffee. If your brother came out right now and asked who wanted freshly squeezed orange juice, everything would be the same as ever.

"Have you got a connection?"

David turns the display to face you. Tanner comes around the table with Leo. The picture is in color. Your brother always loved these electronic toys. The cameras are hidden in various places around the rooms, the picture definition is pin-sharp and vivid. You know some private porn movies have been made with them. Your brother knew no shame. Motion detectors activate the cameras as soon as someone walks through the picture. A two-terabyte hard drive collects the movies. David says he doesn't know how full the drive is, and how many days back the recordings go, but he's going to look into it.

"Show us the basement," says Tanner.

David zaps through the rooms—kitchen, living room, for a moment you see yourselves sitting on the terrace, the downstairs bathroom, the upstairs bathroom, bedroom, loft, garage, and finally the vaulted basement. You see the swimming pool and the boy staring at it as if the pool were an oracle. He hasn't moved from his chair. *This is not going to take long,* you think and are about to set the notebook aside so that you can have breakfast in peace, when Tanner jumps in.

"Go back one."

David clicks back one. You see the garage. Tanner exhales noisily.

"I think we've got a new problem."

You see what he means.

"Where are his cars?" you ask, surprised.

"The Mercedes is in the workshop," says David. "Oskar dropped it off last week, he said the electronics had gone nuts."

"And the Range Rover?"

Nobody answers. You stare at the deserted garage.

"People, where's the fucking Range Rover?"

"I don't know," says David.

"Call the workshop and find out."

David starts to get up, he's overzealous.

"What are you doing?" Tanner asks him.

"I thought—"

"Sit down and let's have breakfast. The boy is more important right now."

David sits down again and pushes the notebook to the end of the table so that he can keep an eye on it. Leo asks if anybody wants the croissant. Tanner shares it with him. You try to concentrate on the food. You can't get your brother's face out of your head. His frozen gaze. You know that gaze. You'd recognize it anywhere.

He looked so surprised.

"Any idea why Oskar is sitting frozen in the basement with a stupid remote control in his hand?"

Of course no one knows what's happened here. It makes you uneasy. If the boy weren't in the basement, you would immediately check the recordings from the last few days yourself. It's your job to know everything, to have everything under control. What did you miss? You assumed the girl would listen to you. You should have been able to predict all possible deviations. Right now the boy in the basement is your only hope of shedding some light on this mystery.

You look at your watch.

The boy has only nineteen minutes left.

Time has always been important to you. For years time was a barbed-wire fence put up by your father, which enclosed your family on five days out of seven and separated you from the outside world. The fence opened at weekends, and normal life returned. In this normal life you met your father after eight unsuspecting years.

Do you remember what it was like running through the streets at fifteen? Do you remember how everything felt transient and how you lived with the fear that there would be nothing afterward? That only the Now existed, and everything had to be savored before it was too late?

You lived for the weekends, because those two days meant freedom. No one talked about where your father disappeared to during that time. Oskar asked once, and your mother pressed her forefinger to her lips as if that answered all the questions. You saw the sadness in her eyes and understood that she was no different from you—your mother endured everything too, and didn't know what was going on around her. Over the years your pity turned into raw rage. A mother has no right to be unsuspecting. She should protect her children. She should know what happened.

On the weekends you disappeared from home without explanation, just like your father. You were fifteen and no longer believed that he was accomplishing secret missions or working for the army. You tried to think about him as little as possible. You spent the night with friends in Bremen and existed in another reality. You drank, you smoked weed, you watched a load of bad videos and just waited to be eighteen so that you could disappear entirely from your old life.

And then he crossed your path.

How surprised you must have been when you were standing in line at the baker's one Sunday morning after partying all night and you saw your father walking past the window. Your reaction was spontaneous. You charged out of the bakery and stared after him. There was nothing special about your father walking past you. Not even in Bremen, had it not been for the little boy on his right-hand side and the woman on his left. The boy was holding your father's hand, the woman had linked arms with him.

Not your mother, not your brother.

It was only when they had disappeared around the corner that you set off running, you followed them four streets to an apartment block. You saw them going down the hall to the backyard. The boy ran ahead, the woman followed your father. You stood in the yard and watched their silhouettes moving up the stairs to the third floor.

The following week was like all weeks. The nightmare of your lives didn't change, although that was exactly what you had expected. You were sure your father would see through you.

Nothing happened.

For five days you gritted your teeth.

On Friday night you left the apartment, on Saturday morning you were on hold, watching the windows of the apartment block.

The boy, the woman, your father.

You just wanted to catch a glimpse of the three of them together.

You lied ruthlessly to yourself on this point, but that was okay, because the situation was unfamiliar. *If something is unfamiliar you have to observe it,* your father taught you. You didn't know what you wanted, you just knew it would hurt in the end.

When they left the house, you were standing on the opposite side of the street. Your father was so different. You saw him laughing, you saw him stroking the boy's head, then kissing the woman. Lovingly.

Your father wasn't your father.

You had to look away.

Outside the cinema and opposite Burger King, outside a bookshop, a flower shop, outside the supermarket and the butcher's. You followed them everywhere and all the way back to the block. You were starving and thirsty, but you didn't drink or eat. You knew it would distract you. From your fury and helplessness, which raged inside you like competing forces, sending out waves of darkness.

Hour after hour.

Only when midnight approached and all the lights went out on the third floor did you turn away and run to a friend. You slept fitfully, and took up your post again at seven o'clock on Sunday morning.

The apartment block was waking up.

You knew they would be having breakfast and talking now, that the radio was on and the toaster was spitting out toast. One more Sunday in your life. You were so lonely that you started crying.

At half past twelve the woman left the house with the boy.

You retreated to the street. You didn't want them to see you in the courtyard. As they walked past you the boy said, "And what if we have the ice cream first?"

The woman laughed and walked on with the boy.

The hall smelled of fresh paint and sisal. On every landing there was a rubber tree, the windows were clean, nothing looked threadbare. You climbed the three flights of stairs and had a choice of two doors.

On the left lived F. Hommer. On the right, in curly letters on a brass plate, was the name Desche. You ran your fingers over your surname and thought: *So this is where I live.*

It took you ten minutes before you could ring the bell.

He was wearing a white shirt and blue linen trousers. He was barefoot and looked like someone who had just come from the beach. You had never seen your father barefoot before. In one hand he held a newspaper, in the other a ballpoint pen. You couldn't look him in the eye. You studied him as if he were a headless creature. The way his toes contracted for a moment. The way the newspaper in his hand trembled. You noticed the wedding ring and you imagined him taking his old ring off every time he left you, and swapping it for this one. You wondered how easy it must be for him to switch from one family to the other. And why? That was the question that wouldn't let you go.

Why?

"Ragnar?"

Even his voice sounded different. Smaller, more insignificant. A voice without threat or danger. Just a voice. And you still couldn't look him in the eye.

"Christ, boy," he said, and took a step backward.

Perhaps it was an invitation, perhaps it wasn't, but anyway you marched past him into the apartment. Shoulders hunched, fists clenched. The door fell shut. The sound of bare feet on the wooden floor. He touched your shoulder. His words were brittle.

"This must come as a bit of a surprise."

He's nervous, you thought, and wanted to ask so many questions, wanted to fire so many accusations at him, but you couldn't do it, because your instincts took over. His hand on your shoulder. *Danger.* You didn't even turn around. Your elbow slammed into his side. When your father doubled up, you grabbed him by the hair and threw him down the hallway. He crashed against one of the cupboards. Two of the doors flew open, some games fell out, a yellow tennis ball rolled over the floor. Your father was gasping. Before he could get up again, you twisted his right arm behind his back. You were your father's son, he had drilled you, you knew what needed to be done. A bit of pressure was all it took and he was standing on tiptoes, his feet squeaked on the floorboards as you pushed him into the living room. Big sofa with matching armchairs, a television set with the sound turned down, a balcony. You wanted to throw him over the balcony. You wanted to hit him with the television. You had so many questions.

You let go of him.

He fell and lay on the floor, he held his arm and didn't say a word as you stood over him and still couldn't look him in the eye. Your breathing didn't quicken, you weren't even nervous, only one mad question made you uneasy.

What if this is his real life and I don't really exist?

His eyes tirelessly sought your gaze, while you had been staring at his chest, the way it rose and fell as he breathed heavily in and out. You wanted to reach in and tear out his rotten heart and ask him how he could do that to you all. He knew what you were thinking, he said, "You wouldn't understand."

"I don't *want* to understand," you heard yourself saying, and as you said it you knew it was the truth. Sometimes any explanations are unnecessary, you learned that day. Since then the following thought has stayed with you:

Some actions are inexcusable.

Then your father attacked you.

You can afford quiet moments of naïveté when you're lying in bed at seventy-five being spoiled by a twenty-year-old girl. Then you can be naïve and unprotected. Then you can close your eyes and believe in the good in people. Then. But not in front of your father. Not there.

He was so quick on his feet that you had no time to register that his weakness was put on to make you drop your guard. One hand grabbed you by the throat, the other arm came across your chest at an angle. He rammed you against the wall like that, once, twice, one of the pictures fell down and shattered on the floor. Your father's eyes were slits. You knew and feared that look. Your ego shrank away, your legs turned to jelly and wouldn't hold you upright.

What had you been thinking? Were you trying to be a judge? So your father led another life, he cheated on your mother and lived in an apartment that was ten times better furnished than yours was. So what? Have you forgotten who this is? Father and teacher and tormentor. He can do as he pleases. He is God, he is the world, he is the air, and if he wants he can take your breath and snuff you out.

He grinned into your face and your fear went up in flames and all those years under your father's fist flowed into that single moment. He shouldn't have grinned. Your knee came up and thumped into his belly. You knocked his hand away, your fist met his Adam's apple. He staggered backward, unable to breathe, but he didn't let go of you, he tried to drag you to the ground. *If he goes down, he's taking me with him.* You kicked his legs away, his grip loosened, he slid along the wall and landed on his back. The sound of the impact echoed noisily around the room. Your father's face turned crimson. He was looking at you the whole time, and there was this surprised expression on his face. It was the same look you would see years later after you'd lifted Oscar's eyelid. The same question after the why. There was something in your father's eyes, a very particular depth that you hadn't noticed before. A heavy, rattling breath left his chest and he lay still. You kept your distance and looked at him. Anything was possible. That he was bluffing again; that he was no longer alive.

That he knows what I'm thinking?

Even that.

You bent carefully over him, again there was that rattling breath, then silence. Your father's mouth gaped open and stayed open. You waited for his next breath.

Nothing.

You brought your face close to his, something looked up at you from the darkness of his eyes, something moved toward you. You held his gaze, you weren't afraid—not of the darkness, not of your father. Then that something disappeared, your father's gaze broke and dimmed. His last breath hit you.

Coffee, dust, something rotten, something sour.

Is that what death stinks like? Can I smell his damned soul?

You stood back up, took a deep breath of fresh air, and walked out.

Perhaps *walked* isn't the right word. Just as you instinctively reacted to your father's presence with violence, now you instinctively took flight. There was no going back now. You had eleven marks and a few small coins in your wallet, nothing more. So you ran aimlessly through Bremen. You didn't want to speak to anyone, you didn't want to see anyone and suddenly you found yourself on a ramp leading up to the Autobahn. You didn't care where the highway went, the only important thing was to make a start.

Six hours later you got out of a car in Berlin. Your older cousin lived here, you didn't know his address, you weren't even sure if you wanted to look him up. He'd doubtless have been delighted to take in his uncle's murderer.

Berlin was a good start, 1981 a good year to move to the city, because everybody was talking about Berlin, the last refuge of the draft dodgers, the wild metropolis. You had your own romantic ideas too. For you, Berlin was the city of freedom, even though it was enclosed by walls. *A city like my life.* You liked the thought.

You spent the first night in the Tiergarten. In the morning you walked through Berlin and the city tried in vain to please you. Everything inside you felt flat and dull. Your anger had taken a backseat and given way to helplessness, but you didn't think about going home for a second.

You had some french fries at a stand at Wittenbergplatz and looked at the people coming out of the subway, disappearing into the subway, hour after hour. There was no relationship. You were not one of them; they ignored you.

Whenever your people talked about Berlin it was all about Kreuzberg, the alternative scene and the dream of being an anarchist. You asked the snack bar owner how to get to Kreuzberg.

The U1 line took you to Kottbusser Tor. You left the station and knew at the sight of the street, the houses, and the people that this was the right place. At last the city reacted to you. It didn't take a minute. A girl asked if you had a light for her cigarette. She became your first angel. There would be so many angels over the next few years that heaven had to close down for a while. Some of them disappeared completely from your life. You know that one angel became a prostitute, two became mothers, and one angel OD'd in Spain.

Angel number 1 was called Natascha and she was a completely new experience for you. Not like the girls in Bremen. More energy, more zest. You thirstily drank her gestures and words, and you couldn't even have said whether she was beautiful or not. It wasn't about beauty, it was about this particular form of energy that hits you when you're fifteen. You gave her a light and joked around, she laughed and listened to you and was so urbane that you felt like a village idiot with shit on his shoes.

Side by side you walked through Kreuzberg, she showed you all the things you had to see. She gave you the feeling she was only there for you, and when she asked if you were looking for a place to stay, you looked down at her and thought: *Am I that transparent?* You didn't want to tell her about the small town and the small life you'd fled. You worried that your problems would seem pathetic and childish. So you shrugged and your angel took you by the hand, really took you by the hand, and so the same day you found yourself in an old building with a view of Görlitzer Park and for the next eight years you were a squatter.

"Ragnar?"

You look up. David is pointing at the screen of his notebook. Fourteen minutes have passed since you left the boy alone. He isn't sitting on the chair anymore. He's walking along the swimming pool, back and forth. He reminds you of animals in the zoo, slowly going mad in their captivity. There's a name for this behavior. Before it comes to your mind, Tanner says, "It's rather sad. Give the little fucker a few minutes and he does what all little fuckers do."

You've left him his phone, it's the oldest trick in the book. If a prisoner sees an open window, he climbs out. David turns the sound up. The boy is on the phone. Your brother has always insisted on high-quality products. You understand every word he says. It would be better if you didn't have sound. You listen and you feel the rage. David turns red. No one says anything, because there's nothing to say. The boy ends his call. David closes the notebook. You've heard everything. Tanner gets up from the table.

"Shall we leave you alone?"

You shake your head. Even though no one can see it, a steep slope has appeared in front of you. Your legs carry you, your heart pumps, and your brain is switched off. You can't stand still. Yield to the pace and hope you don't stumble and fall. You hate having no choice.

"David, find out how far back the CCTV recordings go and where the Range Rover went. And contact that pathologist at the Humboldt Clinic. What's his name again?"

"Fischer."

"Right. We need a death certificate for Oskar and the death registration from the registry. I want those papers on the table today."

David nods and gets up. It's time for you to send him away. He doesn't need to see everything. You wait till he's gone, and only then do you set off for the basement. You yield to the pace. The end of the slope is waiting. You're still breathing calmly.

The boy sits again on the chair and stares into the pool with great concentration. He's a bad bluffer, his shoulders give him away. He turns around as you step through the door.

"I've only known the girl since Tuesday night," he says hastily, as if he's been practicing the sentence and is relieved to say it at last.

"That's a start. So you've known her for three days. Excellent. Where can I find her?"

"I don't know."

"I'm going to ask again. Where can I find her?"

"I said, I don't know."

"That's all you have to say?"

"I said, I've only known her since Tuesday night."

"I haven't known you for half an hour and I know so much about you it gives me a headache."

The boy stares at the floor. You stare into the pool and think enough's enough, and say to Tanner, "Give me your gun."

Tanner takes the automatic out of its shoulder holster and hands it to you. You hear the uneasy scrape of Leo's feet. It's a habit he's developed over the past few weeks and he's going to have to lose it soon, because his unease is getting on your nerves. You release the safety catch and press the barrel to the boy's head.

"Stand up."

He gets to his feet, his knees are trembling.

"One last time. Where is she?"

The boy doesn't dare turn his head toward you.

"Look at me."

He swivels his eyes to get you in range. And then you spot it. Inconspicuous, almost invisible. But you spot it. He's smiling. Hidden in there amid all the fear and panic is a little smile. Even if you can't grasp it, the guy standing in front of you is a goddamn martyr.

MIRKO

How does a normal boy turn into a martyr within only two days? It starts with the boy standing helplessly in the middle of the night on a street in Berlin, with a helmet on his head. He isn't really furious, even though a girl he doesn't know has just driven off on his uncle's Vespa. There's a nervous flutter in his chest, like a bird moving its wings for the first time; there's a longing, even though he doesn't even know the girl's name, and if someone were to tell him now that the girl was called Stink, he would even find something romantic about that. He's happy. She talked to him, she looked at him, she stood beside him. Call it trashy or dazzled, call it dense or call it love. Whatever you call it, the girl has got you hook, line, and sinker. But that doesn't make you a martyr, does it?

The next morning Uncle Runa is sitting at your breakfast table reading the Slovenian sports newspaper *Ekipa*. He gets it from a kiosk on Kaiserdamm that takes deliveries from bus drivers who drive from Zagreb to Berlin and stop over in Slovenia. The paper is often over a week old, but that doesn't bother Uncle Runa. He says he needs the contact with home. You think if he needs contact, then he should go back to Slovenia. The sight of your uncle sitting at the table with the sports newspaper in his hand is a depressing one, because your father did exactly the same thing before he disappeared. Morning after morning.

"How did it go yesterday?" asks Uncle Runa without looking up.

"Same as always," you reply, and think of the Vespa. If your uncle finds out that it has disappeared, you'll just have to act the innocent and you'll get away with it. Uncle Runa gets away with spending every other night at your place, after all. Your mother says he hasn't got anybody else to have breakfast with. The loneliest people in the world are the lousiest liars.

You pour yourself a cup. The coffee tastes burnt. You add some condensed milk, the toast jumps from the toaster, you put it on your plate and spread it with butter. Uncle Runa snorts, clears his throat, and goes on reading. You look out of the window and suppress a yawn. That's your life, and there's nothing in it to suggest that you'll soon be a martyr.

What a boring day. You keep an eye out for the girl at school, but there's no sign of her. In the afternoon you meet your crowd. Darian doesn't mention last night's fiasco. His lower lip is much better, and the cut over his eye has scabbed over. He tells the guys one of the weights came off and nearly took off his head. The guys believe everything, but that isn't much use to you, because Darian keeps you at a distance. You fucked up yesterday, and he's making you pay for it. After school he asks why you didn't call him back this morning, and it's only then that you realize your phone is gone.

"Get yourself a new one," says Darian. "Only tramps don't have phones."

He wants to play billiards, so you go and play billiards. The day slips away, Darian disappears at nine with Marco and Gerd, they want to trudge around the clubs; even though Wednesday's a lame day, it's better than just hanging around doing nothing. Their lives are parting company with your life here, like an Autobahn from a minor road. You head off to work at the pizza stand, agitated and nervous and, for the first time, curious about your night behind the counter.

"Well, on time for once," Uncle Runa greets you.

You take off your jacket and put on the ridiculous apron with the grinning cook on it. Uncle Runa leans against the stack of beer crates and shoos the mosquitoes away with his breath. Since summer began he's been smoking cigarillos, and the stench always reminds you of used diapers that have been left too long in the sun. Your uncle hasn't the faintest idea that the Vespa behind him isn't a Vespa. The bike was parked outside the station, so rusty that the lock fell off the first time you kicked it. No one will miss it. You covered it with the tarpaulin. It looks like the Vespa, just a bit slimmer.

After an hour Uncle Runa leaves you alone at last. The waiting begins. She will come, you know that, she will come and give you the Vespa back and you will find out her name.

You believe that until three o'clock.

The next morning Uncle Runa is sitting at the breakfast table in your flat again, reading the same edition of *Ekipa*.

"How did it go yesterday?"

"Same as always."

You pour yourself a cup. The coffee tastes burnt. You add some condensed milk and spread butter on your toast. It's half past nine, you have two free periods first thing and you're in no hurry. Uncle Runa holds his cup out to you, you top it up, he snorts and goes on reading. Every day is like every other day if you don't catch sight of the girl of your dreams. You look out the window and wish you knew her name.

Ten minutes later you're spitting foam into the basin and wondering why toothpaste has to foam quite so much, when your mother hammers against the wall.

"What is it this time?!" you yell.

She's sitting in the living room, cigarette in her hand, feet on the footstool. Between her toes there are wads of pale blue cotton wool, the freshly applied nail polish gleams damply. The smell makes you feel nauseous, this mixture of chemistry and cigarette smoke in the morning is too much for you. There are already six cigarette butts in the ashtray, but you keep your mouth shut and say nothing about it. Your mother hands you the telephone as if it were a pair of dirty underpants that she found under your bed. She hates it when your friends call on the landline. You should use your cell phone, the line has to stay free. Since your father ran off with another woman, your mother has been waiting for him to call every day. She doesn't want to hear how he is or what he's doing. She just wants to yell at him. Or as she once told you: *I want to tell the swine what I think of him, then I can die in peace.*

"Yes?" you say into the receiver.

"Why didn't you jump on the back?"

You know right away that it's her. You turn away from your mother and go into your room. Your heart is racing and you wonder where she got the number. Your mother calls out that you're going to be late for school. *Yeah, fuck you very much,* you think, shut the bedroom door behind you, and press the receiver harder against your ear.

"Can't you talk, or what?"

"I . . . I can talk. But that Vespa you swiped isn't mine. It belongs to my uncle."

"Oh, poor uncle."

"But—"

"Don't shit your pants, you'll get the thing back, okay?"

"Okay."

"If you help me."

"What?"

"We have a problem here. My girls and me. We need some medicine. I mean, I can't really go into a pharmacy and just ask for prescription drugs, can I? And you, well, you know your way around."

Her words echo in your ears.

You know your way around.

She must know that you're friends with Darian.

Damn.

"Where did you get my number?"

"Guess."

She's confusing you, she's making you nervous, you want to laugh out loud, you want to tell her that you spent minute after minute last night waiting for her at the pizza stand and that you forgive her everything. Just keep your mouth shut.

"The number's stored on your phone under Mom. And you look like somebody who lives with his mom . . ."

She says nothing more, you can figure out the rest. Now she hasn't just got your uncle's Vespa, she's got your cell phone as well. And she's insulted you.

So what?

"And the Vespa isn't stolen," she adds, "it's borrowed. You'll get your phone back too."

"When?" you say far too quickly.

You hear a honk and walk to the window. Another honk. You look down at the street. She's sitting on the Vespa, grinning, her long hair in a ponytail, a pair of those sunglasses with outsized lenses on her nose, so that her face practically disappears behind them. She reminds you of a Mafia bride from one of those '70s movies. She looks up at you, she talks into your cell phone.

"Surprised?" you hear her saying into your ear, and then she makes the engine rattle and you burst out laughing and can't stop. Perhaps it's hysteria. Perhaps you're just happy. You'd like to shout down that she's mad, that she's really and totally mad, when you hear someone roaring.

"HEY, YOU CUNT, WHAT ARE YOU DOING ON MY VESPA?"

You look to the right. Uncle Runa is leaning out of the kitchen window. His face is bright red, he's shaking a fist.

"GET OFF RIGHT NOW OR I'LL KILL YOU!"

The girl does what anyone would do, Mafia bride or not. She puts her foot down and rattles away comfortably. Her red ponytail is a banner waving behind her.

You can forget about school for now, and you should ignore your uncle's outburst as well.

"Did you see that? Was that my Vespa, or what?"

"Bullshit."

"Mirko, what do you mean by bullshit? I'd recognize my Dragica anywhere. How the hell did that bitch get her hands on my Vespa?"

"Uncle Runa, that wasn't your Vespa," you reassure him and murmur that you have to get to school now. You grab your back-pack and run from the apartment before he can ask you any more questions. You expect to see the girl in the street. The street is deserted. Two kids come toward you, kicking a cardboard cup back and forth.

"Have you seen a girl on a Vespa?"

"Hey, I'm still asleep," says one of the boys and dodges you, while the other one dribbles around you as if you were a lamppost. You walk around the block. She needs your help, she called you, she won't just disappear.

Please, not again.

You spit. Since she mentioned Darian, there's been an unpleasant taste in your mouth. Bitter as envy, salty as regret. Your friend's not happy with you. Why did this have to happen right now? Why not two days ago? You were still thick as thieves then, and there was no coward who had crept under a car.

Two corners further on she's sitting on the Vespa at the side of the street.

"I knew you'd come," she says and hands you your cell phone.

"And the Vespa?"

"Will you help me?"

"I'll help you, but I need the Vespa back."

She gets off, puts the Vespa on its kickstand, and hands you the key and a piece of paper.

"This is the list."

You unfold the paper.

Oxazepam. Tilidine. Naloxone. Nemexin. Clomethiazole.

"Wow, what's the plan, are you opening a pharmacy or something?"

She doesn't smile. She puts her sunglasses up on her forehead, the skin under her left eye is swollen.

"Who did that?"

"Not the issue."

"Did someone hit you?"

"Calm down, it was an accident."

She flicks the paper in your hand.

"Can you get me some of this stuff?"

You look at the list again. You don't know what kind of drugs they are and how you would get hold of them, but you keep that to yourself. She could ask you for uranium and you'd find some for her.

"I'm sure I can get some of it," you assure her, and look at her almost pleadingly. "Is that all?"

She smiles suddenly, it's a sad smile. She says that's all, and to your ears it sounds almost as if she's sorry not to want anything more from you. Wishful thinking, Mirko, just wishful thinking.

"When can I collect the stuff?"

"Tonight?"

"Is that a question?"

"A suggestion."

"Tonight, then."

"Seven?"

"Seven's fine. You can take me out for ice cream."

"Ice cream?"

She points at your phone.

"My number's stored in it, call me if you know where there's good ice cream."

With those words she puts her sunglasses back on her nose, straightens the bag over her shoulder, and walks past you. *Tonight at seven,* you think and watch after her until she's disappeared around the corner, and only then do you think about what she said last. You nervously look through the contacts on your phone. The name leaps out at you: Stink.

What? What the hell sort of name is Stink?

She answers after the second ring.

"Did you forget something?"

She doesn't ask who's calling, she knows it must be you.

"The ice cream parlor on Krumme Strasse," you say.

"Fine, I'll be there."

"Are you really called Stink?"

"Are you really called Mirko?"

"But why Stink?"

"Because I smell so good."

You don't know what she smells like. You wish she were standing in front of you so you could bury your nose in the crook of her neck.

"Anything else?"

"Who are the drugs for?"

She is silent, you hear her breathing, the silence stretches out.

"For my friend, she's not in great shape and we're worried she's going to die," she says at last and cuts you off.

You stand at the side of the street and are incredibly pleased with yourself. *Stink*. You kiss your phone, you really kiss your phone. That girl has such a hold over you that you nearly disappear. You don't mind disappearing. You'd do anything for her, you wouldn't even mind becoming nothing at all. See, that's how it goes. A martyr is born.

TAJA

As if from nowhere a hand rests on your forehead and cools you down. As if from nowhere you hear words, and the words are meant only for you.

"Taja, hey, Taja, can you hear me?"

As if out of nowhere you float up and are set down gently as if you were a breathing, quivering soap bubble that would burst immediately if touched too hard. You feel a glass being put to your lips, you drink and cough. There's the hand again, reassuring. There's breathing by your ear.

"Taja, wake up."

I am awake, you want to answer, but you know it's a lie. Being awake means being there, it means being in reality. Reality is a whore who hates you because you've pissed her off. *I don't exist anymore,* you want to say, but your mouth's on strike, your whole head is . . .

"Hey, not so hard."

"That's not hard."

"If I slapped your face as hard as that you'd burst into tears."

"Schnappi, shut up."

"Just saying."

You open your eyes, your friends give a start.

They're real, you think, *they're really there, they—*

"Hi, sweetie," says Nessi.

"What's up with her eyes?" Ruth asks, as if you couldn't hear her. You want to raise your hand and rub your eyes. *What about my eyes?* You can't move.

"Stay calm, now."

Stink puts a hand on your chest as if she has to keep you calm. You want to tell her you are calm, but your teeth click together, your body is all quiver and shake. You tip over sideways and Schnappi already has a bucket ready. You throw up and throw up, and when it's over, when you feel at last that it's finally over, there's a rumble in your gut and you shit yourself helplessly.

When you wake up the second time, you're lying on your side and the balcony door is open. A warm breeze cools your sweat and banishes the stench from the first floor. You hear voices and laughter, then you smell perfume and know that Stink's outside.

"Feeling better?"

You turn around; Nessi is sitting on the other side of the bed. You try to smile at her and pull a face, your lips are brittle and cracked. Nessi hands you a glass of water. You drink greedily and lick your dry lips.

"How . . ."

Your voice is a croak, but it doesn't matter, Nessi knows what you're trying to say. She tells you everyone came straight here after you sent your text. They rang and rang the bell for a while and then came in through the terrace. You nod, you haven't closed the door to the terrace for ages. The smell was too bad.

"What day is it?" you ask, as if time mattered.

"Wednesday. Just after six, the sun's just risen. We found you downstairs on the sofa and carried you up. We're all exhausted."

You nod, you feel the tears welling up.

"I'm sorry, I . . ."

"Calm down. We're here. The important thing is that you're better now, you don't need to worry about anything else. We'd have called a doctor, but Stink said that was a lousy idea."

"Ruth didn't like it either."

You look up, Stink is standing in the door to the terrace, grinning at you. Ruth and Schnappi appear beside her, and suddenly you're enveloped by your girls, you feel their warmth and concern and you realize that you've never felt so secure. Whatever happens next, you're no longer alone.

———

They help you into the bathroom. Your legs are rubber, as soon as you tense a muscle it goes into spasm. You meet your eyes in the mirror for a second. Bloodshot and dull as a scratched spoon. The bathtub is full, the foam crackles, they leave you alone. For a while you just sit there in the water letting the warmth lull you. It's embarrassing. They washed the shit off you, changed your bed-clothes, and scrubbed the vomit off the floor. You're not fit for anything. It feels as if your protective shell has been destroyed and your skin is nothing but a paper-thin membrane. How much weight have you lost? Ten or twelve pounds? You don't want to think about it. Even your hair looks lifeless and your cheekbones are sticking out as if you were incurably ill. Your stomach is on fire and every cell in your body craves the drug. Your nose itches, your tongue is vibrating, the thought of the powder makes your mouth water. You're swallowing your own saliva. Your salvation is in the living room, in a plastic bag.

I could ask the girls if they'd ...

Forget it, your party's over.

But ...

You shut your eyes and listen to the crackling of the foam.

Nessi said it was Wednesday, you think, and don't want to look back at TuesdayMondaySundaySaturdayFridayThursdayWednesday.

No.

You want to start over with this Wednesday. It's the summer when you're all going to leave school. It's a new start. Think of something like that. You manage it for a minute or two, then your body craves the drug again and you plunge slowly under the water as if you could hide. And hold your breath. And hold your breath.

Nessi is waiting for you when you leave the bathroom. She picked out a few clothes. You're grateful, because you couldn't make your mind up what to wear. Nessi helps you dress and finally she brushes the hair off your forehead, pushes it behind your ears, and admits that you look very, very bad.

"Thanks."

She puts her arm around your hips and guides you to the door. She hesitates there for a moment.

"I have to tell you something, but you're not to get excited."

"Nothing excites me at the moment," you reply, and know it's a lie. Deep inside you there lives a hungry animal and it is running wild, tearing at your stomach walls, dashing from your legs to your arms and leaving unpleasant goose bumps all over your body, itching and wanting to be scratched.

Nothing can surprise me.

At least that's what you think.

"I'm pregnant," says Nessi.

Your girls are waiting on the terrace. They are sitting around the same table that four men will gather around in two days' time, before they launch the hunt after you. You can't know that at this time; everything would turn out differently if you knew it right now.

Ruth puts a blanket around your shoulders. Your chair is in the sun. You're freezing, even though it's warm. The air smells sweet of flowers. You're dazzled by the morning light and want to shut your eyes and sleep till summer is over.

"Here."

Schnappi hands you a cup of tea. You'd rather have coffee.

"I'd rather have coffee."

"There's ginger in it. It'll give you strength. I crushed it myself. Here, look at this, I nearly broke a nail and the garlic press is fallen to pieces. Either you drink my tea or I'm going home."

You drink the tea, the heat of the ginger numbs your mouth and makes you sweat, you drink down the cup and can only hope that Schnappi hasn't made a whole pot. Your body yearns for a kick, any kind of kick. Ginger tea doesn't cut it. You set down the empty cup. Schnappi is content, and pushes her coffee toward you.

"Good girl, this one's on the house."

You sip greedily, and feel as if you're going to throw up again. Calm now, breathe, calm now. Your girls are waiting. They have seen the living room and the kitchen. They want to know what this all means and why their best friend disappeared from their lives without a trace for a week. And of course they're also interested in why you got so completely fucked up on drugs. They've got so many questions that they say nothing and just wait.

If only you knew, you think, and look around and look around and realize at that moment what your eyes are doing.

They're looking for the plastic bag.

It isn't on the table in the living room anymore. It isn't on the sofa. *Where is it?* Your lungs clench spasmodically. You feel betrayed, your vision blurs. Pull yourself together. You've shed enough tears in the last days. It's time to accept reality again.

Fuck reality.

You take a deep breath, hold the coffee cup tightly with both hands and want to tell your girls what happened, but not a word comes out. You stare into the coffee. Tears flow down your face. You feel your whole self draining away. You hate yourself for this weakness and want to run off to the sofa and press the plastic bag to your chest.

Where the hell is it . . . ?

Stink leans over the table and slaps you in the face. You look up startled. Everyone looks at Stink, and Stink says: *I had to do this.* You nod. She's right. She had to do that. It does you good, it hurts and does you good.

More, you think, but nothing more comes.

So you get up.

So you walk straight ahead.

So they follow you.

Downstairs to the basement. You hold on to the banisters a few times, leaning your shoulder against the wall to keep from falling. *Weak, how can I be so weak?* The basement is divided into two vaults. You step inside the pantry, which is as big as the kitchen above it. The smell of stored apples is perfume against the stench in the house. Shelves, filled with wine bottles and drinks, cans, boxes, and bags. The things are arranged as they would be in a supermarket. It was always important for your father to be independent. He called the room his bunker. It's so cold that you're shivering. As a child you slept down here on summer nights, as soon as the heat in the house became unbearable. Your father set up a couch, there was a little table and a reading lamp. And if you got really bored, you brought your dolls downstairs, made them a new home among the boxes and imagined bombs raining down on Berlin while you were in safety.

"What are we doing here?" Ruth asks behind you.

You give a start, you'd completely forgotten your girls. Concentrate.

You stop by the chest freezer and rest your hand on the lid. When you speak, your voice is a whisper.

"I didn't know what else to do with him."

Everything begins and ends with death. That's not a special piece of wisdom, it's a fact. Your first life was short and ended with your mother's death. You were two years old, the car came off the road, somersaulted and landed in a ditch. Your mother died in the crash, your father got a scar on his forehead, nothing happened to you. You went on sleeping on the backseat. *It was a miracle*, people said. Ever since then you've hated miracles.

Your father didn't want to stay in Norway after the accident, so he packed everything up and went to Germany. Berlin was the destination because your father's brother lived there. Uncle Ragnar.

The family came together again.

Your second life began.

Your memories of the first few years in Berlin are relatively vague. You lived in Friedenau for a while. You can still see the courtyard in front of your eyes, the tall trees, all the people in the streets. You remember what the girl next door was called, Tina. Nothing more from those days has stayed with you. The memories of your mother overlap with those first years in Berlin, as if she'd been there.

Shortly after your sixth birthday your father bought the house in Frohnau, and you went to school. That autumn your real life began, and your father found his way too. Music had always been his weakness, he composed his first pieces and his passion became a profession. Seen from outside everything looked good and right.

But whatever your father did, whoever he met, the loss of his great love surrounded him like a negative aura and was transferred to you. Suspicion became your closest playmate. It could all come to an end at any moment. Nothing was safe. That's how we are. We learn from our parents. Even if your father assumed both roles, he couldn't replace your mother. And you made life hard for him too. Without really understanding why, most of the time you felt insignificant. As if your mother had died on purpose and left you alone. As if that were the truth and you were worthless.

Until high school you heaped presents on every girl who befriended you. In kindergarten, at school, next door. You gave them everything that was close to you—dolls, books, CDs, toys. You thought you could bind the girls to you like that. The opposite was the case. You hugged them so tightly they could hardly breathe, and soon looked for other friends. And you didn't get your presents back either. There was a deep pain in your soul. You had read that he who gives always gets back twofold. Your father informed you that such sayings were inventions of the Bible and meaningless in real life. He said: *If your heart is bound to something, you cannot give it away, for whatever it is, your heart will miss it.* You were sure that he was talking about your mother. But you didn't understand exactly what he meant, because she was taken from him after all, he hadn't given her away.

Your father's career was unstoppable, and his brother played an important part in making the necessary contacts with television and radio stations. Uncle Ragnar was your father's hero, never yours. He didn't really like you, and made no attempt to hide the fact from you.

Long before you were in secondary school, your father was earning more money than he had ever dreamed of. He was highly regarded as a composer in the world of advertising. Everything he touched turned to gold. But it was never enough. Contentment was not a part of his philosophy of life. *A broken heart is a broken heart, there's nothing you can do about it,* he said over and over, which was in the end only an excuse for the drug excesses and the constant stream of women who came and went and never stayed. And in the middle there was always you—the girl who had lost her mother, the girl who was lonely and could find no place in the world.

Your ego was a disaster, you stumbled from one melancholy to the next, you listened to the appropriate music and wrote poems about loneliness and death. You would inevitably have ended up on a couch with piercings in your face and cuts on your arms, if luck had not been on your side when you went to secondary school, putting you in the right class.

You found your girls.

First of all there was Stink, who leaned over to you in the introductory assembly in the hall and asked if by any chance you had a fucking tampon, she was running out and her underwear was brand-new. Ruth and Schnappi joined you at break on the playground, Nessi switched to your class six months later, and your set was complete.

Your girls accepted you from the start. As far as they're concerned you're interesting and exciting, they love your melancholy and the way your voice trembles when you sing about the end of the world. You're the counterweight to their follies and bring them back down to earth if they float too high in the air. And you're their star, because it helps a bit that your father writes stupid jingles that everybody knows. And then of course there's the Darian connection. Even though you don't like your cousin any more than you like his father, there are advantages to the relationship. Darian ignores you just as his father does, you're the little cousin who gets a present at Christmas, but that's about it. Still the blood bond exists and it gets you and your girls into any club. The bouncers never cause problems once they know who your cousin is.

If you were to claim right now that you get along with your father, it would be a lie. You've more or less lived next to each other in one house. He gave you every freedom so that he could be free himself, and that's the only thing you think highly of him for. Even though it sometimes bothered you that no boundaries were set, you were happy with your arrangement. Until his phones rang a week ago.

You hesitate, you look at your girls, watching you, listening to you. Then you cross an invisible boundary and tell them about last Wednesday. And you don't leave out a single detail.

It was early in the morning, you didn't have to get to school until later, your father was in his studio in the attic, you could hear the music all the way downstairs. The house is big enough, you could easily stay out of each other's way all day. You buttered some rolls and sat down in the living room with a map of Europe. At the end of August you planned to take off along those highways and byways, busking in the streets every now and then and getting to know the different cultures. You were curious and had a feeling that the world was at your feet. You'd marked out a route for yourself and sought out youth hostels. You knew what you wanted to see, and you really hoped your girls would come too. You'd been working on them for a year. Even though they claimed that InterRail sounded exciting, none of them really took your plans very seriously. Or as Schnappi said: *I'd rather sleep in my own bed.* So the way things looked at the moment, you'd have to go on your own, but that was okay too. The adventure awaited.

Paris was a dream, Madrid too, and if you were brave enough you wanted to take a detour to Norway, not just to see the house where you were born, but also to visit your mother's grave. The very thought made your palms moist. Even though in all those years not a single relative from Norway had stayed in contact with you or your father, you've got this vague fantasy—arriving in Ulvtannen and seeing the beach hotel, everyone recognizing you right away and you becoming one of them. Everything seems possible, if you make it possible.

You're free. You have no steady boyfriend, and no interesting internship. Your father was of the opinion that everyone should conquer the world at sixteen, so you had a green light from him. Your curiosity about the world is the only thing you have in common with Uncle Ragnar. When he heard about your plans, he gave you an envelope with five hundred euros in it. It looked as if nothing could stop you. And then the phones rang.

———

You're no fan of ringtones, especially not since people have been downloading them onto their cell phones. Everyone wants his own tune, everyone wants to be special and different, and that very fact makes them all the same. The hunger for originality. Your father was no exception, only he used his own jingles as ringtones. And you particularly loathed this one. It was a jingle for children's toothpaste.

You were sitting on the sofa and traveling across Europe with your finger, you'd just settled in Portugal when the tune rang out.

Your father had four landline phones, scattered around the whole house and all diverted to a single number. He didn't want to be one of those idiots who always have a phone hanging from their belt. So he became one of those idiots who have their phones ringing all over the place and really get on your nerves as a result.

One of them summoned you from the kitchen. After you'd listened to the jingle five times and your father's mailbox still hadn't leapt into action, you stirred yourself and got up.

The ringing stopped.

You marched into the kitchen anyway. The procedure was always the same. You took out the batteries and set them down beside the phone. Your father never complained. You were about to open the flap when the phone rang again. You cursed, the batteries jammed, the phone tinkled, then the jingle fell silent and a woman's voice said:

"*Vi bør snakke.*"

Surprised, you turned the phone over. You must have pressed the answer button after your father took the call. You just stared at the display for several seconds before putting the phone to your ear.

"*. . . med mig tysk,*" said your father.

"As you wish," the woman said, in German now, "but don't forget, she was your grandmother."

"I know who she was, but it has nothing to do with us now."

"Not with *us,*" said the woman. "It has nothing to do with you now."

Your father said nothing, you thought you could hear the grinding of his teeth, perhaps it was just a bad connection.

"It's her legacy," the woman continued, "at least you could allow her that."

Your father exploded.

"Allow her? As if I didn't allow her anything! You know what you can do? You can stick your legacy up your ass! Where did you get this number?"

Now the woman fell silent. The silence started spreading, then your father said in a menacingly quiet voice, "I've warned you. And I'm warning you a second time: never call this number again!"

"I understand."

"What do you mean 'I understand'? Are you even listening? Do you get what it really means when I tell you *never* to call here again?"

"I'm sorry. You know—"

"Go fuck yourself!" your father interrupted. "Go fuck yourself with your stupid explanations. We don't need your shit!"

With those words he hung up and you were left alone with the woman's breathing. At that moment an idea lit up in your head, like a match being struck in the dark. The bad connection, the woman's voice, your father's irritation.

They were speaking Norwegian.

It was like a bad melodrama—relatives looking for you to bring you back into the fold of the family. You were about to say something when the woman hung up as well. *Too late.* You were so stunned that you couldn't take the phone away from your ear. Your thoughts raced. You listened to the hiss on the line and looked out of the window at the driveway. You only reacted when your father appeared in the kitchen doorway and asked why you weren't using your own cell phone.

"Hi there, are you still on this planet?"

You were still there and you proved it to him by throwing the phone at him. It bounced off his shoulder and landed on the floor. The two batteries fell out and rolled at your feet.

"What's up with you?" your father asked and laughed.

He was drunk, and when he was drunk he didn't take anything seriously. He had this stupid grin that was supposed to excuse him for everything.

"Who was that?" you asked.

"What are you talking about?" he asked back and reached past you to open the fridge. You shut the fridge again.

"Who was the woman on the phone?"

He flinched slightly, then pushed you firmly aside, took a bottle of water, and closed the fridge again.

"I have no idea who you're talking about."

He drank straight out of the bottle and looked at you from the corner of his eye.

"I heard everything," you admitted.

"Naughty girl," he said.

"Who was that?"

"One of your aunts."

"Which aunt?"

"Aunt . . ."

He waved his hand around in the air. He was so bad at lying that it was shameful.

"Christ, what's her name?"

"Are you messing with me?"

"How could I?"

He put the cap on the bottle and shrugged.

"I can't remember her name."

"You've *just* spoken to her on the phone and you can't remember her name?!"

"Seems that way."

"What were you arguing about?"

"You know what Norwegians are like."

"I know . . . What? How should I know what Norwegians are like, I've never even met one!"

"Point to you," he said and laughed again.

That was when you took the bottle away from him.

"Hey, I'm still thirsty!"

"Talk to me now."

"I am talking to you."

"Who was that on the phone?"

He looked at you as if he was about to give you an answer, then he shifted into one of those perfect displacement activities that you knew so well. He mumbled that he wanted to watch some TV. So he marched out of the kitchen and sat down in front of the television. You knew the alcohol wasn't his only drug. He'd once told you that no muse in the world was as good as a clean high. Whatever a clean high was, your father needed to top it up with vodka, cocaine, and a whole lot of weed.

You picked the batteries off the floor and put them back in the phone. You tried to calm down, then you followed him into the living room, where he was sitting on the sofa, clicking through the channels. As soon as he found an advertisement, he leaned back contentedly and waited for a commercial with one of his jingles to come on.

"I'm going to bug you all day," you threatened.

"Have fun."

You went and stood in front of the television. Your father furiously raised his arms and whined, "Come on, that's not fair!"

"How old are you?"

He pointed the remote control at you as if to switch you to a different channel.

"Oskar, who was that on the phone?"

"Christ, stop it, you know how much I hate it when you call me Oskar."

"Give me an answer."

He scratched the back of his neck with the remote.

"It's complicated. We'll talk about it tomorrow, okay? Or what about the day after? Or how about I write it down for you?"

You didn't move from the spot. You counted to twenty in your head, then you said, "What have I inherited?"

"Christ, you really were listening!"

"Of course I was listening, I told you I was listening. Are you actually listening to me?"

"I'm listening to you. I hear everything. It's the hotel, okay? You've inherited it. Happy now?"

"The beach hotel?!"

"Don't go nuts on me. It's old and it needs renovating. But if you save up and borrow some money off your good old dad, you might get it back on its feet."

"What?"

You felt dizzy. You sank into one of the armchairs. Your heart raced. The only beach hotel in the world without a beach. *Mine.* You saw the photographs in your head. The gravel in the driveway. The massive Nordmann fir casting its shadow across the façade. Your mother standing in front of it and waving at the camera. A curtain flapping out of one of the windows. The fjord and the mountains in the background.

The beach hotel on the cliff? Mine?

Your mouth was suddenly dry as dust. Norway was calling to you.

"I know it's hard for you right now," your father went on, "but why do you think I didn't want to tell you?"

He turned off the television and set down the remote control. Then he calmly started to roll a joint. Just as he scattered his phones around the place, in every room there were little wooden boxes of cigarette papers and grass. You were familiar with the ritual, your father didn't speak again until the joint was glowing between his lips.

"Maybe we should talk," he said.

"Okay."

"Maybe it's time. You're a big girl, you can cope."

"Christ, what's coming now?"

He offered you the joint, you shook your head, he took a second drag and as he exhaled he said, "We should be honest."

"I hate it when you say things like that."

He looked at you doubtfully.

"Perhaps you're not quite ready yet."

"Oskar, I'm ready."

"Good, good to hear it."

You leaned forward, elbows on your knees, your legs were trembling.

"What's happened?"

"You know the accident and your mother . . ."

Your father took a third drag.

". . . it wasn't quite like that, that was kind of a lie."

"What?"

He touched his forehead.

"I got that scar swimming. An idiot from the other class deliberately threw me off the three-meter board. His name was Roland or something. Afterward he—"

"WHAT DID YOU SAY?"

You didn't mean to scream at him, but your voice came out uncontrolled. Your father fell silent and looked out at the terrace, as if there were someone there who could save him from his situation. Of course there was no one there. When he spoke again, his voice was filled with grief.

"She had a new guy at the time, do you understand that? She wanted to split up and keep you. So I took you and cleared out. You can't really call it desertion. It wasn't kidnapping either, because you were my little one. Your mother thought she could bring charges against me, but she hadn't reckoned with Ragnar's lawyers. And we're still married, so you have to sort out custody and everything."

Your voice was just a breath.

"Mom's alive?"

"That's what I'm saying."

"Mom's alive?"

"Is there an echo in here?"

Now you knew what it was like to be paralyzed. Arms, legs, head. Only your thoughts were moving, repeating those two words: *Mom's alive.* And sometimes it sounded like a question and sometimes like an answer. Then you exploded.

"HOW THE HELL COULD YOU LIE TO ME?"

"It was self-defense."

"SELF-DEFENSE?"

"Taja, she had a new guy, she didn't want me anymore, what choice did I have? Leave you with her and watch her being happy with her new guy? We lived out in the country, it would never have worked. Was I supposed to stand by and watch you calling him Dad and avoiding me in the street? It was out of the question."

"But . . . you could have . . ."

"Of course I should have told you everything before, then you'd probably have emigrated at six years old to go and find your mother. Forget it. Now you've finished school and you can do what you like. You're grown up, you can deal with it all by yourself. I've done my best."

"You've done what?"

He looked at the joint and stubbed it out. He didn't think about repeating himself. You saw him picking up the remote control and turning the television back on as if your conversation was over. Then you got up, bent over the coffee table, and, with suppressed rage, asked your father one last time who that had been on the phone. You needed to hear it.

He didn't take his eyes off you.

"It was your mother, she lives in Ulvtannen and she wanted—"

"YOU MISERABLE PIECE OF SHIT!"

"Hey, listen, it was done with the best of—"

"I HATE YOU, I WISH YOU WERE DEAD!"

He stopped, he saw the tears in your eyes, he saw your fury, and through his haze and his ignorance he must have understood that you were entirely serious. You wanted to pick up the wooden box and smack him with it. You've never been violent, you'd had one fight with a girl from the other class because she'd kicked out at Ruth. Violence isn't a solution, everyone knows that. But on this particular day you understood for the first time what leads to violence.

Disappointment, helplessness, weakness.

Your father saw all those things in your eyes, and a change occurred. In his face, in his eyes. He was shocked. He sank back down on the sofa and sighed. Once. You heard a cracking sound. His right hand was twitching, his left hand was a claw that held the remote control so firmly that the plastic broke.

"Dad?"

He only looked at you. He didn't blink. It was a little as if he'd seen something in you that he'd never seen before. Darkness. His mouth opened and shut again. He sat there motionlessly and his gaze was his gaze for several seconds, until something disappeared.

That day you had no idea what it was that disappeared, and while you tell your girls about it you hear yourself whispering that it might have been his soul—for a moment fear flashed in your father's eyes, a moment later his gaze was blank and lost and still directed at you.

And so it happened that you killed your father.

OSKAR

Of course you've thought about death, but you didn't really expect that it would catch you like that. Your ideal would have been to drift away unnoticed at a great age. A hot bath and the right music in the background, a bottle of red wine, and you would have gone to sleep gently and contentedly. Instead you have this furious daughter yelling at you as if you were the lowest of the low. You should never have let it come to this. What were you thinking of?

Your death takes place in stages. Taja stands in front of you for a moment, shouting at you as you stub out your joint and hope she'll calm down. A moment later there's darkness and you don't understand what's happened. Something's missing. The transition. The switch-off. You're dead, without understanding it. And you always thought there would be an understanding.

Dead?
  Dead.

The darkness persists. And in that darkness your body starts changing. From top to bottom, even though you can't feel it, you know it's happening. As if your body were bidding you a sighing farewell. As if all the light were vanishing from it, flowing and leaking away.

When the light comes back, it happens all of a sudden and you're staring at the ceiling. The colors explode around you and you want to breathe out with relief and tell Taja that this has been the worst trip ever. But the trip isn't over, it's only just started. Everything starts and ends with death. But you really didn't expect that it would catch you like this. If you're honest, there are lots of things in your life that you didn't expect—not a crazed father bringing you and Ragnar up like a dictator; not a brother who abandoned you at the age of twelve; but certainly not a life in Norway and a wife like Majgull. Not to mention your daughter.

"Dad?"

If you could cry, you'd cry now. Christ, how long has it been since she called you Dad? And she means it. It's not her voice that gives it away, it's her thoughts, her feelings. You can read her effortlessly. As if you had a mental connection. It's a world suddenly opening up to you. You have access to every thought, every emotion. And what can you do with it? Nothing. You're just an observer who can't intervene. How fucked is that?

Really fucked.

Taja pulls at you, the ceiling vanishes from your field of vision, you are sitting up again and looking at your little one. Her fingertips stroke your face as if you might shatter if she made a false move, then she recoils and runs away. Shame, fear.

Poor girl.

And as she flees, you suddenly understand what has happened. Her thoughts come fluttering after her like nervous birds, they find you and talk to you and you don't believe them. And don't believe them. And don't want to believe them.

You sense Taja's presence in the room before you see her. Your eyes don't obey you any more than your body does. You stare straight ahead. Taja comes and stands right in front of you as if to catch your eye. She doesn't want to think the word *death*. She thinks everything else. She doesn't want to touch you again. She breathes guilt and vanishes from your field of vision.

Taja is back. She's been thinking. She's been crying. One of her knuckles is dark. She must have hit the wall. She could never keep her feelings under control. Now she's sitting next to you. Her hands touch you.

You feel nothing.

Her hands on your neck.

Nothing.

Her head on your shoulder.

Nothing. But you know what she's thinking.

I hear her thoughts, and if I hear them, perhaps it'll work . . .

No.

But if I can see and hear her, perhaps she can . . .

No, it's over. There's no going forward and there's no going back. You can receive, but you can't transmit. Get used to it.

And so it grows dark outside, and your daughter leans against your lifeless body and sleeps, while you listen to her thoughts as if to a secret radio station broadcasting only to you. You're still stunned. You know you've gone too far, but do you have to end like this? You and your guilt and your shame.

You listen to your daughter's anxieties, her helplessness, her fury. And the question comes back again and again: *Can he forgive me? Will he forgive me?*

You stare a hole into the room. A dead man waiting to see what happens next. And as you're waiting, the dead cells in your body start breaking down. Enzymes rage through your tissue. Rigor mortis leaves you. Only your fist goes on clutching the remote control like a claw, and won't let go of it. The rest of your body gives in. As if it wanted to be a gentle pillow for your daughter one last time.

Daylight comes. Taja wakes with a start and vanishes from your side. She's repelled. She wants to wash and that's fine, you would have done exactly the same. She's revolted by death.

When she comes back the light is different, the sun has reached the opposite wall, hours have passed. Taja pushes the armchair further away from you. You see her arm, her leg, you only see her face at the edge of your field of vision. Your daughter doesn't want you to stare at her. She studies her cell phone as if it holds all the answers. Her thoughts are:

> *What will Stink say . . .*
>> *Shall I call the police . . .*
>>> *Shall I call Uncle Ragnar . . .*
>>>> *Or Ruth . . .*
>>>>> *Shall I wait . . .*
>>>>>> *What will I wait for . . .*
>>>>>>> *How can he just . . .*
>>>>>>>> *What if . . .*
>>>>>>>>> *Perhaps I could . . .*

She gnaws at her thumbnail. You thought she'd have shaken that habit by now, and as if she can hear your thoughts she wipes her thumb on her jeans, draws in her legs and hugs herself. You wish you could hold her, of course you forgive her. She's your daughter. Even if no one deserves to die like that, you can't be angry with your daughter. A father is a father is a father.

Then Taja disappears again.

You see the sun wandering across the living room.

The opposite wall turns dark, the wall turns light.

You hear music from the floor above. Your toothpaste jingle blares twice from the phones, then silence. Taja's probably taken the batteries out. You prefer the music anyway. Alabama 3. You gave her the CD because you thought then she might sit next to you one evening and you could watch *The Sopranos* and enjoy the title song. She thought the series was strangely quiet. That's exactly how she put it. *Strangely quiet.* But she liked the music.

She appears in front of you. She's been drinking. She's plundered the bar. Cognac, Metaxa, schnapps. If you could smell her you'd know she smells bad. She's already thrown up twice and at any moment she's going to go to the fridge and get the vodka out of the freezer. She's like you. Weak and in search of release. Forgetting is the magic formula of the cowards. There's so much she wants to ask you, her head is a book full of questions, then she laughs, because she knows it's stupid to talk to a dead person.

"And now I'll drink your vodka," she says and disappears again.

The living room turns dark.

Your daughter stands in the kitchen drinking your vodka.

The CD comes to an end, the CD starts over again.

Woke up this morning.

Night.

Light in the corridor. Taja staggers through your field of vision. She hasn't slept, her thoughts are overwrought, she's drunk and teary and throws a plastic bag down on the table. Almost as an accusation.

You're surprised that she's found the heroin. Even though you haven't made much of an effort with the grass and it's lying around all over the place, you've always been very careful with the hard drugs. Once again it goes to show how naïve you've been. Your daughter knows everything about you. Where the drugs are, where you hide your dirty secrets. She probably found your private stash of porn ages ago, and knows about the cameras as well. It wouldn't surprise you, everything's possible where Taja's concerned. And if someone doesn't come by soon and save her, your little one could go completely crazy.

To watch your own child going increasingly to pieces over the course of two days is pure pain. But hearing all of her thoughts and being powerless, perhaps that's the true hell after death. Not really disappearing, persisting in a state in which you're aware of everything that's happening around you, observing the decay, helplessly, in a state of nonexistence. And to be carried to the grave like that— knowing, but unable to do anything with your knowledge. After millennia of evolution, finally taking another step forward and not being able to use the knowledge because you've ceased to exist.

On Friday evening Taja turns crazy. Perhaps it's your smell, perhaps it's her doubts. What is she supposed to do? *Hello, my father's been sitting around dead for two days since I killed him, can you come and collect him?* You can see it in her, guilt, and more guilt. She's drinking, she's barely eating, she looks at you, she looks at the heroin. You want to warn her. She doesn't know what she's got in front of her. That heroin's dynamite. Totally pure. Stuff like that is rare on the market. Hardly anyone can cope with quality like that. You ould make neural bombs with that stuff, it's nuclear.

Please, little one, don't.

's done it. She sits there and raises her glass to you. If you could, would look away. You can see everything. Her euphoria and eep, how she gets her strength back and then collapses in on f like an empty balloon. And then how she throws up on the floor, she is not strong enough to make it to the bathroom, she is so tired of herself. Every now and again she explodes with exaggerated activity, running with the cell phone clenched in her fist from one corner of the living room to the other, she doesn't make a single call, wants to sort it all out by herself, doesn't know how, but wants to. Stubborn and guilty. Her face above the table, the straw leaving a clean track on the wood, her contented *ahhh*, rubbing her nose and looking at you and looking at you and then deciding.

She takes you under the armpits and struggles as she drags you down the stairs. She's crying as she does so. Your strong girl is crying. Her plan isn't the dignified departure from this world that you imagined. But it's only temporary. That's what you hope. And besides, she's talking to you again. Her thoughts are one thing, her voice another.

"I don't know what else to do. I . . . I don't want them to come and get me. And . . . I don't want you to . . . I can't bury you either, Dad, I can't . . ."

She clears out the chest freezer and piles up the frozen packets, fish and meat. A lot that you've hunted yourself, with Tanner by your side, early in the morning in the forest north of Berlin, the fairy-tale silence, branches breaking and then the shot. When Taja has made enough room, she heaves you into the freezer. If your body was still in a state of rigor mortis, it wouldn't work. But you bend easily and she lifts you onto a bag of fish and you sit there almost in the same position as you were in on the sofa. When you topple slightly to the side, Taja wedges two packs of sirloin between your shoulder and the wall. That's better, even though you're leaning slightly backward and looking up. Taja tries to free the remote control from your hand. Nothing to be done, you won't let go of it. She bends down to you in the freezer, strokes your head, and promises she'll be back soon.

"I'll be back soon."

There's a *whup*.

It's dark.

You're sitting in the cold.

Soon is just a word.

And you sit in the cold. And you sit in the cold.

And you sit and sit in the cold.

The freezer opens, and there's a scream. First one scream, then three, in the end it's four screaming girls staring down at you. Their screams subside. You're proud of your daughter for finally over-coming her stubbornness and calling her friends for help. You can tell them apart, even though you have to get their thoughts in order first. StinkRuthNessiSchnappi. Taja used to give a pajama party every month. When she did, you left the house voluntarily. Any single father should respect his daughter's wishes.

It would be nice if you could calm the girls down with a few words. *It's not as bad as it looks like,* you would say, but of course that doesn't happen, only the cold from the freezer reacts, it rises into the warmth in threads of mist and settles on the girls' faces as if your soul were stretching its fingers out to them. Feeling nothing has its advantages. After five days you're a lump of deep-frozen meat.

"Is he really dead?" Schnappi asks.

"Do you think he's sitting in there to cool himself down?" Stink asks irritably.

"That's perverse," says Nessi, and as she does so you know that she's pregnant. You also know the name of the boy who deliberately didn't put on a condom because he thought it would be okay without. Nessi trusted him. *Poor Nessi*, you think, and hear the unborn child's heartbeat like whispered drumming. You know what it is going to be.

"Why did you just stick him in there?" Ruth asks. She's the sensible one who always questions everything. Once she asked you if it wasn't incredibly boring, squandering your talent like that. She thought jingles were commercial shit. If she hadn't been your daughter's friend, you'd probably have thrown her out on day one.

You concentrate on Taja. She's completely wrecked. Her body is pulsing greedily for the heroin, it's a dull, weary sound. Her heart's racing, her lungs are sluggish, her jaw is trembling, and there's a rotten taste in her mouth as soon as she thinks about heroin. And she thinks about it almost constantly.

Longing, she's longing.

Taja tells the girls about her fear of ending up with her relatives. She knows your brother will never take her in. She's right to suspect as much. Ragnar has enough to do with his company. As soon as your death is official, your aunt will take care of Taja. Your little one is a minor, what say does she have? It would mean a new life in Dortmund. Her third life. Taja doesn't want a third life.

"And how long were you planning on hiding him here?"

"I don't know. I thought . . ."

Taja hunches her shoulders. Helpless and anxious.

"I really didn't mean to kill him, I was just furious and all of a sudden . . ."

Silence. Stink's snotty voice.

"What's that crap all about?"

"What crap?"

"Who says you killed him?"

"But he *is* dead."

Schnappi joins in.

"Just because you want someone to die, it doesn't mean he dies because you wished for him to die. If that was the case half the city would be dead. Christ, Taja, he could have had a heart attack or one of those stroke things. The amount of drugs he did, it would hardly be a surprise."

Thanks, Schnappi.

Before Taja can process all that, Stink speaks again. Even though she's got on your nerves more than once, you admire her at that moment. Because she never keeps her head down, because she always sees the funny side in every tragedy. Like now, when she says, "Maybe he's just pretending."

Her face suddenly appears in front of yours. Freckles and that little gap between her front teeth. She bats her eyelashes at you and says, "Hello?!"

Hello.

"That's not funny," says Ruth.

Stink disappears from your field of vision. If you were sixteen again, you'd fall in love with her in an instant. Because she's a mystery and nobody knows what she's going to get up to next.

"Was that why you pumped yourself full with drugs?" she asks Taja, and doesn't wait for the answer, but adds: "How stupid are you, by the way? We live in the same city, have you forgotten that? If you've got a problem, you come to us, you don't get shitfaced."

"I know," Taja says in a small voice.

"Leave her be, this isn't going to do any good," Nessi cuts in. "We should be thinking about what to do next."

They all look at you.

"The party is over," says Stink.

She steps forward and slams the freezer shut.

Darkness, my old friend.

STINK

They look at you in horror.

"What's up? Did you want to look at him for longer?" you ask, and you're glad the lid is closed. A corpse is bad enough, but a corpse sitting in a freezer like a popsicle, no, there are limits. Dead is dead.

"You could have closed the lid more gently," says Nessi.

"Have I hurt your feelings?"

"Not mine, but maybe his."

"Honey, he hasn't got any feelings now."

"That's what you say."

"It's what I know."

"Is that really true?"

"Yes, it's really true, I'm an expert on dead people."

You grin at Nessi, Nessi grins back, and then you remember what you're actually doing here, and you look at Taja. Her lower lip is trembling, her eyes are wide. Her father is lying in that awful chest freezer and you're messing around with Nessi. Well done.

Yes, but her father's in there because it's where she put him.

It is a good thing you keep your mouth shut. Schnappi flips you the finger. Ruth puts an arm around Taja and says, "Come on, let's go back up."

Taja feels ill again and goes off to the bathroom on the first floor. Your girls are sitting outside and totally exhausted. You feel like that guy in *Clockwork Orange* when he has his eyelids pinned back and has to watch movies for hours and hours. Cramped, alert, and totally hyped. Every time you pull a face, it takes a while before your expression is back to normal.

It's eight o'clock in the morning and the night is still in your limbs. Even if you wanted to, you couldn't sleep now. Your head is wired, your thoughts won't rest, and then there's this weather — the sunbeams stretch over the hedge and scratch their way across the terrace like a lunatic who hasn't cut his fingernails. It's a dazzling day, which doesn't make any sense whatsoever. It should be stormy and raining. Dazzling days put you in a good mood, and the mood among you girls is anything but dazzling.

"We need to sleep," says Nessi.

Schnappi yawns so hard that her jaw clicks. She rubs her cheek, and has a tear in the corner of her eye.

"Girls, I can't sleep in daylight. Don't look at me like this, I've never been able to. I can only get my eyes shut when it's dark outside."

You're about to tell her you haven't heard such nonsense for a very long time, when you're interrupted by a loud retching noise from the guest bathroom. Nessi immediately gets up, Ruth joins her, and you tag along too, only Schnappi leaves her small ass where it is and says too many cooks spoil the soup.

Taja sits on the toilet seat and can't stand up.

"My legs aren't working properly."

You all help her up. She doesn't want to go back to bed, she wants to be with the rest of you. So you take her outside. Of course Schnappi has gone to sleep, mouth open, like a baby waiting to be fed. Nessi fetches water from the kitchen, while you cushion one of the deck chairs with blankets. Taja's forehead is coated in a greasy film of sweat, her upper arms are patchy and red, and although she washed an hour ago, she's giving off a tangy smell. Nessi comes with the water, Taja drinks greedily. Ruth sets the bag of drugs down on the end of the table.

"Since when have you been taking this stuff?"

The answer is so quiet that you have to lean forward to understand Taja.

"For a few days."

"And how many times a day?"

"Now and again."

"Taja, look at me. How often?"

They look at each other. Taja holds the eye contact for two seconds, then she stares at her hands and admits that she's been living on nothing but the powder for the last five days. Nessi pulls a face and narrows her eyes, which would have looked funny on any other day. You are watching Taja. *How on earth could it come to this? And why didn't she call us?* That's the thing that pisses you off the most. *We were there, after all.* Taja says, "After my father . . . died, at first I did nothing but drink. And then . . . then I discovered that stuff."

She tilts her chin toward the plastic bag. The tip of her tongue darts over her lips, and she gulps as if she has something in her mouth. Nessi tops up her glass. She drinks gratefully.

"It really helped, you know? I calmed down and I could sleep again, and when I was awake I took some more. It helped me, it turned me . . ."

She shrugs her shoulders, lets them slump.

". . . good again."

You pull the bag over to you and take a look at the powder.

"What is this stuff?"

"Coke or something," says Taja.

Ruth thinks she's misheard.

"You don't even know *what* it is?"

Taja lowers her head. You want to put yourself between them. Ruth can kill with words. Perhaps she should become a lawyer. That would fit. And then one day if you end up in court Ruth will be standing there in a business suit, defending you, and in the end you'll be sitting on a terrace, smoking cigars and laughing at the law.

"When did you last take the stuff?" she asks.

"Before I sent you that text."

Ruth looks at her cell phone.

"So, five hours ago. Who knows, maybe you're feeling so shitty because you're suffering withdrawal symptoms."

Taja laughs weakly.

"That's stupid, I'm not a junkie."

You all just look at her. Even though you have barely any experience of hard drugs, it was the only topic at school that you really listened to. Pure self-defense, because you can never know what's going to cross your path.

Schnappi suddenly wakes up and sits upright on the deck chair as if she's been struck by lightning. She looks confusedly around and says, "Girls, I thought I was in a war."

"What sort of war?" you ask.

"I don't know. War is war. We were all trapped. We were in this run-down house, pretty much of a dump, and we couldn't get out."

She points at Nessi and you.

"You and you. We were standing in an ancient kitchen and there was this zombie or something. But not the kind that bites you, it wanted something. And there was blood flowing down one of the walls, it was really steaming, it was so hot. And you . . ."

She points at Taja.

". . . hid yourself. Why did you hide? In the dream it drove me half nuts not knowing where you were. Do you have any idea why it should be me dreaming that kind of shit?"

She points at the water.

"And I'm thirsty."

Nessi passes her the bottle. Schnappi drinks and notices Taja's chalk-white face and asks if she's missed anything. Ruth gives it to her straight.

"Taja's a junkie."

"Crap, I'm not a junkie!"

"How full was that bag before you got going on it?"

"I don't know."

Schnappi looks around, confused.

"What's the problem? Her father's dead, let her be a junkie for a few days."

"Thanks," says Taja, and seriously believes she is off the hook. That means she doesn't know Schnappi very well. Miss Saigon nods contentedly and performs one of those elegant lane changes that you'll never quite get used to.

"Be honest, what's up with your mother?"

Taja looks at you, appealing for help, as if one of you could put the brakes on Schnappi. No one can.

"What ... What do you mean? What should be up with my mother?"

"She's alive, she's in Norway. Aren't you going to phone her and say hello? I'm sure she'll want you to live with her. It's better than moving to the Ruhr. Norway's fantastic. People up there are financially very well-off, even though their country has the highest suicide rate. But so what, you can't have everything. I mean, if I were you and not me, the last thing I would want to do would be to pack my gear and move to Dortmund. Seriously! Why on earth would you go there? So give your mother a call, I'm sure she'll be delighted."

"Dream on," says Ruth.

"Why?"

"Think about it. Taja has no memory of her mother, she wouldn't recognize her if she were standing in an elevator with her. It's not one of those TV series where everyone cries and hugs at the end. Taja can't just call her and start chatting. Forget it. And anyway, who says her mother even wants to see her?"

"A mother is always a mother," Schnappi explains.

"Like your mother?" you can't help saying.

Schnappi keeps her cool.

"No one's as fucked up as my mother," she says and turns back to Taja, eyes wide. "She might even come here."

"Why would she do *that*?" Taja asks, startled.

"Perhaps because you're her daughter? Like if you were my daughter and somebody'd kidnapped you and you'd been missing for fourteen years, I'd be on the next plane out to see you."

Taja's face melts, her fear has gone, her voice softens.

"Thanks."

"I mean it."

"I know."

Ruth, sensitive as ever, ruins the moment.

"But your mother could have done that at any time in the last fourteen years."

"She could have, but she didn't," Schnappi says poisonously, as if it were a pearl of wisdom.

Nessi sighs.

"Christ, Schnappi, I wish you'd go back to sleep. I've been listening to you for over five minutes, and you're giving me a headache."

"But you woke me up, or who was that?" asks Schnappi and looks around, bats a fly away, and wants to know if this is a talk show and whether there's anything to be done about these bloody insects.

End of discussion.

Nessi says the smell is too much for her. Schnappi says she can't stand flies. *Well, you're a lot of help,* you think, and leave the two of them sitting on the terrace. You follow Ruth into the kitchen. Taja insists on coming too. Pale and trembling, she follows you and won't let you shake her off.

The stench is overwhelming. The packets of meat from the freezer are all over the pantry, some of them have leaked and left smeary pools of blood on the floor, others have fallen on it and burst.

"So why didn't you put them in the fridge?" you ask.

"I was going to, but I . . ."

She shrugs.

". . . must have forgotten."

You count the packs and stop at thirty. Rotten meat, rotten fish, the kitchen is buzzing with flies. You wave them away, they get caught in your hair and try to creep into your nostrils. It reminds you of holidays in Crete, when your aunt wanted to barbecue cutlets in the evening. Often you would go out to eat and forget to put the cutlets away. The window was open, it was scorching high summer. In the morning the kitchen was full of flies and the first maggots were moving in the meat.

"The flies must have laid eggs," you say. "We need to get rid of this shit before we puke all over ourselves."

Taja fetches garbage bags and rubber gloves. You pick up all the packages while you breathe through your mouths. The flies rage and cover you as if you were made of light.

After you and Taja have carried out the last garbage bag, you stay outside as Ruth wipes down the walls and cleans the floor. Taja asks you for a cigarette. You lean against her, shoulder to shoulder, and give her a light. The burning tobacco smells better than anything you've smelled recently. How nice it would be now to stand on the playground and have a teacher ream you out, telling you that you can't smoke on the playground. That and no other problems. You sigh. You don't feel as if you're sixteen anymore, you both feel old and tired, you stand beside the garbage cans and look up at the open kitchen window as if it were a painting and you were visiting the most boring exhibition ever. Flies fly in, flies fly out. Taja's hands tremble. You wonder how you'd feel if you'd been wasted for that long. You get a hangover after two glasses of wine. Taja rests her head on your shoulder.

"I feel terrible."

"You should have called."

"I know."

Silence for a moment, you both smoke, you ask, "Where does that stuff come from anyway? I mean, nobody just has a pound of smack in their pantry."

"My father was looking after it."

"Why did he—"

"I don't know, Stink."

She takes her head off your shoulder. You've entered forbidden territory. She drops her cigarette and rubs the ember onto the stone slabs with the tip of her shoe. You shut up and wait to see if she's got anything more to say. She does.

"I once heard him talking about it on the phone. You know, he's always loved that gangster shit. And it wasn't about the money, he had enough of that for four, it was about people trusting him. And he loved stockpiling stuff. You've seen the basement."

For a moment she's your Taja again. Fire in her eyes. Chin jutting. Her pageboy cut reaches her ears and frames her pale face. Not for the first time you're envious of her bravery in having her hair cut. You could kiss her. *My Taja*, you think, when she goes on to ask if you'd like to take a look at his stash.

The hiding place is in her father's studio in a corner between the keyboards and a mixing desk. It's an old metal case with deep scratches in the top. You thought if someone was storing drugs, then in a safe, please. The metal case is ridiculous. It's full to the brim with gear and has a false bottom. You take out nine bags of the white powder. You also find two bags full of pills, six slabs of hash, and several little bottles containing a brown liquid.

"Wow!" you say, surprised.

Of course you'd worked out what was going on here ages ago. Taja is trying to shake off her guilt by showing you everything. You're her witness, and in the end you'll be able to say: *God, there was nothing Taja could have done about it, there was so much stuff, no one could have resisted it.* That's fine by you, you're happy to do that for her. Anything is better than a Taja wandering around the streets with gloomy eyes and feeling guilty. The sight of the drugs has left her wide awake. Maybe she's waiting for you to look away for a moment so that she can have a noseful.

In that case she'll have a long wait.

Taja claps the lid shut and says, "You haven't seen the basement yet."

The second half of the basement is a huge vault that reminds you of those movies where sexy women lie in wait for mean-looking guys to finish them off with a few karate blows. Of course the women are wearing bikinis and they're all oiled up, because there's a swimming pool in the middle of the room. You can see the edge of the pool in the light of the open door. The air conditioning is working, but however well it's working, you'd recognize that smell anywhere.

You take a deep breath as Taja feels her way along the wall and flicks a switch. A blue glow rises from the pool, and from above, spotlights cast soft beams on the floor. Taja stops by the edge of the pool, the blue light flows around her like mist.

"I was never allowed to talk about it, I swore on my life. I had my secrets, he had his. But now . . ."

She falls silent; you know what she wanted to say.

Now that he's gone.

You join her and look into the pool. Your mouth drops open.

"Is that actually real?"

"It's realer than real. He's been working on it for years."

"But in a swimming pool?"

You learn that the swimming pool was a present for an athlete who won some sort of medal for breaststroke at an Olympic Games six years ago. The relationship didn't last long, and when they split up Taja's father didn't know what to do with the pool.

"So he turned it into this."

The bottom of the swimming pool is covered with dark, rich soil. Sodium lamps hang level with the edge of the pool. You see an irrigation system, fans, and floating above it all is the aeration system. You guess that the pool is twenty feet wide and fifty feet long. The plants grow in neat rows.

"He grew the seedlings himself. It was his hobby."

You all smoked your first joint when you were thirteen. Taja never told you where the grass came from, but every time you asked her for more, she brought some along. That mystery's been solved now too.

"We were looking for you everywhere."

You turn around; Ruth and Nessi are standing in the doorway.

"I told you they were still in the house," says Schnappi, and pushes her way past the others, looks around, and declares, "This is pure luxury!"

You point behind you with your thumb.

"Then take a look at that."

The girls come closer. You watch them, their reaction is like yours. Mouth open, eyes wide.

"Is that what I think it is?" asks Nessi.

"It is," you say.

When you come out of the basement, you're all a bit rattled. A marijuana field in a swimming pool has that effect on people. The flies have vanished from the house. It still smells horrible, the stench is probably clinging to the carpet and covering the walls with a thin film. The draft helps a little.

You've taken Taja's father's drug supply out of its hiding place and put it on the table in front of you. Surprisingly, the pills look the most menacing to you. Ruth shakes one of the bottles but doesn't open it.

"What do you think it is?"

None of you has the faintest idea.

"And the pills?"

"Probably a bit of everything," says Taja.

You pick up a bag and weigh the powder in your hand.

"If every bag weighs half a kilo, that's a good five kilos."

"Five kilos," Nessi echoes.

"Five kilos is a lot!" Schnappi suddenly explodes and bursts out laughing, and then Nessi and you laugh, and Ruth hesitates for a moment because she's always thinking, but then she laughs too and in the end Taja agrees, and you only stop laughing when your diaphragms hurt and the first tears flow.

Let's say we've got five kilos of heroin, let's say about three hundred pills including uppers and downers, ecstasy and speed, PCP and LSD, let's say, about eight hundred grams of Moroccan hash in slabs and six 200-milliliter bottles of opium tincture. So let's say, given the exclusiveness and quality of the goods, the whole thing has a real market value of about three million euros.

Let's say that's it.

RUTH

You obviously have no idea of the value of the drugs, although at the moment that isn't important because once again you're the five girls you always wanted to stay. And those five girls laugh about the irony of fate that has dropped five kilos of heavy drugs in your lap. If someone were now to claim that it's the last time and you will never feel like this again, you'd throw him out the door. You don't believe in a tomorrow because you're the now. What counts in the now are your jokes and those sayings that you never seem to run out of. You push the drugs aside and talk, drink orange juice, and eat chips as if Taja's father was still alive, as if getting six lottery numbers right was easy and Nessi wasn't pregnant. You can do that because for the moment you're yourselves again, and that feels good, it feels so damned good.

It would be nice if the story could end there. Like a television series, like the last episode of a television series, and no one knows what happens next. Finale. But chaos awaits, it peels itself out of the background and puts its arms around your shoulders like a good friend who's only popped outside for a quick cigarette in the fresh air, and who's now delighted to be back by your side again.

For another hour things are fine, then Taja topples over. First she starts shivering, then she starts dry-retching. Her muscles are cramping and she can't breathe. You give her water to drink and walk her around the garden. She trembles violently, at the same time she's drenched in sweat, she wants more water, then she suddenly pulls away and just makes it to the toilet in time. Nessi stays by her side, she says: *Shit and vomit don't bother me.* Nessi is your heroine. You stand outside the closed bathroom door and talk about whether it wouldn't be a good idea to call a doctor. You're strictly against the idea.

"He'd see right away what's wrong with Taja. And if he sees that, he'll call the cops. Forget it."

"And her father's still in the freezer," Schnappi adds.

"What's that got to do with it?" Stink asks.

"Nothing, but it'll feel pretty weird if a doctor comes and there's someone lying dead in the basement."

"Schnappi, no one knows he's in there."

"I know, I'm just saying. Bad karma and everything."

"What has that got to do with karma?"

You hold her back.

"Hey, girls, what's up with you?"

"I just can't believe the stuff that Schnappi keeps coming out with," Stink says by way of self-defense.

"Believe it, because there's plenty more where that comes from."

You take them by the hand like two naughty little girls and pull them back out onto the terrace, where you sit down and put your heads together and ask each other how you're going to get Taja back on her feet without having to call an ambulance. Schnappi wants to look on the internet, because you can find everything on the internet, there are bound to be tips on withdrawal as well.

"Why not," you say.

Schnappi disappears upstairs to Taja's computer, while you get out your phone and call your mother to tell her you're going to be spending the weekend at Taja's. Stink also wants to call home; you give her your cell phone and keep an eye on how Taja is.

The bathroom door is shut. You knock.

"Everything okay in there?"

Nessi lets you in. Taja is lying curled up on the floor, covered with a dressing gown.

"Should we put her to bed?"

Nessi shakes her head. She's glad that Taja's asleep at last. So you turn out the bathroom light and leave the door open a crack. In the kitchen you make sandwiches. Nessi goes through the cupboards and discovers a jar of pickled peppers.

When you come back out, Stink is asleep on one of the recliners. Nessi takes the chair beside her and eats the peppers with her fingers. Afterward she sighs contentedly and within a minute has fallen asleep. *Oh great,* you think, and look at your sleeping girlfriends and the table full of drugs. Even if you're not the most experienced—two pills, Eric swore they were LSD, a few joints, and a catastrophic attempt to snort speed at a party—you know that a few dreams lie ahead of you, waiting to be dreamed. You lean forward, open the bag that's already been started, and dip a finger into the white powder. You sniff it and wipe your finger on your jeans.

A small victory is still a victory.

It's important to keep a clear head. You're aware that everything's going to collapse without you here. It's a good feeling, carrying that burden. You're a family, somebody has to hold you all together. *If not me, who?* You listen out for sounds from Taja, and your eyes fall shut. It's a bit like disappearing into a tub full of warm water.

Ten minutes. Fifteen.

The screams from the guest bathroom make you all jump.

Taja is crashing. Cramps, nausea, shivers. You all get her upstairs to bed and cover her with blankets. As soon as she's calmed down a little, you think now it'll get better, the worst is over, and then Taja succumbs once again to a fit of the shivers and it's worse than before. She throws up every sip of water, there's no point even thinking about solid food. Her hands claw at her belly as if she could grab the pain and pull it out. She leaves red scratches. She cries and fights you off. She says she's itching all over. Her elbow catches Stink in the face, knocking her off the bed. You hold Taja tightly, she kicks out and screams at you to leave her alone. She calms down slowly. Her short hair sticks wetly to her head. She's so exhausted that she falls asleep at last. It's not real sleep, it's pure unconsciousness. The sudden silence is scary. You're all breathing heavily. Stink has a swelling under her eye and asks if it looks bad.

"You'll need to put some ice on it," you say and go downstairs with Stink to cool her cheek.

Schnappi has finished her search on the internet, and comes downstairs with a stack of paper. She asks if she's missed anything. Stink takes the ice pack off her eye and shows her the swelling.

"Taja went nuts."

"A good thing I wasn't there."

You want to know what Schnappi has found.

She puts the printouts on the table.

"I don't think it's cocaine. The withdrawal symptoms don't fit. It could be heroin, but heroin's normally brown. So I did a bit of searching and discovered that there's such a thing as white heroin. That stuff's unusually pure."

"Taja used to say her dad did coke," Stink joins in. "That's definitely coke."

"Are you even listening to me?" Schnappi asks crossly, and Schnappi never gets cross. "I just said the withdrawal symptoms don't fit."

"I heard you," Stink replies defiantly.

Schnappi flicks through the pages.

"As I wasn't sure, I just printed out everything I could find about withdrawal. Whether it was coke, speed, or heroin. But mostly I'm worried about Taja's circulation. If we don't do anything, it could fail. And she might . . ."

She breaks off. You guess what she was going to say. Nessi comes out with it: "Taja isn't going to die on us."

"How could you even think something like that?" you yell at her.

"You thought the same thing," Nessi says in self-defense.

"Yes, but we didn't blurt it out."

Schnappi finds the page and holds it out. Black on white.

> Cold turkey withdrawal is not advisable without medical
> help, as the resulting symptoms can lead to death.

"What crap," says Stink, and brings her palm down on the table. "Taja only took the stuff for five days, and that's not going to kill anybody."

"Did you see the way she went crazy before?"

"No, I kept my eyes shut, Ruth. Of course I saw it. But you don't just kick the bucket like that, okay?"

Schnappi fans the printed pages.

"There is more."

You stare at the printout, then you stir yourselves, each of you picks up a stack and you start reading.

The upshot is frightening. All the drugs that could help Taja are prescription-only. Which leaves you with herb tea, vitamins, and mineral pills. One of the articles says that purely physical heroin withdrawal can take up to two weeks, and that in comparison to other drugs heroin leaves the greatest potential for addiction. It doesn't say anywhere how the body reacts after only five days of drug consumption. You all set your pages down. You're so exhausted by all the shop talk that there's nothing more to say.

Taja's attacks continue into the afternoon. Crying, choking, whimpering. Taja can't lie down anymore, so you walk around the garden with her again. It's a good thing the property's screened off by hedges. Walking helps with the cramps and distracts her. When she feels that ants are crawling under her skin, you scrub her down with a loofah. Your girls talk to her, you don't take your eyes off her for a moment.

You read Schnappi's printout for a second time and make a list of the drugs that might help. You want to ask someone who has a clue. You don't know who that might be.

Just before closing time, Schnappi and Stink go shopping for food. Nessi stays with Taja, and while she runs a bath for her and helps her into the tub, you strip the bed for the third time and wash the sheets. Schnappi and Stink come back with fruit, vegetables, and cartons of juice. They've also got some pretzel sticks and Coca-Cola because Schnappi says it always helps. And pizza for the rest of you.

You clear the table on the terrace. You decide the drugs have to go, so you and Stink carry them upstairs. You didn't like Taja having to look at them all the time anyway.

"Who do you think it all belongs to?" you ask, when you're putting the bags back into the metal case.

"Doesn't matter," says Stink. "Some idiot will come and get it if he starts missing it."

Ten minutes later you eat. Taja tries to keep her soup down, crunches on pretzel sticks, and chugs two bottles of Coke. For a while everything's the same as always. As if Taja just had the flu, and might go walking around the neighborhood with you, and just be your Taja again. Chaos is laughing at you. You're tired, you snatch some sleep from time to time, you're troubled and always present in your sleep.

The day goes, the night comes.

In the morning Stink makes a decision and you're not aware of it. Taja's sleeping upstairs, Schnappi is lying down in one of the guest rooms, you're sitting with Nessi and Stink on the terrace, the house is in silence. It's eight in the morning and you have shadows under your eyes. *We're never going to keep this up for two weeks*, you think, when Nessi says, "We could call Taja's mother."

"And what are you going to say to her? That Taja's in withdrawal and has only recently discovered that her mother's still alive? Don't forget to mention that her father's downstairs in the freezer and can't really look after Taja."

"I knew there was a catch," says Nessi and yawns.

You look at her. Maybe it's sleep deprivation, maybe you're about to get your period, but either way Nessi's never been as lovely as she is this morning. *Or else it's her damned pregnancy*, you think and wonder how long Nessi will keep suppressing the truth. None of you has said a sensible word on the subject. Whether she's going to have an abortion or not. Who the father is. Where things go from here.

"You'll be a brilliant mother," you say, "regardless of what happens."

"If I do become a mother."

"Yes, if."

Nessi comes around the table and kisses first you, then Stink, on the cheek. She says that was a nice try on your part, but the discussion's postponed because she can't keep her eyes open and now she's going in to lie down in one of the guest rooms. You'd like to follow her and call it a day, but you know there has to be a solution. Taja urgently needs help. And if nobody comes up with a solution, then nothing will be solved.

"It's just you and me," you say.

"I've been asleep for an hour," Stink says, eyes closed.

You put your feet up and are very glad that no one's got you pregnant. And as you're thinking about your little compact life, you doze off and that's exactly the moment Stink was waiting for. First she blinks, then her eyes open and she's wide awake. You aren't aware of a thing. Stink waits a few minutes for you to sink into deep sleep before she gets up and makes her preparations.

Stink has a plan, but she isn't sure what the rest of you will think of it. *Sometimes you're better off not knowing,* she thinks to herself, and before one of you girls wakes up, she's got on her Vespa and pushed it to the street so that no one hears the noise. In her left jacket pocket is the list of drugs that you've copied down from Schnappi's printout. No one's to say later on that Stink was unprepared. It's a pity you are asleep. You should have seen her riding the Vespa to Charlottenburg through the lukewarm Thursday morning, to turn a boringly normal boy into a boringly normal martyr.

MIRKO

A martyr's job isn't easy. He has to make sacrifices, he has to be selfless and endure an incredible amount of suffering. You will follow this sequence to the letter, and start with the sacrifices. You skip school and try to find out who can get hold of the prescription drugs for you. There are a few sources. You could try Mehmed in Wedding, but you could also try Timo, who only lives two streets away. But you know that isn't going to work. You have to make sure you do it the right way. Nothing happens without Darian's approval. He picks up your call after the second ring.

"Hey, you found your phone."

"It was at the pizza stand."

Darian laughs.

"Your uncle probably shoved it in his pocket and spent the whole night calling Bosnian sex lines."

"We're from Slovenia."

"What?"

You spend the next ten minutes listening to your friend telling you about the new energy food he's found on the internet, then you ask, as if in passing, how you would get hold of prescription drugs.

"What's up? Planning to open a pharmacy?"

You laugh as if you'd never heard anybody say that before, and say the drugs aren't for you. Darian sees through you right away.

"Mirko, you old Casanova, what's her name?"

Of course you blush. A lot of people think you're an errand boy, others think you're a sort of modern slave who does everything his boss tells him to. The fact that your boss is just seventeen doesn't bother anybody. You see yourself as an apprentice. Darian took you under his wing, when you were new at school and a few guys decided to kick your ass. He took them apart and said you looked as if you needed a friend. You've been pals ever since; even after Darian left school nothing changed in that respect, because neighbors stay neighbors, and in this part of town a friend is a friend forever. You do little jobs for him and that's how you've been working your way slowly up the ladder for a year. Step by step. You buy stuff for parties, fill glasses, roll joints, and are errand boy and best friend in one. You don't see any injustice in that, you know your strengths. Darian knows he can talk to you, unlike the guys in the crowd. At some point he discovered you both spoke the same language, and he didn't mean German. Sometimes you wish you could show Darian how loyal you really are. Not by hiding under a car. You're thinking more about a hail of bullets, and you throwing yourself in front of him to save his life. You must have absorbed martyrdom with your mother's milk. Your mother was exactly like that until your father dumped her.

Darian's words are distorted by the connection.

"Come on now, of course it's got to be a girl. When it's a girl, you get this voice like someone's sticking her tongue in your ear."

You laugh shyly, you're as transparent as a pane of glass.

"I'm not allowed to say anything yet."

"Are you a couple?"

"Of course we're a couple, but I'm still not allowed to say anything yet."

"Is she cute?"

"Terribly cute."

You hear Darian rummaging around and cursing that the Goon's number must be lying around here somewhere, then he finds it and says, "Since the Goon moved away, he's had a job as a nurse in the Westend hospital. He can get his hands on anything."

He gives you his landline and cell numbers, and then there's an awkward pause.

"I'll make it up to you," you say, and Darian knows right away what you mean.

"Don't you worry."

"No, I let you down, I'll make it up to you, promise."

"Okay," says Darian, and asks if you'll come to the movies with him tonight.

And simple as that you're part of the family again.

Simple as that.

"Quarter past ten," says Darian. "There's some crap with Denzel Washington and that guy who played Jesus. I missed the movie on Tuesday, but who wants to go to the movies on half-price Tuesday?"

You're grateful and relieved that he's asked you, and promise you'll be there. Even if you have to work at ten, you don't want to miss an evening with the crowd. Your uncle will understand, and if he doesn't then tough luck for him.

After you hang up, you have to do fifty sit-ups to get your feet back on the ground. Then you ring the Goon on his landline. The Goon is actually a gifted musician who screwed up two entrance exams and ended up becoming a nurse. You call him the Goon because he has an IQ of 170 and doesn't do anything with it. He moved to Spandau with his girlfriend six months ago. She wants a kid, and Spandau is cheap. Which proves once again that the Goon has earned his nickname without having to do much in return.

No answer.

You tap in the second number.

"I'm working," says the Goon by way of greeting.

"It's me, Mirko."

"Hey, hi, Mirko. I'm still at work. Right now I'm sticking a spoonful of pea soup up an old man's nose because he won't open his mouth. Yes, I mean you, Granddad. You want this shit up your nose? Is that what you want? Then open your trap or I'll get the tube. Yes, that's better."

"Goon?"

"What?"

"I need something."

You read out the list. He says he can get hold of everything, but if you ask him, then two of the medications will do the trick.

"Are you in withdrawal or something?"

"No, it's not for me."

You're glad he doesn't ask if you're planning to open a pharmacy, or who the drugs are for. The Goon isn't that kind of guy.

You arrange to collect the stuff from his apartment at three. You've still got two hours. The address is in the north of Spandau. The Goon says what he wants for it. You laugh. He is a pal through and through.

At ten past three you ring his doorbell. In your left hand you're holding a paper bag, the smell is heavy and sweet. The door opens. She's wearing nothing but panties and one of those sleeveless shirts so tight that you can see her heartbeat. Her nipples press darkly against the pale fabric. If she wasn't looking at you like that, it could almost be sexy.

"What do you want?"

You hand her the bag. Twenty-four doughnuts, two of each. She looks in and knows. The Goon never puts on an ounce, he eats whatever he gets his hands on. Doughnuts are his curse. Other people need oxygen, he needs fat and sugar.

"Gina, right?" you say.

"Manja," she says and leaves you alone outside the apartment. You hear a rustling sound from inside, you hear a door closing from upstairs, then the sad, quiet whimper of a child. Manja keeps you waiting. Ten minutes later she comes back to the door. There's sugar around her mouth. In one hand she holds a mug of coffee, with the other she hands you the medications and looks at you until you turn and go.

There you are now, with an unsettled stomach that doesn't get any better when you're surrounded by the smell of ice cream and waffles. The heat is scorching, people are lining up at the ice cream parlor, children and wasps, every now and again a dog with its nose stuck to the floor, hoping for leftovers. It's twenty past seven, and she isn't here yet. The ice cream parlor closes at eight, and then you've got a problem. Twice you're tempted to phone her. You know that wouldn't be stylish. You want to show you've got style, you're not twelve years old. Be patient, and leave your phone in your pocket. Wait.

Bernie rides past on his bike and says hi. Jojo buys an ice cream and asks if you're hoping the weather's going to improve. Of course the twins show up too. Tisa and Mel. No one believes they're twins. They never wear the same thing, have different hairstyles, and look like good friends. Someone once claimed you'd only mix them up if they were naked in the shower. Tisa asks you for fifty cents. Mel is having problems with the arm of her sunglasses and wants to know if you wouldn't happen to have one of those little screwdrivers on you. You give Tisa the money; no, you haven't got a screwdriver. Kolja turns up with his new girl, one hand squashed into the back pocket of her jeans; the girl has a tiny tattoo under her left eye. Milka comes in their wake with Gero. They ask if you're coming to the movies too. You start getting seriously nervous. Half the crowd is going for an ice cream and enjoying life, while you sit there waiting. You should have come up with a better meeting place. One where nothing's going on.

"Here."

She hands you an ice cream. Chocolate, two scoops. You choke on the air and cough. Of course you were looking in the other direction. She stands there as if she's waiting for you, as if you're late. *Stink.* You feel your face turning soft, and a stupid smile appearing on it.

"Mmm, delicious, chocolate," you say like a five-year-old who's been waiting all summer for two scoops of chocolate ice cream.

"So? Have you got it?"

"I've got it."

You stroll down the street. You don't talk, you eat your ice cream. In a house doorway you sit down on the top step and you take the medication out of your jacket and repeat what the Goon told you on the phone.

"Two of the drugs are enough."

The Goon has also included instructions for use. Stink is to ignore the piece of paper in the package and administer the medication the way the Goon has written it down.

"What do I owe you?"

"This one's on me."

"Really?"

"Really. If you need more . . ."

You leave the three dots at the end of your sentence. You want to tell her that she must see you again, that the rest of her life will be meaningless if she doesn't, and that she'll be terribly unhappy. But who says something like that?

Stink leans forward and kisses you on the cheek. Some ice cream runs down your fingers. You breathe in quickly and smell her. She smells great.

"I owe you," she says and gets up, and you're sure that's that, you'll never see her again, maybe at school or passing by, and all because you can't open your mouth properly. Then she hesitates and turns around and sits down next to you again. Your heart plays a drum solo. She puts on the sunglasses and says, "What if I had something to sell?"

"What would that be?"

"A few pills."

"Okay."

"Hash."

"Okay."

"And five kilos of cocaine."

You don't say *okay*, you just look at her.

"But it might be speed. Or heroin."

"Five kilos?"

"Just about."

"What do you mean, just about?"

"Just about five kilos. Do you know anyone who'd like to buy it?"

Understanding is a curtain that rises before your eyes. Of course it's possible that it's only just occurred to her, but the likelihood is very small. She wants to sell something. She knows who your best friend is. She has you on a hook. You can work the rest out for yourself. *Maybe she doesn't actually need any medication and just wanted to see if I'd help her, and now she's getting her claws right into me. Shit.* You're suddenly thinking like a grown-up. Your mother's mistrust has infected you. It doesn't suit you, having thoughts like that. You're naïve, you trust anybody and everybody. Cynicism isn't your forte, but a little mistrust never hurt anybody.

"I'll help you," you say with a note of bitterness.

And that's exactly what you did, fourteen hours ago now, and that's why you're standing in this damned basement now, and Darian's father is holding a gun to your head and asking you if you're a god-damn martyr. He's probably never tried thinking straight with a gun to his head. If it wasn't so crazy, it would be funny.

Your mind fills with movies you've seen a hundred times. *Reservoir Dogs. Truth or Consequences.* Even though you know that nothing can happen to you, it isn't much help to you right now. You're Darian's buddy. That counts, for whatever, it counts for something. And fear is in order. If you weren't scared now, it would just mean you were stupid.

"Are you a goddamn martyr?"

"I'm a Slovene," you say too quickly, it's usually a good answer, but it's not the answer Ragnar Desche wants to hear. One of the men behind you laughs, Darian's father stays poker-faced. He looks over your shoulder and tells the man to shut up as if he'd said those words, not you.

You decide never to be smart again. They've kept you waiting for a half hour in this basement, and now you've got a gun at your head and you're trying to be smart. Come on, what's wrong with you? You're doing what animals do when they're threatened, you're freezing. You could roll on your back, too, but how would that look?

"You know very well what a martyr is, don't you?"

You say you know. You might be at technical college but you weren't dropped on your head.

"I'm not a martyr," you lie.

"Then stop acting like one. Have you any idea where she is right now?"

"No idea."

The barrel presses harder against your head, you flinch and try to stay calm. You're breathing shallowly, and staring into the swimming pool and the rows of marijuana plants that seem to be waving at you.

Calm.

Darian's father lowers the gun.

Yes!

You still don't move. Your head is lowered, your eyes are askance. You imagine telling Darian what happened later on. You imagine him laughing at you. *My father isn't a hit man,* he will say.

"Everything okay?" asks one of the men behind you as if he's disappointed that the gun isn't at your forehead anymore. You look over at Darian's father. It's sort of as if he isn't here. He looks past you. You think this is your chance.

"Can I go now?" you ask.

Mistake, oh, boy, what a big mistake. You have dragged Ragnar Desche from his thoughts. He gives you a scathing glance. What are you getting right today? His gaze comes at you from a distance of over six hundred miles and fixes on you again.

"You know what seriously pisses me off about little fuckers like you?"

You don't know, you don't care, you just know he's lowered his gun, and that means everything's okay again. And anyway you don't think Darian's father really wants an answer from you. He likes the sound of his own voice.

"Your generation has everything, but you don't give anything back. You take and you take, and in the end there'll be nothing left to take and then you'll fall on each other like hyenas. Take a look at yourself. You kids think you can make any mistake you like, and that's exactly where you're wrong. You can only really afford to make mistakes when you have something to offer. But you don't offer anything."

"Maybe . . . we're stingy?" you say and immediately shut your eyes tight and want to dissolve into the air. Panic makes a clown of you. You've never had that under control. At primary school, when a boy had you in a headlock, you asked him if you could switch sides.

"Tell me, do you think that's funny?"

"Not really."

"Are you on drugs?"

"No."

"I'm slowly starting to understand why my son is friends with you. He likes hanging out with comedians. It makes him feel he's cleverer than everybody else. You're his little monkey. You know what your problem is, monkey? Look at me."

You look at him. He taps his forehead.

"You're lost in here. Do you think I haven't worked out what's up with you? You like the girl, but the girl isn't interested in you. Have you ever come to the defense of somebody who doesn't give a fuck about you? That's exactly the feeling that's inflating your chest right now. You think you're a hero, but you're really only a goddamn martyr, standing alone on the edge of the street holding out his thumb while the world drifts past him and nobody picks him up. The girl forgot about you ages ago. Now give me your phone."

"I haven't got a—"

"ARE YOU TRYING TO MESS WITH ME? GIVE ME YOUR FUCKING CELL PHONE THIS MINUTE!"

His voice shatters off the walls, the time for talking is over. With trembling hands you pull your cell phone out of your trouser pocket and are about to hand it to him when you realize what he wants it for.

Christ, how can I be so stupid?

You're standing in this bloody basement, seriously believing you could secretly call the girl of your dreams to warn her about this lunatic. Her name and number are stored on your phone as the last call. How could you?

They'll find her, and it's my fault.

Your arm reaches behind you, you're about to throw the phone in the pool, a hand grabs you by the wrist.

"Let go," says the man behind you, and takes it away from you.

And now you haven't got a phone, and there's Darian's father still standing in front of you, except that something's changed. Something fundamental. He's got what he wanted, he doesn't need you anymore. *It's over.* And yet your panic won't subside, there's the unpleasant feeling of having to explain yourself. Quickly, before it's too late. *Too late for what?* You recoil and bump against the chair, which topples over and goes clattering across the tiled floor. Darian's father doesn't move from the spot, his gaze is still fixed firmly on you. *How come he suddenly looks so tired?* He raises the gun and aims it at your face. You know he won't shoot. But you don't know why he's still threatening you. But that makes it worse, that frightens you. *I've got nothing more to offer.* The gun in front of your face is calm. Darian's father's eyes are still. *I'm safe,* you think, you hope. The big question is: how can you fool yourself like that?

DARIAN

Can you imagine your best friend and your father standing by a swimming pool, your father holding a gun in his hand and your best friend practically shitting himself? Even if you wanted, your imagination has limits, like your planning. If you'd known what you were setting in motion, you'd never have canceled that evening at the movie, and you'd have crept under a car two days ago, just like Mirko. You'd have done everything differently, and this meeting would never have taken place.

Every Thursday afternoon at the same time you sit at Pepe's, eating kebabs and drinking ice-cold protein shakes. From five till nine in the evening anyone can get hold of you there. On your left are two cell phones and a book on survival training. You'd rather have an office, but your father reckons you're a long way from being a businessman. Even though you're not working for him, you can't go looking for an office without his permission. Rules are rules. He reckons you have to get to know the streets, because that's how he started. Squatters and revolutionaries—you can really do without that. We're not in the eighties anymore, and not in the nineties either, even though the radio tries to kid you otherwise, with all that endless fucked-up retro music. We're in the new millennium, everything's different, nothing is the way it used to be, and you're sitting in a kebab shop because you still haven't got an office.

On Fridays the guys find you in the park, on the weekends

you're working exclusively for the Brothers. On Mondays you're in the amusements on the Kaiserdamm, you particularly like it there in the summer, because of the air conditioning and the girl on the counter who disappears into the bathroom with you if you ask her. She likes muscles, you've got muscles, and the two of you suit each other perfectly. On Tuesdays you play golf with the Brothers and Wednesday is your very private day in the gym. If this isn't life there is no life.

She sits down opposite you.

Mirko called you twenty minutes ago and said he had something for you. You can see he's got something, probably a massive erection, the way he's standing there. *Like a full shopping bag that someone's left on the edge of the road.* The weirdest images always come into your mind as soon as you see Mirko. He is loyal, he wants to make something of himself, and grows and flourishes in your shadow more than any of the other guys so far. He's your man. You enjoy his guilty conscience. If you threw a stick, he'd be the first to bring it back for you. But if you're perfectly honest you can easily understand why he ran off that night. They were mean bastards, they would have just beaten up Mirko, it was better for him to get out of the picture, it was better for him not to see your humiliation. You've got plans for him. Next year you want to take him on tour with you. He was there when you paid a visit to Bebe, and the guys liked him because he didn't chatter all the time. Sometimes you wish your father had looked after you the way you look after Mirko now. He's a logistics guy, basically. No one provides better security than Ragnar Desche. Recently he's been mostly taking care of the storage and transport of drugs and guns. You know that over the last decade he hasn't lost a single cartridge or a crumb of cocaine.

Be honest, you're proud of your father and respect his consistency, but your true idols are two men of a quite different caliber.

The Brothers, Jonas and Axel Krüger, are the dark souls of Berlin. They wanted to take you under their wing the spring before last when you were only sixteen, and it took your father over a year to give you the green light. Since then you've been dealing, bringing the money in and getting to know the street from the bottom up. You're not a logistics expert, you want to get your hands dirty and be like the Brothers. Everything they teach you, you want to teach

Mirko one day. From violence via discipline to obedience. Humor's a part of it too, of course. That's why you tell Mirko, "Come on, dude. You're standing there like a full shopping bag."

"Very funny."

"Sit down, come on, sit down."

Mirko sits down beside the girl. You give Pepe a sign to bring you another shake. Since his shop has been your base, he's keeping a mixer on the counter. Pepe knows what goes in the shakes. Even if the stuff tastes horrible, you like the fact that Pepe only makes it for you. Healthy doesn't necessarily taste good, every child learns that. *That's why it's so important to grow up,* you think, *then you can eat anything you like.* This kebab, for example, it's exactly right. Not too much sauce, no onions, and enough coleslaw to make a Russian green with envy. You take a bite, look at the girl, thinking, *Well, Mirko's found a hot one.* You know her from somewhere, definitely from around here, you probably saw her in one of the clubs or she bought something from your guys. Superficial as you are, it never occurs to you that she's a good friend of your cousin. You've met her twice at a party, her hair was down and she wasn't wearing sunglasses. Now her eyes are completely hidden behind dark lenses. You can just about make out the pupils.

"Shake?" you ask with your mouth full, tapping against your empty glass.

She says she is not thirsty. You put the kebab on the plate and wipe your mouth. It's time for business.

"Let's do some business," you say.

The girl rummages in her pants pocket and puts a Tic Tac box down on the table. Orange flavor. You've always thought it was ridiculous that Tic Tacs are really white, and only look orange because of the packaging. Someone told you it used to be different. Dyes and stuff. As if there was anything harmful about dyes.

"Aha," you say and take the Tic Tac box and flip it open. The powder is white, you sniff it, it smells like Tic Tacs. Pepe comes with the shake. Green with white foam. You ask him if he wants a Tic Tac. The girl opens her eyes wide. Pepe says, *Sugar no good,* and goes again.

"Did you hear that?" you ask the girl and laugh. "Sugar no good?"

She just looks at you, she obviously has no sense of humor and those oversized sunglasses make her look like an over-the-hill porn star who swallowed too much cum. Mirko, on the other hand, finally has a hint of a grin in the corner of his mouth. Mirko knows what's funny. The girl says, "We've got five kilos."

You don't move a muscle. Whatever Mirko has brought here, it seems to be a gold mine. You don't wonder where the drugs are from, your mouth is too watery and your head is switched to profit. When you ask her about the pills, the girl reaches into her jacket and puts a handful down on the table.

"Are you fucked?" you hiss at her, and sweep the pills from the tabletop into the open palm of your hand. She smiles. Humor is a two-sided blade. You stuff the pills in your jacket. Mirko gives you a funny look, and somehow he reminds you of your mother's top-loader when she took the washing out and left the machine open to dry. As a child you always wanted to get into the machine and travel through time. Your mother always smacked you when she caught you doing that. Now your mother's with a Spaniard half her age and her name's never mentioned at home.

"You look like a washing machine. A top-loader, you know?"

Mirko frowns. Yes, the joke was a bit far-fetched. You look around. It wouldn't be so great if someone from the drug squad was standing at the bar drinking ayran while you were pulling off the deal of your life.

Fuck me, five kilos!

You tap against the Tic Tac box; some powder trickles onto the back of your hand.

"Everybody look away," you say, and inhale it.

If you could see your smile you would take a photograph and have it framed. It does the trick, the drug moves through your head like a cold switchblade and makes you feel good. *Damn good.* You tense your upper arms. Great feeling. Steel and flesh. The girl's probably wondering what it feels like to have arms like that.

"Whoow," you say, blinking away tears. "And you've got five kilos of that? Whoow, that's *the* stuff."

The girl gets up.

"Hey, where are you going?"

"To get the rest. You want to buy it, don't you?"

You bet your sweet ass I do, you think and bite your tongue to keep it to yourself. You're confused, you thought she brought the drugs along. You grin at her stupidly. You really want to call yourself a professional? Do you think she's just going to go walking around the place with five kilos of high-grade drugs?

It's a good thing the Brothers can't see you right now.

The girl says she'll be back at midnight.

She says she wants fifty thousand.

You laugh at her.

"It's worth more than that," you explain, which sounds really unprofessional, but the drugs are making you honest, and besides, you want to be a gentleman, because the little bitch is kind of tasty, and maybe one day she'll feel like snorting a line off your cock. For free, of course.

"I don't want more," she says.

"Ah."

Fifty big ones. Oh my God, the Brothers are going to go crazy. It was so worth canceling the movies for. Mirko hasn't brought you gold, these are diamonds. But Mirko has a few things to make up to you for.

"Shall we meet here?"

You shake your head. It'll be jammed in here in an hour. And midnight's far too early for you. The city's still wide awake at that time of night. You suggest the park. Lietzensee. At two. The little football field is hidden away, and not even tramps go there at night. It wouldn't be the first time you've arranged to meet someone there. The field is hidden way behind an embankment. If two of your guys kept watch, you could hold an orgy there and no one would notice.

"You can have an orgy there at night," you say.

"You can have an orgy at night anywhere at all," the girl says as if she did just that every night. "Two o'clock, then?"

"Two."

She looks from you to Mirko. You'd give a hundred-euro note to see her without those shades.

"Are you coming too?"

"Of course I am."

She looks at you again.

"You're not going to rip me off, are you?"

You put a hand on your heart. Of course you're going to rip her off. She'll settle for twenty thousand, they always do in the end. And the Brothers will never find out that it was five kilos. Three will be enough to make them weep with happiness. And the pills will make their way into your pocket.

"I'm honest," you tell her.

When she leaves, you wait till the door closes behind her, then you explode with laughter.

"God, Mirko, what a bitch!"

"Don't say that."

You get up, you shake hands.

"You've done a great job there, pal, it doesn't get any better than that, we're even now, okay?"

Mirko nods, he smiles, the relief is written on his forehead in capital letters. You pull your friend to you so that his thin chest hits your steel plate.

"I'll pick you up at the pizza stand at a quarter to two."

You slap him on the back, you're so fucking high on the drugs that you feel like grabbing Mirko's backside. *I'm horny,* you think, and let go of Mirko.

"And I can't make the movies tonight," you add, waving the Tic Tac box. "I have to test out this stuff a bit more. Denzel can wait."

Mirko nods, he understands. You hand him your shake as a present, he takes it outside. You look down and seriously have a massive hard-on.

"Hey, Pepe," you call to him. "Look what Tic Tacs can do!"

Two hours later you're lying on your bed exhausted from the drugs, the windows are open, you're king of the city, the wail of an ambulance, a plane heading for Tegel Airport, and the music coming out of the speakers and the deal of the year in your pocket. MTV is on in the background with the sound turned down, a singer is repeatedly slapping herself on the ass as if she is furious that she has an ass. You tap the Tic Tac box, the powder trickles onto the back of your hand.

Christ, what kind of stuff is this?

The last time you spent a day on speed, you had mates from Köpenick staying with you, and you played the hell out of the Play-

Station. Later you went down to the basement and pumped iron until there were rainbows dancing in front of your eyes. Today's not a day for playing. Today's a day when you'd just like to lie in bed listening to music.

The deal of the decade, fuckers!

Later, in the park, you'll show the girl what real business is. You've scraped together ten thousand, you couldn't get more, Bebe threw in five, the rest is from your own pocket. She'll grumble, she'll complain, but she can be glad to get anything at all.

"Darian?"

"Yes?"

"Come down here."

You swing your legs out of bed, your exhaustion dissolves to nothing as if it had never been there. If the old man calls, you run. There's no *later* or *in a minute*. Even as a kid he drummed that one into you, and it didn't get any better after your parents got divorced. You go to the bathroom, splash water in your face, one last look, you try to smile, the smile slips away.

Your father stands in the kitchen getting a cappuccino out of the machine. He's barefoot, wearing linen pants and one of those silk shirts that are like air. He looks relaxed, as if he hadn't a care in the world. You fear and admire him. You want to be like him and then do everything better. You want to give parties and let everyone know that everything's possible because you make it possible. Your father's careful with money. He's careful about who he eats with and who his friends are. He's slim, almost ascetic, while you're exploding with energy and your body takes up twice as much room. And we're talking about not an ounce of fat, all dynamite. Your father has always tried to stay out of the limelight, while you want to grab the world between the legs and shout in its face that you exist. You're very pleased that you're taller than him. Two centimeters. The rest is one great genetic defeat. Even when your father has his back turned to you, as if you are not worth being acknowledged, he gives you the feeling that you're several steps beneath him. But you're young, you're still on the way to becoming great, your father is already there.

He asks what you're doing this weekend, and whether you've given any thought to the rest of the summer. He wants you to repeat your technical diploma next year. You don't think much of the idea, fuck school, fuck diplomas, but you say nothing and hope the Brothers will come to your assistance and support your career. *Career, what an awesome word!* you think and almost burst out laughing. This summer is due to be your last summer in freedom. You plan to visit your mother in Spain. She has insisted on it. Your father wants to know how the plans are looking, whether you've already booked a flight and so on and so on. Then he turns around and looks at you quizzically. It's only then that you realize that you haven't answered a single one of his questions.

You stand there, you stand there, you stand there.

"What have you taken?"

Your father sips from his cappuccino. You want to answer him, but your teeth click together as if someone had released a spring and slammed your mouth shut. *Is it as obvious as that?* you wonder and try not to smile stupidly at your father. You have a lot of questions whirring through your head. You'd love to know why your father never sprinkles cocoa on his cappuccino. *Why, Dad, why?* you want to say. *Tell me why?* Laughter bubbles up inside you. *Cappuccino, what an awesome word!* Just don't start laughing. *Business is business,* you think, and grin at the thought of calling your father *Dad.* You know the rules. Keep off the drugs when you're working. Always. But this isn't work, so you're not worrying about it. What worries you a lot more is the fact that you're talking to your father when you're not under control.

He wants control, his life is control, I know that, he knows that, I . . .

"I've got a deal," you mumble, and fumble around in your jeans and take out the Tic Tac box. You push it across the kitchen counter. It slides into your father's hand. Safe. Cool. Your father sets his cappuccino down, sprinkles a little of the powder on the surface, and dips a finger in it. He tastes it, he looks at you, he says, "What is this?"

"Coke."

You just sense the slap, you don't see it coming.

"What is this, Darian?"

"Co—"

He's too fast. Backhand. The movement hovers in the air like a paper kite tossing in the wind, leaving nothing but a trail of color behind. *Far out,* you think, and here comes the next question: "Darian, what is this?"

"I thought . . ."

You shut up, your head's burning rubber.

Speed?

It isn't speed, you'd recognize speed.

Coke?

You're not about to say coke again.

It couldn't possibly be heroin, could it? you think and your mouth says, "Heroin?"

"Where does it come from?"

You gush it all out, you tell him about the girl and the deal and admit everything, the pills too, you don't even lie about the amount, because your father isn't the buyer, your father is God, and God sees through all lies.

"When?"

"Tonight, two o'clock."

You tell him about Mirko, who got the whole thing going, and where you're meeting the girl. Your father doesn't think much of your plan. He dismisses you with a sentence.

"Get rid of your friend."

"But—"

"And I expect you to have a clear head by two o'clock."

With these words he puts the Tic Tac box in his pocket, takes his cappuccino, and leaves the kitchen without giving you so much as a glance.

By midnight you're sober again. You've sweated out the drug, you've run ten miles on the treadmill, you pumped iron until your body consisted only of pain. Fifteen minutes in the sauna, a cold shower, and here you are.

Just two hours until the meeting.

You go to the Starlight on the Ku'damm. Rico and André come with you. You sell some tabs and a bit of weed. While the customers go off to the bathroom with Rico, you drink one glass of still water after another and keep looking at your phone. Perhaps your father's going to change his mind, yes, and perhaps the moon's made of green cheese. Mirko is waiting for you by the pizza stand at a quarter to two. He's taken the rest of the night off. You know he's only thinking about the girl. You wonder what you're going to say to him without looking like a weak fuck. You're forgetting something. Something fundamental. Keep it in mind.

I'm the boss, the boss can't be a weak fuck.

Well done.

Just before half past one you take the night bus down Kantstrasse, get out by the local court, and walk up Windscheidstrasse. It's really time you got your driver's license and started driving a car. The summer night groans into your face, its breath is rancid, frying fat and corners full of piss. You like the smell, you're sweating nicely. When you get to Stuttgarter Platz, you see the pizza stand like a palely gleaming star by the railway bridge. Mirko is standing outside at one of the tables drinking a Coke Light.

"Artificial sweetener gives you cancer," you say by way of greeting.

"Bullshit," he says and holds out his hand.

It's surprisingly quiet. A scorching Thursday night in Berlin. Mirko's uncle is busying himself with the oven and scrubbing it, the scrape of metal on metal, not a customer to be seen, the lights in the cafés opposite have gone out. Closing time.

"Dead city, right?"

"Totally dead. Shall we go?"

You rub the back of your neck.

"Listen, Mirko, we've got a problem."

"What sort of problem?"

You lie. You lie to him and tell him your father's rejected the deal.

"No cash for the bitch."

Mirko wants to know what your father has to do with it. It's a reasonable question, you're working for the Brothers. Your father's just the logistics guy. You've gone and opened your big mouth. Well done. Time to act the big boss. You laugh at Mirko.

"Nothing's happening without my old man. Ever."

Mirko makes a face.

"Man, she'll go mental!"

Mirko takes out his phone.

"What are you doing?"

"I'm going to call her, so that—"

"Forget it. She knows."

"What? How does she know?"

"Because . . . because I've canceled on her."

Mirko tilts his head a little to the left.

"But you haven't even got her number."

You look at each other. You go on looking at each other. Your mind's racing as if possessed, exploring the database of your messed-up brain and not finding a reasonable answer. Mirko throws in another verbal punch.

"You don't even know her name."

Suddenly you grin. A wolf flashing his fangs. You lean forward slightly. There is the indescribable desire to crush the Coke can into your pal's face till his mother wouldn't recognize him. The desire is just a spark, you'd never do that to Mirko, never.

"Hey, Romeo, if I tell you she knows, then she knows. Do you think I'd lie to you? Come on, put that phone away."

He doesn't react. You grab him by the chin, your great paw covers half his face. Your words are a whisper.

"Mirko, put the fucking phone away. The deal's off. It's over. Finito. Get that?"

You hear his uncle shouting something from the pizza stand and look over at him without letting go of Mirko. His uncle curses and looks the other way.

"Okay," says Mirko.

"Cool?"

"Cool."

You let go of his chin. He stares at the ground.

"Look at me."

He looks at you.

"We take care of each other, have you forgotten that?"

"Of course not."

"I keep an eye out for you, day and night. Never forget that. And we'll go to the movies tomorrow and it's on me, okay?"

You punch him gently on the shoulder, wave to his uncle, and walk back up Windscheidstrasse. Hands in the pockets of your sweatpants, shoulders straight. You can hear Mirko and his uncle talking behind you. Yugo-talk, you don't understand a word. When you get to Kantstrasse, you take a look at your phone. Ten to two. Time to get a move on. Your father's waiting.

RUTH

You're sitting side by side on the subway and your reflections are staring back at you. The sports bag is between you. The zip is closed, Stink's hand rests on the bag like a nervous spider. Black fingernails drumming on the fabric. You want to slap her on the fingers, but in fact you're only furious with yourself. Stink loves chaos, you've known that forever, and it just bugs you that there's nothing you can do about it.

First she disappears this morning without a word of explanation, leaving a little pile of Tic Tacs in the kitchen, then she comes back with medication at nine in the evening, and tells you about this boy whose Vespa she's swiped, and who also just happens to be a friend of Darian's.

Everyone knows who Darian is. No one remembers the boy.

The medication did the trick. Taja felt better after just a few minutes. She slept more soundly, the sweating and itching stopped. Mission accomplished. Or so you'd think. But no, that wasn't nearly enough for Stink, and she told you about her brainstorm. And you haven't thought for a second that she might be lying to you.

"Then I stood there and he gave me the drugs, okay, and I was about to leave again and then I had this brainstorm."

You all looked at her as if she was speaking a foreign language.

"You had *what*?" said Schnappi.

"That's why I've made a date," said Stink.

"With who?" you said.

"I'm meeting Mirko and Darian at two in the morning. It's going to be quick."

"Quick!?" Nessi repeated, confused. "What are you talking about?"

"I'm talking about selling Darian the drugs and making us a shit-load of money."

You were all silent for a moment, and then you said, "I could slap you right now, you stupid bitch."

"Do as you like, but then you'll get no money."

"How much are we talking about?" Schnappi asked.

"Fifty big ones."

"WHAT?"

Schnappi and Nessi staggered backward slightly, they were so impressed. You were less than impressed. You sounded like a grandma whose chair has been whipped out from under her nose: "Stink, you can't do this."

"Sure I can."

"If you do this, I don't know you anymore."

Stink laughed.

"Why don't you know me anymore? What sort of thing is that to say?"

"You're getting us into something dangerous, and I don't want to—"

"Keep your hair on," Schnappi interrupted. "Dangerous is when you're crossing the road or when someone chucks a television in your bath."

"Right," said Stink.

"Darian's Taja's cousin," Schnappi went on. "Why would he want to con Stink? Think about it, Ruth. Fifty grand! Christ, that's ten thousand for each of us!"

"Ten grand's not bad," Nessi admitted, and Schnappi pointed out that some girls would go on the streets for ten grand, and they all laughed and you stood there and just couldn't believe how stupid your girlfriends were. Then Stink went upstairs quickly to get the drugs, and you felt like someone who'd been hit by a hammer. In the middle of the forehead, several times in a row. The worst thing was that Schnappi was beaming at you as if she'd just turned shit into gold. And Nessi was nodding frantically like those idiotic toy dogs you sometimes see in the back windows of cars. You wanted to know how she could possibly think this was a good idea. Nessi replied seriously that nothing comes from nothing. The hammer was still bashing away at your forehead, when Stink came down with a sports bag and said she was ready.

"Stink, you can't do this," you repeated yourself like a cracked record.

So you stood in her way.

Stink laughed.

"What's going on? Are you trying to stop me?"

"Please stay," you said, and Stink promised to be back in two hours. She shoved past you and left the house. The door clicked shut, and Schnappi observed, "Stink's just Stink."

And Nessi added, "Have you ever seriously tried to stop Stink?"

No, you haven't. *But it's time I did,* you thought and did the only thing that seemed sensible—you followed your girl.

Of course there was no way of stopping Stink. On the way to the subway you yelled at each other like washerwomen, tugged at the bag, and finally agreed that you were allowed to come along too. Even though it was a small victory, it was better than letting Stink go on her own.

And now you're on the subway and still have six stops to go. You're going to get out at Kaiserdamm, cross the bridge, and walk up Riehlstrasse to the intersection with Wundtstrasse. By the gates to the Lietzensee Park you'll hesitate for a moment, then go down the path to the football field, exchange the drugs for the money, and then walk back up Riehlstrasse, across the bridge and into the subway, and the whole time you won't be able to believe you've done it. Says Stink.

"You're crazy, you know that?"

Stink nods.

"And you're my bodyguard, how crazy is that?"

You look at each other's reflections, like two gunslingers just waiting to see who'll make the first move. An old woman is sitting at the other end of the car, snoring away. An automatic voice announces the next stop. Deutsche Oper. The walls of the tunnels dart past, the light flickers. The sports bag lies between you like a bomb. Stink sticks out her tongue. Your reflection tries not to smile. Another four stops.

The small football field looks deserted. You're half an hour early and sit on the opposite bank, a hundred meters from your meeting point. The lake is in between. If you could walk on water, you'd be there in a minute.

"Creepy," you say.

"It'll be fine," says Stink.

"Do you really trust Darian?"

Stink laughs.

"He's a dick. You should have seen him, he looked as if he's half Rottweiler and half Mickey Rourke. Pumped up, arms like that."

She shows you what the arms were like.

"He thinks he's one of the tough guys. I can deal with him. And Mirko will be there too. Mirko's fine. He'd do anything for me. He's in love, you understand?"

You understand and say, "Anyone who falls in love with Stink has only himself to blame."

"Tell me about it."

She puts her arm around you.

"That's why you love me so much."

You pull away and the two of you go on waiting, stare at the football field and see shadows and know that your eyes are playing tricks with you in the darkness. The grass is damp, so close to the water your backsides are slowly getting wet. You really hope you don't get cystitis.

"What if they don't come?"

"Then they don't come, but at least it was worth a try," says Stink and looks at you, and as she looks you pray in defiance of all the rules of intelligence that she will never be normal, that she'll always stay this wild creature, and that she'll still be scaring you with her unpredictability when you're old grannies and shitting in diapers again.

"Come on, be honest, Ruth, fifty grand is amazing! Just think! If it works you can buy all the books you want, and Taja can travel till she feels ill, and Schnappi can run away from home and never have to go to Vietnam, and our Nessi won't need some idiot to support her, and she can have her baby in peace."

"And what about you?"

"I'll have my beauty salon."

"Sweetie, I think a salon costs a bit more than that."

"Really?"

"Really."

Stink has her second brainstorm of the day.

"Maybe you'll give me your share."

"Yeah, maybe," you say and you mean it, because you're the only one whose parents are reasonably affluent. And you've got enough books.

"Really?" Stink presses.

"Really."

After a short pause you add: "I might even stay on at school."

It's out now. It might have something to do with the darkness that safely envelops you. You have to say it eventually. The strangest moments are the ones you don't predict. You tense up.

Stink says everyone's worked that one out ages ago.

"What?"

"Christ, Ruth, if anyone knows you, we do. You're our professor. Of course you're going to stay on at school. Your parents would disinherit you if you did some stupid apprenticeship. Don't worry, we'll still love you."

You're lost for words, you've been racking your brain for months about how you're going to tell your girls, and they've known all along.

Who knows who here? you wonder.

Stink glances at her phone.

"I'm off, then."

"Be careful."

"Don't worry, I'm tough."

You laugh, draw her to you by the hand, and kiss her briefly on the mouth; your faces stay close for a second so that you can see the golden sprinkles in her irises.

"Be careful," you repeat, and this time Stink doesn't make a joke, this time she just nods and puts on her sunglasses.

You let her go.

You hear the whoosh of Neue Kantstrasse, the night bus for Zoo rumbles past, then it's silent again, and the only sound is Stink's footsteps. She pauses on the bridge and looks down at you. You wave, she waves back, then you hear her whispering in your ear that it's all going to be fine, before she walks on and the bushes block your view. The cell phone in your hand is wet with sweat. You see Stink walk across the bridge, a little way up Sundtstrasse, and then down the steps to the other side of the park. The football field is still deserted. No one has come, you can see everything, your eyes sting with the effort.

The field is fenced in and looks like a big cage. The goals are a full-length metal pole without a net, the floor a hard rubber surface. Stink stops at the entrance and looks around. She's puzzled. It's five past two. In the distance, with the big sunglasses on her face, she reminds you of a beetle.

Can she see anything?

Stink waits outside the field for a moment before stepping through the entrance. She has promised to leave the cell phone turned on in her jacket. You see her back, she pauses after a few footsteps, you hear a throbbing sound in your ear and curse. Someone's trying to call Stink on her cell phone, and of course she hasn't turned off her call-waiting mode.

Hang up! you think. *Whoever you are, hang up!*

It doesn't occur to you for a second that it might be Mirko. The throbbing stops, it's quiet again, then you hear a man's voice saying, "I thought you'd never come over."

Pause.

"Who the hell are you?" asks Stink.

"Wrong question," the man's voice replies. "The right question is: how does someone like you get hold of this amount of drugs?"

Stink takes two steps back. You can't see the man, there's only darkness in front of your girl.

"Are you a cop?" Stink asks.

Silence. Then the man says, "We're going to have a chat now, but first turn off your phone. Your friend's heard enough. Take out the battery, just so that there are no misunderstandings."

When you hear that, you almost drop your cell phone. Stink hesitates, and you pray that she'll turn around and run away, because the man's voice scares you. Dry, all angles and corners. It's not the voice of someone who's going to put up with Stink's wisecracks.

There's a rustling sound. Stink speaks right in your ear.

"I'll call you, okay?"

"Stink, don't—"

That's as far as you get, because she's hung up. You narrow your eyes slightly to see more clearly. It doesn't help. Stink has stepped forward and disappeared completely into the darkness.

Who is this guy? You wonder and are about to get up and run over there when a hand settles on your shoulder. Silent as a shadow, heavy as a stone. You turn around.

He looks like a wall with a little shaven head. Muscles on muscles and then that face. You recognize him right away. You've seen him on the street and in the clubs. Stink described him very well. His lower lip is slightly swollen and he has a plaster on his forehead. He really does look as if he's half Rottweiler and half Mickey Rourke. *Even if he's related to Taja, there's no family resemblance,* you think, and you're just about to ask him if he eats raw eggs in the morning, when he hits you. A flashlight explodes in your head. You fall sideways, but before you can roll down the slope, he's grabbed you by the hair. His face is close to you. You smell his sweet-and-sour breath and see his eyes, the dilated pupils and the fury behind them. Your cheek glows with the blow, you still have your cell phone in your hand and smash it against the spot where the plaster sticks to his forehead. He lets go of you and clutches his face with surprise. The wound has opened up, his hand is covered with blood. He's stunned. You start to crawl away, he grabs you by the leg, you kick out, hit him in the shoulder and try to pick yourself up, but the ground is too wet and you slide across the grass. You land on your belly and the air escapes you with a dull groan. He grabs your ankle and pulls you to him. Your fingers make furrows in the grass, his fist lands in the back of your knee, the pain paralyzes you, your fingers lose their grip and he drags and drags you along the grass to the bushes. Now you're out of range, now he's pressing the back of your head down so that the left half of your face disappears in the wet grass. You lie there, one eye shut, the other one open, your mouth is full of soil. You hear him say something and can't make out a word because his hand is over your right ear.

"I CAN'T HEAR YOU!"

He takes his hand away and puts it around your throat.

"One more word and I'll finish you off, okay?"

You nod, his hand disappears, you prop yourself up and spit soil and see from the corners of your eyes that he's crouching next to you like some fucking toad.

"Didn't think of this, did you? You thought a backup was a good idea. I'm backup too. We could be a team."

Your knee feels as if someone's constantly pumping it full of air. You wipe the dirt out of your face.

"Can I get up?"

"Sit yes, stand no."

You sit up and spit out blades of grass.

"We're waiting now," he says and looks across to the opposite bank as if you weren't there. There's a stupid grin on his lips. You don't know what he's doing here. *Why isn't he over there, buying the drugs from Stink? If he's here, who's that on the other side?* Five minutes pass, then his phone rings. He listens for a moment and then says: *No, there's nothing here,* before he puts the phone back in his pocket, takes a deep breath and speaks without looking at you.

"This is really going to hurt."

STINK

The man sits leaning forward with his elbows on his knees. Dark linen pants, black shirt, sleeves rolled up. He could be about your father's age. You wish you had a better view of his eyes. Eyes reveal everything. His are black puddles. After you've taken the battery out of your phone, he pats the bench beside him and says, "I've heard about your offer. Take a seat."

"I'd rather stand."

You feel his gaze on you. He's turning your Tic Tac box over and over in his right hand. Gradually it dawns on you that this wasn't such a great idea. He's going to wait until you're sitting next to him. You sit down. He sets the Tic Tac box on his thigh and looks across the football field as if he could make something out in the darkness.

"You're fifteen? Sixteen?"

"Eighteen."

"Take the sunglasses off, it's just us."

You take the sunglasses off, and at last you can see better. Every wrinkle in his face, the color of his eyes. His mouth is mocking you with a smile as if he knows everything about you.

"You're aware that your age is irrelevant. You could be ten years old and I wouldn't care, because at the moment we share the same problem, and that's all that matters."

He looks at you again.

"Do you know how drugs get tested? Some people just need to

taste them. They swear they can define the differences in quality and how much the drugs are cut by tasting them. You follow me? Of course it's all nonsense. No one can establish quality like that. You know what this is?"

He taps the Tic Tac box with his index finger. You don't react.

"I thought you didn't. You probably think this is cocaine or speed. A forgivable mistake. The ordinary citizen doesn't often get to see white heroin. At school I'm sure they've told you that heroin's brown. That's correct as well. Normal heroin is brown and reaches the streets with a purity of twenty percent, and that means it's good gear. Ten percent and below is normal. The more it's cut, the more additives are mixed in with it, usually bitter-tasting materials so as to maintain the supposed authenticity. Have you ever tried heroin?"

You shake your head.

"It's really bitter shit. But let's get back to the problem at hand. People who work seriously with drugs test their product in the laboratory. I have a chemist who's responsible for nothing but that. Can you guess what he discovered an hour ago?"

"That my stuff is crap?"

"No, that your stuff is actually my stuff."

You freeze, he smiles.

"You know what I'm trying to say? What we have here is eighty-eight percent pure heroin. Five kilos of it. We're talking about a market value of two and a half million euros. And this is all in your possession. On a day like today? In a year like this one? You'll have realized that there are no more misunderstandings."

You don't know how he did it, but his arm is around your shoulders now, he's scarily close and speaking into your ear.

"That kind of thing doesn't happen twice in a city like Berlin. Not in these amounts, not with this quality. The question is, how on earth does someone like you get hold of drugs that my little brother is storing?"

His question hangs in the air. You had anticipated everything. You were even sure for a long time that he was really a cop, and that you'd soon be spending three hundred hours doing social work. But this has taken you completely by surprise. *Little brother? Storing?*

The equation is quite a simple one. *Taja's uncle is sitting next to me and his little brother is Oskar, who's lying in a freezer right now, and by the way I'm really fucked.* You quickly dismiss all those thoughts as if Taja's uncle could see inside your head, and start calculating your chances. You've always been good at that. Your mind works best under stress, as if you need trouble to function right. *What now?* If you react right away, you might manage it. A forward jab, catch him in the face with your forehead, and while he's spitting out his teeth, you run off and disappear down Neue Kantstrasse to join Ruth on the opposite bank and—

"Don't even think about it," he interrupts your thoughts. "I could break your neck so fast you wouldn't even notice."

You look at each other. There's an affinity, and the affinity repels you. He's got a deep tan, he's clean-shaven. His mouth smiles amicably, no more mockery, as though he could be nice if he wanted. But it's deceptive, it's all deceptive when you look at those eyes. Metal. Those eyes don't intend to be nice. On his left cheek there's a small sickle-shaped scar, the skin's lighter there. You automatically want to touch your own skin where Taja's elbow caught you. The skin has turned purple there. *What does this asshole see when he looks at me?* you wonder, and find the answer in his eyes.

Nothing, absolutely nothing, because I don't really exist for him.

His hand rests flat on your back, it gives off an unpleasant kind of heat. As if a fire were creeping up your spine.

"Let go of me," you hiss at him.

The hand disappears. You get to your feet. He sits where he is. His voice is still calm, you wish he would show more emotion.

"It's up to you now. Whatever you promise me in the next minute, I'll take you at your word. And if you break your word, I will hunt you down. Have I made myself understood?"

"I'm not afraid of you."

"You should be afraid, girl, you should be shitting yourself in fear."

He gets up. He's a head taller than you. You try to resist looking up at him. You look up. He wants to know what your plan was.

"You turn up without my merchandise, and then?"

"I've got it all in a bag. I'll fetch it once I've got the money."

"Is that so?"

"It's exactly so."

You and your plans. When you got out with Ruth at the station Kaiserdamm, you explained that you didn't trust anyone, and you put the sports bag in a safe-deposit box. Your plan was to swap the key to the box for the money. You were of the opinion that that's what professionals do.

At this moment a professional should look different. Not so surprised. Standing facing Taja's uncle, you understand that it would be the end of the line for you here if you'd brought the drugs. It is a feeling as if someone is standing by your grave waiting for you to lie down in it.

He'd never have let me go.

"Good plan," says Taja's uncle. "In your place I wouldn't have trusted my son either. You can go now. You and I are done."

He looks at his watch.

"I give you till tomorrow morning. You bring my goods back to where you stole them. I don't want to know how you managed to rob my brother. I'll drive out to see him tomorrow morning, and when I ask him where the heroin is, he'll open his metal case and the heroin will be in there and I'll slap him happily on the shoulder and have breakfast with him. After breakfast I'll have forgotten that you and your friend over there ever existed. Have you got all that?"

You grip the safe-deposit box key in your right hand and nod, you've got it, no problem, that's exactly what you'll do. You're almost about to thank him, when your brain processes what he's just said. *After breakfast I'll have forgotten that you and your friend over there ever existed.* You look across to the shore of the Lietzen-see. *How does he know that Ruth's over there?*

". . . involved?"

"What?"

He repeats his question patiently, he's not in any hurry.

"Is Taja involved?"

You hesitate for a moment too long, that's answer enough for him.

"I've never liked that kid," he admits, and turns away from you. He has said what he wanted to say, you can go. You leave the football field. As you're going up the steps to the street, you cast one last glance through the fence — Taja's uncle has his phone to his ear, and is standing with his back to you, legs spread like a footballer defending his goal. *He has already forgotten about me*, you think and then you hear him say, "Hurt her."

He snaps his cell phone shut, turns around and looks at you.

"Run," he says.

And you run as you have never run before.

NESSI

The new day exists for two hours, nineteen minutes, and forty-eight seconds, and no one in the world seems to be interested. You sit wearily on the terrace and wait for Ruth to come back with Stink. You rather regret not having been on Ruth's side. But fifty grand is fifty grand, and if no one gets hurt, then it's a present that shouldn't be tossed aside.

Schnappi is sleeping beside you in the deck chair. Everything is calm. At the moment you don't even need to worry about Taja, she's completely knocked out by the medication. You looked in on her ten minutes ago. She'd kicked the blanket off and pulled her knees up to her chest, as if she wanted to disappear into herself.

It's so sultry that even the mosquitoes are taking time out. There's a storm in the air, the hairs on your arms are standing up. You're on your own and you're pregnant on your own and you feel melancholic. You want to be the soppily romantic girl you were before you fell pregnant. One of those girls who dream of the rural life and a pony in the paddock.

You lean your head back and stare into the night. A nervous starry sky quivers above you, a point of light makes its way toward Tegel Airport, then there's a quick flash of lightning and the sky goes negative for a few seconds. As you gaze up, you're surprised by that overwhelming peace that you always feel when everything stops making sense. Like that summer four years ago. You were standing on the ten-meter board, and behind you was a line of noisy children. At that moment you understood that there was no turning back, because there was no way they were ever going to let you go back down again. So you stepped out onto the springboard and looked down into the pool and knew very well that you would never survive it, that much was certain. *This is the end of me.* And while you were thinking it, that calm swept over you for the first time. The calm of the desperate. *Whatever happens now, it's going to happen,* you thought, and let yourself fall.

The ringing of your cell phone brings the silence to an end. You don't give a start. Something had to happen, and now it has happened. Schnappi, on the other hand, sits up with a jerk and glares at you.

"Are you trying to kill me, or what?"

"It's just the phone," you reassure her.

Schnappi falls back and wants to know why you don't answer it, when it's *just* the phone. You answer it. Stink's on the other end. She sounds hysterical and she doesn't want you to say anything. She speaks so quickly that you only understand half of it.

"Stink, slow down."

She tells you where she is. She takes a deep breath. She tells you what you have to do. You want to ask her what has happened, but she interrupts you and tells you to hurry up. She says it twice.

"Nessi, please, hurry."

The lights in the ceiling flicker on. There's room for four cars in the garage, but there's only one there.

"I thought her father drove a Mercedes," says Schnappi.

"Me too."

"Nessi, that's not a Mercedes, it's a monster."

The Range Rover looks as if it's come straight off the conveyor belt. It gleams coldly in the fluorescent light and looks as remote as the starry sky you were looking at a moment before. There isn't a speck of dust on the black paint, the windshield is an insect eye that stares at you disparagingly.

"It's too big for us," says Schnappi.

"What choice do we have?"

At first Stink wanted you to phone one of the guys from the crowd and arrange for a car. It's half past three on a Friday morning.

You tried. None of the guys answers his phone, and it's hardly likely that they would borrow their parents' car to come to your aid.

How the hell do you arrange for a car after midnight?

Schnappi had the idea of looking in Taja's father's garage. And you're there now and you feel like dwarfs. You can't even see over the roof of the Range Rover.

You pull on the driver's door, which is of course locked. You look at the back tire, because Schnappi says people in movies always hide their keys on the back tire. Not in this movie.

"Nessi, this isn't a good sign."

You want to tape her mouth shut.

"I could ask my father," she offers.

"Do you really think he'd drive us?"

Schnappi shakes her head.

"But I could ask."

"Rather not."

You go back into the house and look through all the drawers. Nothing.

You think about waking Taja.

"But why should Taja know where her father keeps . . ."

Schnappi breaks off; you look at each other and have the same thought.

"Please don't," says Schnappi.

It's time to go back into the basement.

Taja's dad looks just like he did yesterday. Still, stiff, dead.

"I can't do it," you say.

Schnappi groans, leans forward, reaches into the cabinet and, after feeling around for a minute, finds the key ring in his front pants pocket. She snakes two fingers in and pulls a face as if she were rummaging in a bucket full of earthworms. After she's fished out the key ring, she hands it to you. The keys are ice cold.

"And you're sure you can drive that car?"

You nod, what else are you supposed to do, there's no turning back now, Schnappi would never forgive you. Your mother gave you driving lessons when you went with her on holiday to Greece. It was easier than you thought. That's exactly what you say to Schnappi.

"If it's an automatic, I'm fine."

"And if it isn't?"

"Then we'll cross that bridge."

Back into the garage.

The key fits.

You sit down in the car and search with your feet.

Only two pedals.

Bingo.

For a whole five minutes you debate whether Schnappi should stay with Taja, but then Schnappi gets fed up debating and gets in the car.

"So show me what you're made of," she says and puts on her seat belt.

As far as the first traffic light you're terribly nervous, it's weird being so high up, it feels as if you were sitting on a pedestal and not driving the car yourself but being driven. The accelerator is very sensitive, the brake is like a feather. When you finally relax and are about to make a turn, the front tire bumps over the curb and you ram a garbage can, which falls over with a hollow crash and rolls into the street.

"Pull up," says Schnappi.

You brake. The car jolts to a standstill at the side of the street. You take your foot off the brake. The car moves again. You slam your foot down on the brake again. You're thrown forward and fly back, then all of a sudden you're at a standstill and you set the car to park.

"Nessi, take a breath."

Your hands clutch the steering wheel, your knuckles white. You loosen your grip and shake your fingers out. Dark patches have formed under your armpits. Pure panic. Your heart hammers. Schnappi observes dryly, "It's because you're pregnant."

"What's that got to do with anything?"

"Hormones and stuff."

"I'm just fine."

"I bet you're secretly throwing up."

"I'm not secretly throwing up," you answer, and push open the driver's door to throw up in the street.

"See," says Schnappi and strokes your back.

It's really annoying being pregnant, your body's alien to you and does what it wants. It's even more annoying that everyone's solicitous about you and Schnappi's proved right on top of everything else. She reaches into the glove compartment, and points out in passing that her father gave her driving lessons too.

"You tell me that *now*?!"

"It was just a few hours, and it was a car with a stick shift, and anyway I'd never drive a monster like this. You're doing really well."

Schnappi finds a pack of chewing gum and passes you a stick. The taste of mint makes you relax.

"Better?"

"Not bad. Maybe you should train as a midwife."

"Maybe I should give you a kick in the ass to make the baby come out right now."

There's really not much you can say to that, so you slide your seat closer to the steering wheel, put your foot on the brake, and put the car in gear. You're calmer now, and you pull away from the curb like a ninety-five-year-old diva on her way to the hairdresser's. Says Schnappi, at least.

SCHNAPPI

You creep along the city highway. A pensioner on a bike would be quicker. It's a wonder a patrol hasn't stopped you for holding up the traffic. Luckily you're almost the only ones on the road at this time of night, otherwise people would be beeping at you every ten seconds. If you weren't such a dwarf, you could sit behind the wheel, but with your short legs you probably wouldn't even be able to reach the pedals. You don't say a word, Nessi is tense enough. If you were to ask whether she wanted a boy or a girl, she'd be sure to drive the thing off the road. So sit still and look at the lights of the city and get used to the feeling that your whole life is a miserable, endless highway in the remotest corner of Vietnam where you're only allowed to drive ten kilometers an hour. *If they even have miserable, endless highways in Vietnam,* you think and remember how often your mother promised you that your real life would only begin in your homeland. There's no life here in Germany as far as she's concerned. It's a prelude in hell before you're allowed to enter paradise. You like hell, you feel good here, and the thought of no one understanding German in paradise because only the Vietnamese are allowed in really scares you. Your Vietnamese is terrible. And until twenty minutes ago you didn't even believe in hell.

"Do you know what hell is?"

"Driving in a car with me?"

"How do you know that?"

"Thanks, Schnappi."

It takes you fifty-six minutes to get to Charlottenburg. At the

Funkturm you leave the Autobahn and head up the exit at a walking pace. The streets are deserted, the lights are green, a good tailwind might take you up to twenty kilometers an hour. At one point a patrol car draws up alongside you and Nessi nearly faints. She tries to sit especially straight, and asks you out of the corner of her mouth whether the cops are looking over. You put your hand on her knee and tell her not to forget to breathe. But of course she does forget, and only starts breathing normally again when the taillights of the patrol car are tiny dots.

At Lietzensee you stop in a driveway behind the Hotel Seeblick, because there are no parking spaces free around here so late at night. Nessi gets out and leans against the car. Her knees are weak, but at least she's not throwing up again. You take your friend by the hand, and the two of you step inside the park.

Your two girls are sitting on the shore looking at the water, as if they're having a picnic. Ruth's head rests on Stink's shoulder. *Looks okay,* you think as you walk down the grass to the shore, and everything really is okay. Nessi asks what all the stress is about. Stink says: *Stress keeps you young.* The sports bag is on the ground beside Ruth. Ruth pats the grass. You sit down and look at the water and say it's unbelievable that only two days ago Nessi was in the water here. Nessi just laughs, and then you ask what's happened. And Stink points to the bag. *Want to take a look?* You open the zipper, the bag is full of money. All in hundreds, rolled up in bank wrappers, all yours. Your little heart gives a great leap and you say: *Amazing!* And Stink says: *Didn't I tell you?* And then you hear how Stink met Darian at the football pitch and how she handed the bag over and got the money and off she went. *And all we had to do was take a little trip on the subway,* says Ruth. And you laugh again, and then you set off and Nessi drives you to the Mexican place on Krumme Strasse, and you sit there and no sooner have you ordered than your phone rings and it's Taja, and she says she's fine, the medication was a complete success and where have you all gone, she'd have loved to come along and get some fresh air, so you tell her where you are and say she should jump in the next taxi, and before she hangs up you hold up your phone so that the girls could call something to her, and Stink says, "I thought you'd never come."

You blink, you're still standing up on the path beside Nessi,

and the park encloses you in its darkness. You wonder if you're
going to have a blank every day from now on, or what? *Maybe I'm
going mad, maybe I'm about to start time traveling.* Stink and Ruth
haven't moved from the spot down by the water. Stink looks up
at you. Nessi gives you a shove, you snap out of your daze and
walk down the slope. Then Ruth turns around and you both freeze
again and can't take another step. It's as if the air in front of you has
turned into concrete. You must have blanked out because you knew
something was heading your way. You see Ruth's face, and nothing's
okay anymore.

You might be small, but you're tough. How many fights did you
get into in primary school because a bunch of girls thought you
talked too much and had funny eyes? *Too many.* It doesn't help
that your father's a German, in fact that makes it even worse.
You're one of those bastards who look exotic and don't really
fit in anywhere. So you do what all bastards do, you find a niche
for yourself, and you're the girl who won't put up with anything. Your heart is softer than Stink's, but none of your girls is a
match for your rages. Schnappi in a rage is like a bear trap. Everyone knows that. And when everything goes downhill and nothing works, you crush your opponent into the ground by talking
nonstop.

"Darian?"

You say his name as if you can't believe that's really his name.

"That revolting big fucker did this? That bald-headed dickhead?
If I get my hands on him, I'm gonna rip him a new asshole, you hear
me?!"

You kick the grass, a lump of soil comes away, you look around
and wish you had a few stones to smash the hotel windows with.
Even though you couldn't throw that far, it's the thought that
counts, and every thought in your head is like a rocket with a burning fuse. How come Stink's so calm? You don't need to ask, because
you see the answer in her evasive eyes.

Scared, our Stink is scared.

You all support Ruth on the way to the car. She can't really walk

on her right foot, her knee's badly swollen. Nessi wants to take her
to the hospital right away. Ruth says, "No way. I'll stay with you. I
know exactly what'll happen once I end up in the hospital. They'll
call my parents and keep me in for a few days. I don't want to leave
you."

"By the way, we have no time for the hospital," says Stink.
"We've got Taja's uncle on our backs."

Nessi and you stop walking.

"We've got what?"

Stink tells you what happened on the football field, that the
drugs are secure in a safe-deposit box, and Ragnar Desche wants to
show up at Taja's house in the morning to collect his merchandise.

"That's why we can't go to the hospital. We simply don't have
time. We have to move quick. What do you think Taja's uncle's going
to do when he sees his brother's dead in the freezer?"

You're speechless; however much you try, you can't think of a
smart comeback. You only know horrible stories about Taja's uncle.
That he used to be a soldier, and killed over a hundred people as a
sniper during the Balkan war. That almost all cops get kickbacks
from him, and that's why he was able to set fire to a nightclub on
Alexanderplatz and get away scot-free. That he's crazy, and he
scares the other crazies. All made-up stories, a bunch of stupid lies,
but you never know.

"But, Stink, this is Ragnar Desche we're talking about!"

"Yes, Nessi, I know."

"But . . . he's a total nut job, we mustn't get mixed up with him,
he'll kill our parents and then—"

"Nessi, shut up," you cut in. "It's all just rumors. He's only a
human being. And he's Taja's uncle. Shift down a gear. First we need
to look after Ruth, the rest can wait."

The rest, you think, *is a dead man in the freezer and a ton of
drugs in a sports bag. And of course the golden question of how we're
going to get out of this alive.* But you don't say any of that, because
Nessi would probably run away screaming.

When you arrive at the Range Rover, Stink can't believe her eyes.
It's a good feeling, still being able to surprise her every now and
again.

"Do you think you could be any more conspicuous?" she says and kicks the back tire. "You were supposed to get a car, not a tank."

"You can walk if you like," says Nessi and helps Ruth into the car.

Nobody says a word on the way home. You're sitting in the backseat with Ruth, with her head in your lap. Later you'll see the bruises on her arms and her back. In the glow of the passing streetlights you can see only that her left eye is bloodshot, and that there's a nasty cut on her lower lip. Darian has used her as a punching bag, you swear you'll make him lose at least a leg for it.

The city flashes past you as if trying to get away.

Streetcornershouseslightsstreetcornershouseslightscars.

Ruth shuts her eyes. You rest your hand on her forehead and try to send her positive energy. Where you get that positive energy is a mystery to you. Your palm is pulsing, and that has to mean something.

When you stop outside Taja's house, you wake Ruth and help her out. It's half-past four, the sky is a pale bluish gray, morning is so close that you can hear it breathing. You walk Ruth to the terrace and plunder the medicine cabinet, rub ointment on the bruises, and cut Ruth's jeans open from feet to hip. Stink fetches a bag of ice and presses it carefully on the swollen knee. Ruth sighs and says it feels good.

"What are you doing there?"

You give a start. Taja is standing in the terrace doorway, blanket around her shoulders, water bottle in her hand. She was in the kitchen, she noticed the light outside, and now here she is. Barefoot in panties and T-shirt, thin as a rake. There are still shadows under her eyes like thunderclouds, but she's obviously better.

You step aside so that she can get a view of Ruth.

"Honey, what's happened to you?"

You don't know what it is exactly. Perhaps the tone in Taja's voice or just the fact that Taja is standing in front of you like a normal person, and not throwing up over the toilet bowl. At any rate, Ruth shrugs helplessly and bursts into tears.

Ten minutes later Taja knows what's happened, and says to Stink,

"So you were trying to sell my cousin the drugs that his father was storing in my father's house?"

"How was I supposed to know it was his drugs?"

"Stink, why do you always have to cause problems?"

"I thought we could bring in a bit of money."

"You could have asked me."

"Taja, you were in a coma."

"And she didn't want to listen to me," says Ruth.

You fall silent, you look at each other, then Taja says what you're all thinking, "Girls, we're totally fucked."

"What will your uncle do?"

"I don't know."

"He can't do anything to us, can he?"

"No, he can't. And anyway we're related."

"Yes, *you're* related to him," you point out, "but what about the rest of us?"

Taja says nothing. Nessi says, "We could go to the police."

Taja shakes her head.

"Not a good idea to report somebody like my uncle to the police."

"We just have to put the drugs back where we found them."

Stink shakes her head.

"Sorry, Nessi, but I'm not putting anything back."

"What?"

"Take a look at Ruth. That guy doesn't deserve a thing. How could he do that to our girl? If I'd given him the drugs in the park, I wouldn't be here right now. He's that kind of guy."

"Bullshit."

Suddenly Stink explodes, there's panic in her voice.

"How can you say 'bullshit'? I talked to him, Nessi, not you. The guy really scared the shit out of me, and not everybody scares me, you know that. Do you really think he's going to let me get away, and then when I bump into him when I'm out shopping and I say hi, he'll tell his mates: *Hey, that was the girl who tried to sell me my own stuff, but don't worry, she gave it all back, she's okay.* Nessi, do you never go to the movies? When has that ever worked?"

"Never," Nessi says quietly and lowers her head.

"Especially when the guy finds his dead brother here in the

house," says Ruth and tilts her head on one side to spit blood into the flowerbed next to her. Taja strokes her back and says, "Everything okay with you?"

"It's just a nosebleed."

Ruth throws her head back and speaks into the night sky: "People, we should disappear."

Nessi laughs.

"Ruth, we're sixteen. We can't just disappear."

"Who says?"

"That's just how it is."

"But who says we can't try?"

"And where are you going to disappear to?" asks Stink.

"We'll think of something."

"And what are we going to do with the drugs?" asks Taja.

Stink holds a key in the air.

"They're still in the safe-deposit box, and they can stay there as far as I'm concerned. If anyone hurts us, they're going to pay for it."

You want to tear into Stink. You want to tell her she's partly to blame for what happened to Ruth. To your great surprise, Taja agrees with her.

"Stink's right. My uncle should pay you if he wants the stuff back."

You're all lost for words. You look at her, and at that moment you have the feeling that everything's going to be fine, that nothing can go wrong, because this pale-skinned girl, who lost her father a week ago and who's been taking heroin for five days, this girl shows her teeth and beams at you with positivity and says, "I'm in favor of Ruth's plan. What's keeping us all here? Let's disappear."

"But where are we supposed to go?" asks Nessi.

No one has an answer. The question hovers in space. You stretch yourself, raise your arm, and wave it around in the air as if you could grab the question. You look a bit like a little girl who urgently needs to go to the bathroom. They look at you. It's obvious, you've had an idea.

"Listen," you say.

OSKAR

And here comes your last guest appearance. You're still switched to receiving, even though the reception's really terrible. You're increasingly losing contact with yourself, and clinging to memories. The moments fray and pull away as if the past were a train that's dropped you at some bleak railway station and is now slowly pulling out. You hear it, you see it, but you can't follow it. Your biggest fear is that it will disappear forever and leave you alone in this state. So you go through names, places, and dates in your head.

July 1987. Taja. The bower. April 1992. Majgull. Ulvtannen. November 2000. Prenzlauer Berg. Ragnar. Husemannstrasse. April 2005. Gina. Helsinki. March. April? May or . . .

No use. Whatever you do, the facts slip away, the train moves tirelessly on and you stand there and try not to lose sight of it.

Light.

The freezer opens. Two girls look in at you. You try to remember their names. Nessi and . . . You don't recognize the other girl. Asian, she's Asian. Nessi and . . . You can't get there. They look in at you. You hear them thinking. *He looks like he did yesterday.* Nessi reaches past you, stands up again, says: *I can't do it.* Now the Asian girl leans forward. Her hair brushes your face. Her thoughts are a straight line. *Quickquickquickquick.* When she stands up again you hear a clink. She breathes out and says: *And you're sure you can drive that car?* The freezer shuts with a dull thump. Darkness. The girls move away.

Schnappi, her name is . . .

Light.

Schnappi and Stink. They're in a hurry. Schnappi says, "Why me?"

"Do you want Taja to drag her dead father around the place, or what? Come on, get a hold on him."

A third voice.

At last.

"I can do it."

Taja's there. You wish you could feel her hands. She wants to say goodbye and doesn't know how. She doesn't want to leave you alone in the dark and lifts you with Stink's help out of the freezer. You see her shoulders, her chin. The girls carry you into the next room, into the vaulted basement with the swimming pool. You try to find clarity in your daughter's chaotic thoughts. Grief, there's so much grief. *My little girl.* You lose reception, Taja slips away from you and then there's silence and suddenly Stink's thoughts kick off and you can't filter them and for a second the night spreads out in front of you like a troubled landscape. You see your brother in Lietzensee Park, standing on the football pitch, and you hear his words, you see Ruth lying on the grass like a wounded animal, knees up to her chest, then the connection breaks off again and the girls have put you on a chair, they take a step back and look at you.

"Take care, Oskar," says Stink.

"Take care," murmurs Schnappi. Only your daughter doesn't say anything, she's crying, and suddenly her face is back in your field of vision. *Tired, my little one is so tired.* Her hand touches your cheek, her guilt is still her guilt and there's not a thing you can do about it.

They leave, the lights go out.

Darkness.

———

Light.

Stink comes running in, like a raging fire that's out of control.

What's she doing?

She stops at the back wall, by the control panel, twists the buttons, the lights come on. Stink looks and looks before she finds the right button, and then shouts, "Yes!"

The swimming pool starts filling up. The water hisses, it's electrically controlled. As soon as the water reaches a particular level, the system switches off. Chlorine, anti-algae treatment, water hardening stabilizer are added automatically. The system costs you a lot of money. It's a pity, because it's the end of your plants. You fed and nurtured them and now they're going to drown and you're sitting dead on a chair and can't do anything about it. But you understand why Stink is doing this. And be honest, you like her revenge. For Ruth. It's good revenge. Ragnar will go crazy.

The lights go out with a click. The door closes.

You're alone again. And you start thawing. Slowly. And then your eyes close. Slowly. And the darkness is everywhere.

The door to the vaulted basement opens.

Maybe Taja's come back, maybe she wants to . . .

It isn't your daughter. You recognize him by his panting breath. Leo. His thoughts are simple and clear.

What a fucking mess.

The door shuts again, and you know your brother's about to enter.

There he is, and he's in a bad mood. He thinks the fiasco in the swimming pool is his biggest problem. He's so irritated that he disregards you. He punishes you with his ignorance, because he thinks you're drunk and asleep on the chair. Then Tanner comes down, and your brother hears that all the merchandise is gone. He turns to Leo.

"Wake him up."

Leo runs his hand over your face and is confused: *What's up with Oskar?* Your brother works it out as soon as Leo's stood up again.

His panicked understanding chases around the room and meets the miserable remains of your intelligence. And then comes a thought that you really don't understand: *Reptile, I'm turning into a fucking reptile.*

"He's gone," says Leo.

Suddenly your brother is close to you. You're only inches apart. You wish you could see him. *One last time.* Your eyes stay shut.

"What's up with his skin?"

"That's ice. He must have frozen to death."

Wrong, you think.

David joins your brother, and taps you seriously on the forehead as if you were a wax dummy. There's the sound of a dull *tok.*

"Leo's right. Oskar's gone."

Whatever comes next vanishes into a dead zone. The interruptions are coming more and more frequently. It's only when your brother lifts your left eyelid that you come back one more time and see him—gaunt face, sad expression. Then you hear his thoughts and at last you know for sure. All those years you guessed that Ragnar was responsible for your father's death. Only your wife knew about your theory, and you never dared to talk to Ragnar about it. The autopsy showed that your father had suffered a stroke, but no one could say what exactly had happened. Now you can see everything, because your brother's remembering. His own fury, your father's fear and the apartment that you never entered, the life you never had to see. You understand and you're proud of Ragnar. *You're my hero,* you want to say. *How could you disappear to Berlin because of this?* No sooner have you thought that than footsteps ring out and your brother shuts your eye again. Break in transmission.

Like mineral water in a glass, when the bubbles rise and rise and there are fewer and fewer of them, that's what you're like, that's what your thoughts are like. You've just seen your brother, then the darkness came back, and now there's a new voice.

"From here."

"And your parents?"

"Slovenia."

"Do the Slovenians get on with the Serbs?"

"..."

"I asked you a question."

"I ... I don't know."

"You're Slovenian and you *don't know* if the Slovenians get on with the Serbs?"

"I'm from Berlin."

Pause.

Slowly you are beginning to understand. Your brother is looking for your daughter. He doesn't just want Taja, he wants the other girls too. Stink in particular. He doesn't yet know who the girls are. Not their names, and not their relationship to Taja.

That's fine.

The thing with the girls is personal, the rest is business.

Taja would never steal from you, you want to call out to Ragnar, *my daughter isn't like that.* But what do you know? You're dead, your self is just a vanishing bubble in a glass, what do you know?

Pause.

They leave the boy alone. He wants to be a hero and keeps his mouth shut. He's one of those idiots who think love can do anything, that it accomplishes everything and never fades.

Hey, look at me, you want to call out to him.

And your thoughts keep slipping away.

Pause.

You come back when your body slumps, the cold lets go of you and the dead tissue shifts. You're surprised that you can see again. Your left eye opened all by itself. The boy is walking along the pool as if looking for a second exit. Then the idiot actually takes out his phone.

"What? Hello? Why didn't you pick up? Of course I tried to warn you, but you're not ... What? No. Darian's father blew the deal and now I'm in the shit. They've got me, you know? They waited for me outside school and now I'm here in some sort of basement. They want to know who you are ... What? In a house with a swimming pool and the pool's full of drowned weed, if you can imagine that! No, they'll be back in a minute ... Darian's father, yeah ... Do you even know who that is? ... Then you can imagine the mood he's in, because his brother is sitting dead on this chair, and the drugs have disappeared. How could you steal his drugs, how could you do that? ... What? ... Don't worry, he won't see through me. He may be a tough guy, but no one messes with me. The way he walks around. Fucking pussy. He can't do a thing to me. If I tell him he's gay, he's gay, get it? Once I'm out of here he'll be cross-eyed for a week, for messing with me. Where are you now? ... No, thought not. Wait a second."

He goes quiet, he suddenly looks at you.

He knows I'm watching him.

The boy squats down in front of you. He says: *That's really creepy,* then he shuts your open eye, and that's it, that's the farewell, the bubble bursts, the train disappears around the bend and you can't see him anymore, you can't see anything anymore, because it's finished once and for all.

Over.

RAGNAR

The year after your father died you lived in various shared houses and didn't leave Berlin for as much as a day. You were a punk and a revolutionary, you were sixteen years old and deep in your heart hungry for the vile world and yet at the same time you despised it. It took you one year to summon the courage and call home. Oskar picked up after the second ring, as if he'd been waiting for your call. If your mother had come to the phone, you'd have hung up without a word.

"Hey, little brother, did you miss me?"

Oskar didn't think that was funny, he didn't think any of the things you said to him were funny. Your story sounded lame to his ears—that you were fed up with your father, that Berlin had always been your dream. *Being free means being alive.* You murmured something about how you were sorry for not calling before. Oskar said in the middle of your excuses, "He's dead."

No name, no title, just *he*. You knew you had to act surprised. It didn't work. You were you, there was no getting past it. So you just said *good* and felt relieved and had just one thought: *It's really true.*

A dog stopped by the phone booth, lifted its back leg, and peed against the glass. You kicked the windowpane, the dog jumped back with a start and left a zigzagging yellow trail on the pavement.

"How could you leave us alone?" your brother asked.

"I don't know."

"What sort of an answer is that?"

"If no one does anything, nothing happens," you answered.

Oskar hung up. Really, what sort of a stupid answer was that? You couldn't use that kind of revolutionary talk on your little brother, and anyway you'd got the phrase from a calendar. It was hardly original.

You called back. Oskar asked what you wanted this time. You apologized. He told you to shove your apology. You couldn't help laughing. Oskar had a big mouth for a thirteen-year-old, that's exactly what you said to him, even though you knew he turned fourteen a week ago. You wanted to irritate him, so that he'd be your brother again and not some insulted teenager snapping at you.

"Ragnar, I'm fourteen and you're an incredible asshole for somebody who's supposed to be my brother."

"Is that so?"

"That's so. And if my swearing bothers you, you can go fuck yourself."

Silence. You each listened to the other one breathing, then Oskar couldn't keep it up anymore and burst out laughing and you laughed with him. It was such a relief, it was so liberating, that at that moment you'd have given a lot to be there with him.

"I hate you."

"I know."

"How could you just disappear?"

"I'm sorry."

There was that silence again; this time it was you who broke it.

"Is he really dead?"

"Heart attack. They found him at another woman's house."

"What sort of woman?"

"No idea. He had another child. A boy. The bastard had two families, can you imagine that?"

You nodded and dodged his question.

"How's Mom?"

He told you everything, it was like a dam giving way under the pressure of the last year. You found out how they were living, how everything had changed since your father's death. About the friends who were allowed to come by. About the laughter that filled the apartment.

"Aunt Mara and Aunt Joos were there. Half of Norway visited us and you missed it, bro, you miss everything," said Oskar, and you wanted to yell at him: *I'm in fucking Berlin! I'm in the most happening place on the planet, so don't tell me I'm missing something!*

Oskar wanted to know when you were coming back, you explained that you didn't know, you had a job, you'd find a way, soon perhaps. It was another lie. You never wanted to see the dump of a place again. Oskar must have sensed as much. He never asked you that question again.

Over the next nine years the distance between you grew. After Oskar finished school, he and your mother moved to Norway and into the old beach hotel, which was already closed by then and urgently in need of renovation. Ulvtannen, the only beach hotel without a beach. Your mother had always dreamed of going back.

While your brother was starting a new life in Norway, you put down deep roots in Berlin. The jobs were pretty low-rent—handing out flyers, night shift at gas stations, part-time work on building sites, waiting tables, shelf stacking, delivering drinks and turning bratwursts at sausage stalls. There was no job too low for you, and perhaps it would have gone on like that forever, and one day you'd have got one of your angels pregnant. Family with dog and you, pushing a pram through the park and sitting in the bar with the guys in the evening—the infinitely free life of an unemployed person in Berlin who doesn't want anything more because he has so little and needs so little. It all ended the day Flipper stepped into your life.

The eighties were taking their last breath. You were twenty-three, and for a few months you'd been working in a video shop that kept banned movies under the counter and mostly survived on pirate copies. Flipper had just arrived from Vancouver, he was the distant cousin of a good friend, and was stopping off in Berlin for New Year's. In his early forties, he looked sixty and was so exhausted by life that he could barely keep his eyes open. Or as he put it: *God, I've seen so much that I have to take a break.* Flipper wasn't just the most exhausted man who ever crossed your path, he was also the very first dealer.

New Year's Eve 1989.

Your father had been under the ground for almost a decade, and the Wall was about to collapse. Berlin was in an ecstasy of freedom, and Germany didn't yet know that it would one day look at the East as a thing of the past.

The stream of people was endless. They came from everywhere, as if the whole eastern bloc had been emptied, as if Berlin was a swing door that anybody could go marching in and out of whenever they liked.

On every other day you thought the city was the most exciting place in the world, but on this particular New Year's Eve you felt displaced, perhaps not least because you were standing in a smoky pub at Görlitzer station, your mouth was full of blood, and you were listening to an old man who called himself Flipper spreading his life out in front of you.

You were miserable. That evening a particularly brutal dentist had extracted two of your wisdom teeth in an emergency operation, and your head felt like a blocked toilet that gasped for air every few minutes. Normally you would have been in bed ages ago, but stubbornness kept you on your feet. It was only New Year's Eve once a year. And you also enjoyed Flipper's company, even though you could only hear every third word over the noise.

Flipper would have had more fun with a glove puppet. You couldn't speak, you were pumped up with painkillers and weren't allowed to drink alcohol, but you were able to listen. And Flipper talked without interruption. About his life in Tunisia, about his drug experiences, the women and the various bones in his body that were broken. He showed you a scar on the back of his neck and described the knife that had nearly sawn his head off. He said he'd spent four years in an Italian jail, smuggled thousands of Mexican migrants into America, and if fate had anything left for him, he wanted to move to Alaska one day.

"Because of the cold, you know?"

It was the talk of an aging junkie who drank Metaxa and smoked nasty little cigarillos. At the time you had no idea who he really was. At the time you couldn't know that you'd be standing in tears by his grave three years later. Tears over Flipper, over you and your father, but especially over the feeling of having been abandoned.

Flipper stayed by your side the whole evening. He kept you

supplied with bags of ice and looked away when you spat blood into a plastic cup. The pub started to fill up at midnight, and you decided that a little bit of alcohol might back up the painkillers. It helped you over the next hour. You drank eight lemon vodkas and rinsed out the wound with the alcohol. You sucked on ice cubes and numbed the pain with the cold. After the hour you started feeling sick and dragged yourself outside.

Berlin was playing war.

The rain came down like a glittering curtain that was caught by the wind and whipped against the façades. People were standing on the balconies, throwing firecrackers and screaming like banshees. You watched fascinated as a group of drunks tried to pick the firecrackers up and throw them back before they went off. Wiener Strasse was packed. You didn't know where you wanted to go. After ten yards you staggered and nearly fell. Flipper supported you as you leaned between two parked cars. He held your head, kicked the hissing firecrackers away, and wiped the vomit from your mouth with the sleeve of his jacket. A stray rocket landed in the middle of the street, and for a few seconds you were lit up by a red light. Flipper grinned at you, looking like a devil that's just climbed out of a bloodbath. He took you to a house doorway, the air around you stank of sulfur and the rain on the pavement splashed up to your knees.

"Fucking New Year's Eve," said Flipper.

You didn't want to go back to the bar. You wanted to stand here all night inhaling the stench and the cold of the rain. Flipper smoked and looked down the street as if he weren't in Berlin but somewhere far away. Tijuana, Cairo, Rabat. His gray hair was woven into a plait, not a strand was out of place. You studied the wrinkles in his face, which, in the light of the flickering rockets, looked like streaks of mascara. And you swore never to look like that when you were forty. Flipper noticed your expression and smiled at you. His teeth were brilliant white.

"Everything okay?"

You nodded. You started to like the fact that you couldn't speak.

"Do you have a problem with coke?"

You shrugged; until now alcohol and marijuana had been your only sin, but if Flipper thought coke would do you good now, you'd be the last one to say no. It was a new year, new decisions needed to be made.

"I've got a package."

He took a drag on his cigarillo, the smoke puffed from him with every word he said.

"Could you store it for me?"

He spat.

"For a few days?"

You nodded again, and Flipper tousled your hair as if you were ten years old, and asked where you lived. Arm in arm you walked down Skalitzer Strasse. Your days as a squatter had come to an abrupt end a year before, when you met angel number 11. She was a nurse, the apartment was in her name, three rooms in an old building on Prinzenstrasse with a tiny balcony looking out over a courtyard.

"Better a view than no view," said Flipper and left the balcony door open. You heard the city, you heard the rain, and Flipper went on talking until nine in the morning. The pain in your mouth eased after an hour and you managed to speak too. It was your best conversation ever. Flipper was interested, he wanted to know everything about you; and you told him more than you'd ever told anyone. You also spoke about your father, particularly about your father.

"So you killed him," Flipper said at last.

You just looked at him, you didn't know what to say.

"It's fine," Flipper went on. "It's good to let it out. If you ask me, I forgive you. You'll have to do the rest yourself."

"There is nothing to forgive," you replied.

Flipper nodded as if he hadn't expected any other reply, then he said something that won't let go of you even today, something that gives you courage even in your most difficult moments.

"Your father would have done exactly the same. He would have shown you no mercy. You did the right thing."

Angel number 11 came home from emergency service at eight o'clock and made you scrambled eggs, then she said that it was time for sleep and took you to bed. Flipper fetched a blanket and made himself comfortable on the sofa. You slept until the afternoon and then met in the bathroom. Flipper was wearing your dressing gown and bore a strong resemblance to Christopher Lee.

"I've made us coffee," he said.

"How long have you been awake?"

"Ten minutes."

You took a shower, and then you drank the coffee. Flipper didn't once mention the package. He made two phone calls and went to the bathroom for half an hour. When the doorbell rang you opened up, but there was nobody there. A paper bag lay on the doormat.

"Good service."

Flipper stood behind you and pulled up the zipper of his trousers. He reached past you and picked the paper bag up off the floor, weighed it in one hand, and handed it to you. Then he took his lighter and the pack of cigarillos off the table, pulled his coat on, and said goodbye with a handshake.

"I've got to go now, be a good man."

It was the last time you saw him alive. The stench of his cigarillos lingered for four days in the apartment and clung firmly to the curtains and the sofa.

The package was in the bag. You didn't touch it, but put it in your closet and forgot all about it. You knew from the start what had to be done. Instinctively. Six weeks later Flipper called. It was three in the morning. Flipper was making a stopover in Vladivostok and wanted to ask if you could quickly deliver the package to Dahlem.

"Right now?"

"If you have nothing better to do."

You had nothing better to do, so you got on your bike and rode with the package thirteen kilometers to Dahlem. It was unbearably cold, but you enjoyed cycling through the sleeping city in February. It was wild, it was different, it was life.

That morning you met your second dealer. Marcel Tanner welcomed you with a cup of tea and a well-stuffed pipe. It was friendship at first sight, and Tanner became your mentor over the next few years, before he gave up dealing and became a partner in your firm. Since then you've kept things small, because small means safety, small is manageable. Your efforts paid off. Your company now has three partners, as well as an IT guy, a lab assistant, and two lawyers.

You grew into a little family, trusting each other and being closed off to the outside world. And even if you would never admit it, you were already acting along your father's lines. Everything begins and ends with discipline.

The boy in front of you knows what discipline is. The barrel is pressed against his head, his head yields slightly, the boy puts up no resistance and doesn't duck. He reminds you a little of yourself, when you finally stood up to your father and jutted your chin and took the blows and never showed any weakness. Weakness stirred up the fire in your father. Don't let him break you, don't bow the knee. *Bite, keep biting.* Without a bite you'd never have ended up in Berlin, you'd still be sitting in that dump of a house and you'd be one more idiot who was afraid of his father and of life in general.

Perhaps it's the similarity, or perhaps it's the fact that you've already been standing for two minutes beside this boy, holding a gun to his head—eventually the threat loses its effect.

You lower the gun.

The boy doesn't move, he keeps his head at an angle, still suspicious.

Like Oskar and me.

You feel a tingle down your spine and have the feeling your brother's watching you from the chair. *He's dead, he can't see anything anymore,* you say to yourself, and wonder what kind of waves his death will make, and who you're going to have to inform. There are a lot of people who need to know. What are you going to say to them? How are you going to explain this business here?

"Everything okay?" asks Tanner.

You nod, you are so far away in your thoughts that it's shaming. If your dead brother knew what you were thinking about right now, he'd probably come back from the dead to strangle you. Nothing can be made good. And even though you know that, you wish you could casually take out your phone and call Majgull. You miss hearing her voice. She'd know what needed to be done. She'd be a great help to you.

Two years after the Wall came down, your business was flourishing and you'd started working with couriers. Whether it was drugs, guns, or antiques, the product itself didn't matter. You were responsible for the logistics of the operation, and you were one of the best. You'd worked your way up to a position that allowed you to control the market from the background. If someone wanted security for their goods, they didn't get past you. Even in those days you were consistent and hungry in whatever you did. You dictated the rules, no one broke them. Without consistency and hunger you'd have gone on working in the video store.

1992 turned out to be a golden year. Your company had established itself, your contacts extended as far as Australia, and the Asian market was waiting to do business with you. Even in private you couldn't complain. You were with angel number 14. Her name was Helen, she was pregnant, and in the middle of May she would become Darian's mother. The world seemed full of positive surprises, your brother's phone call was definitely one of them. Oskar had had enough of the distance between you, and took a step in your direction.

He invited you to his wedding.

You knew from your few telephone conversations that he'd met a woman, but you had no idea that he was so serious about it. You hadn't seen your brother for eleven years. It was mainly your fault. You stayed away from him for purely intuitive reasons. Perhaps you were just afraid of introducing him to the new Ragnar. Who knows. At any rate no one could have known how fatal a meeting between you two would be after such a long time. It was a mistake you should never have made. You were spontaneous.

Your brother's invitation came at exactly the right time. The success was stressful. You needed a break. Tanner was the only one who put it quite openly: "No phone calls, no questions, no Berlin. Be a stranger in a strange land, I'll deal with everything else."

You took the car. There were three ferries a day from Rostock to Trelleborg. You stood at the railing and thought about the past few years. The company, your pregnant angel, your successes. Taking stock was very cleansing. *I'm going to be a father,* you thought and wondered how that was going to work out. When the ferry landed, you crossed Sweden without a break and only stopped beyond the border, to spend the night on Norwegian soil.

You didn't know what you'd been expecting on your first night. Perhaps a moment of enlightenment, your long-dead ancestors' drunken, jovial voices calling to you, something like that.

It didn't happen, it was a night like any other. The next morning, though, you were filled with a pleasant feeling of calm that stayed with you all the way to the far north. It was important to you to drive the whole way yourself. It was your own kind of meditation. Being alone. Without anyone else's thoughts.

Of course you missed the road to the beach hotel, it would have been too perfect otherwise. You ended up in the little town of Lunnis and asked a boy sitting on the edge of a well with a skinny dog on a leash. The boy jumped down from the well, pulled you around the corner, and pointed to a cliff that looms beside the town like the angry, fist-clenched arm of a giant.

"Ulvtannen!" said the boy.

You looked up, and there was nothing but a rough, rocky wall.

Oskar hadn't been lying: the hotel could only be glimpsed from the fjord.

Who knows, perhaps your ancestors had a warped sense of humor and thought the fjord might eventually climb to the edge of the cliff and then the hotel would actually be a beach hotel. Or else they thought the pebble beach at the bottom of the cliff was enough of a lure for tourists. Whatever your ancestors thought, they refused to be deterred and built a beach hotel on top of the cliff that looks like a grand building from colonial times.

You sat back down in the car and found the right road.

Like something out of a fairy tale, was your first thought when after the final bend the hotel appeared in front of you. A massive Nordmann fir stood to the left of it, casting a shadow on the façade. It reminded you that once upon a time only fir trees had stood here, a whole forest of them. What a view that must have been—hundreds of fir trees stirring in the wind.

Home.

The hotel had gone out of business in the late seventies. The family had scattered around the world and didn't want to invest any more money in the old building. You only knew the hotel from photographs. Your father had never shown any interest in taking you and your brother to your mother's birthplace. Oskar had done fantastic work. Since his arrival in Norway four years ago, your brother had been working on saving the hotel. He had painted the façade, put in new pipes and wiring, and replaced the roof.

It was a new start. The hotel had never looked so good in photographs.

You parked in the driveway and got out. You were just taking your luggage out of the trunk when the double doors flew open, and there he was. If you'd met him on the street, you wouldn't have recognized him. Up until that moment the twelve-year-old Oskar had lived on in your head, the little brother who stole your comic books and pressed himself inconspicuously against your side so that you would protect him against the world.

"Ragnar!"

It was a good feeling to hug him.

It was like coming home.

The beach hotel has twelve rooms spread over the second and third floors. The rooms look out on the water, and a terrace runs around each of the floors like a belt. If you stand on the terrace and look down, the fjord looks up at you.

Your mother lived on the first floor, your brother had converted the second floor for himself and his fiancée. He had knocked walls through and turned the individual bedrooms into airy spaces. The third floor was almost untouched by renovation. You found the only finished room and stood on the terrace for a while, looking down at the fjord before you went to see your mother.

She immediately burst into tears and rushed to touch you as if to see whether you were real. She didn't scold you. She kept repeating over and over how much you looked like your father. It wasn't a flattering comparison, but you didn't say anything.

You couldn't have known that day that a tumor was already spreading in your mother's abdomen. She had eight months to live. Your second visit to Ulvtannen was for her funeral.

After dinner you walked with Oskar down the winding road

into Lunnis. You were introduced to friends and acquaintances and understood hardly a word. Your Norwegian was atrophied, and you had to answer in English. You liked the people, they welcomed you like a prodigal son, but you had quite different problems. No one could tell how this idyll depressed you. It was raining, and the fjord was a threatening shadow. Oskar told you he couldn't imagine living anywhere else. He loved the hotel and the morning mist on the water, he even liked the work—four days a week he drove to the hydraulic power station in Vik, where he had met his Majgull.

"I don't need anything more to live," he said.

Majgull's home was a farm two miles from Lunnis. The family greeted you warmly, a dog jumped up at you, a little boy hugged your left leg and wouldn't let go. Everyone gathered around you in a big living room, aquavit was served and you clinked glasses, answered questions, and then, out of nowhere, fire broke out. You'd never have expected it. You knew the situation from movies and books. You felt unprotected and naked. One glance was enough, and you went up in flames like a bundle of twigs.

Majgull.

Even today you don't think anyone noticed. Not your glances, not the horror in your eyes as she stood opposite you, her hair still wet and her skin red from the shower, with an almost invisible film of sweat on her upper lip. As certain as you are even today that no one noticed, you are equally certain that Majgull alone saw through you right away. She sensed the danger. She sensed your hunger.

"Ragnar," you introduced yourself.

"Majgull," she said and hesitated briefly before leaning in as if to tell you a secret. Her voice was quiet, her words, in English, were meant only for you.

"So you're the one who killed his father."

It wasn't a question, it was a statement. You didn't react, you just looked at her as a clear thought sped like a ricochet through your head: *Oskar knows.* Majgull let go of your hand and turned to your brother. They laughed, he threw his arms around her, and that was all it took, you lowered your gaze almost blinded by their sight and from that moment on you tried to stay out of Majgull's way.

Two days, you thought, *then I'll be gone.*

Oskar didn't mention your father's death and you were clever enough to avoid the subject. Everything between you seemed to have been resolved, and that was how you wanted it to stay.

The ballroom of the hotel was prepared for the wedding day. Since breakfast a band had been practicing hits from the 1960s, and you told Oskar that you had a few calls to make in private. At the time Oskar still thought you were in the building trade. Like father, like son.

You strolled along the fjord. The weather had turned, and the landscape suddenly glowed in a completely new light. You sat in the grass for two hours, looked down at the water, and began to understand Oskar. If you didn't want much, you had more than enough right here.

She was sitting with her bridesmaids on a meadow that you only walked across because you thought it was a shortcut to Ulvtannen. The women were like Sirens waiting for a lonely seafarer. You landed among them like a ship in distress. A rapture of femininity enfolded you. And in the midst of them was Majgull. And in the midst was Majgull.

They offered you things to eat and drink. Their rudimentary English aroused you, their words alone were enough to seduce you. There was so much warmth, and for the first time in your life you became aware that a man needs more than one woman around him.

To try out everything, to miss nothing.

When you had eaten and drunk and were about to go, the bridesmaids told you that the first man who meets the bride with her retinue is the last man the bride kisses before she's given away.

"You have to do this, please, please, please!" the bridesmaids begged you, and your fate was sealed.

Yours, Majgull's, and your brother's.

Majgull's lips pressed firm and hard on yours, then for a second they softened and you looked into her eyes, clear and open and watching as you watched her. The bridesmaids applauded. Majgull touched your arm as if in thanks, then she laughed, and that laughter did send her breath into your mouth.

You still clearly remember that.

Her breath in your mouth.

The ceremony was held in Hopperstad church in Vikøyri. It was cramped and musty, thirty people tried to cram themselves into a historical wooden building that should have fallen in on itself over a hundred years ago. You leaned against one of the pillars and didn't understand a word of the ceremony. You struggled not to stare openly at Majgull. Your hands were behind your back, you didn't want anybody to see your fists.

Afterward the guests drove in a convoy to Ulvtannen, they parked in all directions on the cliff, it looked chaotic, it looked beautiful. Strings of lights and garlands were stretched all over the place, children were running around, the music could be heard all the way to Lunnis. You were barely aware of the party. You drank, you ate. One of the bridesmaids flirted with you, another tried to make you drink homemade aquavit, and again and again Oskar appeared by your side, beaming with joy, putting his arm around your shoulders and saying how happy he was to have you there.

"It wouldn't be real without you."

You left at dawn, when everyone was still asleep. There was mist on the water again, the garlands rustled in the wind, no one encountered you, no one stood and waved at one of the windows. You left a short message. Work calls. Hope to see you soon. And you wished the couple the very best.

Over the next few weeks you headed further north to lose yourself in loneliness. No one knows anything from that time, and no one must know. Your thoughts revolved around that woman who now belonged to your brother. You didn't think about your pregnant angel. Not for a second.

———

On your return to Berlin you were a different person. You plunged into your work with controlled rage, and stopped imagining any kind of future with Majgull. You didn't plan to involve yourself any further in your brother's life. Darian was born in the middle of May, and you became part of a new family.

When your mother died three days after Christmas, you went back to Norway. This time you borrowed Tanner's jeep. A dark winter landscape embraced you, it matched your thoughts. The hotel looked far too inviting, the snow too white.

You spent only one night in Ulvtannen. Oskar didn't leave your side the whole time, which was quite good. It made it easier for you to stay out of Majgull's way. She must have sensed as much, because she let you brothers have your space. You grieved, you drank yourselves into oblivion and got into a fight in a pub. The next morning you carried your mother to the grave, and then you put on your sunglasses and set off for home. You wanted to mourn in private. You drove through Norway without taking a break. Your decision was made: no matter what, you would never come back. It was a pledge. Your family was waiting for you. Your son, your wife. And for a while your life went smoothly again, and it looked as if you no longer had any dreams. For a while you were the hungriest person in a world of the sated.

"Can I go now?"

The words pull you out of your thoughts. You look at the boy who lied to you openly and who wanted to go now. You know he called the girl. You heard what he said about you. You ask him, "Do you know what seriously pisses me off about little fuckers like you?"

He shrugs, and again there's that martyr's smile. If you were thirty years younger, you'd fight him. You tell him what you think of him and his generation, but your words lack fire, you're not really interested in this boy anymore. End it now, enough's enough.

You ask him for his cell phone.

"I haven't got a—"

"ARE YOU TRYING TO MESS WITH ME? GIVE ME YOUR FUCKING CELL PHONE RIGHT NOW!"

He takes it out of his back pocket and is about to hand it to you when he realizes why you want it. His arm swings back, Leo is faster.

"Let go."

Leo takes the phone and steps back again. The boy is uncertain. He's probably wondering if everything's okay again now. Then comes the understanding. He has spotted the connection—the girls, the drugs, the swimming pool, and of course his own part in this story, it all makes sense. His lies, his truth, his pathetic little life. Everything. And that makes him step back, his chair tips over and clatters along the ground, if he could he would run. You don't move from the spot, you read his eyes, every reaction is predictable. He wants to say something, but it's too late for that. You raise the gun and shoot him in the head.

"Well?"

Leo frowns and hands you the boy's phone. The last number dialed is linked to a name.

"Stink?"

"Must be some sort of nickname," says Leo.

You call the number. It rings six times, then you hear a rustle, someone shouts, someone laughs, you recognize her voice immediately, she says, "Girls, will you shut up, I can't hear anything. Hello? Mirko?"

"Hello, Stink," you say.

Silence, the background noises have faded away. She knows now that you're not the boy. She probably knows who's talking to her.

"We had a deal," you remind her.

"Fuck the deal."

"I'll find you. You can try and hide, but I'll find you."

"I told you, you don't scare me."

"You little—"

"Asshole," she says and cuts you off.

PART TWO

I

I'm riding faster than a million
miles per hour
with the motorcycle angels

Kid Loco
MOTORCYCLE ANGELS

THE TRAVELER

We've heard a lot about you and got to know you a little better, but we still don't know where you come from and why you exist. Let's go back a bit. Back to the day when you first discovered that the world turns differently as soon as you take a step outside of reality.

It is December.
   It is 1976.
   It is late afternoon.

A family's having dinner, while outside the winter rages and the streets suffocate beneath the snow with silent resignation. No sounds of cars, no playing children, even the dogs aren't barking at each other on the pavements. Father and son sit silently at the table. Mother leans over the stove. She never sits down. She'd prefer to eat later on her own, because she'll have more peace then. She says. Your mother, your father, you. You are aware that your parents haven't got on for years. They endure one another. Your father sleeps on the sofa. Your mother locks herself in the bathroom. In public they're two shadows that never touch. In the house they act as if one or the other of them is in a bad mood, as if you kids don't understand what's playing out in front of you. They don't believe in divorce. Divorce is for losers. Your father's a winner. He wouldn't dream of letting your mother go. You sit facing one another at the dinner table. Your mother on your right, your sister on your left. Her chair is empty today. She's at dance class. She's allowed to turn up late.

"Sit down, now," says your father, and your mother ignores him and lights a cigarette. She leans against that bloody stove as if she couldn't stand up on her own. You wish they'd yell at each other. It would be nice if your mother won for once. A lot of things would be easier.

The news reaches you when your sister comes back from her dance class. You know when you hear her running along the corridor. The pace of her footsteps, her toneless panic. It's only when she's standing in the doorway that she says, "Robbie's dead!"

Your father looks at you startled, as if you'd said the words. Your mother throws her hands to her mouth, her cigarette slips from her fingers. You lower your eyes because you can't think how to react. You watch the end of the cigarette slowly burning a hole into the linoleum. When you look up, your father is still looking at you, startled.

Ten minutes later. Your father is shoveling the snow from the drive. He doesn't need to do it, you could walk easily across the garden to the Danisch house, but your father needs an excuse. He stalls. He scatters sand. He puts the shovel in the garage. He shuts the garage. He comes into the house. Your mother spoke to Robbie's mother on the phone; your help is needed. You sit in your room and watch the snow pelting the window like a raging swarm of insects. Your parents are talking downstairs. You hear them through the door. Perhaps they'll forget about you.

Your sister looks in and asks if you're coming or what? You get up, push past her, and hear your father say, "This isn't for me."

"What does that mean, this isn't for me?"

"It means what it means."

"But Karen and Thomas are our friends."

"They are not my friends. They are neighbors."

"How can you . . ."

They break off when you come downstairs. Your sister close

behind you. You hear her humming quietly. She always hums when she's anxious.

"You go on ahead," says your father and disappears into the living room.

His boots stand like twin stumps in the corridor. The snow under the soles is firm and lumpy and refuses to melt. Your mother opens the front door and slings the boots outside. The TV comes on in the living room. You want to join him. You wish they'd actually pull knives on each other. And now your father's free to win.

"Coward," you hear your mother mutter.

"What's wrong with Daddy?" your sister asks.

"He's tired," your mother replies.

"I'm tired too," your sister says with a glassy look in her eyes as if there were tears that couldn't get out. Your sister is seven, Robbie was thirteen. Your mother wants you both to put on something black. You go upstairs and get changed.

"What's that?"

You look down at yourself. Your only black sweater is the one with Jaws on the front. Its mouth is wide open.

"You're not serious."

"It's the only one I've got."

"If Robbie's parents see you like that, they'll get . . ."

Your mother breaks off, puts her hand in front of her mouth, and shakes her head as if she doesn't know what to say. You go back into your room and get a dark blue sweater out of the wardrobe.

"Better?"

Your mother stands at the window blowing her nose with her back to you. She couldn't really give a damn about the sweater. In the reflection in the window you see that her eyes are shut. From somewhere there comes the sound of your sister humming. You want to check on her, but you know your mother has to let you go first.

"I don't want to lose you," you hear her saying, as if that had anything to do with anything.

It's terrible. The Danisches are sitting side by side on the sofa, looking miserable. Aunty Henna has come. She's nobody's aunt. She lives two streets away and everybody calls her Aunty. She's always there if you need her. The women say Aunty Henna buried her husband in the cellar because she wanted to keep him to herself. You think that's a lie. Aunty Henna's too good-looking for that. She's got no shortage of men running after her, she doesn't need to bury one in the cellar.

Aunty Henna brings coffee and schnapps and talks quietly. She says all the things the Danisches would say if they were talking to your parents. It's like listening to the radio. After half an hour Frau Danisch leaves the room and goes upstairs. Your mother follows her. After less than a minute, Frau Danisch's grieving wails are heard. You get goose bumps. Everyone else pretends they haven't heard. You drink your fourth cup of coffee and wish you could stick your finger down your throat. Your sister has curled up like a cat on one of the armchairs, she is fast asleep. Aunty Henna tops up your coffee. Herr Danisch holds his hand over his empty cup. He says he has enough. You wish you could creep under the table so that everyone would forget you. It has a glass top. Herr Danisch would see you. He wouldn't forget you. He'd ask you what you were doing there. You drink your coffee. You can't think of anything better to do.

Herr Danisch goes out onto the terrace. You follow him. Snow has collected on the roof. The terrace looks as if someone's dipped it in a glass of milk. The covered pool is the same as ever. It's a mystery to you. It should have changed. You swam in it only recently, you chased each other from one end to the other, while the snow raged around you, and all of a sudden the pool is taboo, even though nothing about it has changed. If you narrow your eyes, you can see Robbie. Arms spread, facedown, naked and motionless.

Nothing.

"I wish we'd never built that pool," Herr Danisch says and turns the switch. The roof slides slowly sideways. Snow comes pelting through the gap and dissolves on the surface of the water.

"It's the best pool in the whole city," you say, and your words are as hollow and empty as the space your brain is sitting in.

"I know, Robbie said the same thing," says Herr Danisch and turns away, without closing the roof again. Snow drifts onto your face, snow is everywhere. The water steams. Robbie turned the temperature up for you this morning. You'd like to turn the switch and watch the roof closing silently again. Like a weary eye. Like your thoughts, if you could think. But you don't dare touch the switch. You don't know if Herr Danisch would go completely nuts.

You hear him saying from the living room: "It happened quickly."

And Aunty Henna replies, "He didn't suffer."

And the sound of Robbie's mother howling comes from upstairs.

"Here."

Your father's come after all. He's shaved and says he's sorry, it took him a while to pull himself together.

"Delayed response time," he calls it, and Herr Danisch nods and shakes his hand. Later the two men will withdraw to the den and sit on two stools and pass a bottle back and forth. Whiskey or vodka or brandy. You know the Danisch family's alcohol supply. You know which pile of books it's hidden behind. You and Robbie drank half the vodka and filled it up with water. The men won't notice. Herr Danisch will tell your father how guilty he feels. He'll look for a pickaxe to destroy the pool. Your father will restrain him. Later. Later isn't now. Now your father's eyes are fixed on you, just as they were when your sister came storming into the house with news of Robbie's death. You know your father's problem. He imagines it had been you. There in the pool. As if something like that would happen to you. Your mother thinks the same thing. They barely communicate now, but when they do, it's on a shared wavelength.

"Go on, have some."

Your father holds a beer bottle out to you. You're too young to drink beer. Thirteen's too young. Coffee's okay, beer's taboo. But the death of the neighbor boy makes your father look at you with different eyes. He doesn't know how old you'll get. From today, anything is possible. Drink.

"Thanks."

You sip at it and then turn the bottle in your hands the way you've seen people doing it on television. Your sister has woken up, she is drinking Coke. What you wouldn't give for a Coke right now.

You're standing by the big plate-glass window. You thought everyone would balk at the idea of looking at the pool. But everybody's looking at it. They're looking at it as if something was suddenly going to happen and time was going to reverse itself, as if Robbie might rise unharmed from the water. The snow pelts through the roof. You wish it would fall more gently. But the snow doesn't want to fall. It's just pelting.

"I still can't believe it," Herr Danisch says quietly, pulling his upper lip into his mouth. All of you are reflected in the window. Your sister turns away first and switches on the television. Aunty Henna whispers to her that that's not quite decent. Your sister tells her what series is about to come on. Aunty Henna says: *Well, if that's the case.* You keep watching the room in the reflection. You keep watching your father on your left and Herr Danisch on your right. No one mentions what's happened. You shut your eyes. Like a jackknife. Like a door. Like a grave that's being sealed.

Dennis waits for you before school the next day and asks, "What happened?"

"Nothing."

"What do you mean nothing?"

You try to walk on, but he grabs you by the arm and drags you into a doorway. Your winter jackets rub against each other and make a whispering sound, as if sharing a secret.

"What do you mean nothing?" Dennis repeats, and presses you against the wall and pushes his forearm against your throat so that you have to stand on tiptoe.

"Don't fuck with me!" he says menacingly, and you can clearly see the fear in his eyes and hear it in his words, and you can smell the smell of fear in his mouth, too.

"If you fuck with me, I'll kill you."

"It . . . was . . . nothing," you manage to say.

Dennis lets go of you, takes a step back, and runs off.

Robbie used to come out with these sayings. He said things like *Not every open door is a way in,* or *He who sees much light, casts a shadow.* At school he was dismissed as a weirdo. The girls liked him because he was always paying them compliments that they never really understood but which always made them laugh. He said: *The way you smell is the way I'd like to dream.* Or *When you laugh, the sun shuts an eye.* The boys told each other that his mother had been X-rayed once too often when she was pregnant. The girls swore it had something to do with the tap water.

You liked Robbie. Perhaps because you drank the same tap water, or perhaps you thought you understood his sayings. He talked a lot of nonsense, but that's better than being quiet. Quiet like you. Like a fish.

Now the seat next to you in the classroom is free, and everybody avoids looking at it. The teachers don't pick you either. You're invisible, because Robbie's invisible. If you got up and left now, no one would say a thing. It's a good feeling. You've always dreamt of it. Being invisible. Two days before Christmas. Like an angel hiding in its angel state. You'd walk through the city and eat what you liked. You'd read comics without buying them, go to the movies for nothing, and feel girls up whenever you felt like it.

Simple as that.

Over the blackboard dangles a Christmas star one of the girls has made. On the right of the door there's a photograph of Robbie. Your classroom teacher has pinned it on some cardboard, and you're allowed to write your names around the photograph. It reminds you of your sister's autographed cast when she fell on a skiing holiday. Six weeks later, the plaster came off and ended up in the trash. Your sister cried for an afternoon because she wanted to save the signatures. You imagine your classroom teacher giving the photograph, cardboard and all, to Robbie's parents. You can clearly see them stuffing the cardboard into the trash can. They'll probably keep the photograph.

Once Robbie tangled with a guy from the senior class. He was a rocker with hair down to his ass, who'd sprayed beer all over the place at the last school party and sold hand-rolled cigarettes at break time. Robbie had no respect. He had this way of looking askance at people so that they thought one of their legs was too short or something. The rocker noticed this and asked Robbie what he wanted. He asked what Robbie thought about minding his own damned business. Robbie shrugged and said: *Lots of hair on the head don't make a hairdo yet.* The rocker just stood there as if someone had pulled his plug out. And Robbie turned away and never so much as looked at the rocker again. He knew what was good for him. He never went too far. He wasn't stupid. If he was challenged, he said: *No, leave it be, or do you think a snowman pees on the fire?* And he would laugh. He was good at laughing, you always thought.

Two girls come up to you in the playground at break time. They ask how you're coping, whether you saw him there in the pool and what sort of feeling it is, you had been friends and everything, after all, it must be a weird feeling, isn't it? And while they're talking you watch their breath, which detaches itself from their lips in wispy clouds and comes together in the air, and you wonder what it would be like if you breathed in one of those clouds of breath, would you know what they'd eaten or drunk or thought over the past few hours? Maybe every cloud of breath is a scrap of soul. If that was so, you'd suck the air out of their lungs in tiny portions to make them shut up for a while.

During second break you stay in the classroom. The school principal shoos a group of boys downstairs and ignores you. You're standing by the window again, you're invisible. It's lonely being invisible on your own. It's a bit like standing wet in the rain. It doesn't make sense.

You cut the last period and go home. You stand up in the middle of class and walk out the door. The teacher doesn't even look at you. It's a good feeling. You're the last soldier of the winter. Christmas will only take place if you want. You don't know what you want. Your mother is over at the Danisches' again, your sister's at school, you shut the front door and you're alone.

"I'm alone," you say, and switch the receiver to the other ear. "We need to talk."

"No."

"If you don't come I'm going to the cops."

"Oh Christ, shit."

Dennis hangs up and you know he'll come. You stand by the window and wait. As you do so, you touch your stinging throat and remember the fear. Everything hides in the eyes, the mouth, the words. Fury and fear and desire. Dennis will weaken. You've seen it before. And if Dennis weakens, everything will collapse. Like a house of cards. Like ice after a long winter. Or like a lie when it meets the truth.

You know each other from the neighborhood. Dennis and Robbie and you. Dennis is two years older. Last summer he took your pocket money in return for letting you touch his cousin. Cousin Rita. And once you spent the night at Dennis's, and he went on and on until you jerked each other off. It was okay as long as you kept your eyes shut and imagined it was Beate from your class. After that Robbie made his jokes, of course. That was when it got embarrassing. And Dennis said Robbie should take a breather, or would he rather take a fist in the face? And Robbie waved him away, as he always waved people away, and kept his mouth shut. Dennis and Robbie and you. You know each other from the neighborhood.

You look at your watch. You need something to counteract the fear in Dennis's eyes. You want to steal his words, leaving him breathless. Anything to keep the fear at bay. You have to convince him there's something worse than an elbow that cuts off air. Something worse than a fist delivering pain.

In your father's den you find exactly the right hammer. It has a hard plastic head and it's as heavy as if it were made of iron. That'll be enough. You take the hammer upstairs and hide it under one of the sofa cushions. You're looking at your watch again when the doorbell rings.

"Come in."

"I don't know."

"Come in, Dennis."

He pushes past you and stands uncertainly in the corridor. He's half a head taller than you, he has no cause for concern.

"Sit down."

Dennis follows you into the living room and sits down. On the edge of the armchair, his eyes darting. You see the wet trails his boots have left on the floor. You'll have to wipe that up later, or your mother will go crazy. Dennis is uneasy. His winter jacket squeaks. You're glad you're not wearing your jacket. You're no longer the same. He's him, you're you.

"What do you want to talk about?" he asks.

"No one's to know anything."

"Sure."

"I don't want you freaking out, Dennis."

"What are you saying, what the hell are you saying?"

"I said I didn't want you freaking out."

"Are you out of your mind? I had nothing to do with it."

"That's exactly what I mean."

"What?"

You pull the hammer out from under the sofa cushion. You don't take your eyes off Dennis. You lean forward and break his elbow with a single blow. It's as easy as answering a question.

It was the second time that year that heavy snowfall had brought the city to a standstill and school was shut. Robbie rang shortly after breakfast and said the water was hot and his parents were away and anyone who wouldn't like to be in a heated pool on a day like this in the middle of winter had a dick like a caraway cat. You had no idea what sort of dick a caraway cat had, you were not even sure if a cat like that existed, but you and Dennis went straight over to the Danisch house.

It was a dream. You opened the roof and lay in the warm water, the icy wind swept over you and froze the tips of your hair, while the snowflakes settled on your faces like a shower of cold kisses. At that point the snow was a treasure that the sky was gently spitting down on you.

You swam naked, you chased each other the full length of the pool and played cockhunting. The hunter had to catch one of the others and tug his cock, then he was free and the other guy became the hunter. It was your turn, and according to the rules you weren't allowed to leave the pool.

Dennis and Robbie jumped screeching over you into the water, and you followed their bare backsides as if they were light-buoys. Robbie was small and agile and incredibly quick. Every time you caught him, you heard one of his sayings.

"A few planks in the fireplace don't make a forest."

"Not every spirit is a bottle."

"He who has lots in his head need not care about gravity."

Dennis laughed at the sayings. At first. But when he was the hunter, and Robbie slipped away from him, Dennis slowly started losing his temper.

"Just shut your trap!" he yelled.

Robbie said, "Not every deep well has good water."

You wanted to warn Robbie, you wanted to remind him that a snowman doesn't pee on the fire, but you kept your mouth shut, because it was a game, it was fun, and you'd had a lot of trouble catching Robbie yourself. You liked the fact that Dennis was suffering a bit as well.

"One more saying and then—" he said and broke off.

"Then what?" Robbie asked in reply and psyched himself up at the edge of the pool, fists pressed to his side, chin jutting defiantly. His dick had shrunk from the cold and looked like a nut with a nose. You stood in front of him shivering. You could have gone on playing cockhunting all day, because the cold didn't matter to you as long as you knew that warmth awaited you in the pool. The anticipation was better than the game itself.

"You want to know what comes next?" asked Dennis.

Robbie nodded.

"A punch in the face, that's what comes next."

"What a spoilsport you are," said Robbie and jumped over Dennis in a high arc. He reemerged at the other end of the pool, long before Dennis had even reached the middle of the pool.

"What was that?" asked Robbie. "Did you even move?"

"Just shut your mouth," Dennis called to him, "or I'll stuff it for you, okay?"

Robbie stayed in the water. He spread his arms and rested them on either side of him, on the edge of the pool. He thought. He tried very hard, this one wasn't off the cuff, he wanted to outdo all the sayings in the world.

"Four inches," he said sagely. "Four inches is a short end."

Dennis leans whimpering against the wall, hugging his elbow. You're sitting on the sofa again, and everything's set out. A splint, a bandage, and a few of the painkillers that your mother always takes when she has a particularly bad period.

"How . . . how could you . . . oh Christ, my . . . my fucking arm!"

Dennis is now younger than you. Weaker. He fears you. You hope that fear is going to keep growing.

"Not a word," you say.

"You fucking . . ."

"Not a word," you say again.

The rubber hammer lies on the coffee table between you. You see Dennis staring at it.

"If you like, I can break your other arm too," you suggest, and Dennis bites his lower lip and goes on quietly whimpering.

He chased Robbie diagonally across the pool. Not pausing, not playing. As he did so, Dennis started climbing out of the water, completely ignoring the rules. But Robbie was still uncatchable. It could have gone on forever. When Robbie swam past you again, you finally grabbed him. It happened, it needed no explanation, your instinct told you: *Grab him.*

Dennis uttered a cry of triumph and came crawling over.

"Don't do anything stupid," said Robbie and tried to escape from your clutches.

"I want a saying," you said.

Dennis came closer and closer.

Robbie started flailing with his fists.

You gripped him tighter.

"I don't know any," he said.

"Just one saying, Robbie," you repeated and laughed, because it was stupid, it was really stupid, and yet it was important to you to hear a saying right here, right now. Robbie was the wordmaster. It was a mystery to you how he could always have a ready saying on his lips. He never repeated himself. Once he claimed it was the Chinese blood in his veins. And he had crossed his fingers, because of course there were no Chinese people in his family.

"Come on," you urged him. "A saying and I'll let you go right away."

Robbie closed his eyes, concentrated, and said, "If a cat was a horse . . ."

He got no further than that. Dennis caught up with you, and Dennis was furious.

"Say that again," he demanded.

Robbie turned around.

"What?"

Dennis thumped him on the ear, there was a splash, water sprayed on your face, Robbie's ear turned red.

"Say that again," said Dennis.

"The one about the well?"

"The one about my cock, you moron."

"I didn't say—"

Another slap, water spraying up, Robbie pulled a face, your hands were still tightly gripping his upper arms. The snow was tattooing your face so that he had to narrow his eyes slightly.

"That's enough," said Robbie suddenly sober and looked at you. At you, as if you were the one who had hit him. You hadn't. So you grinned and said, "Give me a saying first."

"Let me go!"

"Say that again," said Dennis and hit him again.

From that moment Robbie started seriously kicking out around him. You held him tight, Dennis ducked Robbie's head under the water, let him come back up again, and said, "Four inches, hmm, did you say four inches?"

"Did I?"

"Four inches, I heard it, or didn't I?"

"He who asks many questions," Robbie panted, "has no sense of humor."

You exploded with laughter, panic, and nerves. Your blood

was boiling. Dennis ducked Robbie's head under the water again. Your excited blood made you sweat in the water. Robbie kicked out, caught you on the hip, and surfaced again. You couldn't stop laughing.

"Just give me a saying," you said, "one saying and you're free."

You liked this game much more than cockhunting. You liked it because you had a tight hold on Robbie and because you liked Dennis—in his rage and desperation. There were days when you liked Dennis more than Robbie. Days like this. Dennis never laughed when you had an orgasm and wouldn't open your eyes. He understood that you were dreaming about girls. He always said: *Just shut your eyes, it'll feel better.* And Robbie always said: *Just don't come on my shirt, dude.*

Robbie spat in your face, and at last it was your turn to duck his head under.

It went back and forth, back and forth, and you drifted away from the edge of the pool. Robbie was getting weaker, his eyes rolled, he gasped for air. And when Dennis said that was enough, you asked for a saying for the thousandth time, and nothing occurred to Robbie, nothing at all, so you wrapped your legs around his hips and held him tightly in your arms.

And you went under like that.

And Dennis cleared off.

And Robbie and you, you went under.

Just like that.

Dennis doesn't speak. His chin quivers, his eyes are glazed, he has taken three of the tablets. You wonder what his gaze would be like if you'd forced him to swallow them all.

"This stays strictly between us," you say at the door.

Dennis can't look at you. Tears are running down his cheeks. It isn't because of the pain, and it isn't because of Robbie. He's crying out of fear, fear of you.

"Good," you say and close the door.

After that you hid in the snow. You watched Robbie's corpse drifting in the middle of the pool. His butt was paler than his back, his shoulder blades were like narrow hills, and his hair fanned around his head as if it had a life of its own. You were glad he was lying facedown in the water. The snow surrounded him like a raging curtain. Fine mist rose from his back. As if his body could only breathe through its skin now. As if his soul was dissolving into haze.

His mother's car stopped with a crunch of gravel in the drive. She got out. Her footsteps on the way stirred the snow awake. She carried the shopping into the kitchen, and then her voice rang out. She called Robbie's name. She couldn't have known that she would never call his name again. And then she came to the big window that led down to the terrace, and spotted Robbie in the pool. You waited until she spotted him. It had to happen. You couldn't just leave Robbie alone. And when his mother screamed, you hauled yourself up out of the snow and went home.

It's the night after. After Robbie, after Dennis, after you. You crept off and climbed over the garden fence. The key hung on a hook beside the door to the terrace. You got undressed and put your clothes neatly on a chair. The water is lukewarm.

The roof slides open, the night is as wide as if your life had no beginning and no ending. You lie on your back and float. You're naked and calm. After Robbie's death you were sure that lots of things would come to an end. You thought there would never be another starry night. You were also sure the snow would cover the whole world and usher in a new ice age.

There are millions of stars shining above you, and it's stopped snowing.

Every end is a beginning.

You lie still and motionless in the water and stare into the sky above you. Robbie's parents are asleep, your parents are asleep, the world has turned away from you. That's as it should be. It feels as if your soul might break away from your body at any moment and rise into the night. Like snow in reverse. Then your soul would meet Robbie's soul up there. Robbie's probably waiting for you. You move your arms very slightly. You have a thought, and the thought makes you smile. *He will have a long wait,* you think, and move your arms like an angel resting its wings for a while.

And that's how it started.

NEIL

Who thought we'd be seeing you again? Quite honestly, no one. But here you are again, three days later and still with a broken heart. You're sitting completely overtired on a park bench on the shoreline of the Alster, watching the sun rising sluggishly over Hamburg as if it had been diving all night long after gold.

It's half past eight on Friday morning, and you'd be happier if you were in bed. It was a rough night—a concert followed by a party, and you ended up with a woman you'd shared a taxi with. Tina or Gina or whatever. Women like you. You had sex for the first time on your fourteenth birthday after your best friend's sister took you aside and told you she had something to show you. She was the first who left the hole inside you. Perhaps it's a virus, perhaps you're really cursed, at any rate since that day you've been searching tirelessly for your great love. You don't know if the yearning gets more intense with age, and if it does you can understand why people slit their wrists or watch romantic comedies all day. That hole in your heart won't leave you alone. You can wake up next to as many women as you like, it's never the real thing. The soul is missing. That one soul. And sometimes you have to drive two hundred miles to discover that that one soul isn't to be found in Berlin.

This morning you awoke drenched in sweat and your heart was racing. You've always found it hard sleeping in strange apartments. Tina or Gina or whatever didn't wake up when you left her bed and crept into the corridor. Two of the doors were shut, the third was open. A man lay diagonally across a bed, snoring with his mouth open, and opposite him a woman sat by the open window staring into the dawn. She was wearing only a T-shirt and smoking a cigarette. She didn't notice you. A Saint Bernard came trotting out of the kitchen and looked at you reproachfully, as if you'd been neglecting him for years. He stopped in front of you with a snort and blocked your path. You pushed him aside and closed the apartment door behind you.

The party was in Eimsbüttel, but street signs don't lie, you are definitely in Altona. For a while you walked through the area, wired and clueless. The night was still deep in your bones, every footstep felt as if you were moving through Jell-O. You bought a coffee and a croissant at the bakery. You sat at a bus stop and watched the city wake up. Sometimes these moments of exhaustion are like a drug. They make you feel as if you're part of things, as if the people around you are props, the buildings are façades, and the weather is the perfect backdrop for another day in your life. Then there's the soundtrack—footsteps on the pavement, front doors closing, and the dry clap of pigeons' wings fluttering as a dog snaps at them. There was a permanent grin on your lips and not a single thought about the future in your head.

Just as you were about to step onto the bus on the Sternschanze, your phone rang. You had to put a hand over one ear, because a street-cleaning truck drove past you, then you recognized her voice and burst out laughing.

"Don't laugh," she said and couldn't help laughing herself.

She asked if you'd survived Berlin, and you said your heart was still beating, then she wanted to know where she could find you. Just like that. There was nothing more to say.

Two hours have passed since then, and you're sitting on this park bench looking at the sunrise, watching the opposite shore and the way the light breaks against the dome of the mosque. Joggers pant by, a fire engine wails in the distance, and you have a thought that is so clear and so pure that you nearly burst into tears: *If I just dissolved into nothing and became part of the atmosphere right now, it would be a good way to go.*

You're definitely overtired.

A car horn jolts you awake. You've nodded off like one of those old men who spend the whole day on a park bench and go home in the evening with birdshit on their shoulders. The car is parked at the edge of the road, the tinted windows are opaque, the sky is reflected razor-sharp. You rub your eyes. When you look again the passenger-side window slides down, the sky slips away, and there she is.

"Have you been waiting long?"

"A few minutes."

"Will you invite us to breakfast?"

"Who's *us*?"

She doesn't bother answering. The window goes back up, the car doors open, and five girls step out.

You have a table under the spreading branches of a chestnut tree. The girls eat as if they've been fasting for a week. Stink sits opposite you, her hair woven into a braid. There is a purple blotch under one eye and she looks tired, they all look tired. The girl on Stink's left looks like she fell out of a car. She's the only one wearing a long skirt, because her knee is so swollen that she can't get into a pair of jeans. The girl on Stink's right is pale and exhausted. She has a pageboy cut that reveals her long neck. You've never seen such a graceful neck, it's beckoning to be touched. Taja. They tell you that she's had a close encounter with heroin, and that she's slowly getting back on her feet.

"And we saved her," says Schnappi and thrusts her little fist into the air as if she'd just scored a goal.

You've heard a bunch of dumb names in your time. From Zibs to Bozo to Suck and Stink, but you've never met a Schnappi. You don't know whether she comes from China or Japan. Vietnam doesn't even occur to you. All Asians look the same as far as you're concerned, which isn't nice, but then who are you trying to impress with your knowledge of human beings? Schnappi is less than five feet tall, and built like some sort of elfin creature. When she gave you her hand you felt her delicate bones. She talks like a machine gun and says by way of greeting that she's heard about you. She gives you the feeling that she knows more about your life than you do.

"To us!" says Schnappi.

The girls raise glasses and cups and drink to themselves. You still have no idea what's brought them to Hamburg and what they want from you. But they can take all the time they want, because Nessi's sitting on your right and you're perfectly happy if things stay that way for a while.

"I've got to go again," she says and gets up.

It's her third trip to the bathroom. She says she's throwing up so much that she feels bulimic. The seat next to you is suddenly abandoned and cold, as if a cloud had passed over the sun. Of course Nessi's too young for you, of course you're too old for her, but that's not what this is about. When she goes into the café, you ask the girl who the father is. They shrug.

"Just don't make an issue of it," Taja warns you.

Why would I? you think and know the answer, because the answer is your heart and your heart already skipped a beat when Nessi got out of the Range Rover. Yearning crept from your every pore. Is it the face or the body? Is it gestures or is it simply chemistry?

Stink leans forward and pats your hand.

"She'll be back in a minute."

The girls laugh. It doesn't bother you that they can read every thought in your face. Stink grins, you grin back and say, "I knew we'd see each other again."

"Yes, but you didn't know it would happen so soon."

Schnappi touches your arm.

"Tell me more about the curse."

"About what?"

"Come on, we know everything. When you talk to Stink, you're automatically talking to the rest of us as well. It's like in an asylum, all the crazies are watching the same television program. So tell me."

"Not much to tell. My heart's on fire the whole time, I'm always filled with longing and fall in love with every woman who comes my way, that's all."

Of course you could add that your life has been frozen on the spot for a while, that you'll turn twenty-eight this year and that you're tired of being stuck like this. Nothing is happening. But it's good that you keep quiet about that; not all thoughts need to be shared.

"And?" Schnappi wants to know. "Have you fallen in love again?"

Before you can think of an answer, a tune rings out and Stink pulls her phone from her pants pocket and you recognize her ring-tone as "Tongue" by Bell X1. Taja leans over to see who's calling, and says in disbelief, "Mirko?"

Ruth tries to take the phone away from Stink.

"That little jerk!"

Stink holds the phone out of reach and wants to know what Ruth's planning.

"I want to tell him what a fucked-up traitor he is."

"You don't even know what's happened."

"Stink, someone *must* have snitched on us, that's just obvious. Your pal Mirko said he'd be on the football field, and he wasn't there. So who do you think ratted us out?"

"Don't answer," says Schnappi.

"Stink, don't," says Taja.

Stink rolls her eyes as if the girls were ridiculous and takes the call.

"What sort of jerk are you!" she says, and winks at the girls. "Yeah, you heard me right. You said you'd be there and then you dumped us. What?"

Stink listens for a while, then she presses the phone to her chest and says to the rest of you, "They've got Mirko."

She speaks into her phone again.

"Of course I know who Ragnar Desche is. You can tell that shit-head we're going to the cops."

The girls suddenly start shrieking and want to know what on earth Stink's saying. Taja throws a bread roll at her head. Stink says, "Nah, Mirko, that was just a joke, don't tell him that."

Stink moves a little way away from the table. This is the moment when you could ask the girls what's actually happening here. But the girls aren't even looking at you. They are watching Stink, who ends the call and comes back to the table.

"Your uncle caught Mirko," she says to Taja.

"He did *what*?"

"But don't worry, Mirko doesn't know anything."

"Are you sure?"

"Do I look like someone who isn't sure?"

To be quite honest, that's exactly what Stink looks like. You haven't the faintest idea what's going on. Nessi comes back from the bathroom.

"What's wrong with you guys? Did I miss something?"

"Stink's new lover called," says Schnappi.

"He's not my lover, he's not even twelve."

"I was eleven when I had my first boyfriend," says Taja.

"That doesn't count," says Schnappi. "Your friend was nine and didn't know you were so old."

"At least I had a boyfriend, when you were still counting grains of rice in a paddy field."

They joke around, they ignore you as if you were the waiter who'd joined them at the table. They've forgotten about the phone call, it's just them against the rest of the world. You're patient and enjoy their presence. It's only when they've eaten and drunk enough that they tell you, almost in passing, that they're on the run. You learn how Taja's father died and that Taja feels guilty and that's why she knocked herself out with heroin; that the girls found a stash of drugs in the house and how Stink hit on the idea of selling it. You also learn about the fiasco in Lietzensee Park, about how Ruth was beaten up as a warning, and about Ragnar Desche's ultimatum. After that you don't actually know what the problem is.

"So what's the problem?"

They look at you as if you were a cross between a car crash and a miscarriage.

"So you've put the drugs back, right?"

Their faces stay unchanged, then Stink asks you if you've taken a good look at Ruth.

"Darian really fucked her over. For no reason, okay? He nearly ripped her arm off, and one of her teeth is loose. If you think anyone can do that with one of our girls then you're wrong. We've earned those fucking drugs. Taja's uncle is never going to see them again."

You think you've heard wrong.

"Girls, you've *got* to give him the drugs back."

No reaction.

"Where have you hidden them?"

"In a safe-deposit box, and that's where they're staying."

You nod as if that made sense, but it doesn't make sense.

"And what's your plan?"

The girls look at each other. They know exactly what comes next, but they don't want you to find out. They're being careful. How are you supposed to know that you're just a stopover on their flight?

"We're disappearing," Ruth says at last. "We're disappearing never to be seen again."

"No one can do that."

"Just wait."

A barrier has gone up. You doubted the girls and they're not happy. Get to the point before you lose them completely.

"How can I help you?"

"We need money," says Stink, and breathes out with a sigh as if she's been waiting all this time for you to ask. "We threw together everything we had. There was nothing to get at my place, my aunt's stingy and my brother just gave me a pack of cigarettes. Nessi's broke too, and Ruth managed to lift a hundred euros, and that was that."

Schnappi raises her forefinger.

"I put fifty in the pot."

"Show-off," says Nessi.

"Loser," says Schnappi.

"And fifty from Schnappi," Stink goes on, "Taja saved five hundred for her InterRail trip, and with the small change, that makes just under seven hundred. You've seen the car, it's a thirsty beast. If we're going to be on the road for a while, we're going to . . ."

She breaks off and shrugs, she looks at you expectantly, and at last you understand. You're incredibly slow to catch on. You and your mother's Jaguar and all the money you put on the table in that disco. You're an ATM with a heart. Even your lighter is made of gold.

"How much?" you ask.

"How much can you manage?"

You look at your watch. It's half past nine. You need more information, but your father doesn't answer the phone until eleven. You can scrape some money together. If you want to. There's an inheritance from your grandfather in your account. But you have one condition, but that'll come later. All that you need right now is a little time.

"Give me two hours."

They breathe out and thank you. Nessi gives you a smile, and there's so much warmth in that smile that your innards melt away, leaving nothing but a puddle. Get out of here before you spill out some kind of romantic nonsense. You're about to get up when Stink's phone rings again.

"I bet it's your lover boy again," says Schnappi.

"He *isn't* my lover boy."

Stink looks at the display. Taja leans over and grins.

"Of course he's your lover boy."

The girls laugh and agree that Mirko must be really in trouble if he's phoning all the time. You laugh along with them. What would they say if they knew that at that moment Mirko was lying beside a swimming pool with a hole in his forehead, his blood coloring the water? And how would you react if you knew who Taja's uncle really is? You'd probably get up from the table and walk away without a word and never waste another thought on those five girls.

"Girls, will you shut up, I can't hear anything," says Stink, and when it's quiet, she speaks into the phone.

"Hello? Mirko?"

She freezes, turns around, and looks at you. *Why me?* you think. She says, "Fuck the deal."

Nessi frowns, Taja leans forward. Stink says:, "I told you, you don't scare me."

Schnappi gets up. Ruth's fists are clenched.

"Asshole," says Stink and rings off.

The girls wait and don't ask any questions.

"That was Taja's fucked-up uncle," says Stink. "He says he's going to find us."

No reaction, the five girlfriends are only silhouettes in the harsh sunlight shining through the leaves of the chestnut tree. It's suddenly grown cold, you have goose bumps and don't understand how it's possible. Then Stink rouses herself, spreads her arms, and asks what's up.

"Have you all shit yourselves? Girls, anyone who thinks he can intimidate us has shit for brains. Nothing scares us, does it? He wants to find us, let him look. How stupid does he think we are?"

RAGNAR

You take the phone away from your ear and stare at it, then you look over at Tanner and say, "How stupid does she think we are?"

Tanner doesn't react. He knows what a rhetorical question is.

You turn to Leo.

"I want to know everything about this girl Stink. What her real name is, where she lives, who her friends are, and what she has to do with Taja."

You throw him the phone.

"And put Fabrizio onto the last number, tell him to trace the call and find out where this girl Stink is now. We'll meet in the office in an hour. Tell Darian to be there too. And as to this . . ."

You look at the dead boy lying by the pool. You feel nothing but satisfaction. *He who gives nothing gets nothing in return,* you think, *and he who takes must also be able to give.*

". . . we'll deal with it later."

You avoid looking at Oskar. Your emotions aren't called for right now. You need to keep a cool head and solve this problem quickly and cleanly before your emotions get involved. And don't even think about reacting spontaneously again. Watch your every step. You will have enough time later on to mourn Oskar.

An hour later you're sitting alone in your office while your men wait outside. David was successful. The recordings in Oskar's house go back ten days. Three of the eight cameras were active during that time. Living room. Attic. Oskar's bedroom. Every movement was captured. David spliced the most important scenes together for you and burned them onto a DVD. Now you're sitting at the monitor of your PC and turning the player on. David said the relevant recordings begin the Wednesday before last. The date appears on the bottom left of the picture.

Wednesday, July 1, 2009.

You see your brother, you see Taja, you hear them arguing, and you can make out every word. You see what happened. You pause and repeat the scene and watch it again. Your brother dies. After that comes Taja's breakdown. You fast-forward . . .

Friday, July 3, 2009.

. . . and see Taja in the attic, opening the metal case with the gear in it. You see her dragging Oskar's body out of the living room. Perhaps your brother had started smelling, perhaps she could no longer stand the sight of him. Tanner discovered the freezer that Oskar's body was stored in.

Why did she put him in there? you ask yourself and fast-forward through the next few days. You see Taja in the living room, doping up repeatedly, throwing up and tossing and turning in her sleep.

On the night of July 7 four girls turn up and step inside the living room from the terrace. You lean forward and pause the picture.

There you are, Stink.

She still doesn't have the blue patch under her eye, she still hasn't met you. You look at the other girls. You haven't seen any of them before. Your finger taps the space bar and the picture starts moving again . . .

Wednesday, July 8, 2009.

. . . and Taja shows Stink the merchandise in the attic. They take out the drugs. Nine hours later Stink and one of the girls put the drugs back in the metal case . . .

Thursday, July 9, 2009.

. . . and then in the evening Stink is back in the attic, taking the merchandise out of the metal case and cramming it into a sports bag. That's where the DVD ends. An edit of seven minutes and twenty-three seconds. Your brother's death, Taja's breakdown, the theft of your merchandise. You take the DVD out of the PC and look at it for a moment before breaking it on the edge of the table.

"David?"

He opens the door.

"Who else has seen this?"

"Just me."

"Good. Wipe the hard drive."

"I understand."

"And you can all come in."

You throw the broken DVD into the wastebasket under your desk and notice how sweaty you are. You know David won't say a word about the recordings. They all come in. Your son has his hands behind his back and looks like he got called in by the principal. Tanner gets straight to the point.

"What did the cameras get?"

"Let's talk about that later."

Tanner looks at David, David holds his gaze, Tanner turns back to you.

"Ragnar, I want to know what those fucking cameras got. He might have been your brother, but he was also my friend. Did Oskar have a heart attack or—"

"Taja killed him."

"What?"

Tanner jumps up, Darian's mouth gapes open, he comes a few steps closer, his hands open and close, Leo's eyes are closed, his jaw is working. David is the only one who doesn't react. Tanner is speechless.

That's fine.

"But . . ."

"I said we'd talk about it later, that'll have to do. So do me a favor and sit down."

Tanner sits down. You don't like it when people question you.

"What have you found?"

Leo hands David a file. David glances into it quickly, takes out a photograph, and snaps the file shut again. He sums it up, "Stink's real name is Isabell Kramer. She goes to the same school as Taja and took part in a school competition with her girlfriends three months ago. We downloaded the photograph from the school homepage."

He puts the photograph down on the desk and pushes it over to you.

"From left to right they're Sunmi Mehlau, Ruth Wassermann, Isabell Kramer, Vanessa Altenburg, and our Taja. All five have been friends since high school."

You look at the photograph. There they are. Stink, Taja, and the three girls you just saw on the DVD. They're all giving you the finger. You don't take it personally; at their age you were no better.

Under the photograph it says "Happy Losers."

"What sort of competition was it?"

"A poetry slam. They all got up on stage together, joked around the whole time, and had to leave after five minutes."

"Which of them was waiting on the opposite shore?" you ask your son, who's standing by the door because no one's offered him a chair. He looks at the photograph and taps the second girl from the left. It's the girl who put the drugs back in the metal case with Stink.

"You see the problem?" you ask, and before your son can answer, you go on: "The problem is that you didn't scare them enough."

His cheek muscles twitch. The boy can't stand criticism. He needs your attention like a plant needs light, and you treat him like an employee.

"You've got to put that right, do you understand?"

Your son says that he understands. He goes and stands by the door again, legs spread, hands in front of his crotch as if protecting his balls. Tracksuit bottom, tracksuit jacket, running shoes. He reminds you of a bouncer. You notice him glancing at Tanner. Tanner ignores him. He's your son's godfather. Tanner helped him out of a few tight spots while he was at school, but those days are over and Tanner has other problems to deal with right now. You can see it in his face. Taja as a murderer. Never. He can't get it into his head. Unlike you, Tanner likes the kid and doesn't understand your problem with her. And how could he? Whenever he sees Taja, he sees Taja and you see Majgull.

"What else have you got?"

"We know from the school office that Taja was absent all last week. The other girls have been missing for three days, they weren't at home either. From the look of Oskar's living room, it must have been a wild party."

You say nothing, you know better.

"What's with the cell number?"

David looks at Leo. Leo says, "It belongs to this girl Stink. Fabrizio located the phone without any difficulty. The girl isn't in Berlin anymore."

"What?!"

"When you called the number an hour ago, Stink was sitting on the Alster in Hamburg, in a café called the Treasure Chest. Since Fabrizio located her, he's been checking the coordinates every ten minutes; she's still in Hamburg. We got Taja's cell number off Oskar's phone and checked it too. Same location. We're assuming the whole gang's in Hamburg."

"And the missing Range Rover?"

David takes over.

"I talked to the garage. Only the Mercedes is being repaired. They think it wouldn't be a problem to track down the Range Rover. Oskar fitted both cars with tracking devices after the Porsche got jacked last year. As soon as we've found the access code for the Range Rover, we can call the tracking device and it'll text us back its location."

"Simple as that?"

"Simple as that."

They wait for your reaction. Even you are waiting for a sensible reaction, your mind has to process all these facts. However hard you try, you can't see any sense in all of this.

What the hell are they doing?

You want to tell your men to leave you alone, but what comes out of your mouth sounds different, noisy and furious: "ARE YOU TRYING TO TELL ME THAT SOME IDIOTIC SIXTEEN-YEAR-OLD GIRLS HAVE GONE TO HAMBURG IN MY BROTHER'S RANGE ROVER WITH FIVE KILOS OF HEROIN AND WE COULDN'T DO ANYTHING ABOUT IT?"

Your voice rebounds in the room. You see your son lowering his head so that he doesn't have to meet your gaze.

"Perhaps someone's been helping them," Tanner says, openly ignoring your fury because it doesn't get any of you anywhere. You're grateful to him for that. You breathe, you breathe, your clenched fists relax.

"Yes, perhaps," you say with Tanner's calm, and regret your outburst. You thank Leo and David for the good work they've done and ask Tanner who you've got in Hamburg.

"As far as I know, the Greeks are fully occupied again. Markus is back in Fuhlsbüttel. Then we've got the Dietrichs. Their boss is fresh out of jail."

"What about Oswald and Bruno?"

Tanner hesitates.

"I'd rather not."

"Rather not? Why?"

"You know."

Of course you know. The last time you worked with Oswald and Bruno, a failed delivery turned into a bloodbath. Bruno explained later, there was no other way around it; and Oswald said sometimes you have to do what you have to do. You don't much care for that kind of esoteric bullshit, but you do know that Oswald and Bruno get results. They are outposts, they enjoy immunity. Their biggest shortcoming is that they're too violent, which makes them a risk. But they get results.

"Send the picture of the girl to their cell phones and give them the address of the café. With a bit of luck the matter will be sorted out in half an hour."

OSWALD & BRUNO

They're standing beside the shop window wondering if there's something wrong with the colors, or whether it's their eyes. Everything looked different in the shop. Oswald's shirt is too pink, Bruno's T-shirt is too blue. They look like iced lollipops on legs.

"I look like a fucking Smurf," says Bruno.

"Shit," says Oswald.

The day started so well. They were about to sit down in Starbucks when Bruno had to stop by the shop window.

"Nothing looks really good in artificial light," he says.

"Shit," Oswald says again.

While Bruno is changing his clothes in the bathroom, Oswald orders coffee, mineral water, and brownies. And while Oswald is getting changed, Bruno finds a seat outside and stirs milk into his coffee and tries not to light a cigarette. Since he gave up smoking, he's felt terribly healthy. He hates fresh air, and the company could be better. Even though everyone claims they'd died out in the mid-nineties, most of the people sitting around him are yuppies—severe-looking women in shiny polyester blouses that are supposed to make them look ten years younger; guys with tousled hair and the look of eternal students, who earn five-figure sums a month and behave as if they'd just got out of bed. Everything changes. Yuppies have a new disguise. They try to look ordinary. They've given up putting their wealth on display, because even yuppies get lonely, so they try and look young, lost, and casual. Bruno wonders who they're actually trying to fool. They can't change anything about their behavior—they yell into their phones or sit over their Mac-Books and adjust the display every thirty seconds because the sun's so bright. Bruno feels vindicated. When the light is wrong nothing works. Oswald comes outside wearing his old clothes now, and says he feels like himself again.

"Ditto," says Bruno.

They drink their coffee, eat the brownies, and stretch their legs. They can't know that in four minutes they'll get a call from Tanner. They can't even guess how quickly any form of light can make way for darkness.

Bruno's driving today, Oswald's responsible for everything else—air conditioning, music, snacks, drinks. When Bruno's the passenger they mostly listen to Steppenwolf and it's always too hot in the car. Oswald favors a cool breeze, the sound of Ghinzu, and an ice-cold beer in his hand. "Mine" is on at the moment, and even Bruno can't help smiling. They're similar in many ways. They have no conscience, they see brutality as a refined kind of sport, and never doubt one another. And they're learning English together.

"Man, I love that sound."

"It is strange, but strange is good."

"It makes my nerves tingle."

"That's very nicely said."

"Thank you."

For four years Oswald tried to join the fire brigade, but he failed every psychological test. For a while he earned his money as a bodyguard, until one day the Lasser family discovered him. One small job was followed by the next small job, and soon the jobs changed and became too big for Oswald to do on his own. That's when Bruno arrived on the scene.

Bruno served for three years with the French Foreign Legion, and worked his way up to officer. He liked the job, but couldn't cope with the new recruits. Most of them came from Russia and Romania, and he didn't like their mentality. So Bruno went back to Germany, where he met Oswald at a Lasser family party. After that they joined forces and since then they've been doing their jobs together. They are street mercenaries and their big dream is to be hired as real mercenaries by Aegis Defence Services. To pass the admission test, they're polishing up their English and taking language courses. They always sound like tourists as soon as they start talking English to each other.

"There's this new restaurant where you pick everything you want to be fried and then you put it in a little bowl and the chef fries it and a waiter brings it to your table so you can eat it with rice."

"What are you talking about?"

"I'm hungry, that's what I'm talking about."

"You had a brownie."

"I know."

"Guess what."

"What?"

"I'm hungry too."

"What are you thinking about?"

"How about a nice steak with fries and herb butter?"

"Man, shut up, my juices are flowing."

"Yeah, mine too."

Bruno parks the car behind a Range Rover; they get out and put on their sunglasses. Lots of people think they're brothers, the same physique, the same gestures. But that's how it goes when you've been working together for a long time. The differences blur, you're each reflected in the other, and habits overlay one another like transparent foil. Bruno calls it "character assimilation." Oswald doesn't yet know what to make of the definition.

The café has twelve tables outside. The tables are standing around a spreading chestnut tree, all of them are occupied. A sunny day in Hamburg means that the streets are crowded, and anyone who isn't in the street is strolling along the Alster, or sitting in cafés.

"There they are."

Oswald points at one of the tables. The girls are impossible to miss. Bruno licks his lips. Girls are his thing. Oswald prefers older women who have nothing more to lose.

"I'm going for a snack," Bruno says and moves closer like a dark wave. He stops by the table and takes off his sunglasses. The girls look up at the same time and see a bald man in his mid-thirties, leather jacket, goatee beard, twice-broken nose, weary eyes.

"Girls, Ragnar Desche sends us."

Oswald has materialized on the other side of the table at the same time. He watches as the girl with the red hair grabs a fork. *Move once more and I'll break your damn wrist,* Oswald thinks. He knows where to strike. He knows the sound the bone would make as it broke. As if the redhead could read his mind, she looks up and sees a bald man in his mid-thirties in a skin-tight red T-shirt and beige pants, clean-shaven, tattoo on his neck, birthmark in the corner of his mouth. The man isn't smiling. The redhead looks away.

Lucky you, thinks Oswald and hears Bruno saying: "Girls, Ragnar Desche sends us."

"So?"

Bruno thinks he has misheard. The girl reminds him of that actress in *Kill Bill.* He can't think of her name. Lucy something. Her hair is like black ink. He likes the way she says *So?* He imagines her saying *Fuck me!* and *Yes, make me come!* He points over his shoulder with his thumb.

"Our car's out back, we've got to talk."

"Our car's out back as well," says Lucy, "but we're not talking to you."

"Is that so?"

"That's so."

"Oswald?"

"Yes, Bruno."

"Take the blonde."

And then Oswald takes the blonde.

The blonde is the best choice. Beaten and with a black eye, she's the ideal victim. Oswald grabs her hair with his right hand and makes a fist. A second later the blonde is standing on tiptoes and he has his arm around her neck. It's going as smoothly as closing a zipper.

"Hey, what are you doing?" asks a woman from the next table.

"Police," says Bruno and smiles and shows her the gap between his front teeth and the gap in his leather jacket from which the butt of his pistol protrudes. The woman quickly looks elsewhere.

"You're definitely not cops," says the redhead.

Bruno shrugs.

"And you're not nice little girls driving around in Daddy's car, are you?"

"Let me go, you jerk!" hisses the blonde, and tries to break free. Oswald tenses his arm against her throat; she pants, gives up, and raises her hands in defeat, Oswald loosens his grip, Bruno clears his throat and says, "I'm only going to repeat it once. Our car is out back, we need to talk."

This time they obey, this time they stand up. *They actually are good girls,* thinks Bruno and winks at Oswald. Oswald winks back, then his mouth makes an O and he pushes the blonde away as if she were on fire.

"What the—?"

Oswald regrets taking his eyes off the redhead for even a second. He looks down at himself. The fork is sticking out of his inner thigh. It's really stupid. A fork is a fork. Oswald has had worse things in his arm and his back. Knives, screwdrivers, bolt cutters, and once even the broken end of a broomstick. A fork is just a fork. But Oswald hates surprises. He knows what's going to happen next. After he's pulled out the fork, he'll grab hold of the redhead and only let go when she whines for mercy.

"You rotten little bitch!"

Oswald pulls the fork out of his thigh and is about to grab the redhead when something warm trickles down his leg. *I've pissed myself,* he thinks with alarm. His right trouser leg is dark from the thigh to the shoes.

That's not piss, that's . . .

The blood from his wound is spraying bright red across the table. Oswald drops the fork and presses his hand to his leg. His thoughts are reduced to a single sentence that wanders through his head in a panicky loop and doesn't seem to want to end: *The kid's hit my artery The kid's hit my artery The kid's hit my artery The kid's hit The kid's hit The kid's gone and fucking hit my artery.*

It takes Bruno a moment to understand what's actually happening. He sees Oswald's surprised face and then the blood spraying across the table as Oswald pulls out the fork. The girls recoil, a chair tips over, someone screams. Oswald tumbles backward, one hand on his thigh, his face a grimace, and it's only then that Bruno is ready to react. Only then.

That means a delay of about five seconds.

Five seconds that Bruno's lost.

Lucy's so close that he can smell her breath. He doesn't know how she can be so quick. With his left elbow he feels that his gun has gone from his shoulder holster. *How the hell did she do that?* The barrel presses against his belly, he automatically tenses his muscles as if stomach muscles could stop a bullet. Even though Bruno knows for sure that the safety catch was on, there's no guarantee that the safety catch is on right now.

"If you're the cops," says Lucy, "I'm Bruce Lee."

Two of the girls run around the table and past Bruno, only Lucy stays so close to him that he can feel her pointed breasts against his balls. *She's so small,* he thinks, *how can she be so quick if she's so small?* He doesn't move. Nothing like this has ever happened to him.

"Shut your eyes," says Lucy.

Bruno shuts his eyes, he smells her warm chewing gum breath and can't help getting aroused. He would like to tell the girl she really turns him on, that she turns him on so much that he has no words for it, when the gun barrel disappears from his belly. Bruno opens his eyes and sees Lucy running after her girlfriends. He ignores Oswald, he ignores the people gaping at him. All he sees is Lucy's waving hair. He gets his brass knuckles out of his jacket pocket, slips it onto the fingers of his right hand, and sets off in pursuit.

The loss of blood makes Oswald frighteningly light-headed. It's not the first time he's lost blood. Once Bruno couldn't find him for a whole hour after a gang of Albanians picked a fight with them. Oswald was lying in a bush and pressing both hands to a cut in his neck. First you get light-headed, the cold starts with your hands and feet and works its way to your heart, death opens up all around you like a curtain, and the darkness flows in and bathes everything in suffocating silence. Oswald knows it would be a clever idea to let the redhead go; he has to pull his belt out of his trousers and tie his leg. But he also knows he has a job to do here, so he goes on the attack, catches the redhead by the arm and pulls her around. She falls. Oswald can't suppress a smile, he's so fixated on the redhead that he forgot the blonde for a second. She comes down on him like a hellcat, her nails cut into his face, they rip into the corners of his mouth and claw into his eyes, then the blonde lets go of him for a moment and he thinks it's his move. *It's my move now!* He'll never understand how he could have made such a mistake. The blonde rams both fists into his stomach, the air is squeezed out of him and he goes over on his ankle, his knees striking the ground hard.

"Run," he hears the blonde shouting.

"But—"

"Stink, run!"

Oswald knows it's the loss of blood, otherwise he couldn't understand the situation. *This is how it must be.* He's not a pussy, he's a man and the blonde is a girl and she's standing there like a fucking warrior. *Judo or karate,* he thinks, *these damn kids nowadays learn everything far too early.* Oswald shuts his eyes, lowers his head, and stays in that position. He knows how pitiful it looks. Oswald is weak *and* on his knees. He's also a bastard who's pressing the right buttons. The blonde falls for the oldest trick in the book. She knows how to fight, but no one's taught her the rules.

If you injure someone, make sure he can't get up.

The blonde turns away.

Oswald hears the rustle of her skirt and gets up.

Bruno feels old. The three girls in front of him are fast, Lucy in particular seems to have a built-in gear shift, she goes off like a crazy firework and overtakes her girlfriends. Bruno hunches his shoulders, he's nothing now but muscles and lungs. Anything can definitely happen today, but the day has yet to come when a girl leaves him behind.

After three hundred yards he overtakes the tall one who was sitting next to Lucy. She screeches when he draws level with her. Bruno's left arm shoots out, he rams the girl on the chest, she stumbles over a park bench and falls in the grass. Bruno runs on.

In front of him now is the girl who was sitting to the right of the redhead. Bruno knows she's Oskar Desche's daughter. One of those beauties who take your breath away even as a teenager, long legs and a dreamy face and that fucked-up hairdo that he wants to grab and pull her head to him. Bruno can't remember her name, he's never been good with names, Oswald deals with all that. Tanner sent a picture of the girls to his phone. Even though he insisted that they weren't to touch Desche's daughter, the rules don't apply right now. Tanner must never find out. Bruno kicks the girl's legs out from under her. She crashes to the ground, it's a perfect foul. Bruno will take care of her later. He runs on and feels better.

Lucy, I'm coming.

Her hair is a flag, her backside an apple. Bruno imagines putting both hands around that ass and automatically speeds up. Lucy is running toward the crossroads. She only understands her mistake when she's reached the traffic island. The cars start moving, she can't go on, she can't go back. Bruno waits for a gap in the traffic and sprints over. She stands with her back to him. The island is three meters across. They're alone.

"Surprise," says Bruno.

She turns around. Her eyes flash. In her hand she's holding Bruno's Five-Seven Tactical. Bruno fears and respects this weapon. Not only can it be switched to automatic, not only does it have a magazine with twenty cartridges, it also pulverizes most bulletproof jackets as if they were made of papier-mâché, and has such a small kick that it's like being stroked. There are few things in the world that Bruno is seriously afraid of. One of these is his beloved Five-Seven, whose muzzle is right now pointing at his chest. Bruno says, "Take the gun down."

Now Lucy's whole arm is trembling, and she has to use her other hand to support the weapon. Bruno sees a tear running down her cheek and wishes he could wipe it away. He knows she won't shoot. He knows who's capable of that kind of thing and who isn't. She would never stand like that if she was. He's not an idiot. He knows the cowards, the hesitant ones and the killers. She's not a killer. She's a sweet little bitch that he's cornered. She is his now. That's exactly what he says to her.

"You're mine now."

She brings the gun down. The lights change. The cars stop. Bruno senses the drivers' eyes. Lucy has her head lowered.

"Look at me."

She raises her head and looks at him.

"And now come to me."

Just as Bruno recognizes a killer, he also recognizes someone who's broken. She comes closer, five steps, she's standing in front of him. Close. So close that they're touching. Bruno feels how aroused he is.

"Lean against me, it's over."

She leans against him. She's so small that he feels her breath under his heart. The lights change. The cars set off. One driver can't take his eyes off them. The other cars beep their horns. The car sets off with a jolt. Bruno strokes her beautiful black hair. His brass knuckles flash in the sunlight. Her head smells like hot sand. He knows he has to hurt her, but he also knows he'll keep the pain within limits.

"Good girl."

Her right hand rests on his chest, she looks up and there's a smile and the smile doesn't make sense, because she's looking past him. Bruno turns his head to see what she sees and feels the pressure of her fingers. The push comes as such a surprise that Bruno doesn't understand how it's possible. *How could I have been so deceived?* It was all in her eyes, she was broken, she was lost, and it was all a lie. His left foot gets jammed at the curbstone, his right foot kicks back, his fingers slip out of her hair and for a fragment of a second they look each other in the eye, then a van from a flower shop hits him and Bruno is torn off the island and thrown into the oncoming traffic.

Oswald is better off than Bruno, because he doesn't have to run far. The blonde doesn't even know he's behind her. She isn't especially fast in her long skirt, and she's probably thinking he's still kneeling on the pavement, bleeding like a stuck pig.

Girl, you haven't the faintest idea who I am, Oswald thinks and closes his fist around her hair again. For a moment the blonde loses the ground under her feet, her head is pulled back, her mouth is an O, her legs fly forward. Oswald catches her, before she hits the ground. He holds her close, feels the heat of her body, and only now does he sense that something has changed.

I'm shivering. I've got to get a move on before—

The blonde screams, the blonde wriggles, Oswald loses his balance and falls without letting her go. The impact shakes him, his teeth click painfully against each other and bite off the tip of his tongue. The girl reaches back, claws him, pulls on his ears. Oswald is losing control. Pain and fury, fury and pain. His arms are tight around her. He presses hard and hears bones breaking, presses hard and hears her legs dragging along the ground, shifts his weight and rolls onto the girl, while someone is thrashing away at his back, while someone is pulling on his arms, he covers the girl heavily and securely and his tired body starts sucking the warmth from her until they're both lying motionless in a puddle of blood and there's nothing to tell them apart.

No light, no strength, and no warmth.

Oswald isn't aware of them lifting him off the blonde. He isn't aware of the redhead spitting at him and kicking and cursing, or one of the guests from the café dragging the redhead away. He's part of the present that goes on existing without him.

Oswald will never know that the blond girl was called Ruth, that she was incredibly hungry for life and would have given anything to put her mark on the world. And he'll never know that that same day two police officers rang the girl's parents' doorbell, that her mother broke down and clung to the father. He won't be there when her parents arrive in Hamburg to identify their dead daughter in the morgue. And he'll never know how it feels to die pointlessly at sixteen, and lose your friends and still be a hero because that one girl managed to stop a guy like Oswald. Forever. For eternity.

NEIL

"It's me."

"I thought you were coming to Berlin?"

"I've been there."

"What? You've been there?"

"Three days ago. The atmosphere wasn't so great, so I left again."

"Tell me, are you completely stupid? You come to Berlin and you can't even visit your father?"

"I said—"

"That's no excuse, Neil. I'm dying, and you've had a bad day, is that what you're trying to say?"

"I'm sorry."

"Boy, sometimes you're a real idiot."

"I said I was sorry."

"Does your half brother know about this?"

"No, and I haven't seen him either."

"Good. So what's on your mind?"

"Nothing."

"Come on, I know you and I know what makes you tick. You're not phoning me to tell me what sort of idiot you are. What's really going on?"

"Does the name Ragnar Desche mean anything to you?"

"What have you got to do with Desche?!"

"Hey, calm down."

"What have you got to do with Desche is what I want to know!"

"Nothing. I . . . Okay, a girlfriend has a problem with him, and I thought the name might mean something to you."

"Stay away from him."

"Who is he?"

"Neil, I want you to keep away from him, promise me."

"I promise."

"Fine."

"So?"

"Your grandfather and Ragnar Desche worked together, that was at least fifteen years ago. Import, export. It had mostly to do with goods that the customs men weren't supposed to know about. Desche was called the logistics guy. They said you could trust him your own soul, he'd stuff it away and give it back to you unharmed a decade later. There was nothing he didn't store or deliver. Even corpses weren't a problem."

"Drugs too?"

"Drugs too, of course. What's up with you, were you born yesterday, or what? Weapons, antiques, money, and information are goods every bit as much as drugs and people. Desche stayed out of human trafficking, you have to hand him that. Anything that needed to be secured or moved, Desche's company took care of it. Are you getting the picture?"

"I am."

"Neil, who's this girlfriend of yours?"

"A passing acquaintance."

"Get rid of her."

"What?"

"I said, get rid of her. If she has a problem with Desche, no one can help her. What has she done?"

"She took something that didn't belong to her."

"What's *something*?"

"Five kilos of heroin.

" . . . "

"Ritchie, are you still there?"

"Of course I'm still there. I don't understand, where do you keep finding these airheads? I thought you had your life under control. Doesn't your mother teach you anything? Do you want to end up like me? It's no fun being me, you should have learned that by now."

"What should I do now?"

"Stay away from the whole thing. No one takes something from Ragnar Desche and gets away with it. No one, you understand?"

"I understand."

"Does your mother know about this?"

"No, of course not."

"Say hi from me."

"Do you want to talk to her? She's—"

"I'm too tired."

"You're tired, but you can talk to me?"

"You're different."

"Ritchie, I'm your son and—"

"I know you're my son, you're rubbing it in every time we talk."

"But she—"

"I don't want her to hear me like this. I don't care what you think about me, but I want your mother to remember me the way I was. Is that so hard to understand? It's how I protect her."

"And what if she doesn't want to be protected?"

"You don't know your mother, and anyway it's strictly between you and me, grow up and sort out your own shit before you start messing around with mine. And now let's hang up before I go all sentimental on you."

He hangs up before you can say another word. You stand by the phone, and once again you don't know what to make of your father. He's never accepted the role, he's just Ritchie and nothing more. Ten years ago he was diagnosed with cancer, for eight years he's been hiding away in Berlin. He doesn't want to see your mother and he only lets you and your half brother visit him. Ritchie's thin, he's ill and the chemo's made his hair fall out, but as if by magic he clings to life. A dead man walking who doesn't want anyone standing near him.

"You're awake already."

Your mother is standing behind you, tired eyes, tired movements. She turned sixty last year, and you're sure Ritchie wouldn't recognize her. She seems to be enfolded in a constant state of tiredness. Sometimes the cloak lifts, when your mother surrounds herself with people, but as soon as she's alone again, all her strength leaves her and the tiredness settles on her again.

"It's been a long night," you say.

"I can see that. Have you had breakfast?"

You kiss her on the cheek and go with her into the kitchen to keep her company as she makes the breakfast. You can't just disappear now. You've taken your father's place, and that carries obligations. The girls have to wait.

You bring your mother coffee, you hand her the mail and listen. She takes you as you are. Since you finished school, you haven't done much but spend money, watch movies, and meet friends. Nine years on the pause button. It's a mystery to you how time could pass so quickly. You planned to study, you wanted to set up a club with a friend, you even tried your hand as a computer programmer. All your plans stayed just that. Plans. Sometimes you wonder if everything would have been different if your father hadn't left Hamburg. You're not a loser, you're just pleased with this way of life—the world expects nothing from you, you expect nothing from the world. Your mother believes you'll find your way eventually. But what if there is no way? What if you've already got there? The son of a rich heiress and a cancer-ridden crook. The end.

Darkness attracts darkness. Maybe that's why you're part of this story, who knows. The roots go deep. For three decades your father's family was a big player in Hamburg's crime scene. Everyone knew the name of Exner, and it all started with your grandfather Maximilian, also known as Grandpa Max, even better known as the Emperor. He founded his empire in the late 1960s, financed every rising nightclub on the Reeperbahn, and set up a regulation whereby signs were displayed on the barrier to the notorious Herbertstrasse, forbidding access to the prostitute-lined street to minors and women. *The Emperor keeps Hamburg clean* was his motto. Not only did he collect protection money and promise security for everybody, he also controlled prostitution and made sure that the whores underwent regular medical examinations. He was even in charge of farming out cash-in-hand building work. In the early 1970s he put the first fruit machines and pinball machines in pubs, engaged in property speculation, and extended his empire by moving stolen cars. In all those decades he stayed away from the drug and weapons trade. His two sons from his first marriage were Ruprecht and Ritchie. Ritchie never had the ambition to take up the Emperor's legacy. He was useful for small-time deals, like when a car had to be taken from A to B, but when it came to the hard stuff or a few people had missed their payments and needed an arm broken, Ruprecht was your man. Ruprecht was two years older than Ritchie and knew what he was doing. For him, there was only the Emperor's empire, the rest was crumbs from the table.

Who knows where your father would be now if he hadn't met your mother. Perhaps he'd have spent five years in jail like Ruprecht, or hidden himself away in a little Italian mountain village like your Uncle Fredo. At the end of the 1990s your father turned away from the family, and after Grandpa Max's death he gave up on his legacy. Perhaps he was saved by money, because your mother has noble blood, owns a villa on the Alster, and doesn't have to worry what the DAX looks like. But it could also be that your mother showed him another way of enjoying life. Whatever it was, your father's now sick and alone in Berlin, and afraid to look his great love in the eye. No, you're really not interested in being like your father.

"Perhaps you should go there," you say.

Your mother is still holding her cup, even though it's empty. You lean forward to give her a refill. At any moment your mother's going to say *Yes, perhaps.* Your conversations are like games of chess. The openings are always the same.

"Yes, perhaps," your mother replies and doesn't really mean it. She gives you a quizzical look.

"How is he?"

"As always. No better, no worse."

"Do you think his last course of treatment was successful?"

Ask him yourself, you want to answer, but you just shrug. There are days when you want to put your mother in the car and drive to Berlin. You want to ring Ritchie's doorbell, and go as soon as the door opens and leave the two of them alone. If you were brave enough, if your mother wasn't resistant to the idea, if the sun rose in the west one day and your mother could crank herself up a bit and overcome her cowardice. You make the next move and say, "You must hate him for hiding."

"He's not hiding."

"Of course he is."

"He's like an injured wolf licking his wounds."

"Mom, it's been eight years."

"I know."

"Why do you torment each other like this?"

She smiles, you hate that smile, it disarms you, makes you the little son who knows nothing of the world.

"Just wait, once you've found the right woman, you'll think differently about your father."

"You say that every time."

"And you still haven't found her."

Your little dispute is over. Stalemate. Any additional move would lead to superfluous attacks, and you'd rather not expect those of your mother. Let her have her peace. You say you have to go. She doesn't ask where to, because she knows you'll be back. You walk around the table and kiss her on the cheek. The saddest woman in the whole of Hamburg and her son.

You left the bank after ten minutes. You had them give you an envelope, and in the envelope there are now six thousand euros. The sum has to be right, because you're asking a lot in return. You barely know these girls, and don't think you'll ever see the money again. If the sum isn't right, they'll never go along with your deal, and there has to be a deal. You know your father would say you were mad. *I'm doing what I have to do,* you think, and you're about to call Stink when she calls you first.

"Hi," you say. "I was just about to—"

"Did you rat us out?" she cuts in.

"What?"

Her voice is shrill.

"Two guys turned up after you disappeared, did you sell us out or what?"

"Calm down, I didn't—"

"DON'T LIE TO ME!"

"Stink, I'm not lying to you. What's happened?"

Her voice breaks.

"Ruth is . . . our Ruth is . . ."

The line goes dead. You look at your phone and don't know how to react. It rings again. You hear Stink crying, you hear her sobbing.

"Stink, talk to me, what's happened?"

"Ruth . . . they've . . . Ruth's dead . . ."

"What?"

"Our Ruth is dead."

You swallow, you narrow your eyes, open them again.

"Where are you now?"

Stink sniffs.

"As if I'd tell you that."

"Stink, I really have no idea what's happened."

One of the girls says something in the background, Stink answers, you don't understand a word, your thoughts are going round in circles: *How can one of them be dead? I'm just an hour away. If I'd stayed there, then . . .*

"Are you still in the café?" you ask.

"It's crawling with cops now . . ."

She breaks off, she takes a deep breath, she just needs to know: "You really didn't rat us out?"

"I swear."

"Because if you did rat us out, then—"

"Stink, I swear!"

Silence. Voices in the background. Silence.

"Where exactly are *you*?" she asks.

You tell her which intersection you're standing at. She hangs up, and you look at the envelope in your hand and wonder for the hundredth time why you're doing all this. And the answer is right in front of you. If only you could see it.

It takes them ten minutes, they don't look for a parking spot. The Range Rover is double-parked. The passenger window slides down, and you see Stink. Her eyes are red, her mouth so soft it looks like it's melting. She waits for you to come over to her. The girls don't want to risk anything, the engine keeps running, they could take off at any second, so move your ass and get this over with. Go.

You stop beside the car and say you're sorry.

"How did they find us?" Stink wants to know. "Do you have any idea how they were able to find us?"

The anarchy has vanished from her voice. *She was so strong and full of life,* you think and want to apologize for something that wasn't your fault. Say something sensible, psych her up, encourage her.

"I don't know," you say, even though you already have an idea what might have happened. Nowadays no one can really hide and it isn't particularly helpful that they've stolen a car. The surveillance state is a joke, because any individual with a decent computer and a few contacts can access information that should be under lock and key. *And you've had a run-in with Ragnar Desche,* you want to tell them. You're sure that someone like Desche has more than one computer at his disposal to stay on these girls' heels. Or as your father so nicely put it: *No one takes something from Ragnar Desche and gets away with it.*

"What exactly happened?"

Stink tells you about the two guys who appeared in the café. She tells you Ruth saved them, and tears drip from her chin and you have to steel yourself not to hug her through the window.

"Ruth was less than five yards behind me, you know, it was all over already, but when I . . . when I turned around, she was like, she was gone, she was just gone and lying on the ground and that . . . that big fucker was lying on top of her and . . ."

Nessi leans forward from the backseat and pulls Stink to her. She wraps her arms around her and you stand there and the sun is beating down on your neck and you feel Nessi's eyes on you, as she looks over Stink's shoulder. *I had nothing to do with it,* you want to reassure her and you say, "I've spoken to my father."

Stink breaks away from Nessi. Schnappi and Taja lean forward. Their eyes are upon you. Four sixteen-year-old girls who look in their grief as if they were six years old.

Kids, you think, *shit, they're just kids.*

"My father knows who Ragnar Desche is. He said no one takes anything from Ragnar Desche."

"Is he in the Mafia or something?" asks Schnappi.

"My uncle isn't in the Mafia," says Taja.

"I don't know what he is," you lie, "but I think I can help you. I've got six thousand euros here, that'll keep you afloat for a while, and by the time you come back things will be sorted out."

"And how will things be sorted out?" Nessi asks.

"Leave it to me."

They hesitate, they stare holes into your head, they worked out long ago that there had to be a catch. Everything has a catch. Stink articulates it.

"And what do you want in return?"

"The key."

"What?"

"I want the key to the safe-deposit box."

"For six grand?!"

Stink laughs, it's good to see her laughing, even if her laughter is fake.

Better than nothing, you think.

"The drugs are worth twenty times that much," she says. "You know that."

"I know, but that's not what this is about."

"What is it about?"

You speak calmly. You have to convince the girls that you're calm, because if they see through you for a second they'll drive away.

"To be honest, what sort of choice do you have? You get a pile of cash from me. What use are the drugs to you? You're on the run, and the drugs are still in Berlin. Somehow those two things don't go together very well—or are you planning to go back to Berlin?"

Stink avoids your question.

"And what about you? What are you going to do with the drugs?" she asks.

"Some business."

"You're not a dealer."

"Of course I'm not a dealer, but I can still do deals."

Stink lets her window go up, you pull your hand back, the window shuts with a quiet *woop.* Your face is reflected in the tinted glass. For a moment you don't recognize yourself. You look determined, you look like someone who wants something.

If Ritchie could see me now.

When the window comes back down again, you look Nessi in the eyes, and it's a little as if Stink weren't in the passenger seat anymore. There's that tugging in your chest. You wish you could kiss her. Like in a novel where the guy makes time stand still and can do what he wants. Just one kiss would do, you wouldn't want to touch her any more than that. But let us pause for a second. We're a bit confused. What's wrong with you? You're getting all romantic while these girls are grieving over their friend?

"What are you staring at?" Stink asks.

"Nothing."

"He's flirting," says Nessi.

"I'm not flirting," you say far too quickly and lower your eyes. "Have you made your minds up?"

They have.

"If we come back and you've sold the shit, we want thirty percent."

"Okay."

Stink looks stunned.

"What do you mean, okay? Don't you even want to negotiate?"

"I don't like negotiating."

"Fine businessman you are."

"I know."

She holds out her hand.

"Give me the money."

"First the key."

She hands you the key, you put it in your pocket but don't give her the money.

"Neil, please don't fuck with us."

"There's one more thing," you say and open the back door. You get into the car, and you do it so casually that none of the girls can react. Door open, door shut. Schnappi automatically makes room for you. You smell the leather of the car, you smell the girls, their sweetness, their sweat, and their grief; their grief in particular is a cave with velvet walls and hardly enough air to breathe.

"I think you should get out," says Schnappi.

"I just want to—"

You don't get any further than that, because something hard is pressing against your ribs. You look down and see Schnappi's hand and in her hand the black butt of an automatic weapon and at the end of the automatic weapon there is the barrel and it is pressing against your ribs as if there is a secret passage into your soul.

Exactly seven minutes later you get back out of the car and stand on the passenger side. You're still not ready to go. You want to ask the girls where they're headed and whether you'll ever see each other again. You don't do it. It would be a bit like inflicting wounds on yourself. They'd never tell you and you'd be insulted.

Save your breath and get out of here.

You're about to turn away when Nessi reaches past Stink and holds her hand out to you. Your fingers between her fingers. You're sixteen again and your heart pumps and pumps and wants to absorb the moment. You'd like to offer Nessi a new life, you want to say: *Stay here and I'll take care of you and the kid if you save me in return.* Your fingers part, Nessi leans back and puts the car in gear. There's nothing more to say, no last look, nothing. The car moves past you like a boat leaving the shore, and you stand there with your hands buried in your pockets and hope you know what you're doing.

Somebody must know.

Take a look at yourself. You're a hero who has to hold his pants up to keep them from falling down. Although Bruno's beloved Five-Seven Tactical is made mostly of plastic, with the magazine it weighs a good two pounds. Anyone who's shoving that much weight down the back of his pants should have a belt, or else he will look like a sad little gangster taking to the streets for the first time.

Do you seriously think you could raise the gun and fire? For Ruth? For a girl you saw today for the first time? Or for Nessi?

Perhaps.

You watch the Range Rover as it drives off, and gradually have a vague idea why you're doing all this to yourself.

Because it's right?

Perhaps.

DARIAN

Three words can mean so much. More than breathless talking, more than a whole book. Particularly when those three words come out of your father's mouth.

"Deal with it."

He gave you Tanner to take along. Tanner drove you to Frohnau in his car, and parked in the abandoned garage. You entered the house together. Now you're standing in the doorway of the vaulted basement. Blue light gleams from the swimming pool and fractures on the tiles like the thoughts of restless souls. Mirko lies on the edge of the pool with his back toward you, as if he'd turned away so that you didn't have to look at him.

As if he didn't want to show me his face.

Tanner asks you how long you're planning to stand in the doorway.

"It's your job, not mine, so get to work and thank me later."

You step inside the cellar and try to ignore Mirko at first. Your uncle is sitting in one of those deep leather armchairs as if he were sleeping, but you know it's an illusion. No one sleeps as soundly as that, no one sleeping is surrounded by that emptiness.

You take Oskar upstairs. Tanner spreads a blanket on the living room floor. You wrap Oskar in it and carry him into the garage. It's like something in a cheap gangster movie. Trunk open, Oskar inside, back into the house and down into the basement. There's no getting around it now.

Take a look at Mirko. Take a look at what's been done to him.

A black halo surrounds his head, flies buzz around his face and walk across his forehead. You see a fly disappear into his mouth. The puddle of blood looks like dried maple syrup, a dull skin has formed on the surface. Mirko stares across the water. You can only see one eye. You know the right thing to do would be to lean over him and close his eyes, but you can't bring yourself to do it. For a moment you imagine it's you lying here. The flies, the silence. Trapped forever in that moment.

"You know whose fault that is," says Tanner.

"I know," you reply and immediately feel the rage rising, and rage is a good substitute for grief. Of course you can't know that this is another of your father's lessons. He makes you believe what he wants to make you believe. He feeds you with lies and stokes your rage. He's like all fathers. They want to see their sons grow and flourish; and they always want to keep the possibility open of capping their growth if the son becomes a threat. Your father wants to take you to your limits, and you're an obedient dog who trusts only his master's hand and nobody else. If Tanner told you now that your father had punished Mirko with a bullet to the head for his arrogance toward him, you wouldn't believe a word of it.

Doubting your father isn't an option.

The girls are responsible.

For Oskar. For Mirko.

Your father told you they'd found Mirko by the pool. Revenge for the deal that went wrong? Revenge for your failure? Who knows. *He was still warm,* your father said. And there he lies now. Cold. And you don't question a thing.

"Are you ready?"

You try to lift Mirko's head, it sticks, the surface of the puddle cracks, Mirko's mouth flips open, a little fluid seeps out, the fly creeps out over his lower lip and zooms off, you suppress a retch and lower his head again.

"Take his arms."

You take his arms and don't understand how Tanner can stay so calm. He takes Mirko's legs and says, "Just pull away, he can't feel anything now."

You pull on his arms. Mirko's head comes away from the floor and falls back. You regret not closing his eyes. Mirko looks at you, upside down.

"What does he see?"

Absolutely nothing.

Yes, but what if he can see something?

Me. His best friend. The friend who got him involved in all this.

You look past Mirko to Tanner. An empty gaze. A forlorn gaze.

"Everything okay?"

You want to nod, but you can't. Inwardly you're weeping for your friend, you really loved that Yugo and you still can't get your head round what's happened here. He was like a little brother to you. He did everything for you.

"All okay," you reply and blink away the tears, and then Tanner and you carry the corpse upstairs, wrap it in a blanket, and put it with Oskar in the trunk.

After leaving the highway near Oranienburg and driving through the city center, you stop at the Lehnitzsee. From outside, the crematorium looks old and dilapidated, but Tanner says that's just a façade, it's all high-tech inside. Ten years ago the facility was privatized, and your father was involved in the conversion. He was of the opinion that a crematorium is a good investment.

A man in blue overalls stands by the entrance, smoking. Tanner flashes the headlights twice, the man opens the gate. You follow him at a walking pace, park under a massive plane tree, and stay in the car as the man disappears into the crematorium. Tanner lowers the driver's-side window and adjusts the mirror so that he has a view of the entrance. Your hands are damp, you have to wipe them on your sweatpants. You wait for ten minutes and don't say a word, then the man comes back out.

"There he is," says Tanner, and moves the mirror back into its original position.

You get out and shake the man's hand. Tanner hands him an envelope. The man doesn't count the money; he puts the envelope in his pocket and says, "Let's do this."

The trunk opens silently. Tanner watches as you and the man

carry first Mirko's and then Oskar's corpse into the crematorium. Two plain wooden coffins stand ready. The man looks at his watch.

"The incineration chamber's been fired up. We can do this now, as far as I'm concerned."

"Both at the same time?"

"Both at the same time," says the man.

You thought it would be more dignified. You thought you'd stand there and watch first your uncle and then your friend go up in flames.

The man leads you away from the coffins and along a corridor.

"We don't need the boy's ashes," says Tanner.

You don't contradict him. You step into a low-ceilinged room with two monitors and a keyboard on a table. The man points to the monitor on the right-hand side. You see the two coffins starting to move and sliding into the oven chamber. The man looks at his watch again.

"If I can just put the remains through the grinder we'll be finished here in no more than an hour and a half. Will that do?"

"That'll do," says Tanner. "We'll wait outside."

And then you wait outside.

Two hours later you go into a restaurant on Olivaer Platz that is one of your father's favorites. You've spent every birthday and every Christmas here. The cooks are on first-name terms with you, and the owner has been trying to set you up with his daughter forever.

Your father is sitting with Leo by the window, his hand on the menu, his thumb drumming gently on the paper. Even though no one can really see it, your father's psyched up. The calmer he looks, the tenser he is.

You sit down. He asks if it all went well. Tanner opens the menu and doesn't reply. You understand that the question was meant for you. It was your task to deal with the corpses.

"No problems," you say, thinking about the urn on the backseat of the car.

My uncle. Dead. My best friend. Dead.

You want to say it out loud, you want to ask how on earth something like this could happen, even though you know the answer, so it's better to keep your mouth shut. You can be anything. Stupid and anxious aren't in your repertoire. On the way back, when you asked Tanner what sort of grinder the man at the crematorium had been talking about, he laughed and asked you to finally grow up.

"Your father doesn't want you thinking simplistically."

He clapped you on the chest with the flat of his hand.

"You should stop putting your brain into your muscles. If you don't understand something, then try to understand it. The answer will come all by itself."

You looked down at the urn in your lap and felt like a child. Tanner left you dangling in midair for a good five minutes, then he said, "When you cremate someone, not everything always gets burnt. A thousand degrees is no guarantee. And you can be sure that people don't want to see bits of bone or teeth when they're scattering the ashes. So the remains are put through a bone grinder."

Of course you'd already thought of something like that, but you can never keep your trap shut. Tanner's right, you have to grow up. Think everything through, then you can spare yourself all the remaining questions that won't leave you in peace: *What about Mirko? Has he just disappeared now? What will his mother say? And what will I tell the rest of the gang?*

You're like somebody looking out of the window and seeing rain and having to say out loud that it's raining. Death is perfectly self-evident, learn to cope with that, because death is now a part of your life.

"The urn was still warm," you blurt out.

The men look at you. Your eyes are moist again. Seventeen years old, a boy among men. Your father hands you the menu. You take it, you open it. The menu's full of indecipherable signs that have no meaning to you. Find a meaning, give them a meaning. Tanner saves you by flicking you on the ear and saying, "At least they didn't freeze-dry Oskar, or you'd have frozen your balls off on the way back."

The men laugh. You laugh with them. Self-evident.

You're on your appetizers when David comes into the restaurant and wrecks your plans for the whole day. Your father won't be going to the theater this evening, Tanner will disappoint his girlfriend and cancel dinner, Leo will sit at the wheel again, and you'll have to miss your training.

David tells you the Lasser family called.

"Bruno's in a coma, a van hit him. They don't know exactly what's happened. But it gets even better. Oswald bled to death outside the café, and one of the girls bought it too."

"Which one?" asks Tanner.

"The blond one that Darian beat up."

You hiss between your teeth. They look at you, you mustn't bat an eyelid, stay calm, they want you to be cool, so you're cool and ask the right question.

"What about the other girls?"

David spreads his hands.

"Disappeared."

Your father wipes his mouth with his linen napkin and pushes the plate aside. No one's interested in Oswald and Bruno. They're soldiers, they're expendable. The same is true of the girls. They should have known better, they'd been warned. Your father sips his wine and looks out the window. Nobody speaks, nobody moves, the waiters keep their distance. At last your father turns to Tanner and asks him his opinion. Tanner doesn't hesitate.

"We can't let that be."

Your father waves to the waiter for the check, then looks at you one by one.

"Leo, you drive us. Tanner, tell the Lasser family to stay out of this, it's our problem. David, we don't need you. You stay in Berlin and take care of Oskar's house. All traces must disappear, clean the place from top to bottom and find the goddamn access code for the Range Rover. Tell Fabrizio to keep a line open for us and locate the girls' cell phones every five minutes. I want to know if they move an inch from the spot."

He glances quickly at his watch.

"We're leaving in half an hour. Any questions?"

You have no questions.

"Fine. As soon as we've found them we'll head home and scatter Oskar's ashes. And Darian . . ."

He looks at you. *At last.* He hasn't forgotten you.

". . . you will prove to me that you're more than just my son."

He doesn't take his eyes off you, he's no longer your father, he's your boss. You say nothing. Your boss doesn't expect an answer.

NEIL

You know that they will come. You think it's appropriate to go back to the beginning, because everything started here on the shore, so it will end here too. Your head is dull and disconnected. Thinking doesn't help right now, action is required.

The water glitters below you and reminds you of a dress. You were very small at the time and can't remember where the party took place, just that there were unbelievably large quantities of cakes, and what that dress of your mother's felt like. As if her skin had turned liquid. Look, what you're doing, it is very clever. You're thinking your way past your problem. Keep going like that. You consider surprising your father. Perhaps you'll take that journey to Berlin, kidnap your mother and bring the family together. Your father would never forgive you. But it would be a heroic feat. You've felt heroic since abandoning the Range Rover. You're also aware that there will probably be no Later as far as you're concerned.

You shake your head. You know it's nonsense. So much is unresolved. You've achieved so little in your life that it's shaming. You haven't climbed a mountain, and you haven't swum in the ocean. You haven't even solved your problem of falling in love. If you disappear right now, no trace will be left of you.

The footsteps behind you are different. They're not the footsteps of strollers going somewhere. Not those footsteps. *No.* You don't want to be afraid, and no one should be afraid. *Fear is for sissies,* Grandpa Max told you. Remember that. You never wanted to be one of those people who keep their heads down. Not then, not now.

You don't turn round.

Sweat trickles down the back of your neck, your clammy hands cling to the railing. You stare down at the water flowing by, as if the answers to all your questions were hidden in there. The footsteps fall silent behind you. The water flows and flows. The strollers are still walking, the day moves tirelessly toward evening and your instincts yell at you to get yourself in gear.

Run, get away, just do it.

You might be your father's son, but at the same time you're also his opposite—you aren't going to run away and spend eight years licking your wounds.

Not you.

No, not me.

They lean against the railing, one on each side of you. They don't touch you, you don't look at them. You wait. You're playing black, and that means being patient, because white makes the first move, it's always been that way and it always will be. An eternity passes, then the first move is made and a voice on your left says, "We're here."

RAGNAR

You're standing by the Heiligengeistfeld, and the sky is the same crystal blue as the innocent eyes of a newborn baby. You put on your sunglasses. Your car is parked thirty yards from the Millerntor in a no-parking zone. You wait for Tanner to get out and confirm the coordinates again.

The Hummelfest fair is being set up, the stalls and most of the attractions are already standing there, ready for the surge of visitors which is supposedly going to break last year's record. It isn't due to open for another three days, and right now you couldn't be less interested.

"Something smells bad about this," says Leo.

Two and a half hours have passed since you left Berlin. You're so close to the girls that they should be able to feel your breath, but Leo's right, something smells bad. Tanner comes over to you and says, "It isn't a mistake, Fabrizio's checked the coordinates three times."

You set yourselves in motion in sync. You're a smooth machine advancing on eight legs, avoiding a crane, walking past the white-water ride and stopping by the big wheel. You look up. The topmost gondolas are shifting gently in the wind.

"They can't be up there," says your son.

A technician tells you no one's allowed up the big wheel yet. Tanner puts a few bank notes in his hand. The gondolas start to move and rotate slowly past you. Leo checks each individual one.

In the twenty-sixth gondola you find a plastic bag on the seat. The technician gets nervous.

"Is that a bomb or what?"

No one replies. Tanner opens the bag, you all look in, look at each other, look back in the bag. Four cell phones look back at you and one of them lights up. The first notes of a song ring out. You take the phone and press receive.

"We need to talk," says a voice.

You push your sunglasses up on your forehead and look around, you listen to the breathing in your ear and scour the area with your eyes.

Where is he?

You know he needs visual contact. He doesn't wait for your reaction. He tells you where to meet, then the line goes dead. You drop the phone back in the plastic bag. Your mood hits bottom.

It's Friday afternoon, and even in Hamburg no one works at this time of day. The whole of Germany is taking a long weekend and laughing in the face of the global economic crisis. The promenade is crowded. Strollers, joggers, mothers with baby buggies, and a few lunatics with dogs smiling indulgently at other lunatics with dogs. He's chosen a good spot. He's leaning against the railing with his back turned to you as if he didn't have a care in the world. He doesn't deceive you. You stand on his left, Tanner on his right, Leo sits in the car, your son waits a few feet away and keeps an eye on everything.

"We're here."

He looks first at you, then at Tanner, then his eye returns to you. Now he knows who's in charge. You would guess he's in his mid-twenties. His hair is long and well looked after. You can see the film of sweat on his forehead. He smells of expensive aftershave. Whoever he is, you've never seen him before.

"Keep your elbows on the railing," you tell him, "and spread your legs."

His left eyelid twitches.

"Why should I do that?"

"Because I'm not talking to anyone who's carrying a gun in his waistband and thinks I'm not going to notice."

He could run now, he could try to draw the gun. Instead his elbows stay on the railing, and he spreads his legs slightly. Your son steps forward and frisks him, pulls the pistol out of his waistband, shows it to you, you nod, your son puts it in his jacket before stepping back to where he was.

"Good," you say and lean against the railing again, "we've got that out of the way. Who are you?"

"Neil."

"Neil who?"

"Neil Exner."

"Oh, shit," says Tanner from the other side.

You don't move, and search Neil Exner's face for similarities.

The Emperor's grandson? How absurd is that?

You were at the boy's christening, you'd never have recognized him. And how could you? The last time your paths crossed he was nine years old and sitting on a bicycle while you chatted with his grandfather.

Just how small is this world?

You're sure this isn't coincidence. There are lots of Exners in Germany, but running into an Exner on the shores of the Alster after your brother's been murdered and you've had five kilos of heroin stolen has nothing to do with coincidence, there's planning behind it. Suddenly everything makes sense. The girls are just a tool. Put two and two together. Then there's your brother's nervousness over the past few months, as if something was in pursuit of him, as if there was a burden weighing him down. It all fits together. But what is it about? And why would Exner's family want to fuck you over?

Yes, why?

How unprofessional is that? Is there something you've misunderstood?

You know that Ritchie Exner is dying of cancer, his crazy brother Ruprecht is lost in contemplation, and the Emperor is in his grave and hasn't planned anything new for eleven years.

And here we have the little Exner.

Ask him.

"What does your family have to do with this whole business?"

"Nothing."

"I'm going to ask you again, what does your family have to do with this whole business?"

"My family has nothing to do with it, okay?"

Perhaps it's the *okay*, or the way he replies—your fingers itch to smash his head against the railing.

"Does your father know about this?"

"I talked to him this morning, but as I said, the family has nothing to do with it."

"So is it pure chance?"

"Looks that way."

You observe a boat bobbing past, you study a seagull turning languidly in the sunlight like a tossed coin, in defiance of gravity. You're very glad you live in Berlin.

"You know what I think of chance?"

You spit. You spit on Hamburg and on this whole day.

"That's what I think about it. So start from the beginning and convince me your family has nothing to do with it."

He tells you he was in Berlin three days ago. And when he was there he met a girl. Stink. They spent the evening together and this morning she sought him out here in Hamburg because she and her girls needed money.

"And you gave them money?"

"They don't know who I am or who my family is," he says, avoiding your question. "And they don't know I'm talking to you."

"And you gave them money?"

"A bit."

"Did they tell you what they'd done?"

He nods.

"And do you know what will happen to those girls if I find them?"

"That's why I'm here."

He clears his throat and takes a deep breath.

"I want to suggest a deal. I know where the drugs are. The whole package."

You wait for him to say something more. He doesn't. He's waiting for your question.

"What do you want in return?"

"The girls."

You're confused.

"We haven't got the girls."

"I know. I want you to let them go. You will get your merchandise back, and that will be that."

Tanner laughs, his laughter startles Neil Exner, who flinches for a second. He looks at Tanner, who shakes his head as if Exner has made a big mistake. He walks over to your son. Neil Exner now belongs to you alone.

"My brother's dead," you say.

"I'm sorry, but I think—"

"You don't need to think. I said, my brother's dead. After that sentence there's a full stop. After the full stop you have nothing more to say. I don't expect any sympathy from you. You owe it to your grandfather that you're still alive. Do you think these strollers all around us would stop me from pulling your heart out? What's wrong with you? You meet me and you're carrying a gun? Are you completely nuts? Where did you get that gun from, anyway?"

"From the girls."

"How did five girls from Berlin get hold of a gun that's used by a French anti-terrorism unit?"

It's obvious he has no idea.

"If I find out that your family has anything to do with this problem, I advise your clan to hide itself very well or—as your Uncle Ruprecht has already done—disappear without trace. I'm asking you one last time: do you really think that chance brought us here to the Alster?"

"Perhaps it was fate."

You laugh at him.

"Kid, fate is a guy with syphilis and a hard-on, who fucks you in the ass every time you look in the wrong direction. Do you think I'd ever turn my back on fate?"

"Not really."

"Then forget fate. We're here because we feel too much. Me for my brother, you for some girls you don't know . . ."

Suddenly you slam on the brakes and understand what you're doing here. You don't want to tell this boy anything about your anger and feeling of helplessness. Stick to the facts.

"Were the cell phones your idea?"

He nods and says that GPS isn't an obscure bit of terminology these days, and that he thinks you must have tracked the girls down to the café somehow or other.

"And the big wheel? Did you stage all that just to gain some time?"

"I want to protect them, I want—"

"Who do you want to protect them from?"

You laugh at him.

"From me?"

You tap yourself on the chest as if the idea of protecting someone from you were completely ridiculous. He nods, he means you, you shout over your shoulder, "Hey, you hear that, he wants to protect the girls from me."

Tanner and his son don't laugh, Neil Exner smiles wearily, he knows you're fucking with him, and because he knows this you return his smile for a moment, almost apologetically, before burying your fist so deep in his stomach that you can feel his guts rearranging themselves under the impact. Exner gasps for air, steps sideways, and collapses over the railing. A thread of saliva falls from his mouth and lands in the water. You hold the boy, you straighten him back up, standing close beside him. It all went so fast that none of the passersby noticed. Two friends having an intimate conversation.

"Where's the merchandise?"

"I . . ."

Exner coughs.

". . . need a promise . . ."

"There are no promises, you have to trust in faith."

You force his torso further over the railing so that he can see his reflection.

"Where's the damned merchandise?"

He raises a pleading hand, he's had enough. A duck swims up, turns in a circle, and swims away again. Neil Exner takes a key out of his trousers and hands it to you.

"It's in a safe-deposit box at Kaiserdamm underground station. That's—"

"I know where that is."

You put the key in your pocket and let go of Neil Exner. He

wipes the saliva from his chin, straightens up, takes a deep breath, one hand on his stomach, one on the railing. He's as white as a sheet.

"Ragnar?"

You turn round. Tanner is holding his phone up to you.

"It's David, he knows where the girls are."

You smile and look at Exner.

"Surprised? Did you really think we'd lose them just because you took their phones? GPS isn't some obscure terminology anymore, right?"

You hold out your hand, your son steps forward and passes you the plastic bag with the cell phones, you press them against Exner's chest.

"All you had to do was take the batteries out."

"If I'd just taken the batteries out we wouldn't be here right now."

"Clever boy."

"I'm not a boy."

"If you're not a boy, then stop behaving like a boy and forget about the girls. You're finished here. Have you got that into your head? Good. And say hello from me next time you visit your father."

You're about to turn away, Exner's hand grips your elbow, your son wants to intervene, you tell him no with a shake of your head. Exner says, "Please. You've got what you wanted, and one of the girls is dead, surely that must be enough."

At that moment you recognize the Emperor in his eyes. The Emperor on the days when he was weak. You've had enough.

"Do you really think the merchandise is my biggest problem? I mean, do I look like someone who'd drive to Hamburg for a few crappy kilos of heroin? Do I look like a drug runner to you? Do you think I'm an idiot?"

"No, but—"

"I'm only letting you go because your grandfather was my friend a long time ago, so don't push it."

"But they haven't done anything!" he blurts out.

"Can you actually hear yourself? Do you hear that whining noise? Have these bitches told you they haven't done anything? Have they told you my brother had a heart attack or a stroke? Tell me, how old are you, taking some sixteen-year-old girls seriously just because they're sweet and vulnerable?"

Neil Exner looks past you. You've found a sore point. This guy doesn't think with his head, he thinks with his feelings.

"Look at me."

He looks at you.

"Would you put your hand in the fire for these girls?"

"I . . ."

He hesitates, he wants to keep his hand.

"I don't know," he says, finishing his sentence.

"If you're not sure who you're putting your life on the line for, then keep out of it. Didn't you learn anything from your grandfather? The only people who beg are the ones with nothing to offer. And now take a look at yourself. You're begging. It's over. Go home."

He lowers his eyes, right, it's over.

But you haven't finished with him yet.

"Hey, kid, be honest, can you feel it yet?"

He frowns, he doesn't know what you're talking about.

You lean forward until your lips are almost touching his ear.

"Just don't turn around, Neil Exner, because fate's fucking you right now."

With those words you leave him standing there and go back to the car.

Leo holds the door open for you, you sit down, Leo shuts the door and walks around the car. Tanner reaches the phone back and explains that David has found the code for the Range Rover in Oskar's desk. You speak into the phone.

"David, where are they?"

"They're on the North Sea, or more specifically they're in Skagerrak, it's a stretch of the North Sea between—"

You interrupt him impatiently.

"I know where the fucking Skagerrak is. How long have they been on the water?"

"For about half an hour."

"Which direction?"

"It's the ferry to Kristiansand."

You snap the phone shut and hand it to Tanner, who asks you if you have any idea where the girls are headed. You nod. You don't know what they plan to do there, but their goal is clear. *Back to the roots,* you think, and wonder what your next step will be. In this case you're like Neil Exner. You see every action like a game of chess, you look ahead and calculate your opponent's move before you start to drive him into the corner. All strategists do that, but not all strategists have death standing beside them.

"We are returning to Berlin," you say.

Leo starts the car. Tanner wants to know what you should do with Neil Exner. You look over at the riverbank. The Emperor's grandson has disappeared.

"Let him go. He won't cause us any more problems."

Leo puts the car in gear. Your son hands you a mineral water, you drink and ask Tanner to put on some music. Your son asks if he can keep the pistol. You ask him if he knows what kind of gun it is. He knows. He can tell you who made it in Belgium, how much it weighs with and without its magazine, and what its strengths are. He's only stumped by its weaknesses. You tell him. They're the same weaknesses that your son has. The gun suits him. You shut your eyes for a while. Berlin awaits, you have to say goodbye to your brother, and then there's no further delay. The hunt is on.

II

hold my head up everywhere
keep myself right on this train

Kasabian
UNDERDOG

THE TRAVELER

After you wiped out a whole village, Germany went into a total panic. You were the front-page story in *Der Spiegel* and *Stern* hired a team of psychologists to prepare a profile of you, while *Fokus* carried a special piece on the dead of Fennried. *Bild* wrote: *No one came out alive!* The *Berliner Zeitung* matched that with *Welcome to the German Slaughterhouse*. They all thought it was going to go on like that. You were the terror, you were the scourge. No one could have even guessed that you were approaching the end of your journey.

The hunt after you was stepped up. The press wouldn't leave the story alone, there was barely a newspaper that wasn't constantly proclaiming new theories. The nation reacted, the politicians drew conclusions. The special commission was reestablished and expanded by a hundred and fifty policemen after a vote in the Bundestag urged *Intensification of measures to find the perpetrator*. The new team tried to link the murders on the A4 and in the motel with the murders in Fennried. But what exactly was the link? Never had so much money been invested in a police operation. In vain. Your murders seemed random, none of the victims were connected to one another. Even the profile produced was no help. They didn't know what category to put you in—you weren't a serial killer, you weren't a mass murderer, and spree killer didn't fit either. You were somewhere in between, a peculiar creation of hell, killing without an apparent motive. A journalist said on television that your killing would become increasingly terrible in scale because you saw it as a challenge. It's a mystery to you how anyone could hit upon such an abstruse theory. Taking people's lives isn't a competition, after all.

1995. 1997. 2003.

They said the intervals would inevitably get shorter rather than lon-ger. They said there was a pattern, they just couldn't see it. They had clues: they knew that one corpse wasn't enough for you, that you sought out isolated places and apparently operated without a motive. They also knew: when the Traveler kills, he really kills, but never children and he never uses a weapon. But what does that say about you? Are you softhearted? Are you a lover of children? Are you afraid of weapons?

At bottom they knew so little about you that you didn't need to worry. In spite of DNA and fingerprints. All they had were the corpses, and the corpses told them nothing. With every passing week, every month their desperation grew. They knew what you were capable of, but they knew as little about your present as they did about your past, and they had no idea about the boy you'd drowned in a swimming pool, just as they had no idea about your search.

When your son was seven years old he called you up at work once and wanted to know what you were afraid of. He had broken his wrist, and during the night he had dreamt about giant crabs that wanted to cut his arm off. You were speechless for several seconds, because you honestly couldn't think of anything you'd ever been really afraid of. Until a voice came to you from a long way away. The voice belonged to your grandmother, who had escaped from Russia with her family after the First World War. You adored that woman, she supplied your sister and you with comics, you were allowed to sleep in tents in her garden on summer nights, and at bedtime she always told you weird fairy stories that she had heard in her own childhood, and that couldn't be found in any book.

Your sister wanted adventures with horses and princesses, but you couldn't get enough of fairy tales and took every story literally. You looked for fallen angels in hollow tree trunks, suspected there was a weeping witch's eye under every stepping-stone, and crossed your fingers during the seventh chime of the church bell, so that your heart wouldn't turn to stone. You'd been particularly taken with one of the fairy tales.

The story of depth and darkness.

In every deep there dwells a monster that consists entirely of teeth and eats any soul that comes near it. The sinners and the saints, no one is spared. The monster can survive in ice, it can sleep in a volcano, it is indestructible. Whenever it emerges from the depth, it turns light into darkness. It has no soul, so it knows no remorse. It is never angry. And if something knows no guilt, if it never feels fury and devours every soul that comes near it, it can never be stopped. It is like the depth that swallows the light. And there will always be a depth, no light in the world is strong enough to reach all the way down to the darkest hiding place. The monster is everywhere at home.

And then in every darkness there dwells a demon who was born without a heart and eats other hearts to assuage his insatiable hunger. The demon hides in the shadows, you can find him in the corners of the mouth of a cruel child, and even if you close your eyes out of fear, he lurks behind your lids and stretches his fingers out for your heart. There is always a nook where he can hide. There is always a place of darkness. In this way the demon is like the monster. They are inevitably connected. Wherever the monster turns light to darkness, the demon slips out as if a door has opened. Wherever the demon slips out, he leaves an unfathomable depth, and a new home for the monster is thus created.

The monster and the demon are brothers, but they have never met. They have tried to come together for ages, because only when they come together will they find peace. And they yearn for peace. They are weary of their cruelties, because every eaten heart and every swallowed soul leaves a hollow echo behind, like a stone falling into a well, and nothing else happens. But the well fills up. Unnoticed.

So the monster seeks the demon and the demon seeks the monster.

That was the end of the fairy tale. You have never understood why your grandmother couldn't tell you whether the brothers ever found each other or not. She was honest, she didn't know. So you had her tell you this fairy tale over and over again from the beginning, in the hope that a sensible ending might eventually appear. Because even then you knew that stories grow with telling. And perhaps a real ending would sneak its way in. One day. But nothing came. So you decided it was time to take control of this story. You were seven years old and you set off in search of the brothers.

Many people thought you were anxious when they saw you climbing onto a jetty by the lakeside and staring into the water. They were mistaken. You weren't afraid, it was just curiosity. You kept a lookout for the monster, but the monster didn't appear. Even when you jumped into the water and sank to the bottom of the lake, nothing came toward you from the depth, and that didn't make sense to you.

Why would your grandmother lie?

Just as you believed that a monster lurked in every depth, you were sure the demon was waiting hungrily for you in the darkness. The darkness was easier to explore. You didn't have to climb into a well, there was no need to step into a cave and listen to your own breath. Darkness isn't like the depth, it's easier to find. But the darkness disappointed you too, the demon simply wouldn't show himself. Not in curtained rooms or abandoned cellars, not behind the palms of the hands that you pressed to your eyes until lights exploded in front of them. You lured the demon with your heart, but he didn't come.

For a whole five years you kept a lookout for the brothers. It was a game and it was reality and the time passed. How were you

supposed to know that you were looking in the wrong places? You
turned twelve and then thirteen. You were starting to forget the fairy
tale, and then, as if the depth had only been waiting, it showed itself
to you unexpectedly, when you dragged a boy down to the bottom
of a swimming pool. And then you understood the fairy tale. You
opened your eyes wide and looked into the depth. The depth looked
back and you understood where the monster was hiding.

Five days after Robbie's death, two days after the Christmas party,
you took the bus to your grandmother's. You wanted to tell her
you'd discovered the secret, and now you knew who the monster
was and why you weren't scared of the depth or the darkness. You
had understood. Your mouth was full of words.

It's me, you wanted to say. *Grandma, look at me, I'm the monster and now I just have to keep a lookout, then I'll find my brother
in the darkness.*

With that insight in mind, you got out of the bus and walked up
the street through the thick snowfall. You were about to ring your
grandmother's doorbell, then you hesitated. Even today you can't
figure out what made you hesitate. Maybe it was fear. For someone
who doesn't know fear, it must be puzzling when you encounter the
feeling for the first time. You became aware that it would be a big
mistake to tell your grandmother about your discovery. Tell her or
your parents or anyone. No one would have understood you.

You postponed your visit, crossed the street, and waited for the
next bus. You were filled with a calming sense of understanding.
As if God had seen his face in a puddle on a particularly horrible
day, seen that he was still God and nodded contentedly. This understanding felt good. Somewhere outside your brother was waiting
for you in the darkness, and it was up to you to find him.

It is August.
  It is 2006.
  It is night.

You've been in Braunschweig since early afternoon visiting an old friend. You go to the movies with him, then you have dinner at a restaurant before you head back to Hannover. Shortly before you drive onto the Autobahn, a curious rattling sound starts coming from the engine compartment. The car slows and slows and finally comes to a standstill.

You don't think about killing for as much as a second, you think about your apartment.

The breakdown service ADAC promises to be with you in an hour, and comes in thirty minutes. In the meantime you've tried to locate the problem yourself. You're not a clueless idiot who just drives your car and fills it up. You tell the ADAC guy what the problem might be. He looks under the hood, takes the voltage of the battery, and says you're right. The alternator's probably had it. The tow truck arrives fifteen minutes later. You give the ADAC man the address of your garage, tip him ten euros, and get into a taxi.

It starts raining, it's been gloomy all day, you'd give anything for a hot bath right now. The railroad station looks deserted, it's just before eleven, if you're lucky you'll get to Hannover before one. You're looking forward to your apartment, a cup of tea, and perhaps even the late news, if you don't fall asleep immediately after your bath.

The Intercity train pulls out right in front of your nose.

You stand on the platform and watch the lights disappear. The next train for Hannover will be there in fifty-five minutes. You're tired and try to imagine spending the wait with a magazine on a bench. You don't like that prospect. You stand and look at the time-table. In seven minutes there's an Intercity for Berlin. Without really thinking about it you switch platforms. You're aware that you've got to take part in a conference in the morning. That prospect doesn't appeal much either.

The Intercity stops with a long sigh. People get out, people get in, and you're one of them. You're still not thinking about killing, but you've forgotten about your apartment. As if there had never been an apartment.

You're on the move.

The Intercity has seven second-class coaches, an onboard restaurant, and a first-class carriage bringing up the rear. You get in at the front. There are only five passengers in the coach with you. It's a weekday. The people are tired, it's the last train to Berlin.

Ten minutes after departure the conductor passes and you buy a ticket. After the conductor has left the coach, you shut your eyes and concentrate as if to store your thoughts for the lean times when thoughts are in short supply. A woman walks past you twice to go to the toilet. You hear the rustle of her leggings. Minutes later the smell of her perfume still lingers in the air. A man coughs, then there's a crackle and an announcement. The train can't stop in Spandau today because of work on the line. Someone curses, then everything's quiet again. You take a deep breath, open your eyes, and get up.

A train, eight carriages, fifty-six passengers, a conductor, a driver, and a railwayman. Sitting in your coach are the woman with the weak bladder and three men. They keep their distance from one another; no one willingly seeks the company of a stranger late in the evening. The woman doesn't even wake up. One of the men glances up and shuts his eyes again as you walk past him. You pick up his jacket and suffocate him. You break the other two men's necks. You stand behind their seats and grip their heads. One jerk and it's over. Time and again you're surprised at how easy it can be. Easy and quiet.

The second coach takes more effort. You leave a couple sleeping. A man is reading and looks up briefly, you nod to him, he goes back to his book. You walk past him and strangle him with your belt. You spend the most time on an old woman who's stretched out over two seats. When your hand closes around her neck she looks at you with horror. She looks straight at you for two whole minutes while her eyes bulge and her feet scrape on the seat. Then you return to the couple. You don't even think of leaving anyone behind. Something is different. Something isn't right.

—————

In the third coach there are nine passengers. It takes you a quarter of an hour. At the end of it your shirt is soaked, and your jacket is sticking to your back. In the fourth coach there's a problem. A man's on the phone as you sit next to him. He looks up with surprise and asks what's going on. You take his phone out of his hand as if you were taking a toy away from a naughty child, then you strike.

"What are you doing there?"

You overlooked the woman. You walked past her seat and overlooked her. She must have been asleep. Small, curly hair, thin lips. You thought she was just a jacket lying there. When you stand up she notices the blood on your face.

"We need a doctor," you say, "otherwise he'll bleed to death."

"My goodness."

The woman comes along the corridor. She's in her leggings, with her shoes in one hand, the other hand pressed to her mouth. She reminds you of your mother and her startled face when she learned that Robbie was dead. This woman's eyes are different, they're probing lights. She leans forward and looks at the dead man. You grab her by the back of the neck and pull her to you so that she falls over him. Her shoes clatter on the floor. Before she can cry out, you press her face into the seat padding.

Coach five has six passengers. You leave no survivors.

Coach six has four passengers. You leave no survivors.

In the last second-class coach a man sits at a table. He has a book in front of him and he's reading with his fingertips. You sit down opposite him and relax.

"Who's there?"

You don't reply, you look at him and look at him. You're reflected in the lenses of his sunglasses and wonder what color his dead eyes are.

"There's no one here," you say.

"Is that supposed to be funny?"

"Not really."

The blind man snaps the book shut and leans forward. He

reaches out an arm as if to grab you. His fingers move like leaves in the wind. You interlace your fingers with his. Intimate. He tries to pull his arm back, but you hold him tightly.

"Please," says the blind man.

You let go of his hand and take off his sunglasses. You see his dead eyes. Blue. They have no depth, they have no darkness. They are dull and blue with nothing behind them. *So that's what it's like,* you think and get up and go into the restaurant.

When the Intercity pulls into the Berlin Zoologischer Garten shortly after midnight and comes to a standstill with one last jolt, only a single door in the rear first-class coach opens and a man gets out. He carries no luggage, and no one is waiting for him. The man walks down the steps and leaves the station. He washed his hands and face on the train. One pink stain on his shirt is still damp, the knuckles of his right fist are swollen. The man doesn't notice what else is happening on the platform—that no one else gets out of the Intercity and the people on the platform are getting impatient, that they try to look through the windows into the train and get in after a brief hesitation, that they find the corpses and in one of the coaches a blind man with his hands on the table, asking over and over again if there's anybody there.

One of the surveillance cameras on the platform captured you. You're a blurry patch walking purposefully toward the stairs. The police tried to enlarge the footage and failed. They showed the picture on television anyway. You didn't look up once, and your movements are quick. A shadow moving through the light. Over forty callers told the police they knew exactly who the pictures showed. The suspects were questioned over the weeks that followed, they all had alibis.

The second shot wasn't shown on television. A camera by the station exit captured and filmed you from behind as you threw something into one of the rubbish bins in passing. They found the sunglasses that belonged to the blind man, and on the lenses were your finger-prints. Now the police knew for certain that the Traveler was on the road again, and that he was in Berlin. They didn't know how disappointed you were with yourself. For eleven years you had climbed out of the depth again and again and opened countless doors for the darkness, but nothing happened. Perhaps your grandmother was mistaken, and there is no demon. Perhaps there's only you on an endless quest, lonely and alone. You can't find something if there's nothing to find. No matter where your journey takes you. It's a terrifying thought.

On that day in Berlin you grew tired of yourself for the first time. Opposite the station you turned and looked back, like someone checking that the door has shut behind him. A ghost train with fifty-seven corpses remained behind, and you didn't once think about killing.

NESSI

If it weren't for the wind, you could be anywhere. At home on the balcony with your feet on the railing or on the shore of the Lietzensee with your hands in the thick grass and the smell of the city in your nose.

Anywhere, just not here.

The wind exposes everything. Salt-harsh and tangy. You open your eyes and you're miles from Berlin. Your hands grip the railing, the North Sea foams below you, above you the seagulls float like escaped thoughts. You wish you could grab them and put them in your head. Maybe then everything would be back as it should be, and there would still be five of you.

You breathe the wind in deeply, feel it all the way to the tips of your toes and especially in your back. As a child you always slept on your stomach, because you thought your shoulder blades were the beginnings of wings, and needed a lot of room in case they spread in the middle of the night. If you had wings right now, and if time were a landscape, you would fly back and save Ruth. She would be by your side again, and everything would be as it always was.

Footsteps approach and for a moment it's almost true, Ruth joins you at the railing, her arm rests around your hip. You smile, and if your smile had a taste it would be salt-harsh and tangy like the wind. You don't need to look, you know who's standing beside you.

"I could be a madman who's going to throw you overboard."

"No madman smells so good," you say.

Stink leans against you, you look out over the water and feel lost and empty. The murmur of voices around you, music, shouting children, laughing women, the bellow of drunks, and again and again the sigh of the seagulls that never come closer and never disappear.

"What on earth are we doing here?" you ask.

"I have no idea, but we'll manage. If we stick together, we'll manage just fine. Don't worry about it."

She doesn't know how much you'd love to worry, but there's nothing in your head, it's just a vacuum. Every thought fizzles out, nothing makes sense anymore.

"It's just that I don't know what's what anymore, and I'm scared, really scared."

And as you say that, you can no longer tell whether you're scared for yourself or for your girls. Your fears all run together. The day won't end, and that scares you. You don't know what will happen at your destination, and that scares you too. It's the sober realization that nothing is as it was, that there's no going back.

"We can't go back, right?"

Stink presses herself closer to you, that's an answer too. And so you stand there and look across the water as if it were still Tuesday and you were back at the cinema and something was about to happen, the movie was about to take you on a journey. But the movie is just the monotonous surge of the waves against the ferry and nothing else happens. You girls can't even cry anymore. And the day still refuses to come to an end, it claws onto every second, like an exhausted mountain climber who knows very well that if he loosens his grip even once, he will fall to his death. And that's how you all feel too—you're tense and concentrating on not losing each other. So you cling to one another and stand by the railing and breathe grief.

What you really wanted to do was take the ferry from Kiel to Oslo, but just before Kiel Schnappi told one of the cashiers at the filling station about your plan, and he said you would never get a seat on the ferry because it was booked weeks in advance. He advised you to go on to Hirtshals and take the ferry from there to Kristiansand. There's hardly any business out of Hirtshals, he said.

"And where is Hirtshals?" Schnappi wanted to know.

You looked at it on the map. Hirtshals is at the northern tip of Denmark, and directly opposite is the Norwegian port of Kristiansand. It's a short-cut, because on the ferry from Kiel it would have taken you nineteen hours to get to Oslo, while the journey from Hirtshals across Skagerrak to Kristiansand takes just four hours. And Kristiansand is closer to your destination, and that settled it.

After three hours you'd crossed Denmark and reached the completely congested port of Hirtshals. The cashier had neglected to tell you that there's always a big pop festival in Kristiansand this time of year, attracting two hundred thousand visitors. Stink cursed the guy at some length, while Taja said it was the best thing that could have happened to you.

"Take a look. At least no one will notice us."

And that was how it was. No one wanted to check your papers, you were just another four girls in a pretentious Range Rover, who listened to pop music. After only an hour's wait you were able to get onto the ferry.

As soon as you've crossed to Kristiansand, according to your navigation system it's eight and a half hours to Ulvtannen. The plan is very simple. You want to surprise Taja's mother and then move into the beach hotel. Two stories, a room with a view of the fjord, a life in freedom. Even though Taja only knows the hotel from photographs, she's described it so vividly that you can see it in front of you.

Stink pats your belly.

"You're going to have your baby exactly where Taja was born. That would be great."

"I'd rather not imagine it."

"Fresh air and everything."

"Stink, shut up."

You spit on the water and wait for Norway to come closer. You still don't know if you want to keep the child. You see yourself sitting down to breakfast one morning, and looking at your girls and telling them what you've decided. One morning.

An excitable Italian woman joins you and says in English how great it is that you're there too, she comes to the festival every year, only last year was a flop because not enough tickets were sold, but that was last year, this time it's going to be on fire, right? Then a group of guys from Belgium buzz around you, wanting to know what you think of Volbeat, and because you have no idea who Volbeat are they write you off as lesbians. Stink laughs and wants to show off and asks you if you'd like to kiss, tongues and everything. You blush and say: *Rather not.* The Belgians move on. Stink calls you a nun. You kiss her quickly on the lips and tell her to be careful what she wishes for. After that an incredibly thin woman with a basket full of fish sandwiches comes round. When she hears you talking German she reveals herself as born and bred in Leipzig. She's doing odd jobs for her studies and she's on her way to the Quart Festival to sell T-shirts.

"First fish sandwiches, then T-shirts. I'll give you a good price if you're interested. My uncle prints the shirts at home in the basement. That's his car over there. I've got everything, from Manson to the Peas. And if you like I can get you two tickets for next Friday, if you want to see Chris Cornell, and who doesn't? Hahaha."

A quarter of an hour later you buy two fish sandwiches from the woman, and at last she leaves you alone.

"Who's Chris Cornell?" you ask.

"Never mind that, who's going to eat these fish sandwiches?"

The sandwiches are soaking, mayonnaise spills out from the sides of them as if they have had a panic attack and were sweating their souls out.

"No wonder this girl is so thin," you say. You'd really like to throw the sandwiches overboard. But you've never been able to do things like that, so you give them to a woman with four children, who looks at you as if you were handing her a full diaper. But she takes them and puts them in her stroller. Stink has had enough of people talking to you just because you're standing at the railing. So you push your way through the crowd and get back to the car deck. Taja is asleep on the backseat. Schnappi is sitting in the passenger seat, playing with Neil's phone. Her foot is braced against the glove compartment, her black painted toenails are as tiny as raisins, and dart back and forth to the music. Some summer hit is blaring from the radio.

"You haven't called someone, have you," says Stink.

Schnappi rolls her eyes.

"How would I do that? I don't know a single number by heart. Why did we have to give that guy *all* the phones? And my gun, too. I'd earned it. I mean, really."

"Schnappi, that gun was bigger than your head and you could hardly hold it."

"Of course I could hold it. Have I got a child's hands or something?"

She holds out her children hands.

"You know how many idiots have asked me over the last two hours if I play in a band? One thought I was Björk. How dumb is that? Am I really that small? It's really sad. A girl without a gun is completely lost in this world."

You're glad that Schnappi handed over the weapon. You urged her to, Taja was in favor of it as well. You couldn't be armed. And that business with the cell phones made sense, because Taja's uncle must have traced you somehow or other. And Neil didn't exactly look like the sort of guy to pull a fast one on you. He gave you his own phone in return, with instructions—you were to use the phone only in an emergency, he'd call as soon as everything was sorted out. But in the event of an emergency, he'd also given you the number of his new prepaid phone and stressed that it had to be really urgent for you to call him.

Something about Neil felt right to you. You couldn't explain it otherwise. As if he knew what he was doing, without really understanding it.

Like us?

Yes, like you.

"Don't break that phone," you say.

Schnappi ignores you and goes on studying the screen.

"This is expensive crap. There's as much storage space on it as there is on my fingernail. Let's take a look in his address book. Aha, nothing but slags. We've got Gabi and Uschi and Franka and Klara. I mean, who's called Franka?"

"Franka Potente," you say.

"Never heard of her," Schnappi lies and goes on reading. "We've got two Clarissas, one Debo, a Mascha, and three Nicoles. There's hardly a single guy. Either he has no male friends or he never calls them."

"Any music?" Stink asks.

"Not a single song."

You have to ask.

"Do you know Chris Cornell?"

"Never heard of him," says Schnappi.

You yawn and look at the water and see the coast of Norway getting bigger and bigger. Schnappi sets the phone aside and asks how long it's going to take.

"I'm so incredibly hungry."

"There's a girl over there selling fish sandwiches," you say.

"Just because I have slitty eyes, it doesn't mean I have to eat fish every day."

You look at Schnappi in surprise. You have to say it.

"I thought you had slitty eyes *because* you ate fish every day."

Stink explodes with laughter, Taja says wearily from the back-seat that she'd always thought so too. It's your first joke since Ruth died. It's like coming home. All the furniture's in the right place and there's food waiting in the kitchen, but it still hurts because the walls are missing and the floor is full of holes. *How can I make jokes if Ruth isn't here with us anymore? I should grieve for a year and wear black and not say another word.* And while you're thinking that, you become aware that it's the last thing Ruth would have wanted. Grief.

Schnappi gives you the finger and fiddles around with the radio until she's found the right station. She turns the volume up full.

"Who's laughing now?" she yells at you as a string orchestra fills the car with easy listening, and a few guys from the next car boo you.

You're all standing at a stall eating fries with weird burgers that taste of fish and meat at the same time. It's crowded, it's noisy. The ferry landed half an hour ago, and you still can't believe that you've gotten to Norway just like that.

Clouds tower and dusk already covers half the sky as if the day were exhausted and pulling a blanket over its head. That's exactly what you feel like. Last night still fills your bones, and the memory of the morning in Hamburg is like a razor blade wandering about under your skin. You don't think about the unborn child inside you. There's plenty of time for that later on. *There are worse things than having your baby in Norway,* you think, and wonder if abortion is even legal here. You never wanted to have a child out of stupidity. It was supposed to be a child born of love. Whatever's growing in your belly, there was no love during those five minutes.

The girls are waiting for you to decide whether you want to drive on right away or take a break. A break would be good, but you don't want to stand somewhere on the roadside and invite the police to pick you up. They'd just have to ask for your driver's license, and that would be that. You want to keep moving. It's still exactly eight hours and forty-two minutes to Ulvtannen, you're going to manage that, and then you can sleep for three whole days. Promise.

"Let's go," you say.

It's just after nine when you finally get going. You've bought drinks and snacks, you went to the bathroom quickly, and now you're on course. The navigation system guided you out of Kristiansand and you turned off the E18 to Route 41 northbound. The sky is completely starless, the air oppressively close. You've been on the road for a whole twenty minutes, and you've just driven over a bridge when the rain catches you. Rain is the wrong word in this case. It rains in Germany, in Norway it pours. The wind rises, the clouds open without warning, and the road disappears behind a curtain of water. You keep driving for a minute after the first squall before turning off to the right. The windshield wipers fail completely. The rain hammers down on the car and it sounds as if each drop is leaving a dent. You feel as if you're trapped in a tin can. Stink thumps the roof from inside as if to defy the rain.

"Shit, that's noisy!"

"Look, there's light up ahead."

Taja leans past you and points, as if you didn't know front from back. There really is light. You start the engine again. The car advances like a listing snail. The light gets brighter and bigger and reveals itself as a gas station with a restaurant next to it.

Of course all the covered parking spots are full, so you drive past and squeeze yourself in beside a trailer opposite the restaurant.

Through the rain you can just make out the outlines of people at the tables. The place is crowded. What you wouldn't do to be one of them.

"Turn on your hazard lights," says Schnappi, "otherwise someone is going to back into us."

You look in the rearview mirror. The road is awash, the rain is everywhere, and the gas station reminds you of a pale light flickering through seaweed under water. Schnappi's right. You're a few feet away from the driveway. It would be a nasty surprise if a car rammed you in passing. You turn on the hazard lights.

"What's that?" Stink says crossly.

The ticking of the hazard lights is immediately irritating. There is the pouring rain, there is the ticking, and there you are in this tin box called a car. Stink wants you to turn the hazard lights off again. Taja says better safe than sorry. A few people walk past you. They move like sleepwalkers toward the entrance of the restaurant. The women wear bikinis and dance in the rain. Summer in Norway. One man has opened a pink umbrella, and gives you a stupid peace sign. Now you're very glad you're still sitting in the car.

"And how long are we going to be waiting around here?" Schnappi asks.

Nobody answers, you stare into the rain, the hazard lights tick away, and you don't know what's worse—the rattling of the rain or this ticking—when a new noise is suddenly added from the backseat and it startles all four of you and makes you screech like mad.

"GIRLS, SHUT THE FUCK UP, IT'S JUST THE PHONE!" yells Stink, and takes Neil's cell phone out of her jeans. Neil has set the volume extra loud so that you wouldn't miss his call. Stink presses receive and holds the phone to her ear.

"What? Hello? Speak louder, it's pissing down here."

Stink listens, then she puts the phone away again and looks at Schnappi.

"Two hours ago Neil tried to get through to us, but some fish-eating slut must have been playing around with the phone."

"I was just on the internet for a minute," Schnappi says, defending herself.

You don't believe it.

"What were you looking for on the internet?"

"Just checking my mail."

"Schnappi, we're on the run and you're checking your mail?"

"One of us has to keep her feet on the ground."

"I don't believe it."

Taja wants to know what Neil said. Stink replies, "We've got to get rid of the car."

"What?"

You all say it at the same time, you're like one of those Greek choruses announcing the decline of the west. Stink tells you Neil met Taja's uncle and gave him the key to the safe-deposit box. Taja thinks she's misheard.

"What did he do *that* for?"

"Because he's crazy," Schnappi says contentedly. "I've said so the whole time. First he takes our phones away, then my gun, and now he gives Taja's uncle the key to the safe-deposit box. The guy's definitely crazy."

"He isn't crazy," you say. "I bet he was trying to protect us."

"Whatever Neil wanted," says Stink, "he thinks one of those tracking devices is built into our car."

"This isn't a James Bond movie," says Schnappi.

"It's not a toy car either," says Stink. "If it was my ride I'd have put in an alarm *and* a tracking device."

You look around the car.

"If the car has a tracking device, we'll find it," says Taja and opens the glove compartment. There's a pair of sunglasses, a bag of candies, and a few crumpled pieces of paper.

"Give me a candy," says Schnappi.

Taja hands the bag around.

"What do you think it would look like?" you ask.

"It's probably got a blinking red button," says Taja.

"It's probably hidden under one of the seats," says Stink.

You look under the seats, you strain to see, nothing's blinking, nothing looks like a tracking device. You all look at the back. Taja puts it into words.

"We need to examine the trunk."

Schnappi shakes her head energetically.

"I don't want to go into the rain."

"What's that supposed to mean?" asks Stink. "Are you made out of sugar or something?"

"Do you see my hair?"

"Of course I see your hair."

"If it gets wet I turn into a poodle that's been given a hot bath."

Taja doesn't want a discussion.

"Either everyone or no one," she says.

You get out together and you're all drenched in seconds. You open the trunk and stand by your luggage. It's a painful sight, because of course there in the middle of your stuff is Ruth's bag. *No one told her things she's never coming back,* you find yourself thinking, and immediately feel like a total idiot for thinking such a thing.

Before you set off and before Stink came up with the idea of looking Neil up in Hamburg, you all stopped at your homes quickly. It was six in the morning, and it began with Schnappi, who didn't think of waking her parents. She left a note saying she was staying at Taja's for a week. Bag packed and out of the house. After that you drove to your place, and you just left a note as well. Bag packed and out of the house. Ruth's mother sat bolt upright in bed when she tried to creep into the house. Ruth didn't get away so easily. She was interrogated for a quarter of an hour, and tearfully admitted that she was a complete mess because Eric had split up with her. Ruth can do that kind of thing. Her mother gave her a hug and promised always to be there for her. And of course she understood that you girls had to stick together, and as school was over anyway a week at Taja's would do Ruth good and help her forget Eric. Bag packed and out of the house. Stink got the record. Her aunt was asleep, her brother was sitting stoned in front of the TV watching morning cartoons and asked if she wanted a hit. Stink was back in the car before her brother could finish his sentence. And now you're standing in the pouring rain with five suitcases and three rucksacks and Taja says, "It all has to come out."

You put the luggage in the rain. You rummage through the first-aid box and a cardboard box full of odds and ends. Nothing. You open all the doors, shake out a blanket, lean into the car and look under the seats again. If there is a tracking device it doesn't want to be found. The rain creeps down your butt cracks. There is nothing to be found. You put your stuff back in, and wonder whether you should get changed. Every time you move, you smell the fear that seeped from your every pore when those two fuckers appeared by your table. You can still see one of them grabbing Ruth, you see them chasing you . . .

Stink snaps her fingers in front of your face.

"Nessi, what are you still waiting for? We're finished."

You get back into the car, you slam the doors, and the rain is shut out.

"Christ, that was probably the most idiotic thing I've ever done in my whole life," says Schnappi and sneezes. Stink pats her head and says her new hairdo suits her. You've forgotten to take any dry clothes out of your bag. Your T-shirt is almost transparent from the rain. Taja turns the heat up. All four of you look wretched and frustrated. If it had occurred to one of you to lift the mat in the trunk and look under the spare tire, you'd have found the little box with the green blinking light and the day would have been saved.

Taja juts her chin.

"We still haven't checked under the hood."

You stare at the hood. The rain is exploding on the paintwork as if it were New Year's Eve. You're already so wet that it makes no difference. So you get out again and try to open the hood. Nothing happens. The hazard lights make you appear and disappear, appear and disappear. You nearly break your fingernails, but the hood won't open. You get back in.

"Did you get wet?" asks Schnappi.

Taja says there must be a lever somewhere to open the hood. What you'd like to have now is one of those enormous, fluffy towels. Taja rummages around between your legs in search of the lever. You're about to ask her if she couldn't be a bit gentler, when the interior of the car is flooded with dazzling light.

"There's a car coming," says Stink.

"Don't worry, he sees us," you say.

The car parks right in front of you, its headlights stay on so that you can't make anything out. Nothing in front of you, nothing beside you, however hard you stare, you're looking into the middle of the sun. Suddenly there is panic. You want to get out and run away. *This means danger,* you think, and can't react, because it's like in one of those dreams where things happen to you that you'd be able to stop easily, but which are unstoppable because it is a dream.

"We have to get out," you're saying, when you all give a start because there's a knocking on the driver's-side window inches away from your left ear.

TANNER

This day's asking a lot of you. You aren't as young as you once were, and you should be sitting in your house on the Wannsee, enjoying the evening and forgetting the rest of the world out there. You weren't supposed to drive from Berlin to Hamburg and back, then climb the Teufelsberg hill and be irritated by a wasp. You weren't supposed to watch breathlessly as Ragnar bowed his head and cried. You're glad Leo and David weren't there.

No one should see Ragnar like that.

You came back from Hamburg half an hour ago, and now the three of you are standing on the Teufelsberg. Darian is holding the urn, Ragnar is looking down on Berlin as if he's never seen the city before. The Funkturm is a thin line against the sky. Oskar is dead.

"Let's put it behind us," says Ragnar.

Darian hands his father the urn. Over the next few minutes you watch the ash trickling from Ragnar's hand and being carried away. Then he closes the urn again, hands it to Darian, and crouches down to wipe his dirty hand in the grass.

"Darian, you go on ahead."

The boy looks at you in surprise before he turns away. You wait until he's out of sight, then you go and stand next to Ragnar and put your arm around his shoulder. He stiffens, he goes immediately into a defensive posture and holds his breath. Rigid. You feel him carefully breathing in again, his tension eases and he leans against you. You look out over Berlin. *Our city,* you think, and imagine it was

Munich or Hamburg. *No, it has to be Berlin.* A soul of its own, a pulse of its own.

Ragnar Desche has become what he is because he listened to you. You were his teacher, he still looks up to you and respects you. A lot of people think you're his right hand, but you're his arm and shoulder at the same time. Your family is a family of men. Women were never important, they're what comes with it, what gets in the way and is unavoidable. Like a sunrise or a good day after a series of bad days. You've always had difficulties with women, but we're not going to roll out your life right now, we haven't time. We're going to go with you for the next few hours until you bid this story farewell. Like a tired handshake after a long evening or the quiver of an axe when it gets stuck in the wood. But before all this happens you have to talk to Ragnar and his son, otherwise we can't let you go.

"Ragnar, we should leave this be, you know."

"What are you talking about?"

"I've had enough time to think it through. We can't go chasing after them."

"Of course we can. Are you doubting me?"

"I didn't say that. I just think time's on our side. They can't disappear forever. Think about it. How does this look? Why aren't we keeping a clear head and waiting to see whether—"

"I'm not waiting, Tanner. My head is so clear you can't imagine. That slut killed my brother. That's why we're staying here. It's a private matter, and it has to be brought to its conclusion. How can you hesitate when a daughter kills her father?"

Ragnar knows there's only one answer to that. You take your arm off his shoulders and try to find the right words.

"What's really your problem?" he asks.

"We're the problem. The fact that we're getting involved. Let other people do the work. We have rules, and one of the rules is that we never get personally involved. Never. You've got Johannes Melben in Oslo, he could—"

"Forget the rules," Ragnar cuts in. "When I say private, I mean private. Bruno and Oswald failed. We drove to Hamburg and failed. Tanner, we're not a kindergarten here. Either we take charge of the problem ourselves or we chicken out. Do I look like the kind of guy who chickens out? What have you taught me? What did you hammer into me all those years?"

"That you should never lose sight of your goal."

"I see my goal. I want to get there. How can you question my plans for even a second?"

"I'm sorry."

"So you should be."

You don't look at each other. One breath, a second one. You have to ask.

"What did she do to Oskar?"

"She suffocated him with a cushion. They argued, and she suffocated him with a goddamn cushion. He was so high that he probably didn't even notice."

You feel a cold vise around your rib cage.

"She suffocated him? I don't get it. What did she do that for?"

"That's the very question I'm going to ask her when we've found her."

It's the pace that counts. Slowness is for losers. Somebody who says he's got time has no time, he's lying to you. Who stays on the move controls the world. But how does it feel when your own teachings turn on you? You feel like you've betrayed yourself. Like all the verve, like all the risk taking that was keeping you afloat has gone up in a puff of smoke. Or you could say you've got older.

Older and wiser and weaker.

You give yourself another two years. After that you'd like to marvel at the flight of migrating birds. You want to get so slow that the nights never end.

But that is then and this is now.

Now you're standing at a private airport outside Potsdam. You've just dropped your car off and got out when David calls. Even though you know what Taja has done, you hope right up to the last second that you don't have to fly to Norway. Your hope dissolves into nothing when you hear David saying, "There was a sports bag in the safe-deposit box, but there were only books in it."

You look at Ragnar. You could keep it to yourself. The situation is bad enough. *He can find out later,* you think, and wonder when that *later* is going to be. Don't make a mistake now. Hand him the phone. Just do it.

"Ragnar?"

He raises his eyebrows quizzically.

"The merchandise isn't in the safe-deposit box."

He takes the phone, holds it to his ear, listens for a moment and just asks one question, "What color was the bag?"

After he's hung up, he hands you back the phone.

"Do you think Neil Exner's pulled a fast one on us?"

Ragnar shakes his head.

"We've been far too naïve about this whole thing. Those girls just used Exner to buy themselves time. Do you still think we shouldn't go chasing after them?"

You give him the only acceptable answer.

"I'm completely behind you, you know that."

Ragnar smiles and suddenly punches your shoulder, he says he didn't expect anything else. He doesn't say you've dodged his question.

Tomas Zenna has put one of his private jets at your disposal. He's one of your most important customers. Weapon exports, drug imports. One phone call was enough. The pilot greets you with a handshake. Thirty-five minutes later you end up at a tiny airport near Amli. The airport is right on Route 41, which will bring you in an almost straight line down to the south.

It's sultry and humid; summer here has a different smell. It's your first time in Norway. Ragnar went to Oskar's wedding on his own, because he needed some time alone. You're aware that everything would've been different if you'd gone together.

A rental car waits by the runway with its engine running. There's a bag in the trunk. Zenna has prepared everything. You're carrying guns, you don't know what to expect, who the girls are working with or whether they're working on their own. Leo hesitates for a moment, and then he's the only one to put on a bulletproof jacket.

"Better safe than sorry," he says.

You get into the car.

Darian had Fabrizio explain the GPS program, and during the flight he checked where the girls were staying on his notebook. It's just after nine. The girls got off the ferry an hour ago, but they're still in Kristiansand. You're just sixty miles apart.

The timetable stands. Your return flight is booked for one in the morning. Ragnar doesn't plan to go back to Berlin without Taja. He doesn't say what his plans for the other girls are.

Ragnar and Darian sit in the back, Leo drives. If Ragnar is right and the girls really want to go to Ulvtannen, then they have to go past you. You're on course. And it is about time to bring this story to an end so that we never have to talk about it again.

Let's put our cards on the table. Uncertainty has been gnawing away at you since you talked to each other in the office. Fact is, you don't believe Ragnar, or rather you don't want to believe him, because you've known Taja since she was a child and she isn't capable of killing anyone, especially her father. *But why should Ragnar lie to me?* Your doubts trouble you. You can see what's happening here. A man and his wounded pride. Your job is to be there and save what needs to be saved. One dead girl is one too many. And, damn it, you want to know what Ragnar's hiding from you. You miss his rationality. Even though you've spoken out in favor, the trip to Hamburg was a step too far, and now there's this. A goalkeeper is allowed to leave his goal, but he should know how far out he can go. Be prepared. You have an important job to do in this story, and you've got to do it or else everything's going to get out of control. And you really don't want to have that on your conscience.

Darian tells you that the Range Rover has left Kristiansand now and is on the 41, but that it stopped again ten miles later. You know the reason for the stop when you drive past Søre Herefoss and the rain comes crashing down on you. It feels as if you're moving through a wall of water from one moment to the next. Leo turns the fog lights on and leans forward slightly to get a better view. The street is an explosion of light reflections, and the rain hammers on the roof with blunt fingernails as if to drown out not only every word, but your thoughts as well. Leo keeps his foot down. You're very glad you're not at the wheel. Wet tarmac makes you nervous.

Thirty-nine minutes later.

"How does it look?"

You turn around. Ragnar doesn't mean the road or the weather, he's leaned over to Darian, they're both studying the display of the notebook. Their faces are palely lit.

"They're not moving from the spot."

"How far still to go?"

Darian looks up.

"They must be right in front of us."

You look forward, the tarmac steams with its stored heat, you can't see ten yards in front of you, and as you stare into the darkness and try to make something out, a shimmering cloud of light materializes and grows bigger and bigger.

"Gas station," says Leo.

"Another two hundred yards," says Darian.

A car comes toward you, the high beams full on and dazzling, so that for several seconds Leo is driving blind. The car whooshes past you.

"What an asshole!"

Leo curses at length and pulls in at the gas station, which looks a lot like a carnival. People are dancing in the rain, someone has set up a grill under an awning and is turning sausages. Four gaily painted VW buses stand in a row, their side doors are open in spite of the rain. You can hear the music from inside. Teens cross the access road in front of you, holding a plastic sheet over their heads and looking like a walking tent. There are also tired faces staring out of the parked cars as if the rain was holding them prisoner. A dog barks at a puddle, then a flash of lightning splits the sky, thunder crashes and for a few seconds the rain is silent, then its rattle drowns every other sound again.

Leo drives at a walking pace. The restaurant and the gas station drift past like the languid longing of a hippie who's dreaming of the sixties. The smokers under the awning retreat simultaneously when a gust of wind blows the rain in their direction. Everything here looks like a movie set that'll soon be pulled down. The flickering neon light above the entrance to the restaurant makes you particularly nervous. You are tense, your left thumb is twitching. You tell yourself it's the weather and keep a lookout for the Range Rover. The parking lot behind the restaurant is overflowing too. Leo notices that they're already close to the exit.

"We've driven past them," says Darian.

Leo brakes, looks in the rearview mirror, and turns. No one shouts at Darian, it's not his fault. The GPS program works on a delay. They must be somewhere. Darian's arm darts forward.

"There they are!"

You also spot the car well hidden in the shadow of a trailer opposite the restaurant, it's no wonder you all failed to see it. Leo swings out and brakes right in front of the Range Rover. No more chance of escape. It's over.

Nothing is happening in the car in front of you. The tinted windows are dull and dead. You expect the doors to fly open and the girls to come pouring out. That's what you wish would happen.

What are they waiting for?

"I don't see anything," says Leo and turns off the engine.

Apart from the rain and swish of the windshield wipers the only sound is your breathing and the whir of the notebook, then there's a soft click and the whir falls silent because Darian has shut it.

"Stay in the car," says Ragnar.

You don't think of leaving him alone, and get out too.

"For an old man you're amazingly quick," says Ragnar.

"Who are you calling an old man?"

The rain spits in your faces, both of you are pumped with adrenaline.

"I'll sort this one out," says Ragnar, pulling his weapon.

You look over at the restaurant. No one pays you any attention. Ragnar walks up to the Range Rover and stops by the driver's door. He taps on the window and waits. You're ready for anything. You think. You really think you are.

STINK

The guy has black, shoulder-length hair that encloses his head like a helmet and gleams with rain as if it were oiled. He must be drenched through and through, but the weather doesn't seem to bother him, because he grins into your car as if he was standing at the beach buying an ice cream from the stall. You're always suspicious about people who are so damned cheerful all the time. As if the food in your favorite restaurant always tastes good. That's not possible. There are good and bad days. This guy's probably never woken up and seen a bad day.

"I saw you were from Germany. Any problems?"

"What?"

"Your hazard lights are on, I thought you might be having problems with your car."

"Stop the blinking," you say and lean forward to get a better look at the guy. He's older than you, but only by a few years. You like his eyes. No suspicion, just honest eyes. Nessi turns the hazards off. The guy doesn't know who to look at, and turns back to Nessi because she's right in front of his nose.

"Well?" he asks.

"We—"

"The engine keeps stalling," you interrupt Nessi before she tells him her life story. The girls look at you as if you had farted. You ignore them and give the guy a smile. The guy smiles back; what else is he supposed to do?

"Open the hood," he says.

Nessi raises her arms in the air as if to surrender, and says she has no idea how it works. The guy stretches his arm through the window, feels around under the steering wheel, and flips a lever. There's a click. He goes to the front and opens the hood. When he's disappeared from your field of vision, Taja hisses at you, "What are you doing?"

"I think it's nice that someone wants to help us."

"Are you crazy? The guy's already drenched to the skin because of us, don't mess with him more than you need to."

"Who says I'm messing with him?"

The guy looks out from behind the hood and calls, "Start her up!"

Nessi starts the engine, which naturally fires up without any problems at all.

The hood comes down with a crash; the guy shows up cheerfully on the driver's side.

"I jiggled the cables a bit, that always helps, you just have to be careful not to tug them out."

You all nod as if this is a pearl of universal wisdom. It's a good thing that your girls don't know what's going on in your crazy little head right now. You hold your hand out.

"Isabell," you say.

"Marten," he says.

His hand is warm and firm. You introduce your girls, and then you say he's your savior and you'd like to invite him for a coffee, because it doesn't look as if the rain's going to let up and it would be stupid to just sit there in the car while it came battering down on you. Marten grins again. You're not sure if he's flirting or just a bit dense.

"There's really no need," he says.

"Of course there is," says Taja and flutters her eyelashes.

No one says no to Taja.

"Okay, then," the guy gives in and winks at Taja.

Definitely dense, you think and get out first.

The restaurant is overflowing, you hear a murmur of voices, chairs scraping, a clattering of plates and laughter, a jukebox plays hits from the seventies and as always there are a few drunks singing along. You squeeze into a table occupied by two rockers, who make room for you without complaint. You manage to grab the chair next to Marten. You sit down and stare at the tabletop, which is covered with empty beer bottles; cigarette butts are floating in the dregs though there is a clean ashtray in between. The two rockers tell you in broken English that they come from Sweden and that they've been waiting for their buddies for two days. Because it's so cramped, one of them offers to let Schnappi slip onto his lap. Schnappi thanks him and says she's sat on the toilet already today. The rockers laugh. A waitress comes with a green trash bag which she holds up to the edge of the table. The rockers know the drill, and push with their arms so that all the beer bottles fall tinkling into the bag. Only the clean ashtray remains behind.

"Öl!" shouts one rocker.

"Öl!" shouts the other rocker.

When you want the waitress to take your order, she shakes her head and moves on to the next table with her trash bag.

"Self-service," says one rocker.

"Self-service this," says the other one and grabs his balls.

Marten is shivering after the rain. He wants a cup of tea, your girls want coffee. Before anyone can move, you set off with Taja to get the drinks. It's only when you're in line that she asks you, "Since when are you calling yourself Isabell?"

"It's only a disguise, he doesn't need to know what I'm really called."

"Disguise? Will you let me know what's going on here?"

"Secret plan."

"Stink, stop fucking with me. Why are we even having a coffee party?"

You look back at the table, you look at Taja again and ask her, "Have we found that tracker, by any chance?"

"Of course not, we . . ."

Taja breaks off. Her face lights up like a billboard. Even though Taja's still unsteady on her feet, she can put two and two together.

"You're such a bad, bad girl."

"I know, that's why we're best friends."

Marten tells you he turned eighteen two weeks ago, and that his father gave him the trip to Norway for his birthday. Including tickets for the festival. They are staying in an apartment hotel a few miles away, and Marten went to the gas station to get some dessert for their dinner.

"So that car outside isn't yours," you say.

"No, it belongs to my father." Marten laughs. "I'm glad he lets me take the wheel. The car has less than a thousand on the odometer."

You all look outside. The cars stand nose to nose like two dogs sniffing each other. If your car's a bull mastiff, Marten's father's car is a collie.

"Cool car," says Schnappi.

"It's a Peugeot, my dad swears by French cars. He had a Nissan before."

He notices you're getting bored and changes the subject. He asks what concert you're planning to go to.

"Chris Cornell," you say quickly, and Nessi bursts out laughing.

Marten says he couldn't bear it when Soundgarden split up. None of you have the faintest idea what he's talking about, but your heads bob up and down, yeah, that was really shit when Soundgarden split up, you bet.

"And Michael Jackson's dead, too," says Schnappi.

You all look at her. Schnappi mumbles, suddenly unsure of herself.

"He is, isn't he?"

"What's that got to do with Chris Cornell?" you ask her.

"She's talking about 'Billie Jean,'" Marten says, coming to her aid. "Cornell covered 'Billie Jean,' probably the worst cover of all time. That's what you meant, right?"

"That's exactly what I meant," Schnappi lies and grins at you and adds that it was no wonder poor Michael Jackson took an overdose when everybody and his dog was allowed to cover his songs. When nobody says anything, Schnappi raises her coffee and says loudly, "To Michael!"

You clink glasses to Michael Jackson. The two rockers mumble something into their beer bottles and don't even think of clinking. Marten wants to know who you want to see apart from Chris Cornell. As none of you girls know who else is playing at the festival, Schnappi can't keep it up anymore and says you're not really here for the concert.

"Damn it, Schnappi!" you girls groan at the same time.

"Don't listen to them," says Schnappi and tugs on Marten's arm so that he has to look at her. "As soon as it's dark, my girls stop thinking properly. We're really on a secret mission. Taja has inherited a beach hotel from her grandmother, that's where we want to get to. A hotel with a view of a fjord. There's no point sitting on your ass in Berlin forever, is there?"

You really want to slap Schnappi. Taja looks outside and studies the Peugeot, while Nessi stays out of it and tips the third packet of sugar into her coffee.

"Easy on the sugar, Nessi, your teeth will rot," you say.

"I crave something sweet," she says and stirs her sugary broth.

Marten tells you he's never been to Berlin. He probably comes from a village and has only cows and scarecrows in his head, so you all tell him about Berlin and your school and how you found each other. Berlin becomes a place of wonder, your school becomes a dump and you heroines. It's as if you were talking about four girls who once existed and who will never exist again.

"The next round's on me," says Marten and gets to his feet.

When he's out of range, the two rockers lean forward confidentially and say they've got tickets for Ozzy Osbourne and loads of room in their tent. You shake your heads. They stick their beer bottles in their jacket pockets, shake your hands, and promise you'll see each other in Sweden again one day. Then they leave the restaurant.

"What are we doing here, by the way?" Nessi asks.

"Later," you say.

Schnappi tries to decipher the menu.

"He's sweet," she says and throws the menu down on the table and looks across at Marten. "Sweet, but not to my taste. He's more your type, Taja. You like guys who look like movie stars."

"Do not," says Taja defiantly.

"Nico looked like Johnny Depp. Kalle was the spitting image of

Ethan Hawke. And what about Kai, who dumped you for that silly cunt Jenni?"

"He looked like that dwarf out of *Lost.* Charlie," you say.

"He did not!"

Marten comes back with tea and coffee, he's also ordered a large portion of fries and pushes them into the middle of the table. Nessi pulls a face, she's going to stick to the sweet stuff. Marten pulls a Mars bar out of his sleeve and says it's just for Nessi. She's inches away from hugging him. Of course Schnappi has to ask, "You know who you remind me of?"

"Who?"

"Jake Gyllenhaal."

"That guy in *Donnie Darko*?"

"Exactly."

Taja rolls her eyes and gives Schnappi the finger. Marten laughs. You rip open a packet of ketchup. The fries are too salty, the coffee's lukewarm, but it doesn't matter, because this is the brief moment when you can all relax. Taja is resting her chin on both hands, she's turned on her flirty gaze. Every now and again she feeds Marten a fry, and if she isn't careful he'll start massaging her feet in a minute. Schnappi talks about the pizza stand in Stuttgarter Platz as if there was only one pizza stand in the whole of Berlin. You give yourselves ten minutes, ten minutes' fun is fair. You learn what Marten wants to study, and that he grew up with music. He only has eyes for Taja, who also grew up with music, and how much of a coincidence is that? *And if they aren't careful they will have made their own little Mozart by daybreak,* you think, but you say nothing because you're glad Taja's in the spotlight, because if anyone needs attention it's that kid. She slept through most of the journey and feels miserably limp from all that medication. *What would Marten say if he knew what we've been through over the last few days?* you ask yourself as he scribbles his phone number on a receipt and passes it to Taja.

"Let's see if I call you," says Taja. Marten blushes and you decide the ten minutes are over. As if in passing you say, "I've got to use the restroom."

Taja says she's coming too, and squints across at Schnappi, who frowns, then grips her hairdo with her fingers and says she looks like a wet poodle. Only Nessi is frozen in her sugar rush, staring at her coffee until you stretch your claws out under the table and poke them into her thigh.

"Everyone or no one," you say.

Nessi groans and gets up.

"I'll keep your seats," Marten promises.

You march through the restaurant, down the corridor to the bathrooms and past them.

"We've just gone past the toilets," says Nessi and stops.

"Keep walking," says Taja.

"But . . ."

You put your arm around her hips and push her on. You step outside into the wind and the rain, and shove your way past the smokers who reluctantly make room. Once again, Schnappi can't keep her mouth shut.

"Can someone please tell me what's going on here? That guy's okay, so why are we running away?"

"Maybe because we can't find the tracker," says Taja.

You reach the front of the restaurant. When you get to the Range Rover, your girls stand behind the car while you duck down and look carefully over the hood. The turmoil in the restaurant is unchanged. You see Marten sitting at the table, he's got his phone to his ear, he's looking round, looking over at the restrooms. *You'll have a long wait,* you think and duck back down behind the car.

"I don't understand anything anymore," says Nessi.

"Catch!" you say and throw her the key.

Nessi catches it and stares at her hand.

"That's not . . ."

". . . our key," you finish her sentence. "Correct."

MARTEN

"They're driving a new Range Rover."

"Which one?"

"Guess."

"The Vogue?"

"Better."

"Not the Autobiography?"

"Bingo."

"I don't believe it!"

"Crazy, right?"

"Take a picture."

"Why? You know what it looks like."

"Not a picture of the car, Marten, a picture of your girl."

"Her name's Taja and she isn't *my* girl. She's one of four."

"How do four girls get hold of a car like that?"

"I have no idea."

"Either they're rich or they've stolen it."

"No one steals a car like that."

"You have a point there. Where are they now?"

"In the bathroom. At first I thought they were here for the festival, but they're heading further north. Taja's half German and half Norwegian. She inherited a beach hotel from her grandmother. With a view of a fjord."

"If you like, we could drop by on our trip and pay them a visit."

"That sounds good."

"And?"

"*And* what?"

"Did you give her your number?"

"Of course not, what makes you think that?"

You can imagine how pleased your father looks right now. The better you get to know each other, the less he's like your father, the more he becomes your friend. In your childhood he was a stranger who dropped in on weekends and acted as if he enjoyed playing with you for a few hours. Then you got older, puberty set in, and your father was sympathetic in a manly way, which was just embarrassing because he had no idea about your life. The true change only took place over the last two years. You got closer to one another, and your mother doesn't like that one bit.

And then he gave you this birthday present.

He suggested driving to Norway. He's bought a new car and wanted you to test it together. *Together.* It was supposed to be your first big trip. And now he's your passenger, he's making jokes with you about girls and life in general, he treats you like an equal. You expected anything, just not this change.

"Are you sure it's an Autobiography?"

"Of course, I can see it through the window."

Your father whistles through his teeth.

"What color?"

"Metallic gray."

You hear a ringing, your father says he has to get the casserole out of the oven, you're to think about dessert, and say hi to the girls.

"See you in a minute."

Your father has rented an apartment outside Kristiansand because he wanted to avoid the hurly-burly of the festival. You'd rather have been right in the middle of it, but you haven't told him that. It's your second week in Norway, and the festival begins tomorrow. Your father has only bought tickets for you. The music isn't to his taste, and he doesn't want to stand beside you all the time like a guard dog. He thinks you need freedom, so you get freedom. Your mother would go nuts if she knew that. As far as she's concerned, you won't be grown up until you've finished your studies and you're pushing a stroller around the place.

Be honest, you feel as if your real life only began when the ferry pulled in at Kristiansand. The people here are friendly, everyone seems to be having fun, and even though it's raining you can't see any grumpy faces. Your father made it all possible. It's a mystery to you why your mother didn't get on with him.

Perhaps it was the other way round, you think when two women ask if there are seats free at your table. You point to the rockers' chairs, the women sit down. You look across to the bathrooms, then back outside into the rain. Your reflection grins at you, you're as transparent as a ghost. Your father's features, your mother's dark hair. You wink at yourself, take out your phone, and you're about to check your mail when you see the girls coming out in single file from behind the Range Rover. All four of them. They have back-packs and bags and they remind you of the time when you used to creep around the area playing cowboys and Indians. *What are they doing?* you ask as they stop by your father's car, open the trunk, and throw in their bags and backpacks. Then they go round to the front and get in.

For a dull moment you sit there frozen in the restaurant and can't believe what's happening. The car starts, the car leaps forward and then backward a little before the engine stalls. A semi-trailer moves sluggishly past the restaurant, and conceals your dad's car for a few seconds. You get up, reach into your jacket, and feel the key. *Thank God,* you think and pull it out. It's not yours. This key is hanging from a round piece of leather with a monogram—OD. You look outside again. Your dad's car has turned, and finally your paraly-sis dissolves. You run from the restaurant and shove the group of smokers aside. You skid over the curb, the rain turns you wet in seconds. You stumble down the street and pause and . . .

They're gone.

Full stop.

They're seriously gone.

You don't even see the rear lights.

Nothing.

You look around. One of the smokers gives you the finger, another says: *Fucking German.* You stare at the exit and still can't believe it. The trembling starts in your hands, wanders downwards, and when you have the feeling that you're one single great shake, you take your phone out of your jacket and call your father.

He's going to kill me, he's never going to talk to me again, he's going to—

"Say that again."

You repeat what's going on. You stand in the rain and you're the idiot whose father's brand-new car has just been stolen by four girls. No one's going to write a poem about it, it isn't worth a short story, and if it was ever shown in the movies, you can bet a good number of people would walk out.

"And what about the Range Rover?"

"It's still here."

You walk around the car, take a look at the registration plate. On the driver's side you try to peer inside the car, while your father issues instructions. He wants you to stay right there. He's going to call a taxi and he'll be with you in ten minutes.

"The door's open," you interrupt.

"What?"

"The driver's door is open."

You lean into the car, then you look at your left hand, still holding the key. OD.

"I think they've deliberately left me the key to the Range Rover."

"That doesn't make any sense," your father says.

"Maybe the car's stolen," you say and get in, away from the rain, away from the naked reality of being a complete failure. The door closes with a soft click. The inside light dims down as if a movie was about to begin.

What if it isn't the key?

You start the car, the engine fires right away, and for a moment you imagine yourself driving to your apartment hotel, beeping your horn, and your father coming toward you and you getting out of the Range Rover while your father is speechless because he can clearly see now that it really is an Autobiography.

"Marten, are you still there?"

You give a start. *What am I actually doing here?* You completely forgot your father on the phone.

"I'm still here," you say and you're about to get out when you're dazzled by the lights. They're coming straight at you. You suppress a chuckle. It's so simple. It was all a big joke. The girls have come back. And that's exactly what you say to your father.

"They're here again. I'll call you right back."

You turn off the phone. The car stops in front of the Range Rover. Everything's the way it was before. Nose to nose. You screen your eyes against the headlights and wonder what the girls are going to say to you, when there's a knock on the driver's-side window. You flinch. It's really time for you to calm down. You can see only silhouettes through the tinted glass and so you lower the window. The rustle of the rain fills the inside of the car, droplets splash in your face, and a man looks at you unhappily. He's wearing a suit, with a turtleneck pullover underneath. His mouth is a thin line, the rain flows down his face in gleaming trails and collects on his chin. You can see he'd anticipated all kinds of things, just not you sitting in this car.

"Who are you?"

"Nobody," you blurt out and you want to explain why you're sitting here, and all the ridiculous things that have happened, because he might be the true owner of the Autobiography, and obviously you don't want to rile him, when the door is pulled open and from then on it all goes very quickly. You fly through the rain and land on the tarmac. You hear a curse, then a second man appears in front of you. He's wearing a white shirt so drenched with rain that you can clearly see his chest hair through the fabric. He pulls you up from the ground and hammers you against the Range Rover. Once, twice. As if that weren't enough, you get a slap. Your head flies to the left, your ears ring, you taste blood and are like a puppet that's just had its strings cut. An arm holds you pressed against the car. Pause. The two men talk to each other as if you weren't there, their voices are a murmur. The man in the suit appears in front of you again. His mouth moves, you can't hear anything. Your head is filled with water, you cough. The man grabs your throat, you see the gun in his hand, you are pulled up, your shoulders squeak over the back door of the Range Rover. There's a liberating crack, a hissing wind chases through your head and blows your ears free.

"Where are they?"

"I . . . I don't know, they . . ."

"Where are those fucking bitches?"

"... they ... they've stolen ... my father's ... my father's car and ..."

The man strikes. It feels as if his fist is wandering through your stomach and shattering your spine. You become a mouth that's going up and down and waiting to be filled with air. Your lungs are shriveled, your consciousness vanishes.

III

und ich will lichterloh brennen
damit ich leuchte wenn es
    dunkel ist

(and I want to burn bright)
(I want to glow when it's dark)

Pascal Finkenauer
VERDAMMT SEIN
(BEING DAMNED)

THE TRAVELER

And this is the finale. Now we're all in Norway, it's raining on us, and we see you standing there and you're completely helpless. It feels as if someone's pulled the ground out from under your feet. Your posture reveals as much. Your shoulders hang down, your eyes are slits, you're confused.

What's going on here?

You totter in the rain and again you're thirteen years old and just a boy standing by the poolside in the icy wind, goose bumps on his skin; but at the same time you're a man in his mid-forties who went on tirelessly murdering until he realized the senselessness of his action.

Do you feel the ground shaking?

Do you feel reality shifting?

We lost sight of you for three years and thought you'd disappeared forever. The special commission entirely devoted to you was dissolved. The flowers on your victims' graves have gone unchanged for ages now, and the memory of the Traveler is only one more episode in a collection of cruelties with a short half-life. Yesterday's disasters have been replaced by new disasters. It's a flowing change. Sympathy has a short-term memory. You know how the melody goes: We strive for the light, but want to be embraced by the darkness. We hunger for peace and chaos and we are never satisfied, we want more and more. And that's where you fall out of the picture, because you're not a part of us. You're not a *we*. You're an *I*.

That's the reason why we stay by your side right now. We want that *I*. We want your reaction, your helplessness, and we want to see you suffering. Because what could be more charming than a myth that bleeds?

Your chroniclers have wondered what you've been up to over the last few years. Some thought you had died, or become weary of yourself. *How much cruelty can an individual person endure?* they wrote in their blogs but never received an answer. A lot of people thought you'd left the country and resumed your traveling elsewhere. Spain. Africa. Maybe India. None of it is true. You got out of a train in Berlin. That was your last stop.

You are still on the road a lot. Every morning you spend half an hour on the toilet, laugh at good jokes and out of politeness at bad ones, and shake your head when someone dies. You still drink your coffee black and feel uneasy when you have to see the doctor. You make love, you curse, you try not to think ill of other people. On election day you stand in line; you feel your balls in the shower for undesirable swellings. Every Sunday you run one extra time around the park because your doctor says it does you good. It's a pleasant existence. You looked in the darkness for a long time and didn't find the demon. You learned to live with that disappointment, because you know everything you wanted to know about yourself. Your life is no longer a mystery to you. Millions of people strive to discover the point of their lives. See the goal, reach the goals. Fail and win. You've done all that. You are in a perfect state of consciousness. Your account is filled, your future is secure, the years have been good to you.

The big question is why this had to happen to you right here, right now.

You haven't riled anybody, you haven't insulted any gods or been guilty of misconduct. Is fate suddenly spitting back after all that time? Is this the final reckoning?

Whatever the answer, you're in Norway now, you're standing in the rain, while people openly gape at you, while the sky falls down on you. You look in all directions. However hard you look, your son has disappeared without a trace.

Since your journey to Berlin on the Intercity train, you've deliberately worked at getting closer to your boy. Your wife was very suspicious. You were living in another city, and then you were suddenly back as an alien body in the family, with a reawakened interest in your son. Your wife wanted an explanation. You spoke of change. Your wife laughed at you. You knew your son was the only reason you'd never got divorced. She didn't love you anymore, she just wanted to give Marten a sense of equilibrium. And at the age of sixteen he sounded so grown-up that it brought tears to your eyes.

You had proper boys' nights out when you went to the movies together, went to handball games and enjoyed your love of cars. Your son opened up hesitantly, but he opened up and that was what mattered.

You didn't want to repeat the mistakes of your parents—a neurotic mother and a remote father. No, that wasn't going to happen to you.

As Marten's eighteenth birthday approached, while searching the internet you happened upon an article about the Quart Festival in Kristiansand. You told Marten about the idea you had of driving the new car to Norway. You saw it in your mind's eye—wide streets, solitude, and your son at your side. Your first big trip was to be your shared adventure. Eight weeks, four in Kristiansand, four on the west coast. A perfect plan. You and your son.

And now you are soaked to the bone and you enter the restaurant and speak to a waitress in your clumsy English. You say your son was here with four girls, and hold up four fingers. The waitress points around the room. Her English isn't any better than yours. *Too many people, too many talk*, she says and turns away. You go from table to table, questioning the people and constantly looking outside as if your son might appear at one of the windows and wave at you. You tried his phone, you left him a message, his voicemail comes on at the sixth ring.

No one has seen him, no one remembers.

You walk back out into the rain. You urgently need to calm down, your throat is tight, the situation makes you sweat. This is new to you.

Say welcome to fear.

"Excuse me . . ."

The smokers shake their heads, a cleaning woman goes past with a bucket, you barely get half a sentence out and she's raising her hand. *Sorry.* She doesn't speak English. You look in the toilets and run twice through the gas station shop. You ask at the register and stand by the exit again, opposite the restaurant, right beside the Range Rover. Marten was at one of these tables and talked to you, he looked at the Range Rover and said: *Of course, I can see it through the window.*

You don't understand, and call his number again. He won't have run off with the girls. Marten isn't like that. You press the phone to your ear and look around.

Please answer.

The ringing sound comes to you like a whisper. You follow it around the Range Rover. Your son's phone has slipped a little way under a trailer and glows green to the rhythm of the ringtone. You pick it up.

What's happened here?

You see dark patches on the tarmac. You touch them, hold your fingers to the light. Blood. You feel dizzy, you lean your back against the Range Rover, unaware that your son was standing in this very spot a quarter of an hour ago. Your eyes are shut so tightly that lights explode in your head. In your head you run through every detail of your conversation.

"The door's open."

"What?"

"The driver's door is open."

You blink, look at the door, and pull on the handle. The door swings open, the light inside goes on. You can see the driver's seat is still wet.

He sat here.

You put your hand on the seat as if you could feel your son's warmth. It was a quarter of an hour ago. No more than that. You get into the car and have the pleasant feeling of getting closer to your son that way. You close the door and take a deep breath. The rain is locked out. The light dims.

"I think they've deliberately left me the key to the Range Rover."

Your hand seeks and finds the key. It's in the ignition. You lean your head back, the rain drums on the roof. You're sitting in a bloody Autobiography, hearing Marten's voice like a distant radio station: *Her name's Taja and she's not my girl.* Every word echoes in your head: *She inherited a beach hotel from her grandmother. With a view of a fjord.* You still don't get it. What's the connection? Why would they steal your car of all cars, and then come back?

"They're here again."

None of it makes any sense. Marten would never have gone with them.

"I'll call you right back."

He said he'd call you right back. And why is his phone lying in the road? And what about the blood? You look at your fingertips. There's no point sitting round here, just do something.

You search the car. There's an empty candy wrapper on the back-seat, some bits of paper on the floor, empty plastic bottles. You open the glove compartment. Sunglasses, five gas station receipts, a blunt pencil, nothing more than that.

You slam the glove compartment shut again and look at the instrument panel. It's all high-tech. You turn the ignition. The CD player comes on, you turn the sound down. The navigation system lights up and tells you it's another eight hours and eleven minutes to Ulvtannen. You tap on the display and see the route. It leads north.

"They're heading further north."

You start the car. Wherever your son has disappeared to, you're setting off to bring him back. Because that's what fathers do for their sons. They protect them.

DARIAN

He's soaked through with rain and quivering, he's bleeding from his mouth and every few seconds he gasps for air like there isn't enough oxygen in the car. He's older than you, bigger, one of those gangling types with shoulder-length hair that everyone likes. They write poems, listen to Damien Rice, and are adored by all the girls because they're so understanding. You must weigh twice as much as he does. Muscles versus brain. You grab the back of his neck and shake him. He starts whimpering. *Fine.* Now he knows who's in charge here. He stinks. The inside of the car fills with his smell and you remember the night three days ago when the gang roughed you up and Mirko ran away. You smelled just as bad when that happened, and even after a shower the stench didn't leave you and clung to your hands.

You don't want to think about Mirko, but your thoughts do what they want. You try to imagine one of the girls putting a gun to his head and then BOOM. The picture refuses to come into focus, as if it's trying to deny reality, but you'll find out what really happened. In detail. Which of the girls shot him, what she was thinking as she did so. And you will smell the same smell on her skin.

The doors open. Your father and Tanner get in. Your father slips in next to the boy. They've just been looking through the Range Rover and they've come back out empty-handed. Now their heavy breathing fills the interior of the car. Tanner opens the window a little to let the stench out. Leo starts the engine and turns on the heating. Your father asks the boy what his name is. The boy tells him.

"Okay, Marten, I'd like you to listen to me very closely now. I need to know how you're involved with the girls."

The boy tells you, stammering and nervous. How he thought the girls had problems with their car. How they had coffee together and then went off to the restroom and a moment later stole his father's car. How he came running out.

"But they were gone."

You nod. The story makes sense, it fits those sluts, but your father doesn't like it. He has a very different question.

"And why did you get into the Range Rover?"

The boy says it was raining and the driver's door had been open, so he'd thought he could get in.

"They left me the key."

He shouldn't have said that. It sounds so false that you want to knock his teeth out. Your father asks Tanner what he thinks. Tanner says it sounds ridiculous. *Me too,* you think, and say, "What if he's just putting on a show and they're all in it together?"

Back in Berlin, Tanner suggested that the girls had probably had help. The way it looks, Neil Exner wasn't the only one supporting those bitches. You take the same line. Your father gives you a look of approval. It's good that you're adding your bit.

"Maybe his job was to get rid of the Range Rover," you say.

The boy shrinks by nine inches. Your father asks him if he knows where the girls were going. The boy doesn't react. His eyes are shut tight, he for sure wishes the day would start over again and he would wake up in his bed. You grab the back of his neck again. He recoils and whimpers. Snot flows from his nose, Tanner and Leo turn round for the first time. This is going on too long for them. Your father repeats the question.

"Where were they going?"

"To the north . . . I think . . . They . . . they wanted to get to a beach hotel . . . on a fjord . . ."

You're impressed. It's a mystery to you how your father could have known where the girls were going. You admire him so much it hurts.

"She inherited it," the boy adds.

"Who inherited what?" your father asks.

"Taja, she inherited the hotel."

Leo whistles through his teeth, and you have no idea why he does it. Your father looks out the window into the rain for a moment, before turning back to the boy.

"What kind of car are they driving?"

"An 807."

"A what?" you all say at the same time.

"It's a Peugeot," says the boy. "A Peugeot 807."

Leo turns round and wants to know what color the car is.

"Red."

"Shit!"

Leo hammers twice on the steering wheel.

"Shit! Fucking shit!"

You don't know what's going on. Leo calms himself and says, "The car back there, the one at the exit that dazzled us, you know? Red. Shit, the car was red. I'm sure it was them."

Tanner looks at his watch.

"They can't be more than twenty minutes ahead of us. We'll get them."

Your father doesn't react. In the semi-darkness of the car you see him wiping the rain from his face as if it had only just begun to bother him. He's in no hurry, no one ever escapes him. He looks at you.

"Darian, show him your gun."

You draw the Five-Seven from your jacket. When you took it from Neil Exner and felt the grip in your hand, you knew immediately that it was a beauty. A Herstal, top Belgian model, light and elegant. You know it from gun magazines, NATO stock. Your boys in Berlin will shit themselves when you show it to them. You know Neil Exner got it off the girls, and you wonder if it's the same gun that killed Mirko.

The boy stares big-eyed at the Five-Seven, which is now on your knees. You feel him shaking beside you, it comes and goes in phases, you find it surprisingly arousing. If you're discovering your homo-erotic side right now, you really are in trouble.

Your father's explaining the rules to the boy.

"Darian's going to take care of you now, Marten, do you under-stand that?"

The boy doesn't understand, but he nods.

"The risk that you work with these girls is simply too high for us."

The boy stops nodding. *Now* he's understood. You smile. Leo puts the car in gear, reverses a little way, and turns. You leave the restaurant and you're back on Route 41. Twenty minutes pass, then the boy dares to break the silence.

"Please, let me go."

No one reacts, it isn't their problem anymore, it's up to you now, so you bring your mouth close to the boy's ear and whisper, "Say one more word, one single word, and I'll blow you away. I don't care whether you have anything to do with those bitches or not. I'm on your case now, and when I'm on your case you're mine and mine alone till the end of your fucking days. You're my responsibility, got that?"

The boy's eyes are closed again, but he's understood. Good. *Nothing works without rules,* you think. It would be interesting to hear what your thoughts would be if you knew what a big mistake you've just made. Because fear isn't always fear. There's also fear that awakes courage.

MARTEN

To understand you, we need a story from your life that you're not proud of. Your father doesn't know anything about it and your mother would probably have gone to the police if she'd known.

It's your very private story.

Once upon a time there was a boy who didn't defend himself. That boy was you. For years you kept your mouth shut. A psychologist would have established that you lacked the support of your father. A pal would have called you a pussy. Once upon a time there was another boy, who liked the fact that you kept your mouth shut and didn't defend yourself. He slugged you whenever he felt like it. In school, after school. No one did anything. He stuck his tongue in your ear and called you a faggot. He ate your recess-time snacks, poured Coca-Cola into your schoolbag, and threw darts at you. Sometimes friends tried to help you, sometimes a teacher came or a passerby stopped and intervened. Their help made things worse. He stole your bicycle and sold it. He kicked your legs away on the street, your arm broke in two places when you fell, and your mother was surprised that you could be so clumsy.

In a book you read about the transmigration of souls and wondered what would happen if this boy was your archenemy in a previous life. Could it be that your fates were intertwined? Was he your scourge and you his victim? The idea that supernatural powers might be involved gave you courage. Anything was better than reality. Every spell has a counterspell.

The year you turned fourteen, your archenemy did something unexpected. He hit a different boy. That confused you. You thought you were his special, personal adversary. You wanted him to tell you why he'd done it. He didn't understand what you were talking about, and smacked you. But you didn't let go, you went running after him across the playground and followed him into the boys' bathroom. He wanted to have a quick smoke in there, you needed an answer. He punched you in the stomach a few times and asked you if that was answer enough for you. You slid down the door. He asked you if that was what you'd wanted. He said you now belonged to him alone, forever and ever, and that from now on he'd just wait for you to have a girlfriend so that he could fuck her while you were forced to watch.

He was the same age as you, he was four inches shorter than you, it was going to be the last time he hit you.

When he leaned over you, you grabbed him by the shoulders. It looked as if you wanted to hug him. It took him by surprise. It was all you needed. You smacked your face against his. Again and again. You didn't let go of him. He couldn't find a grip, his sneakers slipped around on the tiles, he tried to push himself away from you, you didn't give in, your nose broke, you didn't yield an inch, and by the time you finally let him go he had lost his fighting spirit. He fell on top of you, and you lay there just like that.

Since that day you haven't belonged to anybody, you're your own man and you've found your counterspells — pride and violence. You never had to use them ever again, once was quite enough.

And now you're sitting in a moving car with four strange men and your skull is about to burst and that muscleman next to you is waving a gun around, pressing his body against yours, not letting you breathe. The whole thing's going too fast for you. A moment before you were on your way to the filling station to get ice cream for dessert, you were just flirting with a black-haired girl who knew almost all the bands you like. Until that moment your life had been an exciting sequence of great events. All of a sudden that collapsed and became this situation from which there seems to be no way out—you, crying; you, scared and summoning your voice and say-ing, "Please, let me go."

It sounds as if there's a dwarf sitting in your mouth and speaking on your behalf. You want to clear your throat, but the blood from your nose won't stop flowing down your esophagus. You swallow and want to spit, but you don't dare, you don't dare to do anything, you're just a pile of misery in a car racing through the night and planning to cross the whole of Norway in search of a beach hotel.

With me, shit, with me!

You know that isn't okay. *This isn't okay,* you want to say out loud, then muscleman leans over you and whispers in your ear as if he'd read your mind.

"Say one more word, one single word . . ."

Your brain registers the threat, your brain switches off and erects a mental barrier, but whatever your brain tries to do, the words filter through and your body pulls itself together. You're twelve again and then thirteen and then fourteen, and all the threats echo in your head and make you close your eyes. *Never again.* When you open them again, the sound of the rain has gone. From one second to the next the car is quiet, the only sound comes from the rolling of the tires. Everyone looks upwards with surprise, as if the car roof alone were responsible for the silence. Everyone apart from you, because that's the moment when you react. Your arms come up and you push mus-cleman against the window, his face hits the glass, there's a smacking sound and you scream at him, you scream into his face and feel the clammy, shaven scalp beneath your fingers and have no idea what words are coming out of your mouth. You push and scream, and then the shots go off ONETWOTHREE and the car starts swerv-ing and brakes hard, but you don't care. The spell is your spell and you're defending yourself, you want justice rather than enemies who are on your tail your whole life. Once was enough. Once was easily enough.

Never, ever again.

The car stops, you hear heavy breathing, you feel the wind blow-ing damp and warm into the car, and then you hear whimpering. Muscleman beside you has disappeared, the door is wide open.

Freedom.

You get out legs trembling, the car has stopped in the middle of the road, the headlights cut two breaches into the darkness, the tarmac steams and glistens like the skin of a reptile. You register everything, your senses are alert and receptive. The men in the car are moving. You hear groaning and cursing and you know you've got to get out of here, you've got to get away as fast as possible. Just do it.

Muscleman rams you from the side, you crash against the open door, bounce back, the air is pressed out of your lungs. You try to cling onto the door frame, the car door swings shut, you let go at the last moment, the door misses your fingers by a fraction of an inch. Muscleman grabs you by the back of the neck again, pulls you to him, and presses your head down as if you were a disobedient dog. You look at his running shoes, lift your foot, and stamp your heel down on his toes. He yells, he flinches, without letting go of you, then he slips on the wet tarmac. You both fall against the car and land in the road. You're lying under him, his face is a raging moon, blood flows from his nose and drips down on you. You turn your head away, your knee comes up and slams into his balls. He bends double and slips off you. You start creeping under the car. Your plan is to come out the other side and then run, run faster than ever before. You've half disappeared under the car when he grabs your ankle. You kick out, kick against his fingers, lose a sneaker, kick with your other foot, he lets you go. You're now right under the car, you slip through and come out on the other side where the man in the suit is waiting. He crouches down in front of you like someone who's been waiting for a while, and is now looking at the animal that's fallen into his trap. He has no gun, he doesn't come any closer, he doesn't need to touch you, he is the weapon.

"How could you?" you hear him say.

And then you give up. You put your arms over your head and give up. Enough is enough.

RAGNAR

The first bullet hits the back of Leo's head, a bloody crater glistens where his eye used to be. Leo leans against the driver's door, his shattered face pressing against the window, his other eye wide open and staring into the road. One hand lies on the steering wheel, as if he still had everything under control. You see the scars around his knuckles, his other hand rests on his knee, palm up. You've never seen Leo so motionless. No nervous twitching, nothing anymore.

The second bullet left a clean hole in the windshield.

It was the third bullet that caught Tanner from the side. It smashed two of his ribs and tore a pinhead-sized piece out of his heart and shredded his right lung. Tanner's head has dropped back, his breath rattles, and he stares at the roof of the car. His right hand grips the door handle, his finger bones shine white through the skin. The smell of urine hangs in the air like a spilled perfume.

You hear footsteps, your son comes running round the car, blood on his face, that damned gun in his hand. He sees you standing on the driver's side, he sees the boy at your feet. You hit him, one blow on the left, one on the right, then you grab your son by the ear, pull him around the car, and point at Leo.

"You see that, you little fucker? You see that?"

Your son pants, your son nods. The gun falls out of his hand; you should never have let him keep it. All this happened just because he was taken by surprise.

All this.

You let go of him and go back to the boy. He hasn't moved

from the spot. With his arms over his head he lies on the tarmac and shakes as if it is freezing cold.

What a fuckup, you think and take your jacket off. You fold it and lay it on the backseat. Then you roll up the sleeves of your sweater and try to open the driver's door. Tanner's still clutching the handle. You tell him to let go. Tanner doesn't react. So you knock against the glass. Tanner doesn't look at you. His eyes flicker. You wait a few seconds and try again. Tanner's grip has loosened, the door swings open. His pupils are dilated and moving, they try to settle on you, his head stays rigid. You lean into his field of vision, he sighs and looks at you. A tear dislodges from his left eye and flows down his cheek. The rattling in his lungs makes the hairs stand up on the back of your neck.

"What a mess," Tanner says and coughs blood.

"Calm now," you say, grabbing him under the arms and heaving him carefully out of the car. "Just be calm now, Tanner, I've got you."

"What can I do?"

Your son's there again. At least he has the guts to show up. He's wiped the blood off his face. You tell him what he needs to do.

"And clean the seat and the window."

You help Tanner to the edge of the road, ten yards away there's a rock, you sit Tanner carefully down on the ground so that he's sitting upright, with his back to the stone. Now no one can see him from the road. You sit down beside him and wipe the drool off his chin. The ground is soft and damp. It's all wrong. You could be back in Berlin right now. You could be at the theater, chatting over dinner, lying in bed.

"It's stopped raining," says Tanner.

You feel a stinging in your eyes and press his hand.

It's stopped raining, that's right.

"Typical Norway," says Tanner quietly. "It would have . . ."

"I know, it would have been nice if I'd taken you along to the wedding."

". . . been better."

"What?"

Tanner's thoughts are already elsewhere, his eyes look for the road and the car, he knows why he's sitting here.

"Leo?"

"Dead," you say.

Tanner sighs again, his eyes close, the rattling grows quieter.

"Poor Leo," Tanner says after a long pause. "Poor, poor Leo."

You hear the trunk slamming shut. Your son's footsteps.

". . . to me," says Tanner.

"What?"

"Bring Darian to me."

You hesitate, then you get up and call your son. You leave the two of them alone, go back to the car and crouch down beside the boy, who hasn't budged an inch from the spot. His arms are wrapped around his head, his knees pulled up to his chest. He doesn't hear you when you say his name. You look at his body, trembling and quaking, one sneaker is missing, his jeans are damp at the crotch, he looks pitiful, and you think: *He's someone's son.* You also think: *Every man is someone's son, you idiot!*

A minute passes, then another.

You hear Tanner, his voice is a long way off.

Farewell.

Your thoughts slip away from you as you study the boy's shaking back. You're no longer in the south of Norway, crouching by the roadside, you're standing in a cemetery in Berlin, Charlottenburg. It's drizzling and Tanner hasn't a shredded lung, he's talking to you and has to repeat his words three times before you really hear his voice.

"Ragnar, it's enough!"

You flinch. A man lies curled up on the ground in front of you, unmoving, except his back is like a bellows, it goes up, it goes down. You spit and turn away. It's spring 1993, and you're at Flipper's funeral, your son is nine months old, Oskar's been married for a year, and Majgull sticks in your head like a tick that's slowly but surely sucking out your brain.

Tanner passes you a cigarette, your hand is trembling. You thank him and ask for a light. The funeral's over, and you still don't know why all this is taking its toll on you. Last year went smoothly, even though you never had the feeling of being really present. A wife, a child, and you, somehow never quite part of the equation.

And now this funeral.

Tanner was quite relaxed when he heard about Flipper's death, although he was close friends with him. You knew Flipper had specialized as a courier in precious stones over the past few years. No one was really surprised when the news came in five days ago that Flipper had died of an overdose in a hotel in Geneva. You know it was murder. The consignment of precious stones wasn't in his luggage, and no one mentioned it. There will always be risks in this job.

The funeral is well attended for someone everybody thought was a junkie, and who wasn't really at home anywhere. Anyone in this city who'd had anything to do with Flipper is here today. Grief hasn't brought them together, they're all taking advantage of his death and looking out for new contacts. Business is business. This is a meeting that's all about profits. Businessmen among businessmen. Until five minutes ago one of those businessmen was still standing right beside you, saying that it served Flipper's looks taking all those drugs over the years.

"He looks like a bloody mummy, you could probably make money by putting him on display."

You asked the businessman to step aside from the others. Once he was lying on the ground, you kicked him until he couldn't get up again. Apart from Tanner, no one intervened. Now your fist is sore, but you don't regret losing your composure. It felt good. Tanner is completely clueless and doesn't understand what happened. At least that's what you think.

"What's up with you?" he asks.

"Nothing."

"You'd only known Flipper for one day, so what's up with you?"

The answer lies heavy and thick in your mouth. Spit it out.

"Was Flipper his real name?"

Tanner laughs a sad laugh.

"No, his name's Felipe. He hated the name, even in kindergarten he called himself Flipper."

"In kindergarten? You'd known each other that long?"

"We were neighbors, sometimes you just know people. But that's not important. Ragnar, stop avoiding the issue. What's your problem?"

You clench your aching fist, you try to sound as matter-of-fact as possible.

"He was like a father to me."

"What?"

"I know it sounds crazy, but he felt like my father never had done. When I was out of it on New Year's Eve, he wiped the puke off my face. He looked after me. Like a father, in fact. Not like you, you're a friend; not like just anybody, do you get that?"

"Shit, Ragnar, you only knew him for a day."

"I know, that's the weird thing. Something strange happened on that day."

"He slept over at your place, he used the toilet, what else have I missed?"

"Flipper showed me a way."

Tanner laughs.

"You found this way by yourself. He gave you drugs to deliver. You delivered them. That's all that happened."

"He knew what he was doing."

"Flipper knew a lot of things, that's why he's in that hole there."

"That's probably true."

Tanner looks at you quizzically.

"You're not going to have a breakdown on me, are you?"

"'Course not."

"Flipper was a nice guy, that's all."

"But without him we'd never have met. You think that happened by chance?"

You smile. You know the answer, yet you want to hear it again. Tanner obliges.

"Chance is the sister of fate. And fate is a guy with syphilis and a hard-on, fucking you in the ass as soon as you look in the wrong direction."

"I'll remember that one."

"You say that every time."

You look across at the businessman. He's clutching his stomach, supported by two of his colleagues. He doesn't glance in your direction.

"You can be thankful you didn't break any of his ribs."

"Did you hear what he said?"

"I was standing beside you."

Tanner waits; at this point he's only known you for three years, but he always knows when to wait and when to talk. You look over at the mourners who are on the way to their cars. Business cards are exchanged, conversations ended, hands shaken. Life goes on. Your funeral will be exactly the same. Pure business.

As you watch the procession, you realize what's just happened. Your frustration is over a year old. It's been fermenting away and now it's looking for an outlet. It didn't really have anything to do with Flipper or your father. Tanner was right not to believe you. These are all just alibis that are supposed to put your mind at rest. Open your eyes. Your problem lies elsewhere, and Tanner expects you to recognize that.

"Tanner?"

"I'm listening."

"I've got to call her."

"Oh, shit."

That's all either of you needs to say.

You call her two days later. It takes you two days, to understand what you're actually doing. After you've jogged six miles through the forest and had a cold shower, after you've worked your body until your head was able to work properly again, you're ready and you call her number.

She picks up after the fourth ring. You knew she was there. Anything else would have been unacceptable. Your voice sounds unfamiliar to yourself when you say in English, "It's me."

She breathes out.

She breathes in.

Nothing else happens.

You feel your jaw quivering, you listen out for background noises. Nothing. As if she were in a bell jar and you were her only contact with the outside world. At last she speaks.

"I know."

As if everything inside you were suddenly blossoming. *She knew I'd call.* As if a previously hidden world were opening up. You know it's ridiculous, you know it's a cliché and irrational. But that's exactly how it is. You're twenty-eight, and that's exactly how it is.

"I need to see you."

"Where?"

"Can you get away?"

"I can."

You name a hotel in Amsterdam. Amsterdam is the first city that comes into your mind. It could just as well have been Istanbul or Skopje. You couldn't think of a city in Norway. Her reaction is like a surgeon's first incision. Without hesitation.

"See you there."

She hangs up. You look at your phone. The whole conversation took twenty-two seconds. No more, no less.

The same day you go to Amsterdam and wait for her. You leave your cell phone number for her at reception and wander aimlessly through the city. In the evening you eat in the hotel bar and read. She arrives on the third day, just before midnight. You look up from your book, and there she is. You don't know how long she's been standing there. She has no luggage, just a handbag over her shoulder.

You pull the bar stool next to you out a little way. She comes over and sits down. You don't touch each other, you just look at each other, and then she asks in German how many coffees you've had already. You love it when she speaks German to you. From the very first moment there's a special charm in the fact that you can switch languages whenever you feel like it. As if you had a very private connection that extends across continents. You look at the counter. There are four empty coffee cups sitting on it, and you can't remember drinking even one of them.

"More than four," you say.

She looks at the book.

"How's the book?"

You push it away.

"Like all books."

She smiles. She pretends to read the title. Her voice sounds as if she's asking the time.

"I'm pregnant."

And she says, "I'm in the sixth month."

And you can't think of a better answer than, "I'm glad."

She laughs. Suddenly. As if it had just occurred to her that laughter's permitted.

"I'm really here."

"Yes, you're really here."

It sounds absurd, but everything between you sounds absurd. The fact that she's speaking German to you, that you're sitting side by side at a hotel bar in Amsterdam and that the waiter's left your empty coffee cups there. Especially the fact that you don't touch each other. Especially that.

"Come," you say.

You leave the bar and walk past the lobby. You step into the elevator and stand side by side, familiar yet strange to one another. The elevator starts moving, the floor shakes, and nothing else happens. On the fifth floor you open the door to your suite and let her walk ahead. Her scent hovers in the air, sandalwood and oranges, you inhale it deeply before you follow her.

In the morning she travels back to Norway. She never mentions love. She never mentions the future. *Your brother mustn't know,* she says at one point. She doesn't want you to come and get her from Norway, everything's to stay the way it is. And you believe her and don't see through her lie for a second. *It is the way it is,* you think. In another age you'd have been dismissed as a fool.

She comes to Holland another four times, and you wait for her in the hotel, open the door to the suite and let her walk ahead. You don't know what she's told Oskar about where she is at those times, and you aren't really interested. You don't question your actions. When she's in the ninth month, you meet in a hotel in Bergen that's just three hours away from Ulvtannen. She's excited, they're nearly there and it's going to be a girl. She tells you her name. Taja. You make love very carefully.

Six days later Oskar calls you.

You're in Munich, you hear your brother's excited voice through the phone and wonder how you're ever going to get back out of this mess.

"A daughter! I've got a daughter!"

You laugh with him. He wants to know when you're coming to Ulvtannen. You mumble something about a lot of work and then ask if you could congratulate Majgull. Oskar walks through the hotel, no, he runs, you hear his footsteps echoing down the stairwell.

"See you soon, brother," he says.

"See you soon, Dad," you say.

The footsteps move away, there's a hiss on the line.

"Majgull?"

"Hello."

Silence.

"Are you okay?"

"Wonderful."

Silence.

"Good luck."

"Thanks."

She breathes in your ear and you don't dare say anything wrong. You just sit there and have an erection. After another moment of silence you hang up without a word.

Two years of silence follow. Two long, miserable years of silence in which you don't call, in which you get harder and harder inside, like a diamond that lies in the depths like a dead man who can't let go of life. Tanner's the only one who knows.

"Stay away from the woman," he says.

You have a son you have to look after, and your work demands your full attention. There can be no more lapses.

You listen to Tanner.

Two years' silence and then there's a short message on your phone. Majgull calls at three o'clock in the morning and says the Plaza Hotel in Oslo. She wants you to understand her lies. She wants you to see her as she really is. You have no idea what she's talking about. A fool is always a fool, and that fool needs to see Majgull. Without Tanner's knowledge. You don't want an argument, and you know there's definitely going to be an argument if you tell him. So you fly out that same day. *I need to see you.* You can't guess that she doesn't plan to come on her own.

"Father?"

Your son's standing in front of you, and we're back in the here and now. Your drifting thoughts have been rudely interrupted. Your son's face is wet with tears. You don't know how much time has passed. There's a stale taste in your mouth that makes you think of Majgull—sweet and sharp at the same time, the taste of loss. The boy is still lying on the ground in front of you. His back rises and falls. You're still crouching next to him like a big cat guarding its catch. A few minutes have passed. You look down at your son, you see his tears and think he's weeping over Tanner. You're not concentrating. Every time you remember Majgull, you lose your contact with reality. Like now, when you misinterpret your son's tears. It's unforgivable. If you were focused right now, you might be able to save your life. But you took your eye off the ball, and for that moment's inattention you will pay later on.

"I—"

"Don't say anything," you cut him off and stand up.

Your son says nothing, you go back to Tanner. His torso has slipped slightly sideways off the rock. You straighten him up, smooth his hair. He's almost white in the face. The rattling in his lungs sounds damp. It won't be long now.

"Hold me."

You sit down next to him again, you take a breath and hold Tanner in your arms. The only light comes from the headlights of the car. Only now do you notice that the engine's been running the whole time. The storm has passed. No stars. No traffic. Wherever God is now, he should stay there. Tanner shivers in your arms. Something damp runs down your hand, you don't move, you hold him and don't move. You give him warmth.

"Ragnar?"

"Yes?"

"Ragnar?"

"I hear you."

"Let me . . ."

You wait.

". . . let me . . ."

You wait.

". . . please."

"Of course, my friend, of course."

Tanner shuts his eyes, his head presses hard against your shoulder, you kiss his forehead and put your hand gently over his mouth. His nostrils flare, you close them with your thumb and forefinger, Tanner presses himself against your chest as if he wanted to merge with you. One minute. A second. The rattling falls silent. Tanner's mouth moves one last time as if to kiss your hand. The shaking fades, then Tanner falls still into your arm, just as the night falls still on this damned day. No pain anymore.

You pull away and stand up. Your body is vibrating as if connected to an electric line. You lean forward and pick Tanner up. He's smaller and heavier than you. You carry him in your arms to the car. Your son is sitting on the hood. He understands you without a word and opens the trunk. You put Tanner inside with Leo.

"Where's your gun?" you ask your son.

He thumps his jacket. You can see that he's in shock, and that's okay. He should go on living in shock, for a whole century, because two men have died on his account.

"Take the boy behind the rock."

SCHNAPPI

For a few seconds you're like panicked chickens, running about in a minefield, before you turn back into four girls sitting in a brand-new car that doesn't belong to you and isn't budging an inch.

"Shit, it's not an automatic!"

"Just drive, drive!" yells Stink.

"Are you deaf or what?" says Nessi shrilly. "I can't drive this thing, it's not an automatic!"

"Shit, he's looking at us!" Taja shouts next to you and smiles anxiously outside as if Marten could seriously see her from this distance. You all lean forward and look over at the restaurant. Four chickens pausing for a photograph in the middle of a minefield. Marten's mouth is gaping. He's a good fifteen yards away from you in the restaurant and can't believe his eyes. As far as he's concerned you're still in the bathroom. As far as he's concerned this isn't really happening.

"DRIVE!" you suddenly screech and break the spell and sound like one of those girls in the manga cartoons. "DRIVE, DRIVE, DRIVE!"

Nessi turns the ignition. The engine comes to life. Nessi puts her foot on the accelerator, the engine wails, Nessi's so nervous that she's forgetting the simplest hand motions, she tugs on the gearshift, the car jumps forward and bumps with a crash against the nose of the Range Rover, before the engine stalls.

Stink slaps Nessi on the back of the head.

"PULL YOURSELF TOGETHER, YOU SILLY TART, WE'VE GOT TO GET OUT OF HERE."

"I'M TRYING, CAN'T YOU SEE THAT? I'M TRYING."

"REVERSE!" yells Taja. "PUT IT IN REVERSE!"

Nessi shakes her hands out as if she's got a cramp, then she starts the engine again and shifts the stick to R. The car jumps back and stalls again.

"I CAN'T DRIVE THIS THING!"

Nessi sounds as if she's about to burst into tears. You can see that Marten's up from the table.

"HE'S COMING!" cries Taja.

You burst out laughing.

"Stop it," she says.

"That sounded as if someone had tied a knot in your ovaries."

Stink drums her feet on the floor.

"NESSI, DO IT, JUST DO IT, OR DO YOU WANT THE GUY TO DRIVE THE CAR FOR YOU?"

Nessi jiggles the gearshift, tries to work the clutch, pumps with both feet as if this weren't a car but a paddleboat.

"You've got to lift the clutch gently," you say as calmly as you can from the backseat.

"The what?"

"The clutch, Nessi, gently."

Nessi starts wailing. The engine stalls. Nessi holds both hands in the air and says she can't and she doesn't want to and could Stink stop annoying her. Stink looks back at you.

"You do it."

"I'm too small."

"There's no such thing as too small!"

Stink pulls you forward as she herself climbs into the back. Nessi makes room for you and slips into the passenger seat. Behind the wheel you feel like a dwarf in the land of giants. You stretch and the tip of your left foot finds the clutch and your right the brake, while your spine stretches and strains. Now you've got to pretend you know what you're doing. When your father gave you driving lessons, you sat on a pillow and drove across a parking lot. Back then it was all a game.

You concentrate and start the car. You put it in reverse, bring the clutch up slowly, and you move back at a snail's pace. Your girls cheer. You brake, put the clutch down, and shift into first gear. You slowly bring the clutch back up. You do it very elegantly and then you destroy the moment when you tap the accelerator. The car shoots off, your girls screech, you pull the wheel to the left, miss the restaurant by inches, manage to turn and race toward the exit without leaving a scratch on the car. The rain seems to applaud you, the windshield is a steeply flowing river.

"I CAN'T SEE ANYTHING! THIS FUCKING RAIN, I CAN'T SEE ANYTHING!"

Nessi reaches under your arms and the windshield wipers come on, but you still can't see anything, because it's dark, because it's night. There's something missing. Stink shouts in your ear, "LIGHT! DAMN IT, SCHNAPPI, TURN THE LIGHTS ON!"

You shove all the levers on the steering wheel up and down and at last a light comes on and the road flares up and of course at that very moment a car comes charging straight at you and a voice in your head yells: *THAT WAS IT!* You pull the wheel to the right and the car speeds past you.

The road in front of you is empty and as brightly lit as a football stadium.

"Your high beams are on," says Nessi.

"So," you say, and think you can taste the adrenaline on your tongue. You enjoy being in the role of the crazy driver. Nessi reaches past you again and finds the right switch.

The high beams come off, but the dipped headlights stay on.

"Everything okay back there?" you ask and reach for the rear-view mirror the way you've seen people do in movies, but your arm's too short. You can't even reach the mirror. Hell, why are you so small? You glance over your shoulder. Taja's turned pale from all the rocking, and Stink looks as if she's bitten a lemon. She looks at her right hand and wails, "One of my fingernails is broken!"

"Pussy," says Nessi.

"Double pussy," you say.

Stink kicks your seat, you swerve deliberately from left to right, the girls screech again and then laugh, because you've got everything under control and it's always reassuring when someone has something under control. If your father could see you now, you know what he'd say:

Little, but wow!

After half an hour it suddenly stops raining, you look suspiciously out the window, it feels as if someone has turned the power off on the night. The storm has passed, and you're still on the road. Driving is easier now, but your shoulders are tense because you still have to stretch to see the road ahead.

Taja says she's got to pee, suddenly you all have to pee. You stop at the side of the road and you find a place behind the bushes, squat down, and pee. You can't help grinning. Four girls in a circle, panties around their knees and butts sticking out. Nessi passes tissues around, you wipe yourselves and drop them on the ground. You know Nessi's thinking about picking them all up.

"It's cellulose, it's biodegradable," says Taja and pulls her trousers back up.

"Says you."

"Knows I."

In the car Nessi's supposed to be taking over. You show her how the clutch works, and feel cocky. You're in a floating state as if nothing can happen to you as long as you keep moving. But what sort of lie is that? Ruth's death caught you totally unprepared even though you were in motion. For a while you even wanted to give up. Lie down on the ground and never get up again, never breathe again, just disappear. Taja and Nessi were ahead of you on that one. When you saw them both crying, you knew that giving up wasn't an option, because there was only Stink and you to keep you all together. Lying down on the ground and giving up breathing wouldn't have been fair to Stink.

"Let's drive on," says Taja.

She's nervous, she keeps looking back, because who knows what Marten will do when he works out that you aren't planning on coming back.

"I feel really mean, he was so nice."

Stink pats Taja's arm.

"Next time we'll find somebody who's a total asshole."

"Next time we'll all stay at home," you say.

Nessi smells her rain-soaked T-shirt and says she needs some fresh clothes. Stink asks her to bring a sweatshirt. Nessi goes to the back of the car. The trunk opens, you hear her rummaging in the bags. In the meantime you do something sensible and fiddle around with the navigation system and ask Taja what that funny place is called again.

"Ulvtannen," she says.

"Spell it."

Taja spells it; she's lying down on the backseat with her legs in Stink's lap. All that's missing is a hot tub and a minibar. The navigation system indicates the route and you're about to tell your girls that you're right on course when Nessi shouts from the back, "Stink, you're the biggest asshole of all time!"

Taja and you freeze and look at Stink.

Stink pulls a surprised face.

"I haven't done anything," she says.

"Could everybody please get out of the car," says Nessi.

You get out of the car and go to the back. Two of the backpacks are open. In one of them is a yellow sports bag. Nessi is holding a white package in her right hand.

"No way!" says Taja.

"Come on, Stink!" you yell and try to sound angry, but your tone gives you away. It's incredibly hard to be angry with Stink.

"How could you?" Nessi wants to know.

Stink shrugs.

"I was sure Darian would fuck me over, so I packed two bags. There were books in one. It wasn't so stupid, was it? Imagine the look on their faces when they took the wrong sports bag out of the safe-deposit box!"

Nessi gets a weird gleam in her eyes, and then she throws the package at Stink, who steps casually aside. The heroin flies past her head and lands in the road, where it slides across the tarmac with a slithering noise. The plastic wrapping tears open. The white powder immediately turns gray on the wet road surface.

"Yeah, great," complains Stink. "Just keep chucking our retirement money around."

You see Taja making big eyes. She is probably wondering whether it's worth licking the wet powder off the road. You don't understand why Nessi is making such a fuss. It doesn't matter how Stink managed to get the drugs into her backpack now, because the stuff's here and not in Berlin, so you should really be celebrating the fact.

Nessi doesn't look as if she wants to celebrate anything.

"No wonder they won't leave us alone," she says. "And now you've fucked over Neil too."

"What? How have I fucked him over?"

"You stupid cow, he gave Taja's uncle the key to the safe-deposit box, he was trying to protect us, and now—"

"Now we're safe and in Norway," Stink interrupts. "No one needs to protect us anymore, Nessi, we're protecting ourselves. Neil will be able to talk his way out of it, he wasn't born yesterday. If you like, we'll stop at the next post office, package it all up, and send the whole shitload back to Taja's uncle. I don't care."

"Great idea," says Taja, "as if customs doesn't check packages coming from abroad. My uncle will dance with joy when he sees the cops standing at his door and asking him who his dealer is."

"He'd have deserved it."

"He'd definitely have deserved it," Taja agrees, "but that's not the point."

Cease-fire. No one asks what the point is. Taja buries her hands in the front pockets of her jeans and asks if you could now please, please drive on. Nessi thinks she's misheard.

"What? Is that all? Stink idiotically brings the drugs along without saying a word, and you just want to drive on?"

"What else are you going to do?" you ask. "Are you going to punish her now, or what?"

"Just try it," says Stink, and assumes the boxing posture, both fists in front of her face so that only her eyes can be seen.

"You're such a jerk," says Nessi, and there's no humor in the insult, it's meant seriously. Stink lowers her fists and tries to sound sincere.

"I'm sorry."

"I don't believe you."

"Okay, I'm not really sorry, but it's happened now."

Nessi nods, yes, it's happened now, then she says something none of you wants to hear.

"You know what, girls, I'd like to go home. I'm fed up. I've had enough of this chaos. We're lying to each other, we're fucking with people who are kind to us, and we're making more and more of a shitstorm with every passing minute, and we're not even there for Ruth's funeral. Is that really what you want?"

You all look away; of course you don't want that.

"No one wants that," says Taja, "but we can't turn back now."

"I know that. I just wanted you to know. You're my girls, but I'd really like to be back in Berlin."

Nessi throws Stink a clean sweatshirt and says you can drive on now. You haven't got a good feeling, something is different, right now you don't want to put an axe in Nessi's hands. You get back into the car. Stink nudges you and whispers that it's all going to get a lot worse when Nessi's got a belly on her.

"Shut up," Taja hisses back, and Stink actually does shut up. Nessi waits until you're all comfortably back in the car, and only then does she get going. You hear a slapping sound and look out the back window. One plastic bag after the next lands in the road. You like that, you like it when your girls go a bit nuts. They're not your friends for nothing. And everyone needs a valve for letting off steam, even if that steam is worth several million euros.

Taja curses and jumps out of the car. Stink follows, you come after them, but of course you're too slow, and before you've set foot on the road Nessi's thrown out the seventh bag and the tarmac looks as if it's just snowed after rain.

"Don't come any closer!" warns Nessi.

She's holding the next bag in her hand. She looks totally insane; if you touch her now, she'll probably explode with rage.

"You're insane," says Stink.

Nessi throws, Stink tries to catch the bag, it tears between her fingers and covers her jeans from her feet up to her knees. It looks as if Stink's wearing white boots. Nessi chucks the last two bags into the road. One of them stays intact. Nessi goes and stamps it flat. Then she comes and plants herself in front of Stink.

"Where are the pills and the other shit?"

Stink says under her breath that she left them down at the bottom of the sports bag. Nessi chucks the pills and the other shit into the bushes. When she's finished, she's breathing heavily and slams the trunk shut. For a moment she stands behind the car so that you can't see her throwing up, then she comes back and says, "That was for Ruth."

Immediately all of you have tears in your eyes. Stink lowers her gaze, she has understood. Nessi walks past you and sits down at the wheel. A minute later you're on the road again. The mood is gloomy. Stink mumbles that she didn't mean that thing about the belly. Nessi mumbles back that it's okay. Silence settles on you again. You look through the CD box from the glove compartment. It's up to you to save the moment. You choose the CD with the weirdest name. Experimental Pop Band. You put it in the player and hope it isn't some stupid classical orchestra pretending to be modern and playing Bach sonatas with a chainsaw. Music and lyrics have to be right. You want your girls to smile again, so you put your trust in the gods, and that they're looking mercifully down on you, as your mother always used to preach to you: *Stay close to your home, and the gods will look down mercifully upon you.* As if the gods had nothing better to do with their time.

The CD player starts, you turn up the volume and close your eyes. For a breath nothing comes out of the speakers and the gods start wondering what's going on. At last there's a crackle and a woman's voice whispers: *Bang, bang, you're dead.*

THE TRAVELER

Half an hour later you see something pale in the road and brake. You stop six feet away and get out. It's a sneaker. You pick it up and look round. Lights come toward you from a long way off. You stand there and wait. The lights approach and turn into four motorbikes. They keep accelerating and race past, only a few feet away from you. One of the drivers gives you the finger, then they're gone. You stand there, holding the sneaker. Every fiber in your body is in flames. You can't move. You see the skid marks on the tarmac. A car has gone into a swerve here and then stopped on the dotted line.

Right here.

You look to the right, it hurts, every inch hurts, but you leave the road and look through the bushes. Shoe prints on the damp earth. Further off, a rock. Something keeps you from going over there. You go over there. Blood on the soil, blood on the stone. Someone's been sitting here. You should get back to the road. You walk around the rock, and there lies your son with his face pressed into the damp soil. His arms are bent and lie close to his body, his hands have clawed into the soil next to his head as if he wanted to cling onto it. Beside his hips you see deep prints made by knees. Whoever was sitting on your son was stopping him from moving.

You turn him over. His eyes are open, his eyes are full of dirt. You wipe the dirt carefully away with your thumbs, you close his eyes. And look at him. And look at him. You sit down on the ground and put the sneaker on him. You make a bow, it goes wrong, you make it again, and only then do you wipe the rest of the dirt out of his face.

Reach into his mouth. Take the soil out. Run your finger over his lips. He's clean now.

You wait.

You don't look at the sky, you don't murmur a prayer. You're a man whose dead son is lying next to him, and nothing else is ever going to happen in this world. No disaster will be unleashed because of it, no one will set himself on fire, no pop star will write a song.

In the trunk of the Range Rover you find a blanket. You wrap Marten up in it and carry him to the car. After you've laid him down on the backseat, you take your jacket off and put it under his head. You want him to be comfortable, it's his last journey. You close the door and stand beside the car in a T-shirt that belonged to your son. He lent it to you and dared you to wear it for a whole day. Today is that day. A white cross in a circle on a black background. Like you see on ballots. And under that the word *deselected.* You look very silly. Like someone who's become something he never wanted to be.

You get back into the car and are about to start the engine when the shaking begins. First your jaw, your teeth chatter against each other, then it wanders downward, and within seconds your whole body is shaking so hard that you have to hold on tight to the steering wheel. Your balls contract painfully as if trying to hide in your abdomen, your guts want to spill their contents, you control them, you control yourself, the car rocks, the shaking turns into a hurricane that rushes through your life and drags away everything that isn't nailed or bolted down. Including your son.

A few minutes later you're calm and bathed in sweat. The windows are covered with condensation from inside, the car stands still. You carefully peel your fingers off the steering wheel and reach for the ignition key. The peace remains. You start the engine, put the car in gear. The car starts moving. You lower the window, the wind cools the sweat on your face. The monster in the deep jolts awake and rises to the surface. The Traveler is on the road once more.

PART THREE

you think the world owes you
it don't owe you a thing

Sean Hayes
ROSEBUSH INSIDE

THE TRAVELER

The night is a narrow tunnel that you're moving through with great determination. Everything about you is efficient. Even your breathing, even your glances, every movement has a purpose. You stop twice. Once to fill up, once to stretch your back. While you're filling up you drink water and eat a cheese sandwich. You see, you breathe, you move. Nothing else happens.

At the age of seven Marten wanted to know what you were scared of. You didn't have a good answer for him. So you said the stupidest thing a father can say to his fearful child.

"There's nothing to be afraid of. When you've grown up, you'll see for yourself that there's nothing in life to be afraid of."

Apart from the death of your own child.

While you were looking for Marten at the restaurant, true fear gripped you for the first time. Only after you'd lifted his corpse out of the dirt and laid it in the Range Rover did your fear melt away again. Like an illness leaving you. Forever. There's no one now that you need to look after. There's no reason for you ever to be afraid again.

Seven hours later the sky lightens. You drive through Vik, morning comes hesitantly, on your left side a fjord peels away from the landscape, misty and gray. You stop at an abandoned crossroads. The navigation system lets you know that you've reached your destination. The car stops, the engine is running, you look in the rearview mirror and meet your own gaze. A stranger looks at you and the stranger is your best friend. You tap on *recalculate destination*. The result is the same. You haven't driven all the way across Norway to arrive at a crossroads. You turn off the navigation system. You have a choice of two roads. One leads up on the right, the other leads further along the fjord. A sign says LUNNIS 1 KM. No mention of Ulvtannen. You drive further along the fjord.

It's Saturday, seven in the morning, even the bakeries are still shut. A delivery guy beeps at you because you've stopped in the middle of the street. You get out, walk to the back of the car, and ask the man if he knows where Ulvtannen is. He shakes his head, he's not from around here. You get back into the Range Rover and pull over. What now? For a quarter of an hour you just sit in the car and stare into the street. You try and work out what you're doing in Lunnis.

A man with a greyhound on a leash taps on the glass. You lower the window. The greyhound looks at you with its head tilted as if it wants to say something to you. The man is in his mid-twenties, he has a pockmarked face and smells of woodsmoke.

"Good morning," he says in English.

"Good morning."

"Do you need help?"

"I'm looking for a place called Ulvtannen."

"You are looking for the hotel?"

Before you can answer, the man laughs and speaks to his dog in Norwegian, the dog yawns, the man looks at you again and says, "Sorry. My dog is tired."

"I'm tired, too," you say.

The man jabs his thumb over his shoulder.

"You see the building behind the church? There's a path to the water. You climb the hill. Up and up. You don't need your car. You can walk it easily. Fifteen minutes."

"Thank you."

"No problem."

You park the Range Rover outside the closed post office, walk past the church and an old building, and climb a path that consists largely of broken stone slabs. The fjord appears again on your left. It could also be a football field; the view doesn't interest you. Thick mist floats like a layer of cream on the water. By the shore you see a boathouse and next to it a flagpole with the Norwegian flag hanging slackly from it. A beaten path replaces the stone slabs, leading up between the cliffs and disappearing behind a bend.

After twenty minutes you reach a knoll and there is your car waiting for you. You stop. Nothing happens. You go over and see four girls. They're asleep and look so innocent that your heart contracts.

The window on the driver's side is open. One of the girls is leaning against the door, she has golden hair, a few strands blowing out of the open window. In her lap is the head of a red-haired girl, and in the back a fine-boned Asian girl is sleeping arm in arm with a pale beauty. The girls look as if they'd belonged together forever. You know there's something not quite right about this situation, but you don't yet know what it is. You can hear the girls breathing and wonder which one of them is Taja and whether that has any significance. You thought you'd find them and make them pay for what they did to your son. You didn't expect a sight like this. You look round. There is a road leading up to the top of the cliff.

If this is Ulvtannen, what are they doing here? And where's the hotel?

So many questions, so few answers.

You reach through the window and pull out the ignition key.

Later.

TAJA

The water below you, the sky above you and you're sitting in the grass, your feet dangling over the edge, and nothing is as it was in your dream—the day isn't gray, no snow is falling, and the valley walls shimmer in the morning sun like liquid silver and don't look in the slightest like Japanese ink-wash drawings.

It's nine in the morning, and your girls are still asleep in the car. You woke up half an hour ago and looked outside. And there it was, there was everything. The earth and the sky, the cliff and the fjord.

Home.

In front of you the cliff climbs higher, twenty yards to your left you see a narrow, overgrown path leading down to the pebble beach. On the beach there's a boathouse, the boards are painted green, the paint has faded on the lower edge. The shadow of a flagpole draws a sharp line across the façade. You sit very still, you look at the line and wait for it to wander on. The sunbeams are tireless, they tear holes in the pale gray carpet of mist, letting the surface of the water shine through. A high-pitched cry makes you start. It echoes for several seconds over the fjord, then silence falls again. You look into the clouds. Perhaps a bird of prey, perhaps a seagull.

Or my father, calling to me.

You sniff hard. Since you've been sitting here, the tears won't stop flowing. Tears for your father, tears for Ruth, and most particularly tears for yourself. Melodramatic and so pathetic that you get a pain in the back of your head. But the tears help and release the pressure that weighs down on you like a great hand, trying to make you smaller.

"Brilliant!"

You hastily wipe your face dry. Schnappi comes and stands next to you and looks at the fjord.

"This isn't a place, this is a fairy tale!"

The passenger door opens. Stink blinks around suspiciously, then braces her feet against the dashboard and puts on her boots. She's the only one you're really afraid of. Nessi and Schnappi are the ideal listeners, full of sympathy and love. Stink's always critical, she only ever sees the dark side, but she's fair, you particularly like that about her. If she sees a lie, she gets her teeth into it and tears it to pieces. Which doesn't stop her lying like a loon herself. You love and hate it in her. There's always a bit of distance between you two. As if you mustn't get too close to each other. Even the way she jumps out of the car and runs both hands furiously through her mane, as if she were washing her hair. She reminds you of a warrior who's escaped from a Viking movie. After she's stretched she says, "I'm in urgent need of coffee. Coffee and a roll."

"First take a look at this," says Schnappi, "it's fantastic."

"Yeah, yeah, in a minute."

Stink pulls her pants down and squats beside a bush. She yawns, winks at you, and says, "So, are you a voyeur or something?"

"You look awful."

"Take a look in the mirror, bitch."

"You're really pale," says Schnappi and points at her hairdo. "How do I look?"

You wave her over, Schnappi leans forward and you comb her sticking-out hair behind her ears, and after that she looks tolerable again.

Stink snaps her fingers.

"Hey, I don't suppose one of you could . . . ?"

You rummage in your jacket and hand Schnappi a pack of tissues. She throws them to Stink. Stink joins you a minute later and says, "Funny lake."

Schnappi rolls her eyes.

"Girl, that's not a lake, that's a fjord."

Stink gives her a shove with her backside.

"Oh, is that right?"

"Where do you think we are?"

"In the country where you can mess with little Vietnamese girls?"

Schnappi shoves back.

"Ever fallen in a fjord?"

"Ever had the worst hairdo of all time?"

"Sit down and shut up," you interrupt them, and your girls listen to you and sit down, let their legs dangle and say nothing. A whole two minutes.

"And the coffee?"

You sigh. A seagull lands on the flagpole. Stink yawns and asks who wants a cigarette. Schnappi throws her head back and spits into the fjord in a high arc.

"That hit the spot!"

"Yeah, and I got half of it in my face."

Stink makes a show of wiping her face on her sweatshirt. You look down between your feet.

"Do you think if we jumped we'd die?"

Your girls take a look too, Stink stretches her hand out and drops the used tissue. You watch it curving, sweeping down and landing on the water like a clumsy bird.

"No, that wouldn't kill anybody," says Stink. "You'd just make a big splash and go swimming around. Where are we, by the way?"

In my dream, you want to answer, but you know how stupid it would sound. And your friends don't know anything about your dream. Your sense of longing is as alien to them as you yourself have been to them for quite some time.

"Nessi will know where we are," you say and get to your feet.

Of course you can't wait until Nessi wakes up of her own accord. While you stand beside the car, talking about who's going to wake her, Nessi sits up.

"You're talking so loud I'd wake up if I'd been in a coma."

"So, had enough sleep?" asks Stink.

"Not really. How is it?"

"How's what?"

"We're here."

"Where's *here*, Nessi?"

She frowns.

"Well, the address. Ulvtannen."

Nessi leans out of the window and looks around; you look around too. There isn't much to see, a knoll looming out into the fjord, and beside it rocks and a cliff.

"So where's this village?" asks Stink.

"You'd be better off asking where the hotel is," says Schnappi.

They look at you. You have no answer. Being here feels as if you'd found something and lost it again right away. From euphoria to depression in two seconds. Wherever you look, there's definitely never been a hotel here, and the boathouse down at the beach doesn't count.

"Maybe the navigation system is acting up," says Schnappi.

"Why would it act up?" asks Nessi and gets out. Schnappi climbs into the car, Nessi takes a deep breath and says the air's amazing. She stretches the way Stink did before. Nessi is the only one who's never had trouble with her hair. She looks like a fresh-baked angel. Schnappi's hand comes out of the window. She wiggles her fingers.

"I can't start the navigation system without the keys."

"They're in there," says Nessi.

"Nope."

Schnappi looks around the floor, checks under the seats. Nothing. Nessi rummages in her jeans.

"I don't understand it. I definitely didn't take the key out. And it can't have come flying out on the drive, either."

"I think that's impossible," says Schnappi.

"Oh, is it really?"

"Guys, the key can't just disappear," says Stink, and drags Schnappi out of the car to do a bit of looking herself.

"Is this like a horror movie or something?" says Schnappi. "One of you is about to go crazy and you're just waiting for night to fall?"

You look at each other helplessly. You look at the road leading down. Then you look at the road winding its way back around the bend between the rocks and up to the cliff.

"What's up there?"

"No idea. I listened to the navigation system, that's why we're here."

"Let's take a look," you decide, and go on ahead.

The euphoria is still there, and it sweeps the bad mood away. You know you're in the right place. You can feel it. And you have to prove it to your girls so that everything's all right again.

"And what about the key?" Stink calls after you.

You turn round and hold out your hand for her.

"We'll find it, come on."

After the first bend the road leads into a second bend. Fifty yards further on you see the summit in front of you; the sky all around it looks as if it's been cut with a blunt knife. You're glad to be moving. Over the past few days you've either been lying in bed or sitting in the car. Stink is cursing constantly, she's out of breath after less than a minute. She says she's absolutely had it, and she's going to spit her lungs up if the rest of you don't slow down.

"I need coffee, I've got to fill up my batteries."

Schnappi links arms with her, Nessi does the same on the other side. They support Stink like a grandma who's lost her walking stick. You go and stand behind Stink, grab her ass with both hands, and start pushing. Stink screeches and runs off. You all go after her and could be four girls who've run away from summer camp. And so you reach the peak and stop as if you'd walked into a glass wall. The cliff is in front of you, and Stink says, "That's impossible . . ."

"But . . ."

You don't get another word out.

Nessi throws her hand over her mouth as if to keep her words in.

Schnappi has no words left.

You stand there and don't believe what you see.

DARIAN

"Boy, listen to me."

You wake up with a start and gasp for air. It feels as if a great weight is lifted off your chest. The seat belt cuts into your ribs, you unfasten it and look around, register your environment and breathe out with relief. Your fists are clenched, you open them and wonder how long you've been sitting like that. In the yellow light of the filling station your fingers look dead. They're ice-cold and filthy, black soil is stuck under your nails. It tingles as the blood starts flowing again. Slowly the rest of your body wakes up. An unpleasant clamminess creeps up from your feet as if you were standing in water. You touch your knees. Dry. You look at your hands. Dirty. You shut your eyes again and try to make everything around you disappear. Your arms tense, you're in your cellar lifting weights. For a few seconds.

"Your father wants to train you."

Tanner's last words won't leave you in peace. The thought that your father still wants to train you. The thought that Tanner was telling the truth.

"He does what he has to do."

You jolt upright, you have nodded off again. Tanner's voice falls silent, your car is still at the filling station, moths flutter around the pale yellow light, and your father is a silhouette ringing a doorbell beside the closed gas station shop. He's put his jacket on again, he means business.

The house looks as if it's been yielding to the wind for a decade.

It leans slightly to the side, even the window frames look crooked. In another life you'd have been messing about with your mates and taken a picture of them—Darian, supporting the house. In this life you stare at the façade, and imagine everything going up in flames.

Upstairs there's a television on, the first floor is in darkness. A low-energy bulb flickers on. How you hate that lifeless light. A shadow passes by one of the windows. You can just imagine one of those old shits muttering and cursing his way through the house in his slippers and coming downstairs, a shotgun in the crook of his arm, spitting with rage. *But he doesn't know my father.* No one knows your father, who knows whether your father even knows himself after tonight.

You wonder, not for the first time, where you'd be if your mother had taken you to Spain. You'd probably be running one of her boutiques in Madrid, and you'd have biceps like a girl.

I'd probably be gay.

You are who you are because your father made you what you are.

I am who I am because my father made me who I am?

You're not sure what to make of that thought. Perhaps you will love this summer with your mother so much that you won't be coming back. Anything is possible.

The front door opens. The woman has put a woolen jacket around her shoulders, and rather than a shotgun she's holding a cup. For a moment it looks as if she's bringing your father some tea. You wait for an explosion of rage, the clock says six in the morning, and instead the woman laughs. Ragnar Desche and his charm. Your father opens his briefcase, the woman waves him away and drinks from her cup. She spots you in the car, you look in the other direction.

The night is fraying at the edges, a gloomy gray flows into the black while the road remains a colorless strip leading all the way across Norway to Ulvtannen. You only know your destination from stories, your father never talked about his origins, that was your uncle's job. You wish he'd kept his trap shut.

———

When Oskar left Norway with Taja and moved from Ulvtannen to Berlin, you were four years old and your uncle told you all about the beach hotel overlooking the fjord, about the people from the next village and their peculiarities, but what impressed you most was how the cliff got its name.

Ulvtannen means wolf's tooth.

Winter after winter a wolf pack used to assemble here at full moon. In those days the ground was still densely covered with fir trees. Then one summer your great-great-grandfather came with his four brothers. They felled the firs and built a massive house for their family, a house that would one day become the beach hotel. They left a single Nordmann fir standing; it became the family tree. At the time everybody thought the wolves had been driven away, but in the winter they arrived right on time every full moon and stared at the house. The wolf pack would not be driven away by noise or gunshots. It only disappeared with the waning moon. Since then every generation has put up with the wolf pack in the winter months, and watched the wolves lying patiently in the snow or pacing around the house and rubbing against the fence, leaving clumps of fur hanging on it. As soon as winter was over, the clumps of fur were collected by the children and thrown into the big fire for the spring festival to keep the wolves' hunger at bay.

You wish your uncle had never told you those stories because by doing that he gave you attention and got closer to you than your father did. Without your uncle's interest you would never have been so aware of your distance from your father. The yearning began. The longing for a father who would talk to you, who would take an interest in you, and at the same time it was the longing for Ulvtannen, a place at the end of the world. Although you hardly had anything in common with Taja, in those days you had the same longing and wanted to spend your winters in the beach hotel—by a big hearth with ice flowers on the windows and a wolf pack outside the door, howling and wailing. How were you supposed to know that Taja had more in common with you than just that sense of yearning? Both of you yearned so much for your fathers that you lost yourselves.

A car speeds past the filling station and drags you from your thoughts. For a moment you could swear it was the Range Rover, but of course that's silly. Oskar's car is a good four hundred miles away in front of the restaurant and will stay there until your father deals with it.

My father.

You look over at the house. Your father is handing the woman a few bank notes. The woman goes back into the house and shuts the door behind her. Your father comes back to the car and opens the fuel tank flap. You hear the gasoline flowing. Three minutes later you're still sitting in the car and your father is a little way off at the tap washing his face and hands. He has hung his jacket on top of a young tree that leans slightly under the weight. *That's exactly what I feel like,* you think and want to slip over, start the car, and just drive off.

As if.

After your father turns the tap off, he shakes his hands out, tugs the sleeves of his sweater back down, and pulls on his jacket. When he gets into the car, you smell the water on his skin. Rusty and cold. You smell your father, too. That familiar mixture of sweat and energy. You don't look at him. You've made your decision. He will never know what Tanner told you. Because if he finds out, you'll have to react to him, and if you react to him, his world will keel over and everything will be different and you're not sure if you can bear that.

You haven't spoken for hours, not since all the white appeared in the road and you thought it was slush. Your father took his foot off the accelerator, and you saw the burst bags glittering in the headlights. Your father hesitated for a moment before putting his foot down and driving on. In the rearview mirror you saw the heroin floating in the air like fog.

Your father didn't waste a word on it. He didn't ask what you were thinking, and for the first time you were happy about his lack of interest. The sight of the heroin had made you feel calmer. As if it was right for your father to fail too. Satisfaction was the right word.

Over the next few hours you kept falling asleep, because there was nothing to say. Now you're fifty miles away from your destination at a closed filling station. Dawn is breaking, and the silence has made itself comfortable on the backseat, and won't think about leaving you alone.

"You should wash too," says your father and starts the car but doesn't put it in gear, as if he wants to give you a chance to jump out quickly. You don't move, you stare straight ahead, your hands are still dirty, there's no reason to leave the car.

The car moves into gear, you drive away from the gas station.

Fifteen minutes later.

"Well?"

He takes a break, the break is like an airless space that you're suddenly standing in and don't know where to go next. Everything within you contracts, you don't want to ask, you ask.

"Well what?"

"How did it feel?"

You look at your hands, which are fists again. It happens automatically. As if your hands wanted to take the answers from you.

"It was okay."

"Okay?"

"It was . . ."

The oxygen turns to lead in your lungs, you try to find the right word, a manly word. And you know you'll only say the wrong thing. And you say, ". . . a relief?"

Your father doesn't react. For a brief moment you're sure you didn't answer, that the word has got stuck in the convolutions of your brain, then your father says, "Give me the gun."

He sticks his right hand out. You hesitate. How can you hesitate? His hand stays in the air, waiting. When your father speaks again, you give a start.

"You are responsible for the deaths of two important people. Leo looked after you, he taught you to box and was beside you when your mad mother wandered around the house at night. And Tanner was your godfather. He'd have done anything for you. He . . ."

He stops, you both know what he wanted to say, the words "loved you" hang like a gentle sound in the air. Your father changes the subject, this isn't a space for gentle sounds.

"Give me the gun."

You draw the gun and rest it in your father's open palm, grip first. He's right. You don't deserve the gun. Your father weighs the weapon in his hand as if checking whether it has lost weight. He doesn't look at you once, he looks at the road and looks at the road and suddenly the barrel of the gun is pressed to your temple and pushes your head aside so that you have to look straight ahead.

You tense up, you freeze.

"How could you."

It isn't a question, it's an observation, but you still try and defend yourself like an idiot.

"I'm. I'm sorry. The boy . . ."

"It wasn't the boy's fault."

Your chest is covered with sweat and you even feel it running down the back of your neck, but that's very unlikely, it's more likely that it's your soul saying goodbye.

"Then why did he have to die?" you blurt out, and you understand that you're calling your father into question. *What on earth am I doing here?* The pressure against your temple increases, you sit still, just don't show any weakness.

"It was a punishment," says your father.

"But I thought he wasn't to blame."

"Who said *he* was the one being punished?"

You understand, you want to lower your head. Shame. You keep your head up.

"I will never forgive you," says your father. "Never."

Your father pulls the trigger. Once. Twice. Each movement of the trigger is like an electric shock that travels into your brain on one side and shoots out on the other. You think about Mirko, you think about Gina and Nadine and that you'll probably never decide which is the right one for you. You think everything at the same time and sit still and wait.

Your father takes the gun from your temple. It leaves a deep imprint on your temple.

"You can thank me because *I* didn't forget the safety catch."

"Thanks," you say quietly.

He hands you back the gun. *It's over,* you think, then he looks at you, both hands rest on the steering wheel, he isn't interested in the road anymore, he looks at you and there's sheer rage in his eyes and at that moment you realize that he despises you, that your own father deeply and fervently despises you. You want to explain yourself, you somehow want to react to that gaze, when he looks ahead again as if nothing had happened, and the gun is in your hand. Everything's going too quickly. Like Timo, who got stuck on LSD two years ago, ended up spending a few months in the bin and later told you the world was a record player turning too fast. You need something to come down. Gear down. Take a break. A bit of weed would be good. Just a couple of drags. Something to relax you. Your father doesn't plan to let you take a break. He says, "At least you've understood what it means to be a man. You know the relief. You know the loneliness. Did you look him in the eye?"

You react far too quickly.

"Of course."

Your father laughs, it's like the barking of a dog that you some-times hear in the city at night, short and dry. And then you feel his hand pressing your knee.

"That's my boy. A damned ice-cold killer who can't even look his victims in the eye."

It's so terrifyingly intimate that you get goose bumps.

How can he know me so well?

Your father lowers the window and spits, spits his rage and his closeness to you into the road. You look at your knee, from which his hand has disappeared, and don't know what's going on with you. Love and hate are raging in you, and you're filled with pride. You've been close to your father, he's touched you. Be honest, how sad is that? The man who's bringing you up the way you bring up a fucking pit bull. The man who makes you murder, and who is tire-lessly bringing you toward chaos at sixty miles an hour. This man has made you proud.

You eat breakfast in a café that a taxi driver recommended to you. Vik wakes up slowly. Oskar worked in the hydraulic power station here, and met Majgull on the night shift. *Love at first breath,* he called it. You ask your father if he knows anything more about the story. Your father doesn't react and you go on eating in silence.

It makes you nervous that you're not getting a move on. You have no idea why your father is taking his time. It's a bit as if he'd lost his sense of logic. Even in Berlin you had a sense of that when you were standing on the Teufelsberg watching him scattering Oskar's ashes. Tanner must have felt it too. And now all this creeping along. Since you've been on the road he hasn't driven above the speed limit, he's eaten his omelet in slow motion and seems to be as calm as anything. On the other hand you feel as if you're sitting on a pile of burning firecrackers.

Of course your father doesn't miss any of that.

"We have all the time in the world. They're not going to run away, they're going to wait for us. Finish your coffee, then we can get going."

You could ask what makes him so sure, but you've got Tanner's voice in your head: *If you don't understand something, then try to understand it. The answer will come all by itself.* You drink your coffee and wish your father's confidence was infectious. You have a bad feeling, you don't like Norway. Until today Norway was the memory of your uncle, which took place entirely in Ulvtannen. You don't want to take the magic away from that memory and tear it down into reality, it should stay a memory. You miss Berlin, because Berlin is reality and a safe place, your place, which you know and control. So much has changed in your life. Death travels with you now. It hides in the corners of your eyes and in the shadows that surround you and accompany every one of your thoughts. You've already noticed the change. Ask your father, he'll know what's happening to you. He's responsible for the fact that you have a companion. Death has devoured your innocence. From now on every moment of your life will feel as if you're running across a frozen lake, knowing quite clearly: *Every moment the ice is about to break, every moment it will happen.* And you run and run, because it would be a mistake to stop. As soon as you stop, it's all over. Your father shares this feeling with you. In his case it's a steep slope plunging ceaselessly down. You on the other hand are running over ice.

NESSI

The house isn't a house anymore. It's a dog that's been hit by a car, lying by the roadside, guts spilled, unable to move. The roof has been torn away, and the exposed rafters look like the ribs of a whale you once saw in the natural history museum. A fir tree collapsed into one side of it long ago, seedlings have fought their way through the rubble and point their gaunt branches defiantly at the sky. The windows are broken, the masonry is fragile, even the graffiti is decayed, and the painting of the façade, once blue, is a dingy gray. On your right there towers a public rubbish dump. You see washbasins, mattresses, washstands, and chairs. There's a pyramid of bulging black garbage sacks, a bright red and yellow IKEA bag gleaming among them with bits of cable sticking out. It hurts to look. As if someone had opened a corpse and forgotten to close it again.

"Pinch me," says Stink.

"Shit, that looks like shit," says Schnappi.

"Taja, what is it?" you ask.

"I . . . I don't know."

"We must have taken a wrong turn," Schnappi says firmly, looking round. "Taja, where are we?"

Taja doesn't reply, she stares at the ruin.

"I don't understand. We . . ."

She walks closer.

"We're in the right place."

"Are you sure?"

Taja points at a pile of stones.

"There's the old well I told you about, and over there, where the fence has collapsed, was the dog kennel. Where all the trash is, that was the parking area. I know it all from the photographs. Even the tree—that used to be a giant fir. And right here there was a fence. You see? But . . . I don't understand this."

The trunk of the fallen fir has flattened a quarter of the hotel, and brought down the roof. You're sure that if nature could murder deliberately, it would look exactly like this.

"And where's your mother?" asks Stink.

"I don't know."

"She certainly doesn't live here," says Schnappi.

"Do you think anyone might know where your mother is?"

"I have no idea, Stink," Taja replies irritably. "I don't know anyone here."

"But you're going to—"

"Have you gone deaf?" you cut in. "If Taja says she doesn't know, then she doesn't know."

You turn to Taja.

"Maybe we could ask down in the village. Everybody here's bound to know everybody else."

"Maybe." Taja softens her tone, and for a moment the situation relaxes, and you're glad you opened your mouth. Your stomach doesn't need any extra tension, it's already been turning itself inside out for a while, and at the moment there are lots of things you want—like a shower and breakfast—but throwing up like a pregnant bitch isn't one of them.

Everything'll probably sort itself out, you think. *Taja's mother probably has one of those beautiful houses right down by the water, and she's laughing because we went up to the dump.*

You stare at the ruin for a while, then Schnappi stirs herself and turns away.

"Off we go. Anyone who wants coffee . . ."

She pauses. You feel a tingle in your back, just below your left shoulder blade. You don't want to turn round.

I don't want to.

If you could stop this moment and see it from outside, you would know what a surreal scene this is—the sun laughs down at you, the mist above the fjord has melted away, the morning air is refreshingly clear. It's a magnificent summer day in Norway, the birds are singing, and you're standing by an ugly ruin, but that's okay, because everything seems to be in harmony, and if everything's in harmony it makes life a lot easier.

I still don't want to.

You reluctantly turn round and look darkness in the face.

DARIAN

You leave Vik and after a couple of miles the fjord appears on your left. Your father ignores the sign for Lunnis, he turns right at the crossroads and reaches a narrow road leading up a small hill. A church appears in front of you. It's made of dark wood and reminds you of old Japanese movies and samurais barking their orders like dogs. You can't know that it's a stave church, and you can't know that your father stood in this church at Oskar and Majgull's wedding, and couldn't take his eyes off the bride. Beside the church there's a little graveyard that looks as if people only died here every hundred years. You drive past the church and find yourselves on a forest path.

"And where are we going now?" you ask.

"Surprise."

After a few minutes you're surrounded by pine trees. The forest is dense and dark. You lower the window slightly, the scent of resin settles coolly on your face and fills the car. Five hundred yards further on, the forest clears and you see a chapel with a dome. In front of the chapel there's an abandoned parking lot. You get out, walk down the stone path past the chapel, and reach a second graveyard. Now you know where all the dead end up. A graveyard, surrounded by a pine forest. You follow your father along the rows. He stops by your grandmother's grave. She's dropped the name Desche and returned to her maiden name. Sinding. Your father says, "If you die before me, I'll bury you here."

"I want to be cremated."

He laughs.

"You must have loved that crematorium."

"I don't want to lie down there and get eaten by worms."

"Fine, we'll cremate you, then."

"And you?"

"I don't intend to die."

He looks at the headstone as if he's looking for something. You were seven months old when your grandmother died. Your father never talked about Norway, or about his mother either. You only know her from Oskar's stories.

"Do you miss her?"

Your father shrugs.

"She betrayed us when we were children. She stood by our father. A mother should always stand by her children."

"And what about fathers?"

"Fathers stand by themselves. That's how it's always been. When you're a father you'll understand."

He spits on the ground beneath which his mother lies.

"She was a cowardly woman. You don't miss someone who's betrayed you."

"So why are we here?"

He smiles.

"Not because of her."

Your father sits down on his mother's gravestone and points to the graves to his left.

"From here over to the statue of the angel, that's all your relatives. They built Ulvtannen. And this . . ."

He points to his right, where there is nothing.

". . . is reserved for us. Past and future, you see?"

Before you can answer, your father waves his hand dismissively.

"You don't need to understand. Go back down the path. Beside the chapel there's a shed. You'll find spades in there. Fetch us two."

You don't move.

"The grave isn't for you," says your father, and in his eyes you can read that anything's possible, even a grave for you if you don't jump to it.

You go to the shed, the door isn't locked. There are tools hanging on one wall, standing against the other there are three wheelbarrows, rakes, spades, and a brand-new lawnmower. There are stacked-up buckets and several zinc watering cans. You take two spades and try to imagine burying Tanner and Leo. You know it's wrong. They deserve a decent burial. When you come back, your father has taken off his jacket and hung it on his mother's gravestone. You have to ask him.

"What are we doing here?"

Your father takes one of the spades, moves a little way away from his mother's grave, and sticks it in the ground before he answers.

"We're going to dig a grave. A nice deep grave for four girls."

You spend the next hour and a half in the graveyard. The ground feels as soft as if it were dug over every week. You're working back to back. You have no more questions. You're on a collision course. You're only a part of the whole, your father knows the formula and isn't planning on telling you about it. He scares you, but you know the feeling, and you're still surprised every time. Like watching a horror movie over and over. You know exactly what's going to happen and yet the fear won't leave you.

You climb out of the grave, drenched in sweat, your muscles feel good. You wash yourselves in a water trough beside the shed and your father remarks how lucky you are.

"If it was a Sunday we wouldn't be alone here."

You go back to the hole; your father puts his jacket back on and crouches down with his back against the gravestone. He sighs. The sun shines in his face, it's pleasantly cool, the summer heat hasn't yet invaded the patch of forest.

"Sit down, rest for a moment."

You stop and look across the graveyard. You deliberately turn your back on your father. *If he takes a nap right now, I'm going to lose it.* Your father sighs again. He has all the time in the world. He isn't planning to die.

You set the spades down by the grave and leave the cemetery, but you don't go back to the car. Your father heads off in the opposite direction and you walk side by side through the wood until you see water. The fjord is a sliver of blue that gets bigger and bigger with every step. You'd like to sit down on its bank and hold your hand in the water.

"Along here."

Before you get to the water your father leads you to a steep cliff. A footpath winds its way up. You don't know how your father knows his way around here. You're a clueless dork taking a quick holiday in Norway. It would be nice if the bit about the holiday were true.

You climb the cliff. It's tough, the sun is scorching, you don't say a word. Before you reach the top, your father grabs you by the arm, so that you have to stop.

"It's going to be a very nice view."

"What's going to be a very nice view?"

"The past . . ."

He looks to his right. The fjord, the opposite shore and individual houses. All that's missing is a sailboat drifting gently along the water, and it would be perfect. Your father finishes his sentence.

". . . however you look at the past, in the end it always looks shabby."

Your father lets go of your hand and invites you to walk ahead of him. Six steps and you're up at the top, and give a start. Your father's behind you, and rests a hand on your shoulder, there's no going back.

There it is.

There are all the stories your uncle told you condensed into a single moment: the hotel on the cliff. The mountains on the other side of the fjord. Everything.

Ulvtannen, you think, while your uncle's stories flee your head with a sudden shriek. Your father was right. It looks as if the Norwegian past had crouched down up here and taken a shit. But of course that's not enough, because four girls are standing in front of the ruined hotel and all four girls are looking at you in amazement.

SCHNAPPI

At first only a head appears. It floats above the knoll like a furious balloon, then the rest follows. Shiny shaven head, pale face. Darian wears a black and red tracksuit and white sneakers. He looks at you and freezes. Behind him comes a man in a dark suit and a gray polo-neck sweater. He's the first guy ever to wear a sweater like that and not look like he writes poems. He's slim, with a narrow face and weird gleam in his eyes—if you saw someone like that in the street, you'd cross to the other side. You learned that from your mother. *Pay attention to the eyes.* That gleam is naked and furious. No warmth. He only has eyes for Taja. You don't need an IQ of 200 to know who's standing in front of you. Your brain has much more trouble processing how Darian and his father managed to track you down.

We got rid of the car, you think. *We did everything right.* You're about to call out to the girls that it would be a good idea to get out of here as fast as possible, when Taja's uncle gets moving. In his fury he's so fast that you don't know how he does it. Suddenly he's standing a few yards away from Taja, and he says, "Are you running away from me?"

He taps his chest.

"From me?"

He doesn't come any closer, he just stands motionlessly in front of Taja, as if he'd traveled halfway around the world to say those two sentences. You've all automatically taken a step back instead of gathering around Taja, but there's this gleam in his eyes, and if someone doesn't recoil from that, then it's your own fault. Taja starts breathing frantically.

"What the hell do you think you're doing here?" her uncle wants to know.

Stink starts to lunge forward, Nessi holds her back by the arm; you're about to move too, you're about to grab Taja's hand to pull her out of her uncle's spell, when your girl speaks, and her words are a loud whisper, if there is such a thing, because that's exactly what it is. She says, "I want to visit my mother."

"What?"

Taja clears her throat and says in a louder voice, "I . . . We want to visit my mother."

"Are you fucking with me?"

All of a sudden her uncle's voice is loud, spit flies from his mouth.

"Tell me, you fucking with me?"

Taja shakes her head.

Stink's had enough, and pulls away from Nessi. Taja's uncle snarls at Stink, without deigning even to look at her.

"Move one more inch and Darian's going to shoot off your kneecaps."

Your heads whip round, you look up at Darian, who stands in the background holding a gun like a cop in an American movie—both hands, one hand under the grip, one around it, finger on the trigger, arms outstretched at chest height, the barrel pointing at Stink.

"What on earth have you done?" Taja's uncle continues. "Did you think I wouldn't find you if you switched cars? And how the hell did you get Neil Exner involved? At first I was sure he was part of your plan, but then I worked out that you haven't got a plan. You do whatever you like, with no regard for anyone else, and this is how it ends up. Take a look at your cousin. He's become a murderer because you had to steal that car from that boy, from a complete stranger. Your cousin's a killer now, Taja. He killed for me. And it would be amazing if he could remember the boy's name. We all make mistakes . . ."

He turns round and spits his words at Darian.

". . . but we're not all leaving three fucking corpses behind!"

You stand there like someone has turned you into stone.

Marten, you think, *is this fucker talking about Marten?*

Taja's uncle turns back to Taja.

"Are you surprised by all this? Does anything surprise you? What if I tell you those dead bodies are on your account, would *that* surprise you?"

Stink can't keep her mouth shut.

"She hasn't done any—"

"SHUT YOUR FUCKING TRAP!"

Stink shuts up. What works on Stink doesn't always work on you. Sometimes you wish it were the other way around. *If wishes were horses,* your mother used to say. Scared or not, you don't like it when other people talk for more than two minutes without making sense. Taja's uncle exceeded that limit ages ago.

"Chill out," you say.

"What?"

He looks at you. That bloody gleam in his eyes makes you shiver, but you're not a bastard for nothing. You wear thick armor. And yet you have a wish. *If that guy would just shut his eyes everything would be okay.* You're about ten feet apart. If he gets closer, you can put on a sprint. You're fast, you proved that yesterday, you can prove it again. But unfortunately speed isn't called for at the moment. First you've got to assert yourself here. Eye to eye. You know what this guy's problem is. It's not about Taja's mother or poor Marten, it's about Oskar, who you and the girls fished frozen out of the freezer. At least that's what you hope, because if it isn't the case you may as well throw in your cards right now. Your voice tries to sound bigger.

"Chill out, I said. Taja hasn't done anything. Oskar's heart stopped. Or his brain. A stroke or something, get me?"

Taja's uncle looks at you as if he's been confronted with a new species. Then he asks you, "Says who?"

You are lost for a second, you ask back, "What do you mean, says who?"

RAGNAR

"Who says my brother's heart stopped?"

Schnappi looks at you as if you're an idiot. You have to admit that you admire her cheek, which wouldn't stop you from smashing her face in.

"Taja, of course," she answers. "Who else? She was there when it happened."

"Is that so?"

You focus your attention on Taja again. You control yourself, you've been controlling yourself the whole time. You'd like to grab that little piece of shit and strangle her until the tenderness and innocence fades from her face and the truth beneath emerges.

"And what happened after you stuffed Oskar in the freezer?" you ask her. "Did you think you'd just clear off with my merchandise and visit your mother? Was that the plan? If that was the plan, then let me repeat my question: what the hell are you doing here?"

"I . . . I thought she still lived in the hotel. I didn't know . . ."

Taja hunches her shoulders, looks at the ruin, looks at you again, and for a few seconds you have your doubts, for a few seconds you believe her naïveté and you believe in her innocence. She gives you the warm feeling of being wrong, of making a mistake. How could she know you were the kind of person who never makes mistakes?

"I didn't know anything about what's happened here," she says.

"And now you do. So what do you think, shall I bring you to your mother now?"

Taja stares at you, no further reaction, the naïveté has vanished from her face. She shakes her head, she doesn't want to.

"How about you tell your girlfriends why you don't want to come with me?"

She starts weeping silently. She exudes invisible threads that try to clutch your heart. As she does so, she looks so like Majgull that your heart contracts. You have to look away, you say to the girls, "You have no idea what's going on here, do you? You're the good friends who join in all kinds of crap because they've known each other forever. Loyal to the end. One for all, all for one."

You shake your head, you can't believe it.

"You've caused me so many problems, so unbelievably many problems, and you're such idiots there ought to be a law against it. Do you want to know why your Taja suddenly doesn't want to see her mother anymore? It's because her mother—"

Taja interrupts him, stressing every word.

"My mother isn't dead."

"Says who?"

"Oskar. He . . . he lied to me all those years. My mother wasn't allowed to see me. He . . . he kidnapped me. My mother isn't dead, she never had an accident."

You come so close to her as if you wanted to kiss her. She stares right through you. It's a mystery to you. They look so similar. Mother and daughter. The faint scent of sandalwood and oranges. You deliberately kept your distance from Taja all those years because that resemblance was too much for you.

"You want to know why I know better than anyone else that your mother is dead?"

Taja narrows her eyes and nods. She really wants to know, and juts her chin defiantly. Your gaze, her gaze. She asks, "Why?"

"Because I killed her fourteen years ago."

We're back in 1995, it's the end of silence between Majgull and you. She left you a message on your answering machine. She wants you to understand her lie, so she wants to meet you at the Plaza Hotel in Oslo. *What lie?* The question won't leave you in peace.

You flew back to Norway the same day. No one knew. Majgull

and you. Your nervousness felt like a controlled high. You were your father's son, and you didn't lose control, but deep inside you'd been severely unbalanced for some time. Without that woman you are only half of what you are—half-present, half-happy, half-full. With her, everything was whole. She made you dream. She made you yearn. Your own marriage felt worthless in comparison, and your son was just a piece of luggage that you could take along or leave behind.

After you got to the Plaza Hotel you swam in the hotel pool until you were exhausted. You went to the sauna and had a massage. Giving your body all that attention helped, it meant your head was silenced for a while. When you got out of the shower, your phone was ringing. You were prepared for everything—problems with the company, a confused Tanner wanting to know where you were, or your wife, fed up waiting for you all day. Anything was possible, but you hadn't bargained on your brother. He had broken down in tears and didn't know what to do.

"Take a deep breath," you said.

The situation felt unreal. You'd been in Berlin what seemed like a moment ago, and now all of a sudden you were standing dressed only in a towel in a room in the Plaza Hotel, Oslo, talking to your brother whom you'd last talked to at Christmas, and who couldn't have had any idea how close to him you were.

"She's got somebody else," said Oskar.

"Who?"

"Majgull, of course."

"Oh."

"I knew it, Ragnar, I guessed it a while back and now she's admitted it. What should I do now? What can I do? I love her, what am I going to do?"

"First of all, calm down."

"She wants me to meet him today."

"What?"

"She . . . she says she wants to explain everything, she . . ."

He was gasping for air, taking deep breaths.

"What am I supposed to do, Ragnar?"

"Where are you now?"

"I'm at the hotel, I'm racing like mad along the terrace, and I'm just about to throw myself into the fjord. It's my fourth circuit, I've run around this hotel four times and I've got side stitches."

"Stop, then."

"I can't."

"Oskar, stop!"

"Okay. Fine. I've stopped. What now?"

"Where's Majgull?"

"She's putting a diaper on Taja, she wants us to go right away. She's arranged to see this bastard in Oslo. She wants . . . she wants us all to go together. As a family. Isn't that sick? I wish you were here. I don't know if I can cope on my own. She wants to have the kid there too. She says she's not going without Taja. What happens if she leaves me?"

"She's not going to leave you."

"Ragnar, I'm so scared."

A shrill noise sounded in your ears, pleading with you to get out of Oslo as soon as possible. *Clear off, it's too much for you, run.* But Ragnar Desche doesn't run. That's the law.

"Couldn't you talk to her?"

"What?"

"Please, Ragnar, couldn't you talk to her? She likes you, maybe you could bring her back down to earth."

You wanted to ask him what you had to do with it, you of all people, but it would have been pure hypocrisy. You shook your head. There was no question of your speaking to Majgull. You saw it right in front of you. Her coming to the phone and asking you why you're getting involved. Passing the receiver to your brother and saying, *My new lover wants to talk to you.* You and your brother never seeing each other again, and you dying of shame. You were aware you would have to make a sacrifice.

Majgull or Oskar.

"Oskar, I can't talk to her right now. I'm at work right now, the conference room is full, people are waiting for me. Try to calm Majgull, tell her you're not going."

"But I *want* to go."

"What? Why do you want to go?"

"I want to see him. I want to know who is daring to tear my family apart."

"Oskar, leave it."

"You don't understand what it's like. You've got a good life in Berlin and your wife loves you—"

"Majgull loves you too," you interrupted him, feeling acid rising up in your stomach. Even those simple words hurt. Majgull belonged to you.

"She's calling, I've got to go," said Oskar.

"Wait."

"Thank you for listening to me. I'll call you as soon as I've met this bastard. I don't want to lose her, Ragnar, I'll do anything not to leave her."

With those words he hung up.

You wanted to call Majgull and ask her what she was playing at. Instead you treated your phone as an oracle and looked for Majgull's last message in your inbox. Nine hours previously, you had still had no idea what lie she was talking about, but now you were starting to work it out. Majgull wanted to reveal herself to you, she wanted to hold up the facts in front of Oskar and give up her family for you. Oskar was to see you, speak to you, everything would be explained. Her detachment, her pretense that her interest in you had been only sexual, had been a lie all along. She wanted to give up her family, she wanted you to give up your family. You didn't know if that pleased or frightened you.

Action was important, you couldn't just sit around waiting to be crushed by events. So you hired a car and drove north. A six-hour journey and then? You didn't know what then. You could hardly tell Oskar you'd just hopped on a plane to solve the problem with Majgull. Even a credulous person like Oskar would have seen through that one.

What on earth am I doing here?

Six hours is a long time to forge a plan. Your phone was on the passenger seat all the time. Perhaps she'd call you, perhaps she'd cancel everything. It could be so easy. You could take the next flight back to Berlin. Her name could vanish from your memory. Her number from your phone. But there was this pull, there was this boundless hunger. You wanted that woman. Damn it, you wanted that woman.

Two cars on the road, two planets that were never supposed to touch.

Oskar drove, Taja was asleep on the backseat, Majgull didn't say a word. If you'd seen that, you'd have seen the pain in your little brother's face, who knows whether you mightn't have turned round on the spot. Majgull's face, on the other hand, gave nothing away. She leaned against the passenger door as if to keep her distance from Oskar.

Your brother knew he was losing his wife, he knew it and he was keeping himself under control. Who knows how different things might have been if Taja hadn't been lying on the backseat. Oskar didn't want to make a scene in front of his daughter. He wanted to look his enemy in the face and then decide what happened next. You've always been very similar. In true crisis situations you've waited until the last minute before deciding on your reaction. Your brother and you.

And maybe you would have just driven past one another and in that way everyone would have reached his destination. You in Ulvtannen, they in Oslo. You on the steps of the beach hotel, them in the lobby of the Plaza Hotel. Maybe all that dark energy would have gone up in smoke, but you know that's not what happened.

Less than two hours on the road, you couldn't bear it any longer, you took your phone and called her number. You just needed to know if they were on the way. You didn't even think of calling Oskar. You just needed to talk to Majgull.

She picked up after the second ring. Her words were warm, she smiled at you through the phone.

"We'll be in Oslo in four hours," she said in English. "I'm looking forward to it."

She said twice more, "I am happy, I am so happy."

And then you heard Oskar saying in German, "Give it to me."

And Majgull said, "I don't think so."

And Oskar cursed and demanded the phone.

And Majgull told him to keep his eye on the road.

"GIVE ME THE PHONE OR I'LL SLAP YOU!"

"YOU ARE NOT GOING TO HIT ME. NOT YOU!"

Oskar had never planned to hit her, he swore afterward, he said he'd only threatened to because he'd wanted to have the damn phone. She ignored his threat, so he grabbed for it. He missed the phone and grabbed her wrist. She pulled, he pulled, the car started swerving, Oskar was driving fast. When a car starts swerving at a hundred miles an hour, you need control to get back on track. Oskar lost control. Luckily there was no traffic coming in the opposite direction.

The car slewed into the opposite lane, slewed back, came off the road and drove into a ditch, ran up the embankment and turned over twice before settling on its side.

You heard your brother shouting into the phone, the screech of the tires and the dull thud as the car turned over. Then it was suddenly quiet and in the midst of the silence there was the quiet weeping of a child.

Even today you don't understand your reaction. You opened the window and threw your phone out. You saw it bounce twice on the tarmac before breaking apart. Only then did you brake and drive to the side of the road. Your arms were shaking, your heartbeat was irregular. You sat in the car and went through every second that had passed over and over again in your head. After fifteen minutes you turned the car and set off back to Oslo. You drove straight to the airport and had to wait less than an hour before catching a plane back to Berlin. Just before eight you got out of a taxi in front of your home and turned up in time to read a bedtime story to your son, while in a hotel in Oslo a damp towel hung drying over a towel rack.

No one asked where you'd been.

No one knew you'd been away.

The call came just before midnight. Oskar called you from the hospital in Laedal. He had a cut on his head, but Taja had got away without as much as a scratch. It was a miracle. The doctors had pumped your hysterical brother full of tranquilizers, and he could only mumble incoherent stuff, but the sense seeped through, the sense reached you and so you learned that Majgull had broken her neck when the car turned over. And time and again Oskar said he should have listened to you, everything would have been different if he'd listened to you.

And so ends our little story of Ragnar, who destroyed the love of his life with a single phone call. And of course we keep that to ourselves, because this story has nothing to do with anybody.

Because I killed her fourteen years ago is testimony enough.

No more truth is needed.

STINK

"What the fuck?"

Once again you can't keep your trap shut, you step forward and push Taja's uncle aside like a piece of furniture that's in the way. No idea when the guy was last pushed aside. Out of the corner of your eye you see his face slipping away like some stupid pancake falling out of the pan. You don't care. You've got a completely different kind of problem. The Eiffel Tower is a matchbox in comparison.

"Taja, give me an answer!"

She doesn't react. You push her on the chest with both hands, making her stagger back and nearly fall. In fact she doesn't need to answer. Her face tells you everything you need to know. And you don't believe it, you just don't believe it. Your good friend lied to you. You saved her life and wiped up after her and she's seriously lied to you. You point at Ragnar Desche, your voice is shrill: "So your mother *is* dead, and that bastard *killed* her? Is that right? So when were you going to tell us *that*?"

A moment later your head explodes. It feels as if you've just been french-kissed by a bomb. You don't understand what's happened. *I was standing up a second ago.* You try to get up again, your arm slips away, your sense of balance has just been on a roller-coaster ride, you're lying flat on the ground. Let that be a lesson to you, unpredictable violence is a little fucker who lives on surprise. This fucker is wearing a smart suit, he has hit you with his fist, and now he says, "I've been looking forward to this all this time."

Taja's uncle shakes his fingers out, and at the same moment Taja clears out. She wants to get to the road, she really thinks she'll manage to get past her uncle, who only needs to stretch his arm out to grab her. He pulls Taja roughly to him, so that her chest hits his.

"Where do you think you're going? We've only just got here."

He turns around with Taja in front of him, so that you can see her. Your girls pull you to your feet, Nessi keeps an arm around you. There's a shrill ringing in your left ear that only slowly subsides. *He's using Taja as a human shield,* you think, and you follow your logic through: *If you need a human shield, it means you're scared.*

"We're not finished here, not by a long way," says Taja's uncle. "We haven't heard the whole story. Have we, Taja? Now you're going to tell us what really happened to Oskar."

"It . . . it was an accident," says Taja, and looks at you pleadingly. *Save me, hurry up, save me,* her eyes say.

"What sort of accident?" asks her uncle.

"He . . . Oskar was sitting there and . . . we argued and suddenly . . . he was gone . . . he stopped breathing. It was . . . it was just over. Like when Grandpa died . . . Grandpa died like that too, didn't he? Oskar told me that—"

"Taja—"

"I swear! I really swear!"

Her uncle draws a gun and aims it right at you, of course. It was obvious, this guy has a private feud with you, it was perfectly obvious. He should try wrestling with you, you'd twist his balls till he sounded like Mickey Mouse.

"Take a good look at your friend," he says. "I'm going to blow this arrogant mouth of hers away if you don't tell me what really happened."

"I said—"

"STOP LYING, I'VE SEEN IT!"

Taja closes her eyes.

"I've seen everything," her uncle whispers suddenly, but you understand every word, because all of a sudden it's quiet on the cliff, no seagulls, no wind disturbs the scene as he whispers in Taja's ear, "Three of the cameras were running. They'd been running for the last ten days. It's as if I was there. Are you going to risk your friend's life for your lies?"

You girls stare at Taja, you have no idea what cameras he's talk-ing about, but you can see that Taja knows. Her face goes so sad that you're sure she's about to burst into tears again. Her eyes open, but there are no tears in them, she looks at you and in this short moment something happens to your friend, as if a part of her was getting loose and disappearing forever. And then she says the two words you don't want to hear. You want to hear: *Run, he's nuts.* You want to hear what a miserable fucker Ragnar Desche is and that it's all a bunch of stupid lies. Everything, but not these two words. But there they are. Live with it.

"I'm sorry."

TAJA

It isn't a heroic moment for you. Look at your girlfriends, they still don't understand exactly what has hit them, but they smell the corruption in the air, they feel it with every fiber of their bodies, as if the corruption had wings and was about to plunge down on them from thirty thousand feet up.

Did you really think it wouldn't come out? By the time you were standing outside the derelict beach hotel, you must have understood how brittle your reality was.

Of course you were surprised.

You thought the hotel would still look as it did in the photographs. But why should time be good to a place that's been empty for twelve years? Time isn't good to anybody. Even if you turn time into God, it just laughs at you. Like now. You hear? Her laughter sounds like a storm, like the storm that came down on Berlin exactly a year ago, with a cooling summer rain. The thunder kept you awake for a while, as if the weather knew exactly what you intended to do. It spurred you on.

You summoned your courage and went downstairs to drink a glass of water. You thought you could have a look at what your father was doing. There were nights when he stayed in the attic till the early hours, working on his new jingles. And there were nights when he had visitors.

You knew he was alone that night.

You went upstairs and looked in his bedroom. He was lying on his side, his back was rising and falling as he breathed calmly. Sometimes he twitched when a crack of thunder made the sky outside tremble. You heard the rain on the plank flooring and closed the door. Now you were in his room, you'd taken the first step. You hesitated for a few minutes and watched him, you listened to his breath before you lay down next to him. As you had always done when you were little. At the age of ten you knew it had to stop. *I'm not a child anymore,* you had said. Tonight you aren't a child anymore either, but you want to be with your father. For a while. In safety. And perhaps it had something to do with the fact that your boyfriend had split up with you, perhaps you were lonely and wanted to hear that everything was okay. Perhaps even that is just a lie.

You lay down behind your father and it felt proper and warm. He was aware of your presence, he turned round and looked at you in surprise. Before he could say anything, you threw your arms around him and pressed him to you as if you were lost and he was your salvation. Your heart was thumping wild and confused, and your leg pushed its way between his legs. Only then did he slowly start to understand that you weren't his little girl anymore. He tried to pull away from you, he actually recoiled, and that was too much for you, that wasn't right, he couldn't push you away, so you held him tight, your hands on his back, your breath on his neck. You felt his erection, and it was shockingly beautiful and right, because an erection meant something, it meant he was aroused, it meant you were arousing him.

He hurled you out of bed and gathered the blanket between his legs as you sat bewildered on the floor in your T-shirt and black knickers that you'd chosen specially for this evening. Planning is everything. Only those who are brave reach their goal.

"You . . . It's you?"

Your father tried to laugh.

"Who did you think it was?" you asked him and rubbed your bottom and thought of his erection and wondered if it was still there. Until then you'd only slept with Kai and you always had to hurry, because his erections came and went, as if he had to think every few minutes about whether he actually wanted to have sex.

"Were you afraid of the storm?" your father asked in a falsely chatty tone, and you could tell by his eyes that he wanted to say something else. Something like *Are you crazy? How the hell could you even think of this? I'm your father!*

But he didn't say it, and that encouraged you.

"Nightmare," you replied and got up. You turned round and showed him your sweet ass and asked him if there was a bruise on it, and as you did so you looked at him over your shoulder. He didn't risk a glance, he stared at the bedcovers and said there wasn't a bruise and did you want some hot milk with honey.

That was how the night ended—the two of you in the kitchen, each holding a cup of hot milk, candles burned, a summer storm raged outside and you talked about music.

For two days there was peace.

For two days he studied you out of the corner of his eye.

On the third day you stood by his bed again in the middle of the night.

"Dad?"

"Yes."

He wasn't asleep. He must have heard you coming in. Perhaps he'd been waiting. You liked that idea. His back was turned to you.

"Can I get into bed with you?"

"Taja, no, it's not right."

"I'm so alone."

"Sweetheart, that . . ."

You started crying. It was real, you weren't acting. You couldn't deal with rejection. You stood by the side of the bed and cried and held your hand out to him. *Help me.* He turned around. Your hand was trembling. He pulled you into bed and held you in his arms as he had held his little girl in his arms six years before. Your back was turned toward him, he held you tight. It was lovely, but it wasn't what you wanted. *More.* You slowly started pressing your ass against his crotch. He shrank back, he tried to hide his erection, you held his arms tight, he couldn't get away. *Stay.* You heard him groaning, his breath burned the back of your neck and smelled of pot and slightly of vodka. *Mine,* you thought, as your bottom rubbed against him and then you took his sweaty hand and stuck his thumb in your mouth. It was as simple as that.

———

It wasn't love, it wasn't passion, it was pure power. And of course we want to hear that it was despair that drove you to it. Loneliness, abuse, violence. Give us something so that we can understand and forgive you. But there's nothing. There's just a fifteen-year-old girl who wanted to test her power and whose only excuse was that her boyfriend dumped her.

You wanted it; it made you grow. Each time it happened your value increased, while your father's attempts to resist got weaker and weaker. When you got into the shower with him, when you stuck your hand down his trousers in the kitchen in the morning. Discreet, always discreet. Never when you had visitors, never when he was composing. You could still be the daughter who loved her life and didn't get in her father's way; but you could also be the little slut who seduced him and felt triumphant.

When women stayed overnight, you asked him in the morning if it had been any good. He blushed, tried to defend himself, and you walked away mid-sentence. You enjoyed it. You were taking your mother's place without even thinking about it. And perhaps at some point you'd have had enough, normality would have returned, and you could have dumped your father like a boy who didn't interest you anymore. It didn't come to that, because your father started losing himself.

He couldn't do it anymore, he didn't want to do it anymore.

Six months had passed. No one noticed anything, even your girls hadn't a clue. There was just you and your father in the house, you lived in a cocoon of lust. Your father knew it was wrong. He said he didn't want to be a square, but it couldn't go on like this. You knew your weapons and you used them. You look so like your mother and you pulled out all the stops. Clothes and hairdos. At Christmas you had your hair cut because your mother had a pageboy cut at her wedding. You became a second Majgull, and your father would have been a liar if he'd claimed he didn't like it.

It didn't last long. He avoided you until the summer, then he broke down completely, he took more drugs, drank vodka for breakfast, and wanted you both to see a psychologist. Your father became paranoid with guilt. He didn't want to be alone with you in a room anymore, he was ashamed and said he'd go voluntarily to jail if it had to be.

And then came that Wednesday.

He hadn't slept that night, he'd been fiddling about with various songs and taken tons of amphetamines because he was worried you might surprise him in his sleep. In the morning he stood in your room and just looked at you. You woke up with a start as he lay down next to you. You had swapped roles, he couldn't live without you anymore, however much he resisted, he couldn't. He said it. He said: *I'm giving up.* Now he was you, and he wanted you to hold him. You held him until he had fallen asleep, then you got up and showered. Something was wrong, your triumph had a stale after-taste, something was definitely wrong.

When you came back out of the bathroom, he wasn't in your bed anymore. You were relieved. It was like waking from a dream. Then you heard him downstairs on the telephone. His voice sounded as if he might burst out laughing at any moment. You crouched on the stairs and listened.

"Maybe a week, maybe longer. A holiday will do me good. Diana's always wanted to go to the Côte d'Azur. No, without Taja. What did you think? She'll manage, you know what kids are like."

He hung up, and you went downstairs. He was standing in the kitchen drinking orange juice. You were so furious, so incredibly furious, and you wanted to know what he was up to. He laughed.

"Didn't I tell you about it?"

He was messing with you and he didn't even hide it. It was as if his helplessness had been wiped away, he was in control of you again. A cool, detached indifference was looking at you. Your father said, "We need a break."

"I don't need a break."

"Too bad."

And then he gave that laugh again.

He walked past you into the living room and slumped on the sofa. He put his feet up, picked up the remote control, and zapped through the channels. Whatever had given him back his sense of balance, it sent you back to the start. You couldn't get past Go, no one gave you a get-out-of-jail card, it was wrong, even your voice sounded pitiful.

"You can't leave me alone here."

You were his daughter again, and you needed him. He sat up and rolled a joint, didn't look at you, lit it and took a drag, sighed, still not looking at you, and then said, "You're a big girl. Invite your girlfriends. Have a party."

"Oskar, you can't just run away from me."

"Don't call me Oskar."

"That's your name."

At last he looked at you.

"You're a slut. Just like your mother. Do you know that?"

You thought you'd misheard. He could disrespect you as much as he liked, but he couldn't talk like that about your mother.

"Mom wasn't a slut."

"She was unfaithful, so she was a slut."

"She was what?"

"Do you think I'm such a shitty driver that I'd just lose control like that and drive into the ditch? Your mother broke her fucking neck because she wanted to leave me. You get that? She wanted to leave me and you. God punished her for it. If there is a God, he did a good job."

"What are you talking about?"

"She was a slut, Taja. Get that into your head. It's all you need to know. It's in your blood too."

"You're lying, you're a fucking liar!"

"Believe what you will. I should have seen it coming from the start. Your mother always did what she wanted."

"At least she didn't let her father fuck her."

He fell silent and stared at the television, his eyes wide. He'd stopped breathing and you were satisfied because you'd hit the bull's-eye, he wanted to hide it from you, his voice sounded dull: "You're no better than your mother, just get out of here, I can't look at you anymore."

So you got out, you disappeared deep into yourself and walked round the table and stood in front of him so that he couldn't see the television. He didn't dare look up, his eyes were focused on your crotch, because your crotch was level with his eyes. No thoughts of sex now, nothing at all. You spread your legs and sat down on his thigh.

"Shit, go away."

He didn't really resist, his hands found your hips, but he was weak, he was stoned and exhausted and couldn't get you off him.

"Taja, what the hell's going on? Piss off!"

You took one of the cushions and pressed it down on his face. You wanted to scare him, you wanted him to be really terrified and understand how bad it all was for you. He immediately lost it and started flailing his arms at you. It was ridiculous. You'd fought stronger girls. He tried to press his hands against your belly, he tried to push you away. Then you got really furious. What was he doing? You were just trying to scare him, why was he freaking out? His right fist struck your face, the remote control scratched your forehead open. It hurt, blood flowed into your eye, it hurt like hell. You yelled at him to calm down.

"CALM DOWN, DAMN IT!"

Not a chance, he was pure panic, rearing up against you. So you lay down on the cushion with all your weight. You knew you didn't deserve this, not the panic, not the blows, not all this damned unfairness. You'd done so much for him, you'd even had your hair cut, and you were always there for him, you gave him your love and he dumped you, just like one of his many women.

And he wanted to go to fucking France.

Without you.

In the end his leg twitched once more, then he sat still, head thrown back, no panic now, just calm. But you couldn't ease the pressure, the switch had broken, you couldn't just let go, and you kept the cushion pressed on his face, minute after minute. Eventually your body gave up and you collapsed exhausted over your father, and leaned your forehead against his. There was only the cushion between you.

For a whole day. For a whole day you didn't take the cushion away. You looked at your father, you stalked through the house like a cat and took the batteries out of his phones. Silence was important. You drank everything you could find in the bar, and looked at him sitting there with the cushion on his face.

On the second day you took the cushion away. He was so peaceful. You sat your father up, his eyes were open, you didn't want him to stare at the ceiling. You looked into his eyes and it felt as if he could see you, as if he could understand you. You didn't want to close his eyes. It meant bringing it all to an end, really parting. You didn't want it to come to an end. Your father sat on the sofa as he always did, with the remote in his hand. Only his eyes stared absently past you.

On the third day you took the drugs from the metal case. They made the situation bearable, but soon they led to the fact that you couldn't bear the sight of your father any longer.

After you'd dragged him to the cellar, a century went by in slow motion. You lived on sleep and heroin, the sofa was your ship, the days' light playing on the walls. And that was how your girls found you.

They were shocked and sympathetic, and even though you'd sworn to tell them everything, in the end you just couldn't. They would have hated you, they would never have been the way they'd always been with you. No admiration, no love, nothing.

They'd have called you *fatherfucker,* and you couldn't risk that.

The lies spilled from your lips like new truths. And so you won your girls over. You were the victim, they wanted to save you, you allowed yourself to be saved and made a new reality for yourself.

Stink went along perfectly. You knew the buttons you had to press, you predicted her reactions. That was why you showed her the drugs in your father's hiding place. You wanted to disappear with your girls, but on no account could it look like your plan. It would have been too striking, it would have been wrong. You goal was your dream, your goal was Ulvtannen. You were sure that if you could start all over again far, far away from Berlin, everyone would forget you, and then your soul would have a chance of a new beginning and everything would be forgiven. You wouldn't lose each other after school, and you'd be able to stay together. Every cloud has a silver lining. You and your girls. There wasn't really anything to keep you in Berlin. Somewhere in Oslo or Bergen you'd be bound to find a dealer who would pay good money for your uncle's drugs. If Darian could do it as a matter of course in the clubs, you were bound to pick it up without much trouble. And then there was the beach hotel that you could live in. It belonged to the family, and you were family. You firmly believed that Norway would welcome you with open arms. And if the money ran out, you'd get a job at the power station. Like your father, like your mother. You wanted to grow vegetables and become a real Norwegian. And you were sure your girls would love it. You'd always have a full house, you'd be inseparable and that would be your new life.

You wanted so much.

Your first mistake was not telling your girls who the drugs belonged to. Your second mistake was that you thought you knew what made Stink tick. How could you have been so stupid? Stink is unpredictable. She took the drugs and offered them to your cousin. You'd never have seen that one coming. Never. The worse the situation got, the tighter you clung to your lie. And you lost Ruth.

It really isn't a heroic moment for you. You lied to us. To protect your own dark soul, you sullied our souls. And we believed you, naïve as we are—we fell for the lie about the phone call from Norway, we swallowed the argument with your father, the idea that your grandmother had died and left the hotel to you, and also that your father was a vile liar who hid your mother from you fourteen years before—we swallowed all that, because you're sixteen and sweet and you were in need of help, who wouldn't have fallen for that? You could have done that to us, we are standing here on the sidelines, it would have been okay, but lying to your girls, making them believe that your mother was still alive, who knows if they'll ever forgive you that.

———

But you did give us one truth. It really was your sense of guilt that drove you to drugs. You couldn't sleep, you were eaten away inside by guilt and looked for an emergency exit. Your guilt was and is genuine. Your father was never supposed to die. You're sorry. You know you can't take it back. It's the only truth you gave us.

You tell your girls every single detail because you hope they'll understand. During those minutes your uncle stops existing. There's just you and your girls. After the last sentence silence falls, a genuine silence. Your uncle lowers the gun and lets you go. Then Stink steps forward. Of course it would have to be Stink. The warrior is there. You fear her judgment most of all. Her judgment. Her fury. She steps forward and hits you. With the flat of her hand, right across the face. Once. Then once again. And you don't turn your face away. Your sweet Stink, with tears in her eyes, your beloved Stink, whom you have betrayed. When she raises her hand for the third time, your girls hold her back. Stink scolds and curses.

"And what about Ruth, you piece of shit? Just because you couldn't keep your panties on, Ruth had to die!"

She struggles to break free.

"Damn it, let go of me, she lied to us, I'm going to kill the bitch, let go of me, damn it."

"Let her go," says your uncle and puts his gun away. "She has a right to be furious."

Schnappi and Nessi reluctantly let go of Stink. Your eyes meet. You're not going to defend yourself, whatever happens, Stink can do what she wants with you. For Ruth, for all the shit you've come out with.

Stink walks past you to the rubbish heap and picks up a pipe the length of her arm. She holds it like a sword, utters a growl, and runs toward you. You weren't expecting this. You have no time to react. You stand there helplessly and keep your eyes shut tight.

That's it.

DARIAN

Your arms are heavy, your muscles dead, your blood boils and your eyes hurt as your brain tries to understand what's going on here.

Taja did what?

You try to understand it, but there's nothing to understand, however you twist and turn it. And then Stink starts laying into Taja, one slap, then another, and the other girls intervene and hold Stink back and your father says, "Let her go. She has a right to be furious."

Your father's wrong. It's *your* job to be furious. Yours alone. *How could she do it?* You want to step in, you want to say you're the one who should be beating your psychopathic cousin. Without her you wouldn't be here. She's destroyed everything, she's destroyed the fairy tale of Ulvtannen. Before you can say a word, Stink grabs a pipe and runs at Taja.

That's it, you think.

You can see your father's pleased, he doesn't have to get his hands dirty, Stink's doing it for him. He looks at you, standing there helplessly with the gun in your hand, unable to make sense of the world. Your father did his homework, he knew all along and he didn't warn you. That's why you never got to see the camera recordings. He didn't want to give it away. Not even to Tanner. And now he's smiling at you contentedly. *That's how you do it, son,* his face says to you.

You miserable fucker, you think as Stink runs past Taja and brings the pipe crashing down against your father's temple. He crashes to the ground, and you stand there and simply can't process any of this anymore.

What . . .

Your arms sink down, a dull groan leaves your mouth. The girls look at you in horror, as if they don't know what's just happened here either. Stink stands beside your father, there's blood on the end of the pipe, she too looks at you and looks at you, then she drops the pipe, turns around, and yells to her girls, "RUN!"

They run to the hotel. You have their backs right in front of you, you have the gun in your hand and you raise your arms, you support the gun and hold it still. Nessi brings up the rear, pushing Schnappi in front of her. Taja's right behind Stink. Red and black and blond hair. Your finger is on the trigger, their footsteps are barely audible on the ground, it's only when they reach the paved area in front of the hotel entrance that a hectic rhythm rings out from under their feet and this noise releases you from your frozen posture. You breathe in and hold the air in your lungs. There's ice under your feet again, and the sky is over your head and you know, *If I hesitate now it's over.* That's what the rules are, so don't think, don't even think about hesitating.

SCHNAPPI

It feels as if you're moving under water, with those tenacious strokes that you always hated because they hardly got you anywhere. Swimming is not your passion, it's something for retirees with back pains, or people who like secretly peeing in the water. Yesterday you were a rocket, today a butterfly with a suitcase could overtake you. Even though it feels as if you aren't getting anywhere, surprisingly you aren't bringing up the rear, which certainly isn't due to your fabulously long legs. Nessi pushes you onwards. Her hand is on the small of your back, but it isn't getting you any closer to the hotel.

"Run, Schnappi! Shit, keep running!"

She pushes, you stumble and nearly fall, and then time takes pity on you and your legs are your legs again and everything goes incredibly quickly from then on. Stink disappears into the house, and when Taja tries to get through the rickety double door, you hear the first shot ring out. All of a sudden your back is hot and wet and you stop abruptly, you nearly fall headlong.

Then the second, then the third shot.

You turn around.

Nessi isn't behind you now, there's no one behind you. You look at the ground. And there lies Nessi, her left shoulder is nothing but shredded flesh, you see the shimmer of bone, the blood pumps and pumps and forms a pool around Nessi. You can't take your eyes off that white shimmer, and feel the warmth on your back and something running down your arm. You don't want to look, but you look and there's a scrap of skin on your upper arm, right where the sleeve of your T-shirt stops.

You look up. Darian is still aiming the gun at you, and you know that's it. *The fucker's going to blow my head off now, and I'm just standing there and there's nothing I can do, and what sort of a stupid ending is that?* Darian pulls the trigger, the shot crashes through your stomach with searing heat, and Nessi says, "Everything okay?"

You blink, you're standing in the hotel lobby and it's hazy, the air around you glitters with the dust particles that you've swirled up with your feet. You look down at her, a sunbeam has pierced your stomach and is warming it up. Stink shuts the other half of the double door with a bang, the sun is closed out, she comes over to you and wants to know if you've seen a ghost or what. You grab Nessi by the shoulders and turn her around.

"What's up with you?" asks Nessi.

You hug her, press her to you.

"Honey, what's up?"

"Stop chatting, you two," says Stink. "The bastard almost got us. We can't stand around here waiting for the next bus. Perhaps there's a rear exit."

"No."

You turn round. Taja is sitting at the foot of a sweeping staircase that leads to the second floor and looks as if someone's been working at it with a jackhammer. Taja has put her arms around herself as if it's incredibly cold in here, she's rocking gently back and forth.

"The house is built right on the cliff," she says. "There's no rear exit."

You stare at her, your blank is forgotten, now you can just see Taja, pale and miserable, rocking back and forth, and for that moment even Darian and his father are forgotten. You want to ask her to stop rocking like that. It's weird, as if Taja's inner balance is broken. Nessi asks the question that's troubling all of you.

"But why, Taja?"

And she doesn't mean Taja's father and what happened between you. You don't care about that, if you're honest; it's Taja's business.

"I thought we'd start over," she replies. "I thought it would be okay."

You could give her encouragement now, and say that everything is forgiven and you'll be able to have a new start. You could, but you don't, because it would be a lie. The wounds are too fresh. You feel the tension rising. Stink might tear into Taja again at any moment. Do something.

"We've got to hide," you say quickly. "The hotel's huge; if they come in search of us, we'll definitely find a way of creeping past them."

It's not exactly a foolproof plan, but it's better than nothing. You do the same thing as Taja did when she decided to run up the road to the cliff—you run ahead, your girls follow you, even Taja. *Thank God, even Taja,* you think and run down the corridor on the left, run through rooms full of rubbish and detritus. The fir trunk finally blocks your path, the wall around it has collapsed and you can't get past the rubble.

You turn round and come back to the entrance hall. You don't really know what you're looking for. A door leading to the emergency exit? A cellar you could hide in? You know you'd never hide in a cellar.

I'd rather die.

There's a room that must once have been the library. Warped shelves, stained books everywhere, a fireplace with a broken chair in it, the graffito of a huge pirate runs like a painting across one of the walls. The room overlooks the fjord. You step onto the terrace and stand by the railing. There's a steep drop. Nope, not an emergency exit.

You run on.

A toilet, a tiny room, a ballroom, a big room, more rubble. Everything's been cleared away. Cables hanging from the ceiling, tattered curtains, more graffiti. At the end of the corridor you see a locked door. The first one. All the other doors are missing, or else they hang into the room at an angle. You push the door open. It's the back room, it doesn't go any further. A huge kitchen opens up in front of you, and it's completely intact. There are cracks in the ceiling, mildew has formed in one corner, and the windows are all broken, but otherwise the kitchen looks untouched—two stoves, a ceramic sink the size of a bathtub, lamps, pots and pans on the walls, and in the middle of the kitchen a massive table with twelve chairs.

At the end of the table sits a man with his hands flat on the tabletop as if to keep the table from floating away. You're not sure if this isn't another of your blanks. Maybe your father's about to come in and ask which of you wants some pizza.

"Just come in," says the man.

He looks as if he's been waiting for you. It's weird. He doesn't smile, he doesn't do anything, he just watches you, hands flat on the tabletop, no tricks behind it. You feel you can't breathe anymore. The man's eyes look as if a light's been turned off. *Cold,* you think, *so damned cold.* You all cram together in the doorway and stare and stare back. Then Stink says what you're all thinking.

"Deselected?!"

DARIAN

The girls have disappeared into the house, and you didn't hit any of them. Three shots, and you seriously didn't hit them. You switch the gun from one hand to another and shake out your cramped fingers. Your body was too stiff. You wished you had the agility of a cat, but you were just a clumsy piece of wood without elegance.

You walk over to your father, who is lying motionless on the ground. You can't tell if he's breathing. The blood gleams dully where the pipe hit him on the head. You kick the pipe away and crouch down. You want to ask your father if he can hear you, where it hurts, and what you should do. The three questions produce one simple statement. It startles you just as much as the truth that you've heard from Taja's mouth.

"You shot my best friend!"

Your voice sounds shrill. It's the adrenaline, the echo of the gunshots, and of course the sobering feeling of failure. *It's out now.* You're wired up and you switch the gun back to your firing hand. Your father is lying in front of you and he might be dead and he might be alive, but whichever he is, your thoughts left your mouth unfiltered, and now you're seriously waiting for the reality around you to blow apart with a bang. Nothing happens, of course, so you go on, "You lied to me because you wanted to train me. I know that. Tanner told me, he told me everything."

It's a new feeling, you squat down beside your father, you say what you're thinking and nothing happens. Fuck the ice beneath you, let it break, fuck your father, let him be dead. *Dead,* you think, and it's a sense of relief the like of which you've never felt before. Like you feel after an orgasm, like a swig of water after being thirsty for a week. Your father has failed, he let one of the girls knock him down. And he lied to you. That carries some weight. You wanted to keep it to yourself and now it's out. You pussy.

"He was my best friend."

You look at the gun in your hand and move the safety catch up and down, up and down. How easy it would be to shoot your father right now. That really would be the end. No more you, no more him.

When he's dead, I'll live.

Then you would throw the gun into the fjord, put your father over your shoulder, and go back to the cemetery. Then you'd lay him in the open grave and add Tanner and Leo to it. It would give you a great sense of relief to fill the grave yourself, put the spades back in the shed, and then go to the car. Maybe you'd drive back to Berlin, maybe you'd disappear into the Norwegian wilderness and become a legend.

Anything is possible.

You take your eyes away from the gun and look at your father. His eyes are open, his voice is hoarse.

"What . . . what happened?"

"You shot Mirko."

"Shit, Darian, what just happened?"

"Stink knocked you down."

He doesn't move, only his eyes, his mouth.

"What?"

"She clobbered you. With that pipe there. You didn't see it coming."

He blinks, licks his lips, rolls his eyes, tries to look round, but he can't move his head, his right hand is trembling, he tries to clench his fist, gives up.

"And you shot Mirko. Tanner told me. You shot my best friend."

Your father coughs, takes a deep breath, he looks pained, he doesn't want to hear that, but he has no choice, he's helpless.

"Why did you lie to me? Why did you say it was the girls?"

"It made sense."

"It made sense? What does that mean?"

"You've got to learn to direct your anger. I gave you a direction to go in. And Mirko was a coward. He insulted me. Apparently Tanner didn't tell you that. Your friend was giving us all the runaround. You'd have done the same thing if—"

"You can't just shoot my best friend!" you interrupt the man nobody interrupts, and add softly, "It's not cool."

"Of course it's cool. I'm your father. I can do anything. Have you forgotten who I am? Are you starting to cry? Where's your cock? Are you a eunuch? You killed a boy and you couldn't even look him in the eye. Think about that. Think about it, damn it, and open your eyes and look at me. What's up? Is your hand twitching? Are you going to take your revenge on me and put a bullet in my head?"

You just look at him, your hand won't stop twitching, you pull the safety catch up and down, up and down. And think about Leo. And think about Tanner. How the gun went off in your hand because the boy went nuts. Three shots and two corpses.

Because I fucked up.

"Help me up, I can't feel my legs."

"I want an apology."

"What?"

"I want you to apologize to me."

"Darian, stop all this nonsense, my head's about to explode and I can't move my fucking arms and legs. Help me up!"

"Apologize."

Your father stares at you, his right hand claws in the earth, he isn't capable of doing anything else. His voice is a hiss.

"You little shit, just so you know, I have no reason to apologize, I . . ."

He breaks off, his eyes bulge, he turns pale, then he turns his head to the side and throws up. It's pitiful. Nothing about your father is working anymore. Stink really whacked him, he can't even wipe his own puke off his chin. His head whips around, spit goes flying through the air.

"Help me up, Darian! I'm not going to say it again, help me up, you muscle-bound jerk. HELP ME UP, I'M YOUR FATHER!"

You know if he could he'd grab you now. *He can't.* You crouch down in front of him, unmoved, there's no reason to move back even an inch. *So weak.* You grab your chest, put your hand over your heart, you really want to cry now, because you've just understood something, and that understanding is full of emotion and it makes you sad. You think you've understood your father for the first time.

"I don't think you have a heart," you say. "That's why you don't feel anything, that's why you can be the way you are. They forgot to give you a heart."

Your father laughs.

"Stop talking such bullshit. Everybody has a heart. Nothing's possible without a heart. Perhaps I should send you back to school, you idiot."

It's a bad laugh, it doesn't even reach his eyes. The fingers of his right hand move a few inches toward you, the dead arm holds them back. You can't take your eyes off your father.

"Darian, help me up, I'm lying in my own vomit, can't you see that? Help me up and let's get out of here."

"I don't think so."

"What?"

"I said, I don't think so."

"What do you mean, *I don't think so*? No one wants you to think."

He's right; it hurts, but he's right. So keep it short and snappy. Spit it out.

"I don't think you're my father anymore."

THE TRAVELER

After you've left the sleeping girls on their own, you look up the cliff, all you can see is rocks, occasional bushes, but no hotel. You follow the road, reach the summit, and don't believe your eyes. Where the girls will see decay and chaos two hours later, you see something completely different.

What is that?

It reminds you of a beach hotel that you saw in Montenegro years ago. The house could be from colonial times, it doesn't fit here at all. Now you can understand why the man with the greyhound laughed a little while ago. Who would take the trouble of climbing up this cliff to see a wreck like this?

The rooms are dilapidated, cracks in the ceiling, holes in the walls, the floors covered with rubbish. But you can see that they're good floors. Floorboards that have defied the elements and not warped. The entrance hall is tiled and supported by four pillars; a wide staircase leads upward, the banisters are missing in several places, and it looks as if the steps would give way under the slightest weight. You're careful and climb up to the first floor. Empty rooms, in the bathroom even the toilets and fittings have been torn out. You run your hand over the wallpaper as if looking for a pulse. On the second floor you throw back your head and look up into the sky. The roof has been torn away completely, the rafters revealed, the withered branches of a fir dangle in and remind you of the Christ-

mas trees that lie sadly by the edge of the road at the beginning of
January.

On the way down you imagine how many guests have walked
up and down the stairs here. What they felt, what they thought.
Every house has its own soul. The hotel's soul hasn't fled. It is still
breathing, and lives hidden in the walls. Even though you haven't
yet found the pulse, you know it's there.

Back on the first floor, you find a closed door at the end of the corridor. It's jammed, the wood must have warped. You slam your shoulder against it and the door swings open.

The kitchen is massive and almost undamaged. A table with
chairs, broken glass and stones on the floor, a kitten calendar from
1997. In the sink there's the skeleton of a dead pigeon that must have
flown in through the window and been too stupid to find its way
out again. An old station clock hangs on the wall, the minute hand
missing. *Who would steal a minute hand?* you wonder and open the
cupboards. Plates. Cups. Glasses. You find cans whose use-by date
ran out ten years ago. The kitchen is a time capsule. You go to the
door and close it again, the capsule is sealed, the present only comes
in through the broken windows and breathes in your face. You sit
down and lay your hands flat on the tabletop. Dust and dirt don't
bother you. You're quite still and listen to the house and wait for
the pulse.

It feels like minutes, but you've been sitting here for over two hours,
and you'd probably hold out for even longer if you didn't hear the
voices.

They've found the house, you think and don't move.

It's like a radio play. You hear the girls arguing. Then it falls
silent. A man speaks. Sharply, furiously. You like the sound. You
can make out every word, and slowly, very slowly, you work out
the connections.

My son's murderer is standing outside.

You don't move. The girl Taja confesses. And you hear and don't
move, both hands on the tabletop, eyes on the closed door. Patient.

———

You can imagine staying here forever. You would start on the first floor and breathe life into the hotel, one step at a time. Clear away the dirt, cover the roof, entice past glories from the ruin. When you were on the second floor, you stepped out onto the terrace. In front of you was the fjord, below you there were rocks.

Not even the end of civilization could be more beautiful.

A place to stay.

The shots make you flinch. No shouts, nothing. Just three sharp shots and then silence. You go on waiting. Hands on the tabletop, silent. You look at the door and the door flies open and the girls are standing in the doorway. The door bangs against the wall, swings back, the delicate Asian girl holds it open with one hand. They look at you in alarm. You say, "Just come in."

They don't move. They expected anything, but not you. The red-haired girl frowns and says, "Deselected?"

You look at your chest, look back at the girls.

"My son lent me the T-shirt. He thought I'd never wear it, he was wrong. Sit down."

The Asian girl shakes her head. It's the last thing she wants to do. You're going to have to be a bit more persuasive. Tell them the truth, give them the feeling they've arrived.

"You'll be safe here."

No reaction; they probably don't think much of the safety promised them by a stranger who's sitting in a dilapidated house, wearing a stupid T-shirt.

"Which one of you is Taja?"

At last they react and look at each other and turn around. The girl with the golden hair says, "Where's Taja?"

TAJA

You stand in the middle of the corridor, while your girls go on running. They don't notice, they look into the rooms and leave you behind. It's the end of the sweet bitches. Your biggest fear has come true. You're no longer part of them. You're no longer part of anything. Even if you've been pretending over the past few days that everything would be as it always was, you were living only on the memory of a Taja who was once part of it.

Once upon a time there were five girls and I was one of them.

Shame floods over you, and you'd probably cry again if it wasn't for this pain. The bullet hit you a couple of inches above the left of your pelvis. It got you just as you were running through the front door. At first there was just a dull stitch, you staggered and bumped your shoulder against one of the pillars, but then came the pain. You clutched your hip and blood stuck to your fingers. Your girls mustn't find out anything about this, you don't want their sympathy and concern. *It's just a scratch,* you lie to yourself while the wound pulses like a strobe light, frantic and nervous.

And sometimes you're there and sometimes you're gone.

Your girls haven't noticed anything, not even Nessi, who's normally alert to everything. It must be the fear, the fear is too deep in their bones, Darian and your uncle could come charging in at any moment, and it doesn't help that Stink has shut the double doors, because if your uncle comes, nothing in the world is going to help. So you went running through the hotel looking for a hiding place and you followed your girls for a while, as if a hiding place could save you. When they ended up in a blind alley, they turned around and you followed them to the entrance hall and that's where you put on the brakes. You didn't want to do this anymore, you let your girls go on.

Since you stepped inside the hotel you've only had one single destination.

The stairs groan under every step. You avoid the holes in the floor and hold on to the wall with your right hand, you don't dare take your other hand away from your injury. Your lips move, you're murmuring your very own mantra.

A house among rocks. Water below me, sky above me.

On the second floor you choose the first room you come to that looks out over the fjord. Here too the glass in the door onto the terrace has disappeared, only a single shard hangs in the frame like a comma. Your father told you the glass in the windows and the glass doors are from the days of art nouveau. You break the shard out of the frame and hold it against the light. It has a soft orange glow.

I was born here, you think and step outside.

The terrace is six feet wide and leads all the way around the building. You'd like to walk its full length, but in one direction the floor has broken away, in the other the wall has fallen outward, dragging the terrace and its railing away with it. When you were teething, your mother always pushed you around the house because you would only calm down in the moving stroller. Night after night. Her record is supposed to have been sixteen circuits of the terrace. You won't be doing a single circuit, you're trapped.

A house among rocks.

You shiver, even though there's sweat on your forehead and the air is warm. The sunlight lies like a halo on the fjord. The mist has vanished, on the opposite shore you see the mountains and a road with two cars advancing slowly along it. You lean forward, the railing creaks and bends slightly outward. There's the pebble beach with the boathouse. It's all as your father described it to you. You look straight down. It's high, really high. A drop of sweat falls from the tip of your nose. At this point Stink would say: *This is definitely high enough.* You wonder what it would be like to land down there. The glass slips from your hand and vanishes. *No.* You're not planning on dying, but you're not planning on living either. You want to stay in this intermediate stage. With pain, guilt, and suffering. You deserve to feel as miserable as this.

If your mother were here, she would understand you and your loneliness. You believe in that, you cling to it. Your mother would have understood you wanting to bring her back to life for a few days. For a few days you were really on the way to her.

Behind you, leaning against the wall of the house, are six deck chairs which are as weathered as the façade and have assumed the same gray color. When you were in your delirious state and traveled here in your mind, the deck chairs were green and yielded slightly under your weight. You unfold one of them, it comes to pieces in your hands. You pick up the chair behind it. It creaks and trembles when you sit down and stretch your legs out. The linen fabric holds, you lean all the way back, it's the most relaxing feeling you've had for ages. Better than any drug, better than any hand touching you. You look down at the fjord. It's like coming home.

Water below me, sky above me.

STINK

You look down the corridor, you call her name, Taja doesn't reply. You look at the man as if he might know what's going on here. And it slowly dawns on you how crazy all this is. Meeting someone in this dilapidated house. Someone who speaks German.

Someone who knows us.

"How do you know about Taja?"

"Sit down, then we can talk."

You don't move.

"We'd rather stand," you say, "because we have no time to chat, there are two lunatics out there who want to kill us."

None of this affects the man, he is tranquillity personified, he repeats that you're safe here. Nessi stands beside you and she is as nervous as if she needs to go to the bathroom, she whispers to you that the guy's weird. *That's not really news to me,* you want to tell her. All of a sudden Schnappi can't keep it in any longer: "Excuse me, why are we safe here? And who are you anyway?"

The man puts a key on the table.

"You've been traveling in my car."

So there is the key! you think and know right away that it must be nonsense, because you stole the car from Marten and not from a man in his late forties, wearing an idiotic T-shirt. *That's never his car.* Then it clicks, then all of a sudden you know who you've got sitting in front of you. Schnappi works it out at the same moment.

"No way," she says.

Nessi is missing it again.

"What?"

"This is Marten's father," you say.

"What?"

Nessi looks at you with big eyes and then she looks at Marten's father and then she starts stammering.

"We . . . we never wanted this to happen. You see . . . We needed the car because . . ."

"It's okay," says the man, and for one brief moment you see a cloud drifting across his eyes, then the cloud has disappeared again, leaving behind a coldness that you hadn't noticed before.

He's here, and at the same time he's very far away.

"We didn't do anything to him," you say.

"I think you did. Without you, Marten would be in Kristiansand right now."

You don't know what to say to that. His calm voice makes you nervous, you almost wish he'd get angry. But good luck with that, he sits and touches the key with his fingertips. If it came to it, you could outpace this guy in ten seconds flat. But where would you go? Marten's father in the hotel and Taja's uncle out there, and to crown it all you've got Darian, shooting away like an idiot all over the place. Life isn't exactly showing you its sweetest side, but as it hasn't been doing that for a few days now, it hardly matters.

The man looks over to the window, then he asks you who the two people out there are. You tell him, you tell him exactly what kind of a mess you've got yourselves into. First you speak, then Nessi, but in the end Schnappi does most of the talking. When she mentions the drugs, Marten's father interrupts her.

"That's not the issue."

Of course not, you want to say, *it's not about pride and revenge, and it's not about a few million euros that our Nessi scattered on the tarmac, because I couldn't help taking the fucking drugs with me, because Taja couldn't help fucking her father and then suffocating him under a cushion.*

"Here's the key to my car," the man goes on, "I'd give you back the Range Rover, but Marten's lying on the backseat and I don't yet feel like moving him off it. And anyway, it's an Autobiography."

He smiles wearily. You haven't the faintest idea what he's talking about.

"You can keep my car as long as you want. Drive away and don't look back."

"You want us to do what?" you ask as if he'd been speaking Greek the whole time.

"Get out of here."

"We can't go outside, they'll shoot us down."

The man shakes his head.

"They won't do anything to you."

At that moment you hear voices from outside. Schnappi goes to one of the windows and jumps back immediately.

"What is it?" you ask.

"Darian's crouching beside his father and they're talking. You really messed him up, the bastard's still lying on the ground."

"You knocked him down?" the man says to you.

"He threatened us."

"You could have killed him."

"At that moment it didn't matter."

"And if he was dead now?"

"That wouldn't matter either," you admit, and know it's true, because Taja's uncle deserved more than being hit with a pipe. The man nods appreciatively. He respects your fury, and when has anyone ever respected your fury?

He likes me.

You're not sure if that's good or bad. Schnappi knows something's happening between you, she tilts her head at an angle and says to Marten's father, "My mother told me about you."

The man takes his eye off you, you're free again. He sounds surprised when he asks, "Did she?"

Schnappi nods.

"My mother says if you see someone who's missing a soul, you've got to run. Faster than the wind, faster than light. Because the ones who are missing a soul, they'll steal your breath, they have nothing to lose and that's why they aren't scared of anything or anyone."

"Your mother must be a clever woman."

"My mother's a witch, and I can't stand her."

"No one likes witches."

"No, no one likes witches."

"So . . ."

Schnappi takes a deep breath.

". . . are you one of the ones who are missing a soul?"

"I'm one of those," the man confirms, and however hard you try you have no idea what the two of them are talking about.

The man pushes the car keys away from him, they slide across the table toward you. Nessi picks them up. You have to ask, "How did you find us?"

The man smiled.

"That's a misunderstanding. You found me, I didn't look for you."

"What? Is that supposed to be an answer?"

"That's an answer. Now go, and shut the door behind you."

Of course the answer isn't enough for you, but Nessi pulls you by the arm on one side and Schnappi pushes you from the other. You leave the kitchen, Nessi shuts the door behind you.

"What was that?" she asks quietly.

"He's nuts," Schnappi says loudly.

"Shh, he can still hear us," says Nessi and pulls you down the corridor toward the hall.

"What did you mean by he's 'missing a soul'?" you ask Schnappi.

"He's without a soul, haven't you noticed?"

"He's what?"

"Didn't you see?"

You can't describe what you saw in Marten's father, just that it was cold and distant, but what's that going to sound like?

Better than without a soul, *anyway.*

Yeah, you've got a point.

You reach the hall. No trace of Taja. You look at the entrance. The doors hang at a bit of an angle, so that the sun can push its thin fingers through.

"Are they coming to get us?"

"If they come, let's send them to see Marten's father in the kitchen."

No one laughs. None of you can take your eyes off the door. You could stand there gaping all day. Like before school when there were exams and you kept your cigarette going till the filter charred.

"No way am I going out there," says Schnappi.

"We can't just hide like rabbits and wait till they come and get us," you say.

"We've got to find Taja first," says Nessi.

You knew she'd mention that one. Schnappi bites her lower lip, you try to ignore Nessi and think: *I'd rather go outside and take a bullet.* When Nessi adds, "Guys, this is *our* Taja we're talking about."

"*Our* Taja lied to us," you remind her. "We're only here because she lied to us. Don't you get that, Nessi? She's fake."

Schnappi nods, she agrees with you. It's the worst judgment you can make about any of the girls, but you have to be honest, because without honesty nothing keeps you together anymore.

"I know she's messed up," says Nessi. "She messed up big-time, okay, but the way I see it she can mess up as much as you like, she's still one of us. That's how we are, that's how we always wanted to be, have you forgotten that?"

Of course you haven't forgotten, and you're about to let her have a few choice arguments, when Taja's uncle suddenly yells outside.

Schnappi wants to go and see what's going on.

"Schnappi, keep out of it," you say.

The yelling stops. Silence. Schnappi steps over to the door.

"Schnappi, don't!" says Nessi.

"Don't be pussies," says Schnappi and peers through the crack. One second, two, and suddenly a piece of the door beside her head is pulverized and bits of wood fly in your faces.

"Get down!"

You throw yourselves on the floor, and after that it's shot after shot, fist-sized holes open up in the front door and let the sun in, while the hotel quakes and quivers under the impact.

DARIAN

The man who's no longer your father lies on the floor and looks up at you. You defied him. You said *no* to him. You fucked up Judas. The satisfaction sets off little explosions in your body.

The man who's no longer your father turns red in the face, his chin trembles, a thin thread of blood runs from his nose, the blood is almost black, he yells at you,

"THEN FUCK OFF! GET OUT OF HERE! AND IF I EVER GET BACK ON MY FEET, I'LL FINISH YOU OFF, YOU GET THAT? YOU CAN HIDE WHERE YOU LIKE, I'LL FINISH YOU OFF, DO YOU UNDERSTAND WHAT I'M SAYING?"

You nod, you understand, you're a boy without muscles again, who sees his mother standing at the roadside with two suitcases, waiting for a taxi and promising she'll call you soon. Again you're a boy with no muscles, running in tears to his father because he hopes for a hug and instead he gets laughed at. You've been a boy with muscles for too long. You don't want to be you anymore. You get up and look across at the hotel, and in that moment the hotel represents everything you once were. Your uncle and his stories about the wolves and the memory of a time that will never come again, because your uncle stopped existing. Only this hotel remains, and your despair has a target. You raise the gun with both hands, release the safety catch, and fire and fire and fill the front door with holes as if this pitiful door is to blame for everything. After fourteen shots the magazine's empty, only the echo of your despair floats in the air.

It's over.

You turn away and walk over to the slope that you climbed with your father. Your life in reverse. You hear the man who's no longer your father yelling after you, but he no longer speaks your language.

You go, because you're no longer furious with anyone. Not with Taja and what she's done, not with your father, who never wanted you. You forgive them. Your mother. Your first girlfriend, who dumped you without a word of explanation after two weeks. Those bastards, lying in wait for you and Mirko. Everybody. Even Mirko, who went and got shot. And particularly your father, who is no longer your father. You've changed, whatever that means, you're no longer the person you were this morning. You forgive everybody, but you keep hold of your own guilt, because you still can't forgive the murder of the boy, and even the fact that you've forgotten his name is inexcusable. His death will stay with you for ages yet. Eventually you'll be standing at a crossroads in Berlin, watching after a bus that beeped at you. And at that moment the boy's name will come to your mind. Twenty-one years will pass before that happens. Twenty-one years without forgiveness. Take time with your guilt, the wounds need to heal. And look around you every time you get to a crossroads.

SCHNAPPI

"Is he dead?"

"Looks that way."

"Christ, he scared the shit out of me."

"Imagine if he got up right now."

"Keep your mouth shut."

"Do you think he can hear you?"

"Not if he's dead."

You keep your distance, because you've seen enough horror movies. You keep glancing over at the slope that Darian's disappeared behind, after firing at the hotel like a lunatic. You lay down flat on the floor in the hall, arms over your head, and you thought: *This is exactly what war must be like.* You'd have liked to have Marten's father by your side, to ask him if he meant it when he said you were safe. Then everything outside fell silent. Nothing. No voices, no footsteps, the shooting was over. Somewhere a bird was singing, and when birds sing it usually means everything's okay.

You got up and looked carefully through one of the bullet holes. The wood was rotten and smelled of burnt paper. You saw Darian heading toward the slope.

"Darian's leaving."

"And what about his father?" Stink asked.

"He's still there."

You wanted to clear out before Darian came back. Nessi wouldn't think of it, and handed you the key to the car.

"What are you doing?"

"You two can go where you like, but I'm not going anywhere without Taja."

Stink turned pale.

"Come on, Nessi, she's fucking left, or can you see her anywhere?"

Nessi looked up the stairs.

"Where could she have got to? She must be in the hotel. You two can leave. I'm not abandoning Taja."

"Shit, I hate it when you're like this," Stink said.

"What's that supposed to mean?"

"It means we'll wait outside for you," you said quickly, because if anyone can interpret Stink's words, it's you.

"Thanks," said Nessi and was about to turn around, but Stink held her back.

"Just in case there's any misunderstanding, I'm not going to forgive Taja. She's still one of us, and that will never change, but I'll never forgive her."

"And you don't have to," Nessi replied. "I think the only person who can forgive Taja is Taja herself."

With those words Nessi went upstairs, and Stink looked at you quizzically and you shrugged and then you all left the hotel. Since then you've been standing in the sun, ten feet away from Ragnar Desche, waiting for Nessi and Taja and hoping with all your heart that Darian's not going to come back. You walk to the edge of the slope. No sign of Darian. You look around the place. No sign of anyone. No cars on the road, no one walking a dog, not even an elk standing by the water and drinking. Probably all the Norwegians have emigrated and you're the last people left in the country. You look over at the hotel and wonder if Marten's father is still sitting at the kitchen table.

When you return to Stink, she's standing bent over, hands on her knees. She's taking a closer look at Ragnar Desche.

"He's not breathing. He's not bleeding anymore, either."

"Did you really have to use a pipe?"

"What are you thinking of? Should I have tried to find something softer, or what?"

"Nah, it's fine."

"I didn't plan him to break down like this."

"You saved our lives, and now shut up."

"What about Taja?"

"What do you mean?"

"I don't know, do you think we can save her?"

You nearly said there was nothing to save, but even a Schnappi sometimes manages to keep her mouth shut. You stand there and don't know what to do next. You look at Ragnar Desche for another minute, then you turn away and look over at the hotel. Nothing. No Nessi, no Taja. You imagine Marten's father suddenly deciding he's been sitting here for long enough.

"What happens if Marten's father goes berserk?"

"Schnappi, I hate it when you say stuff like that."

"I'm just thinking out loud."

"Then think quietly."

You purse your lips, draw a cross on the ground with your heel, and spit on it.

"What the hell was that? Voodoo?"

"Nope, just bored. Where have they got to?"

"Perhaps Nessi can't find her."

"Perhaps Taja doesn't want to be found."

Both of you look over at the beach hotel.

I hope so, you think and immediately regret the thought.

TAJA

And then it's over, the shots from the first floor fall silent, and you're still lying stretched out on the deck chair. The sun has wandered around the corner and covers your legs like a blanket of light. It feels as if your batteries are being charged. From a distance you think you can hear your father. He talks to you, and although you don't understand a word, it's a good feeling that he's there. You listen, drift off, and feel through the woodwork of the terrace the vibration of footsteps coming toward you.

If it is my father, I'll ask him if he forgives me.

"Taja?"

You can't answer, you lie there and can't even open your eyes. You can't sleep now, look up.

You look up.

Nessi is standing in the doorway, a hand over her mouth in fright, the other a fist that doesn't know what to do.

Typical Nessi, you think and attempt a smile. It doesn't work, your mouth is too tired for a smile. Nessi steps outside, she's so quick, a moment ago she was still standing in the door and now she's crouching down beside you. You sigh and make a sound like a baby waking up.

"I'm okay," you say and can't see what Nessi sees—the dark puddle spreading under your chair and drenching the dry wood.

"You're bleeding."

"I'm okay, Nessi, it feels . . . good."

"That can't feel good. You've lost a ton of blood."

She lays her hand on your forehead. Clammy and wet. You're in shock, your body's slowly running down, the system's saying goodbye. Nessi grips your arm.

"You've got to stand up, we'll get you to a hospital."

"Nessi, don't!"

A firmness in your tone startles Nessi.

"I'm staying here."

"But—"

"There's no *but*. I'm staying here. It's fine. Really."

"But, sweetie—"

Nessi starts crying. You're finding it difficult to keep her in focus. Your eyes flicker like reflections of light on the water, now bright, now dark, you could just go to sleep like that with the sun covering you slowly, and Nessi by your side. Her tears do you good. *She's grieving over me.* You want to tell her to grab another deck chair and—

"Taja, do you hear me?"

She shakes your shoulder, your head slips to one side, your cheek touches her hand.

Peace.

". . . exactly did he hit you?"

"What?"

Nessi touches your injury, you cry out, Nessi pulls her hand away as if she'd burnt herself, her fingers are red. You look at each other, and there's suddenly a terrifying clarity in your eyes, that stops Nessi crying for a moment.

"I can't leave you behind, Taja, please, I can't do it."

"Nessi, I'm going to jail, you know that."

"But if no one knows that you—"

"I'm going to jail whether anyone knows or not. My father is dead and I'm going to jail. Can you imagine that? Me and jail?"

"You're underage."

"My uncle will see to it that I'm punished. Or else he'll kill me himself. I'd rather stay here."

"But—"

"It's okay, really. I'm glad to be here."

"But you're bleeding to death."

"It's just a scratch, Nessi. It looks worse than it is. I swear."

Nessi knows you're lying, you know you're lying. You need that, otherwise you'll never part. And the parting has to be.

"And call him, promise me that."

Nessi knows immediately who you mean; she promises.

"And tell the girls I love them and that I'm sorry. Please don't forget, I really love you all."

Nessi strokes your head, she squats down next to you and you lean against each other, forehead to forehead. It's warm and safe, and it would be nice if Nessi stayed with you like that forever, because this way you can endure everything, cold, heat, loneliness. You fade away, come to again, thirsty and tired, the sun scratches your thighs and tries to get at your lap like an excited puppy, you sit up, you'd like to drink from the fjord.

Just one sip.

"Give me a farewell kiss," you say.

Nessi kisses you, her breath enters your mouth, a warm, long kiss. *Longing, I'm dying of longing,* you think, and hear your father's voice saying in the distance: *If your heart is bound to something, you cannot give it away, for whatever it is, your heart will miss it.* He was wrong. You listened to him, you wanted to keep him with you, and chaos broke out. He misunderstood. It's real love when you let go of something that's close to your heart.

"It'd be nice if there were a few more chairs here," says a voice on your left, and Stink sits down on the floor, saying that her sweet little ass won't stand it for long.

"You don't look, you don't find," says Schnappi from the terrace door. She has three brand-new chairs wedged under her arms, and she winks at you. A moment later your girls are sitting next to you, their legs outstretched, and sighing because the view is so beautiful, and you're glad your girls are sharing this place with you. It's quiet, nobody's talking about guilt, there's no past, just four girlfriends in the here and now. Everything is as it was always supposed to be. And sometimes you hear your father speaking as if from far away, sometimes you hear the gentle rolling of wheels as your mother begins the next circuit and pushes the stroller through the night, even though it's day. Time is good to you and your girls are by your side, and it can stay that way. Maybe somebody will bring tea and biscuits, a few blankets wouldn't be bad for the cold times, then you'd sit here forever and look at the fjord, and there would be no better life than this one.

NESSI

She can't hear you, she hasn't been able to hear you for a while now, all the promises and all the forgivings in the world are pointless if she can't hear you. Her head leans against your head. You still have her taste on your lips, as if with her kiss she had passed part of herself to you. You stroke her cheek, feel her neck for a pulse. You don't shake her, even though everything within you cries out to shake her and bring her back to life, you let her go.

Enough's enough.

You lay her head back gently, take your jacket off, and cover her up with it. The sun has reached her hands now, they look bare and unprotected. You can't stand up yet. You take her hands in yours and protect them. Her eyes are open a crack, she looks down at the fjord, and that's how you're going to leave her.

At peace with herself, in a place that now belongs to her alone.

You let go of her hands, stand up, and kiss her on the forehead before you leave.

They're waiting outside the hotel.

"Girl, what took you so long?" asks Stink.

"Imagine if Darian had come back," Schnappi whines, then she sees your face, frowns, and wants to know what's happened.

"Nothing, I didn't find her."

"You've been in that dump for an hour and you didn't find her?"

"Stink, the hotel is big."

"So's my ass, if I'm lying. And where's your jacket?"

Stink shuts up, Schnappi says quietly, "And why do you have blood on your hand?"

You look at your hand with surprise, you're really a rotten liar. Without giving your girls an answer, you walk past them. They don't follow you. After a few steps you turn around.

"Are you coming now or are you not?"

"And Taja?"

Stink sounds as if she's about to burst into tears.

"Taja's okay," you say and swallow the tears down and summon all your courage and go on talking: "Taja doesn't want to come. She's up to her eyeballs in guilt, and I'm to tell you that she loves you, and you're to know that she never wanted to be fake, but it's happened and she regrets it and hopes you can forgive her, but you don't have to, because as I've said, she has to forgive herself, that's all that's important."

"What . . . what are you saying?" stammers Schnappi, and when Schnappi stammers it means there's a good chance the world's about to end. She looks back at the hotel, she looks at you almost pleadingly.

"Nessi, what happened in there?"

"Nothing. I want you girls to turn around, okay? We're going, and if we don't go now I'm going to get hysterical and scream so loud they'll hear me in Berlin. Please, let's get going."

They've never seen you like this, you don't know yourself, you stand there and wait, you want to be you again, soft and tender and not hard and resolute. At last your girls get moving.

"Relax," says Schnappi and takes your hand.

"We're coming," says Stink and takes your other hand.

The way down the winding road to the car is a sluggish dream in reverse. You can't feel your footsteps. Sometimes Stink says something, sometimes Schnappi does, you keep quiet and try not to think, not to feel. You get into the car, the doors close, you take a deep breath and start the engine and then you just sit there without putting the car in gear, hands on the steering wheel and leaning slightly forward as if waiting for a signal to go. Schnappi asks if everything's all right, and you almost burst out laughing, because everything's never going to be all right ever again, but you don't tell your girls that, you just turn to Stink and ask for the phone. She hands it to you and you take your hands off the wheel and keep the promise you made to Taja.

NEIL

We've got to let you go too now. You were our very special guest, stolen from another story, thrown into this chaos. Without you everything would have gone quite differently, without us no one would know how much you've changed. We've seen you grow and now it's time to say goodbye. The beginning is like the ending. You're sitting in the car, you're on the road again. Your mother sleeps throughout the whole journey as if she knew what lay ahead, and that she needed strength for it. She didn't believe you for a second when you said you wanted to take her for a quick drive into the countryside. And here you are now.

You drive, she sleeps, the landscape passes by.

Three hours later you stop on a side street off the Schlesisches Tor U-Bahn station and have lunch in an Indian restaurant. You talk about everything except what's happening right now.

The apartment block is old, and the façade is under restoration. Your mother follows you up the stairs. Just once, she holds you tightly by the arm. You wait. She isn't out of breath, she's thinking.

"We can go on now," she says.

You go on.

———

There's no nameplate on the door, the wood around the lock is scratched and the letter box dented.

"It's all exactly as I imagined," says your mother.

"Okay?" you ask.

She nods.

You ring.

You wait.

The sound of footsteps.

The door opens.

You turn away and go downstairs.

"Richard," you hear your mother say.

"Oh, Kristin," you hear your father say, not surprised or disappointed; he says it like someone who's been carrying around a chest full of thoughts on his shoulders and now at last he can set the chest down.

You leave them alone.

Outside the building you blink into the sunlight as if you'd only just woken up. You're in Friedrichshain, the whole of Berlin is at your feet, and you don't know what to do with yourself. Last time you were here, you ran into Stink. It feels like a decade ago, it's like yesterday, it's exactly four days ago. Nessi has left deep traces in your memory.

As if she'd been there forever and I'd never noticed her.

The previous evening you tried to get through to the girls twice, but the phone was switched off. Who knows, maybe they've thrown it away, that would be better anyway. You also hope they were clever enough to get rid of the car.

You walk toward Alexanderplatz, buy yourself an ice cream, and take a look at the shop windows. You mingle among the people and wait for your mother's phone call. What will your parents decide? Will they continue their lives together or not? You don't really want to think about it, you've done what you could.

Two hours become three and then your phone rings. It isn't your mother. On the display you see your old phone number. You cautiously take the call.

"Neil?"

"Yes."

"It's me, Nessi."

You stop, people push past you, you just stand there.

"Hello? Can you hear me?"

"I can hear you."

"I . . . I just wanted to say we're on the way back."

"Good. That's good. Are you okay?"

"We . . . I just wanted to ask if you . . . Can you . . . Will you be there?"

You say nothing, you know what she means, sometimes a few words can mean so much. *Will you be there?* And for a moment you're sure that when she touched her hand to say goodbye that morning, she read your thoughts: *Stay here and I'll look after you and the child, if you save my soul in return.* Your soul still wants to be saved. Now you just need to be there.

"I will be there," you say.

"Thank you. That's . . ."

She breaks off, you hear rustling, then Stink's on the line and she says, "Holy fuck, she's crying again now. I hope you said something nice?"

"It was nice."

"Lucky for you, otherwise you'd have to deal with me."

"I'd never do that."

"Glad we've sorted that one out."

You laugh, you're standing in the middle of Berlin on the footpath and you burst out laughing. The people look at you crossly and push you aside like a leper. It feels as if your life has only just begun, and anyone who isn't laughing doesn't know what it means. You put your phone away and look into the sky, stretch your back, and feel four inches taller. Being a leper has never felt so good.

STINK

Two minutes later.

"What did you do?" Schnappi asks.

"I kept a promise, that's all," Nessi replies, wipes the tears away, and puts the car in gear. You speak up from the back. Your voice is quiet because you actually don't want to hear what exactly happened in the hotel, but what must be must be. So speak louder, "And when are you going to tell us everything?"

"First let me drive a bit, please."

You breathe out with relief. The car rolls down the road. It's pleasantly quiet. Only the engine and the tires. Only your heads and the thoughts locked inside them.

"Sweetie, don't cry again."

Schnappi hands Nessi a tissue, she drops it, Schnappi picks it up again, leans over, and starts dabbing away the tears from Nessi's right eye. Nessi laughs. You offer to do her left eye. Nessi warns you that she's going to crash into the next tree if you don't stop treating her like a baby. Schnappi decides it's been quiet long enough and puts on a CD. You hear a guitar that sounds like waves coming closer and receding again, coming closer and receding again. Then Damien Rice sings *tiredness fuels empty thoughts,* and Ulvtannen disappears in the rearview mirror, and you know that Nessi will tell you everything after the song. You think the same during the next song and the one after that. You wait for her words. Words that don't hurt. Words that will make everything better. Words that no one has yet pronounced.

RAGNAR

You're lying on a barren piece of land that was once dense with fir trees, where wolf packs once gathered on winter nights, before your forefathers cleared the land to build a beach hotel without a beach. You feel nothing of the old times, and soon you will be part of this damned land if the sun goes on burning down on you like this. If you get heatstroke on top of your concussion, we'll soon be able to leave you to the seagulls. But it's looking good, something's happening. There's a shaking in your leg, and your fingers are twitching too. Your body's waking up as if it had been frozen.

Like Oskar.

Your world has gotten out of joint. Your son denied you, two of your best friends are dead in the trunk of the car, and you're seething with rage. It is diverted from your head to your belly, because you're going to need all your wits about you to get out of this wretched situation. Whatever you do now, you should gather your strength for the finale, because you're going to need a lot of strength.

The pain has faded, the nausea has gone, your stomach has calmed down. You're slipping away into a healing unconsciousness, and for a while you disappear into a café in Bregenz with a view of Lake Constance that you visited years ago when one of your customers flew you in for the opening of the festival. You're sitting by the window with Oskar and Tanner, the sun is shining in, everything is dazzlingly bright. Tanner raises his glass to you, you look up, Leo walks past outside, but he's in a hurry and just waves at you in passing. You drink cold lemonade, Oskar eats his third piece of cake, and you're amazed that he hasn't put on an ounce over the years. Tanner pats his stomach. He's almost always on a diet. *And what good did that do? I'm not even breathing anymore,* he says. Oskar nods, he knows the feeling. You look into your lemonade and can't move. *Now you know how I felt,* says Oskar, *nothing's working anymore, the body is down.* The waitress brings a plate with even more pieces of cake and says: *These are from the boss.* You look over at the bar; the boss is a boy in an apron with a hole in his forehead. You nod your thanks. He nods back. You don't want to say it. Tanner says it: *Isn't that Mirko?* Oskar says: *At least he has a job.* You take a sip of your lemonade and try not to laugh. The dead are all around you, and if you look up right now Ruth will come in and she'll be holding hands with Marten, but that's something you don't really want to see at the moment. The darkness saves you. The sun disappears behind the night as if the night were a curtain. It becomes pleasantly cool, and when you open your eyes you're no longer alone. A man is leaning over you, the sun lurks behind his shoulder, you can't make his face out. The man asks, "Do you remember me?"

"What?"

"Do you remember who I am?"

You swallow, your tongue feels as if it's three times its usual size. Your eyes have gotten used to the light. The man's face is hovering clearly and distinctly above you. You can hardly hear yourself, your voice is so faint.

"I have no idea who you are."

The man nods, he expected this.

"It's on its way."

"What is?"

"The memory. It sometimes gets lost."

You try to keep him in focus. He's wearing a T-shirt with a cross on it. He's the same age as you. He says, "But I know who you are. You're the man who gets his son to kill people. Because of you my son lay with his face in the dirt."

You feel a quiver in your right hand and clench it. *Wake up, you stupid fucking body, wake up and do something before this guy does me in!* A muscle in your thigh twitches, your heel scrapes over the ground.

"Marten," you say.

"Right, his name was Marten."

Of course you could lie to him, but that wouldn't be you. Ragnar Desche doesn't lie. Ragnar Desche is honest and says, "It was his fault."

"No."

"He—"

"I said no. My son wasn't guilty of anything. Whatever happened, I know he wasn't to blame. But whose fault was it?"

You look at each other. He knows the answer and still wants to hear it from you. Your son Judas. It's easy for you to betray him.

"It was my son."

"Thank you."

The man leans forward.

"This is definitely going to hurt."

He pushes one hand under your back, the other under your leg, and lifts you up. It's a bit like someone sticking a red-hot stake up your backside. The pain spreads, shoots up your spine, and you greet it like an old friend that you haven't seen for ages. Pain means that there's still hope, no paralysis, no life in a bed with a straw in your mouth. So the connections haven't been cut yet. Your eyes fill with tears. A hundred-year-old man would have more dignity. Your head hangs down, your arms and legs don't really exist, only your right hand clutches at the air, spittle trickles from your mouth, and after a few steps the pain's too much even for your stubborn consciousness and you black out.

You blink. There's a dirty glass of water in front of you. You're sitting at a table, your head manages to move, your muscles work, your left arm doesn't react, your right comes up slowly, your fingers grip the glass. Your arm trembles. You drink and look at the man. He's sitting at the other end, his hands are flat on the table, he's looking at you expectantly.

The glass is empty and you set it down again.

"We're alone," says the man.

"My son will come back."

"I don't think so. Your son won't come back any more than my son will come back. We're fathers without sons now."

For a moment you're sure that the man must have captured Darian. Then you remember Darian speaking to you and leaving.

After the idiot had emptied the whole magazine at the hotel.

"We have plenty of time," says the man.

"I don't think so. As soon as my body's working again, I'm out of here."

He shakes his head.

"What's that supposed to mean?" you ask.

"It means you aren't leaving here. This is the place where you will die. This is the end of you."

"What?"

"You heard me."

He smiles. Not cruel, not arrogant; kind.

You think you can feel time breathing down your neck. Of course it's only the summer wind blowing through the broken windows. Of course the man in front of you is a comedian. You laugh and say exactly that.

"What are you? A comedian?"

"You know me, you know who I am."

Your fist comes down on the table, the glass leaps into the air, rolls along the tabletop, and shatters on the floor. Your voice is a growl. Ragnar Desche slowly wakes up.

"You little fucker, what do you think you're doing here? Do you think you can drag me around the place, sit down at this table, and tell me I'm going to die here? No one threatens me. No one, is that clear?"

"I haven't threatened you."

"What?"

"No one's threatening you, these are just the facts."

Your hand searches, the gun's not in the belt holster anymore. The man picks your automatic from one of the chairs. He leans forward and pushes it into the middle of the table. The table is sixteen feet long. If you stand up now, you'll be holding the gun in two seconds, and that'll be that for this comedian. But what if he's only trying to make you look ridiculous? What if he's taken out the magazine? It could be an embarrassing moment.

"The gun's loaded."

The man isn't just making you nervous, he's reading your mind.

"What's to stop me from grabbing it?" you ask.

"Your legs. You'll have to wait a while before they work again."

"Who says they don't already?"

"If they worked, you'd have grabbed the gun long ago."

He's right, and you hate him being right.

"And what happens then?"

"As soon as you've got the gun, I'll kill you."

You look at him in disbelief.

"What with?"

He looks at his hands.

You look at his hands.

They're lying flat on the tabletop.

You laugh.

"What's that supposed to mean? Is that all you have to offer? Your fucking hands? Have you any idea who's sitting here in front of you? You're going to need more than those hands to finish me off."

He doesn't react. You go on, it's always the same game with you. Wind up your adversary, see how far you can go.

"Do you think the table's going to go flying up in the air if you take your hands away?"

The man thinks for a second before he says, "If I take my hands away, they will kill you."

He smiles and adds, "That's the kind of hands they are."

There's really nothing more to say on the matter. You feel a trembling in your legs. *Wake up, damn it, just wake up!* Even though you don't want to, you have to ask, "Who the fuck are you?"

THE TRAVELER

"I'm going to tell you a story, and then you'll know who I am," you say, leaning forward slightly.

It's a wonderful feeling. The pulse of the house flows through your fingers, you knew there was still some life in it, you go on.

"The summer I turned twelve, I was secretly reading by candlelight one night, when a moth flew through the window into my room. It circled the candle flame, and after less than a minute it burned up. I wondered how the moth could be so stupid. And then it occurred to me that the moth might have seen something in the flame that I couldn't see. Did it want to die, or did it know nothing of the danger? And what if it had known about the danger and flown deliberately into it? I thought about it a lot and wondered what it would be like to fly into the flames without burning up. Where would I be then? Would I be at the center of the fire? And what if nothing happened to me there, and if from that moment onwards I was untouchable? And if I was untouchable, would I still be me?"

Ragnar Desche looks at you, he begins to understand, you can read it in his eyes. Where you see the flame, he sees his father. You go on talking.

"For a year and a half I've thought about it, for a year and a half I've thought about these questions and nothing else. One day I pulled a boy down to the bottom of a swimming pool and let him die. It was very simple, it wasn't planned and it wasn't an accident. I flew right into the flames and nothing happened. At that moment

I became invincible, do you understand that? I became the person I am now. No guilt, no regret, and no morals either. I became a part of the flames and there was no retaliation, there was no punishment. No god came down from heaven to strike me dead. No one pointed a finger at me. The impossible became possible. This experience ran against all the rules of our society. It was intoxicating. And I asked myself the most important question you can ask yourself as an individual: *If the flames can do nothing to me, how can I stay away from the flames?*"

You pause for a moment, before you add, "That's why we're sitting here."

Silence. You don't know what he's thinking, his face gives nothing away, his left hand has woken up now too, it's opening and closing. And if you could look into his head, you'd see a fifteen-year-old Ragnar Desche leaving the apartment block after his father's death and walking away. Not on the pavement, he's walking down the middle of the road, because he needs space because he's suddenly big and violent and the pavement isn't big enough for him. You stepped into the flames in your way, he did in his. The result is the same, you have both grown with it. And now he's sitting opposite you, and he's not taking his eyes off you. He's reliving his own moment, standing in the flames and looking out at you.

"We're the same," you say.

No reaction. Perhaps everything really is very different and he's not thinking anything and wondering how quickly he can get to his gun. Everything's possible.

At last he speaks.

"What makes you think we're the same?"

"The darkness and the depth," you answer.

"You're a sick fuck," he says.

"And you have no heart."

"What?"

"And I have no soul. You and me, me and you. We've found each other. Now we'll come to rest."

And so you tell him who the Traveler is, you don't leave out a single victim, you tell him every detail and describe your quest. And tell him of the depth from which you always had to rise to open the door to the darkness.

After thirty-four years your search has brought you here to this place.

To this room.

To this table.

Arrived.

Ragnar Desche just looks at you. He doesn't reveal himself. He is not interested if you've been looking for him for a hundred or a thousand years. You know it can take a while. He will show you his true face. It will just take a while. His facial expression gives nothing away, only his body reacts. His shoulders hunch, his hands lie flat on the table so that he's sitting there like you. One foot drums, you can feel it through the floor. His breathing grows faster and more confident, ready for anything.

The drumming stops.

"Now we've arrived," you say.

"Now we've arrived," he says.

Two men in a kitchen.

In a ruined hotel.

On a cliff.

Alone.

No Me anymore, no Him anymore.

Only one thing is left.

You.

My Thanks To

Gregor, you lit the flame and let those sweet bitches
  from the first sentence on into your heart. They thank you too.

Martin, you brought me closer to my own novel,
  your friendship shines and shines.

Daniela, once again you've helped me mull over my doubts in long
  conversations, stroked my head reassuringly, and grinned away
  the insecurities.

Christine & Peter & Ulrike & Stephanie & Martina, you read as if
  possessed, while I sat at home as if possessed and waited for your
  comments.

Evi & Felix for the confidence you give my writing.

Arnon Grünberg & Larry McMurtry & George R. R. Martin,
  it's a joy to learn from you.

Misophone & William Fitzsimmons & Lloyd Cole,
  whatever it is, you've got it.

Corinna, my greatest heroine,
  who puts every sun in the shade.

SRRY

'SURPRISES, SHOCKS AND THRILLS'
SUNDAY EXPRESS

sorry
YOUR WORST NIGHTMARES
ARE ABOUT TO BEGIN

Zoran Drvenkar
INTERNATIONAL BESTSELLER

BERLIN. FOUR FRIENDS.
ONE EXTREME IDEA.

Kris, Tamara, Wolf and Frauke set up an agency called
SORRY. An agency to right wrongs. Unfair dismissals,
the wrongly accused: everyone has a price, and SORRY
will find out what it is. Simple as that.

What they hadn't counted on was their next client
being a cold-hearted killer. But who is the killer and
why has he killed? Someone is mocking them and their
hell is only just beginning.

KILLER READS

DISCOVER THE BEST IN CRIME AND THRILLER.

SIGN UP TO OUR NEWSLETTER FOR YOUR CHANCE TO WIN A FREE BOOK EVERY MONTH.

FIND OUT MORE AT
WWW.KILLERREADS.COM/NEWSLETTER

Want more? Get to know the team behind the books, hear from our authors, find out about new crime and thriller books and lots more by following us on social media:

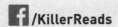 /KillerReads   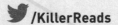 /KillerReads